THE
STORE

~~~~~~

BENTLEY LITTLE

A SIGNET BOOK

SIGNET
Published by New American Library, a division of
Penguin Group (USA) Inc., 375 Hudson Street,
New York, New York 10014, USA
Penguin Group (Canada), 10 Alcorn Avenue, Toronto,
Ontario M4V 3B2, Canada (a division of Pearson Penguin Canada Inc.)
Penguin Books Ltd., 80 Strand, London WC2R 0RL, England
Penguin Ireland, 25 St. Stephen's Green, Dublin 2,
Ireland (a division of Penguin Books Ltd.)
Penguin Group (Australia), 250 Camberwell Road, Camberwell, Victoria 3124,
Australia (a division of Pearson Australia Group Pty. Ltd.)
Penguin Books India Pvt. Ltd., 11 Community Centre, Panchsheel Park,
New Delhi - 110 017, India
Penguin Group (NZ), cnr Airborne and Rosedale Roads, Albany,
Auckland 1310, New Zealand (a division of Pearson New Zealand Ltd.)
Penguin Books (South Africa) (Pty.) Ltd., 24 Sturdee Avenue,
Rosebank, Johannesburg 2196, South Africa

Penguin Books Ltd., Registered Offices:
80 Strand, London WC2R 0RL, England

First published by Signet, an imprint of New American Library,
a division of Penguin Group (USA) Inc.

First Printing, July 1998
10 9

Copyright © Bentley Little, 1998
All rights reserved

 REGISTERED TRADEMARK—MARCA REGISTRADA

Printed in the United States of America

For my wife, Wai Sau

PROLOGUE

The DeSoto drove along the rutted dirt road through the series of low desert hills that signaled an end to the Texas flatlands. A cloud of dust accompanied the car—enveloping the vehicle, not merely following in its wake—but the dust was preferable to the heat, and the windows remained open.

It was the third day of their honeymoon, and although Nancy didn't want to admit it, she and Paul seemed to have run out of things to say to each other. They had not spoken since Houston, save for Paul's occasional requests to hand him the map, and though she tried to come up with something that they could talk about, there seemed to be no subjects that would sustain a conversation more than a few minutes. She figured she'd better save those for El Paso and dinner.

She fanned herself with the map. The unbearable temperature didn't help any, either. She couldn't think in weather like this. She'd never been so hot and uncomfortable in her life. She would've liked to take off her top and her bra. The old Paul would've liked it, too. It was the type of wild spontaneity that newlyweds were supposed to engage in, the sort of madcap antic that would make the honeymoon memorable, that they would be able to look back at and laugh about years later. No one else would see her—they hadn't come across a single other car for the past two hours—but even without asking, she knew that Paul would not approve.

They were supposed to have been married three years ago, but he'd been drafted, sent off to Korea, and though she'd wanted to marry before he shipped out, he wanted to wait . . . just in case. Each time she mentioned it, he'd remind her of Scarlett O'Hara's first husband in *Gone With the Wind,* the boy she'd married just before he'd gone off to his death in the Civil War, and though Nancy knew he was joking, his underlying meaning was serious, and it terrified her to think that he might not return.

Return he had, though. Alive and unharmed. But there'd been something different about him after the war. He seemed changed somehow, although it wasn't anything she could really put her finger on. She'd noticed it immediately, had considered asking him about it, but she figured if he wanted to talk he would, and she decided to let him be. She was just happy that they were together again. Man and wife. And if the silences were a little too long, they were comfortable silences and she knew that once they started their new life in California, once they made friends and had kids and settled into marriage, those silences would disappear.

Ahead, at the foot of a sandstone cliff on the right side of the road, was a small brick building that appeared incongruous out here in the middle of nowhere. A strip of green grass fronted the structure, bisected by a short white sidewalk. There were no windows on the building, only a large black-on-white sign on the wall to the right of the door.

"That's odd," Paul said, slowing the car.

Nancy nodded.

This close, they could read the words on the sign:

THE STORE

GROCERIES—PHARMACEUTICS—MERCANTILE

Paul laughed. " 'The Store?' What kind of name is that?"

"It's straightforward and honest," she pointed out.

"Yeah. I guess it is that. But you'd never make it in a big city with a name like 'The Store.' You'd need something catchier, something with more pizzazz." He laughed again, shook his head. "The Store."

"Why don't we stop?" Nancy suggested. "Maybe they have cold soda. A nice cold soda sounds real good right now."

"Okay." There was no parking lot, but Paul pulled off the side of the dirt road and stopped directly in front of the small building. He turned toward Nancy. "What do you want?"

"I'll go in with you," she said.

He placed a firm hand on her arm. "No. You stay here in the car. I'll get us the sodas. What do you want?"

"Yoo-Hoo," she said.

"Yoo-Hoo it is." He opened the driver's door, got out. "I'll be back in a flash."

He smiled at her, and she smiled back as he walked down the short sidewalk, but her smile faded as she watched him open the glass door and step into the store, disappearing into the murky dimness of the building. She suddenly realized just *how* odd this place was. They were fifty, maybe a hundred miles from the nearest town, there were no visible telephone lines or electrical wires, she could not believe that there was water, and there certainly was not any traffic. Yet the store was open and ready for business—as if it were in the middle of downtown Pittsburgh and not in the middle of the Texas desert.

Something about that made her uneasy.

She stared hard at the door, trying to see into the store, but she could make out nothing. No shapes. No sign of movement. It was the glass, she told herself, and the angle of the sun. That was all. Besides, if the interior of the building were really as dark as it looked from out here, Paul would not have gone inside.

She tried to make herself believe it.

Paul emerged several minutes later looking stunned, carrying a large paper sack. He opened the driver's door of the DeSoto and sat down, placing the sack between them.

"You were just supposed to get sodas," she said.

He started the car.

"Paul?"

He didn't respond, and she began digging through the sack. "Light bulbs? What do we need light bulbs for? We're on vacation. Tissue paper? Whisk broom? Masking tape? What is all this?"

He glanced furtively back toward The Store as he put the car into gear. "Let's just get out of here."

Nancy felt a chill pass through her. "But I don't understand. Why did you buy all this? And where are our sodas? You didn't even buy our sodas."

He looked over at her, and there was fear on his face, fear and anger, and for the first time since they'd gotten married, for the first time since she'd known Paul, she was afraid of him. "Shut up, Nancy. Just shut the hell up."

She said nothing but turned around to look as they sped away. Before the car rounded the curve of the hill, before the dust completely obscured the scene behind them, she saw the door of the building open.

And, in a sight she would remember until her dying day, she thought she saw the proprietor of The Store.

ONE

1

Bill Davis quietly closed the front door of the house behind him as he stepped outside. He walked off the porch and stood for a moment at the head of the drive, doing knee bends and breathing deeply, the air exhaling from his lungs in bursts of visible steam. When he reached the count of fifty, he stopped. Standing straight, he bent to the left, bent to the right, then walked down the drive to the road, where he inhaled and exhaled one last time before beginning his morning jog.

The dirt changed to asphalt at the bottom of the hill, and he ran past Goodwin's meadow and turned onto Main.

He liked running at this time of morning. He didn't like the running itself—that was a necessary evil—but he enjoyed being out and about at this hour. The streets were virtually empty. Len Madson was in the donut shop finishing up the morning's baking as the first few customers straggled in, Chris Schneider was loading up the newspaper racks, and here and there individual trucks were heading off to construction sites, but otherwise the town was quiet, the streets clear, and that was the way he liked it.

He ran through downtown Juniper and kept going until he hit the highway. The air was chill but heavy, weighted with the rich scent of moist vegetation, the smell of newly cut grass. He breathed deeply as he jogged. He could see his breath as he ran, and the brisk air felt invigorating, made him glad to be alive.

On the highway, the view opened up, the close-set trees that had been lining the road falling back, making visible the sloping landscape. Ahead, the sun was rising behind broken clouds that floated, unmoving, over the mountains, the clouds silhouetted against the pale sky, black in the center, pink-orange at the edges. In front of the sunrise, a flock of geese was flying south in a morphing V-formation, the shape of the flight pattern varying every few seconds as a different bird moved into the lead and the other members of the flock fell in behind it. Shafts of yellow light slanted downward through the clouds, through the pine branches, highlighting objects and areas unused to attention: a boulder, a gully, a collapsed barn.

This was his favorite part of the jog—the open land between the end of the town proper and the small unincorporated subdivision known as Creekside Acres. The dirt control road on the other side of the Acres that looped back to his street was wider and more forested, but there was something about this mile or so stretch that appealed to him. Here, the tall trees ringed an overgrown meadow that sloped up the side of a low hill. An outcropping of rock on the south side of the meadow stood like some primitive idol, its erosion-carved facade giving it the appearance of something deliberately sculptured.

He slowed down a little, not because he was tired but because he wanted to savor the moment. Glancing to his left, he saw the brightening sunlight captured and amplified by the brilliant yellow aspens that were interspersed among the pines. He shifted his gaze across the highway, to his right, toward the meadow, but something here was different, something was wrong. He couldn't put his finger on it, but he noticed instantly that there was an element in the meadow that was out of place and did not fit.

The sign had changed.

Yes. That was it. He stopped jogging, breathing heavily. The weatherworn sign announcing "BAYLESS! OPENING IN SIX MONTHS!" that had been posted in the meadow for the past decade was gone, replaced with a new sign, a stark white rectangle with black lettering that sat solidly atop twin supports sunk deep into the ground.

THE STORE IS COMING
FEBRUARY

He stared for a moment at the sign. It had not been here yesterday, and something about the cold precision of the type and the flat declarative promise of the message made him feel a little uneasy—although he wasn't quite sure why. It was stupid, he knew, and ordinarily he was not one to go by hunches or intuition or anything so nonconcrete, but the sign bothered him. It was, he supposed, a reaction to the idea of something—anything—being built here in the meadow, in what he considered *his* spot. Sure, a Bayless grocery store was supposed to have been built at this location, but ground for the construction had never been broken and the sign had been there for so long that its promise was empty, its words had ceased to have any meaning. The sign had become part of the landscape and was now merely another picturesque relic by the side of the road, like the fallen barn up ahead or the old Blakey gas station that had collapsed into the brush on the highway west of town.

He glanced around, trying to imagine a huge, new building in the middle of the meadow, the grass around it paved over for a parking lot, and it was depressingly easy to conjure up such a picture in his mind. Instead of seeing the glistening sparkle of dew on the grass, he'd see black asphalt and white paint lines stretching before him as he jogged each morning. His view of the hill and the rocks would probably be blocked by the square concrete bulk of the store. The mountains up ahead would be unchanged, but they were only a small part of the beauty of this spot. It was the convergence of everything, the perfect integration of all elements that had made this stretch such a special place for him.

He looked again at the sign. Behind it, between the posts, he saw the body of a dead deer. He had not noticed it before, but the shifting clouds and the rising sun had changed the emphasis of the light and the brown form was now clearly visible, its distended stomach and unmoving head protruding from the meadow grass. The animal had obviously died recently. Probably during the night. There were no flies anywhere, no sign of decay, no wounds. The death was clean, and that somehow seemed more ominous to him than if it had been shot, or hit by a car, or crippled and attacked by wolves.

How often did animals drop dead of natural causes next to construction announcement signs?

He would have called it an omen, had he believed in omens, but he did not, and he felt stupid for even thinking about it, for even pretending in his mind that there was a causal connection between the two. Taking a deep breath, he resumed jogging, heading down the sloping highway toward the Acres, looking ahead at the mountains.

But he remained troubled.

2

Ginny was already up and had cooked breakfast by the time he returned. Samantha was peacefully eating her Cream of Wheat in front of the television, but Ginny and Shannon were arguing in the kitchen, Shannon insisting that she didn't have to eat breakfast if she didn't want to, that she was old enough to decide for herself whether or not she was hungry, Ginny lecturing her about bulimia and anorexia.

Both of them assaulted him the second he walked into the house.

"Dad!" Shannon said. "Tell Mom that I don't have to eat a big breakfast every single day. We had a huge dinner last night and I'm not even hungry."

"And tell Shannon," Ginny said, "that she's going to end up with an eating disorder if she doesn't stop obsessing over her weight."

He held up his hands. "I'm not stepping into this. This is between you two. I'm taking a shower."

"Dad!"

"You're always chickening out," Ginny said.

"You're not dragging me into this!" He grabbed a towel form the hall closet and hurried into the bathroom, locking the door. He turned on the water, drowning out the noise from the kitchen, then quickly took off his jogging suit and got into the steaming shower.

The hot spray felt good. He closed his eyes and faced into the water, the tiny streams simultaneously hitting his forehead, his eyelids, his nose, his cheeks, his lips, his chin. The water ran down his body, pooling around his feet. Low rainfall in the spring/summer months and low snowfall last winter had led to a reduction in the water table and rationing for the houses in town, but they had their own water from their own well, and he stood there for a long time, luxuriating in the shower, letting the heated liquid caress his tired muscles.

The girls had taken off for school by the time he finished his shower, and he walked into the kitchen and poured himself a cup of coffee.

"I could've used some support," Ginny said as she put the girls' dishes into the dishwasher.

"She's not anorexic, for God's sake."

"But she could be."

"You're overreacting."

"Am I? She skips lunch now. Almost every day. And now she wants to skip breakfast. Dinner's the only meal she eats anymore."

"I don't want to burst your bubble, Gin, but she's chubby."

Ginny looked quickly around, as though Shannon might have surreptitiously returned in order to eavesdrop on their conversation. "Don't let her hear you say that."

"I won't. But it's true. She's obviously eating more than dinner."

"I just don't like the way she's always worrying about the number of meals she eats and the size of her food portions and her weight and her appearance."

"Then stop harping about it. You're the one drawing attention to her. She probably wouldn't be as conscious of it if you weren't focusing on her all the time."

"Bullshit. She'd eat one meal a week if I let her get away with it."

Bill shrugged. "Your call." He checked the pot on the stove. A small dollop of hardened Cream of Wheat lay clumped against one rounded side of the metal cookware. He grimaced.

"It's not as bad as it looks," Ginny said. "Pour in a bit of milk and heat it up."

He shook his head. "I'll just have toast." The open bread sack was still on the counter, and he took out two pieces, popping them in the toaster. "I saw a new sign when I was out jogging. It said The Store was coming—"

"That's right! I forgot to tell you. Charlinda told me about it Friday. Ted's company is bidding on the roofing contract, and she said that he stands to make more from this one project than he did all last year. If he gets it."

"I'm sure a lot of construction workers around here'll be happy."

"I thought you'd be happy, too. You're always complaining about the high prices in town and moaning that we have to drive down to Phoenix in order to find a decent selection of anything."

"I am happy," he told her.

But he was not. Intellectually, he supposed he could appreciate the coming of The Store. It would be a big boost to the local economy and would mean not only a temporary increase in construction jobs, but a permanent expansion of sales and service positions, particularly for teenagers. It would also be good for consumers. It would bring big-city discount prices and a big-city selection of products to their small town.

On a gut level, however, the arrival of The Store did not sit well with him—and not just because it was going to be built on his scenic spot. For no reason that he could rationally justify, he did not want the chain store in Juniper.

He thought of the sign.

Thought of the deer.

"Well, I'm sure local shop owners aren't too thrilled," Ginny said. "The Store'll probably put some of them out of business."

"That's true."

"Just what we need in town. More abandoned buildings."

His toast popped up, and Bill took a butter knife out of the silverware drawer, grabbed a jar of jam from the refrigerator.

"I'd better get ready," Ginny said, walking around him. She went into the bathroom, and he heard her brushing her teeth as he prepared his toast. She emerged a few minutes later, makeup on, purse in hand. "Hi ho, hi ho. It's off to work I go."

"Me, too." He walked over, kissed her.

"Will you be home for lunch?"

He smiled. "I think that's a safe bet."

"Good. Then you can finish the dishes."

"Ah, the joys of telecommuting." He followed her to the front door, kissed her again, then watched through the screen as she walked down the porch steps and across the drive to the car. He waved as she drove away, then closed the door, finished eating his toast, washed his hands in the kitchen sink, and walked through the living room and down the hall to his office.

He sat down at his desk, turning on the PC. As always, he felt a thrill of almost guilty pleasure as the computer booted up, as though he was getting away with something he shouldn't. He swiveled in his chair, looked out the window. This might not be *exactly* the life he had imagined—but it was pretty damn close. In his mind, the house had been a large, glass-walled, Frank Lloyd Wrightish structure, and he'd been seated at a huge oak desk, looking out a giant window into the forest while classical music wafted into the room from a state-of-the-art stereo. In reality, he worked out of this cramped back room, the walls of the office little more than an extension of his bulletin board, with magazine articles and Post-It notes affixed to nearly every conceivable space. And he wasn't nearly as cultured in his real life as he was in his fantasies—instead of classical music, he usually listened to classic rock on a portable radio his daughters had discarded.

But everything else was on the mark. The room did

indeed have a big window, and that big window did look out onto the forest. And, most importantly, he was doing what he wanted, where he wanted. His reach may have exceeded his grasp, but he had not sold out. He had not given up his dream and settled for a lesser fate, choosing the least offensive alternative. He had stuck to his guns and here he was, a telecommuting technical writer, working for one of the country's largest software firms a thousand miles away from the corporate office, communicating with his superiors by modem and fax.

The computer finished booting up, and he checked his E-mail. There were two messages from the company—reminding him of his deadline, no doubt—and a message from Street McHenry, who owned the electronics store in town. Smiling, he called up Street's message. It was two words long: "Chess tonight?"

Bill typed a quick reply and sent it back: "See you there."

He and Street had had two separate chess matches going for most of the past year—one online and one on a traditional board. Neither of them were really chess fanatics, and they probably would have stopped long ago were it not for an interesting and unexplainable fact: he won all the computer games; Street won all the board games.

It shouldn't have worked out that way. The mediums were different but the game was exactly the same. Chess was chess, no matter what pieces were used or where it was played. Still, that was the way it broke down.

Every time.

That oddity was enough to keep both of them interested in the matches.

Bill fired off a quick E-mail message to Ben Anderson, informing him of tonight's game. The newspaper editor, the other member of their online triumverate, had only recently learned of the Great Juniper Chess Mystery, as he called it, but he was fascinated by it and wanted to be present at all board games and eavesdrop on all online matches to see if he could detect any patterns in their playing, any logical reason why they won and lost as they did.

The situation until this point had seemed lighthearted, their approach to it curious but not serious, their manner half-joking, but as Bill stared at his E-mail screen and thought of their past year of chess games, he was reminded for some reason of The Store.

The sign.

The deer.

Suddenly, their win-loss pattern didn't seem quite so benign, and he wished he had canceled out on tonight's match instead of agreeing to it. He already knew what the outcome would be, and he now found that a little unsettling.

He looked out at the trees for a moment before finally turning back to the computer. He wasn't in the mood to jump straight into work, so instead of calling up his two messages from the company, he exited E-mail and logged on to Freelink, his online service, in order to check out this morning's news.

He scanned the wire service headlines.

THIRD STORE MASSACRE IN A MONTH.

The words jumped out at him. There were other headlines, more important stories, but he did not see them and did not care. Feeling cold, he displayed the text of the article. Apparently, a sales clerk from The Store in Las Canos, New Mexico, had come to work with a .45 caliber pistol tucked into the waste band of his pants, hidden beneath his uniform jacket. The clerk had worked from eight to ten in the morning, as always, then, on his break, had taken out the gun and started shooting his fellow employees. Six people were hit before the clerk stopped to reload and members of The Store's security team wrestled him to the ground. Five of those six people were dead. The sixth was in critical condition at a local hospital.

According to the article, similar incidents had occurred at the chain's stores in Denton, Texas, and Red Bluff, Utah, within the past month. In the Texas store, it was a customer who had started firing on employees, killing three and wounding two. In Utah, it was a stock boy who had opened fire on customers. The stock boy had had a semiautomatic weapon, and he had managed to mow down fifteen people before being shot by an off-duty policeman.

Corporate officials of The Store would not comment on the incidents but had issued a press release stating that the possibility that the occurrences were related was being investigated.

Bill read the story again, still feeling cold.

The deer.

He signed off Freelink and stared at the blank screen in front of him for several long minutes before finally getting back into E-mail and accessing his messages from the company to start his morning's work.

TWO

1

Greg Hargrove looked down at the contract on his desk, frowning. He didn't like doing business this way. It might be the wave of the future and all, but he still liked to deal with his clients the old-fashioned way—in person. All this faxing and phoning and Fed Exing might be fine for Wall Street investment firms, but, damn it, the construction business wasn't a service occupation, or a paper-pushing job. It was manual labor. It involved real work by real men. Men who created something with their hands, who produced something tangible.

And it didn't seem right to approach it this way.

He picked up the contract. This was the biggest job he'd ever had, maybe the biggest job he ever would have, and it just didn't sit well with him to be communicating through paperwork. He wanted to see a face, to feel a handshake, to hear a voice.

Well, he'd heard a voice. Several voices, actually. All talking to him over the phone. Official-sounding corporate voices that talked at him, not to him, and didn't seem to give a damn what he had to say.

The past few days, there hadn't even been that. There'd been only the forms and the lists and the specifications and the requirements.

It was especially annoying that so much of the paperwork was faxed to him overnight. It was bad enough not being able to do business with an honest-to-God human being, but doing it when he wasn't even there? Having to find out in the morning, after the fact, what was going on? That really bugged the shit out of him.

He was used to being able to show a client around a

site, to explain what was being done and why, to walk him through the various stages and steps, to answer questions and allay fears.

He wasn't used to filing reports.

And having his reports critiqued.

That was what bothered him the most. The loss of control. On all projects before this one, he had been the one in charge. He had been the one to call the shots. Sure, he had built to suit, he had carried out the client's will, but within that broad framework, he had been the one making the decisions. Now, though, he was just another worker, following orders, not allowed to think.

He didn't like that.

And they were just in the planning stages now. God knew what it would be like when actual construction started.

Better, he told himself. It had to be better.

There was a knock on the doorframe behind him, and Greg turned around. Tad Buckman stood on the porch of the office, grinding his cigarette into the cement slab with his work boot. "Ready to roll, boss? We're going to start surveying."

Greg sighed, nodded. "Yeah," he said. "I'll be right with you. Just let me get my spec sheets." He dropped the contract back on the desk and walked over to the file cabinet for the specs, stopping by the fax machine to pick up this morning's modifications.

2

Her period was late.

Shannon closed her locker and twirled the combination lock, shifting the textbooks from her left hand to her right. She was never late. Some girls, she knew, varied all the time. But she was as regular as clockwork. Her menstrual cycle had never been so much as a day off in her life.

Now her period was three days overdue.

She held the books in front of her as she headed down the hall toward Algebra, her first class. It was stupid, and she knew it was impossible, but she felt unbearably conspicuous, as though she were already showing, and she tried to cover her belly as she walked.

Maybe her mom was right. Maybe she should be eating more. That way she could attribute her expanding abdomen to weight gain rather than pregnancy.

Maybe she wasn't pregnant.

She sighed. With her luck?

No, she was almost certainly pregnant.

Probably with twins.

In movies, in books, in magazines, girls always shared this stuff with their sisters, but there was no way she could do that with Sam. She'd like to be able to have one of those after-hours bedroom conversations while their parents were asleep, to be able to explain her problem to her sister and get some sympathy and advice, but there was no way that was going to happen. Sam was just too perfect. She was pretty, she was popular, her grades were always good, she never got in trouble. Although boys had been chasing after her since she was fifteen, Shannon doubted that her sister had had sex yet. She'd probably wait until she was married.

If anything, Sam would be even more disapproving of her than her parents.

No, she couldn't talk about it to her sister.

She couldn't talk to Diane about it, either. Diane was her best friend, but she was still a blabbermouth, and Shannon knew that if she even hinted about her fears to Diane, the news would be all over school by the next day. And greatly exaggerated.

She didn't want that.

The only one she could tell was Jake. And she knew he wouldn't be happy to hear it. She didn't know exactly what his reaction would be, but she had a pretty good idea, and just the thought of the ensuing conversation made her stomach knot up with tension.

She wished she knew for sure. That would make it easier. It was the not knowing that was the worst part of it. If she knew that she was definitely pregnant, at least she could make plans, plot a course of action. As

it was, she could only worry and wonder, her mind vacil-
lating back and forth between scenarios.

She'd buy one of those home pregnancy tests and perform the test here in the bathroom at school, but she
knew that no matter where she bought it, word of the
purchase would eventually get back to her parents.

One of the many disadvantages of living in a small
town.

That was one good thing The Store would bring, she
thought. Anonymity.

The Store.

It was pathetic how excited everyone here was about
The Store. You'd think Neiman Marcus was coming to
Juniper, the way everyone was talking, not just some
chain discount retailer. It was like—

Her left foot slid backward beneath her.

She hadn't been paying attention to where she was
walking, and she realized instantly that someone had
spilled something on the floor and that she'd slipped in
it. Scrambling to maintain purchase, trying not to fall,
she clutched her books hard and stumbled backward,
accidentally bumping into Mindy Hargrove.

"Hey!" Mindy said, pushing her away. "Watch it,
Davis."

Shannon regained her footing. "Sorry. I slipped."

"I'll bet."

"It was an accident."

"Right."

Shannon frowned, moving way. "Oh, eat me, Mindy."

"You'd like that, wouldn't you?"

There was a chorus of whoops from the smattering of
kids still in the hall. Shannon held up her middle finger
and continued walking toward Algebra. Seconds later,
Diane came running up next to her, laughing. "That
was great."

"You saw that, huh?"

"You smacked right into her. Practically knocked
her over."

"There was water on the floor or something. I was
spacing and I slipped on it."

"Serves that stuck-up bitch right."

Shannon looked mock-offended. "Stuck-up? Mindy?"

Diane laughed, and the two of them walked into class just as the bell rang.

She didn't see Jake until History. She'd been half hoping that her period would come sometime during the morning, during one of her classes, but it hadn't. She desperately wanted to talk to him, wanted to tell him, but though they sat together in class, there were too many people around and it was not a good place to bring it up.

She decided to wait for lunch, but when the time came, she couldn't think of a way to broach the subject. The two of them sat alone together, on a wall near the Junior Circle, eating in silence, and Shannon started to tell him several times, but then she thought of the way he'd probably react to the news, and she couldn't decide how to begin.

Her distress must have been obvious, because halfway through lunch he took her hands in his and asked, "Is something wrong?"

She almost told him.

Almost.

But then she thought that her period might come at any minute, might come before the end of lunch, might come during her next class, and she shook her head and forced herself to smile and said, "No. Nothing's wrong. Why?"

3

Ginny sat in the staff lounge, eating her lunch as she watched the kids on the playground. The blinds were half-closed, but she could still see the tetherball and hopscotch courts as well as the bottom portions of the slide and monkey bars. Amidst the chaos of activity, she saw Larry Douglas chase Shaun Gilbert across the asphalt and through a hopscotch game, causing the girls involved in the game to scream for one of the lunch monitors.

Ginny smiled as she finished her Cup O' Noodles. Meg Silva, who taught sixth grade and had been staring out the window as well, shook her head. "Those Douglas kids are all troublemakers. I had Billy Douglas last year. I heard he just got suspended from junior high for vandalizing school property."

"Larry's not a troublemaker," Ginny said. "A little overactive maybe, but he's not a bad kid."

Meg snorted. "You learn to spot 'em. Talk to me in another fifteen years." The older woman crumpled up her sandwich wrapper and threw it in the trash can under the table before getting up from her seat and walking slowly over to the couch.

Ginny watched Meg settle in, then looked back toward the playground. She wondered if she would be as burntout when she was Meg's age. She didn't think so.

It was possible.

But she didn't think so.

She liked teaching grammar school. Her father wondered why she didn't teach high school, thought she was wasting her talents here, but she enjoyed working with young children. She felt as though she had more of an influence on them at this age, that she could do more to help mold and shape the way they turned out. Besides, grammar school kids were nice. Junior high students were brats, and high school students were too involved in their own teenage world to pay any attention to adults. But students this age still listened to her, still respected her authority. And, most importantly, she genuinely liked working with them. Sure, there were a few bad apples. There always were. But overall, they were good kids.

Mark French, the principal, walked into the staff room and over to the coffee machine. "Looks like culture is finally coming to Juniper," he said.

Ginny looked over at him. "What?"

"The Store." He held up the newspaper in his hand. "It says they're going to have a cappuccino and sushi bar instead of a regular snack bar. And they're going to carry videotapes of foreign films. For sale and rental. Northern Arizona is finally entering the twentieth century."

"Just as it's ending," Meg said.

"Better late than never." The principal finished pouring his coffee and walked out of the lounge, nodding good-bye. "Ladies."

"Ladies?" Meg snorted.

Ginny laughed.

She stared back out the window at the playground, feeling good. Cappuccino? Sushi? Foreign films? This was like a dream come true.

She couldn't wait to tell Bill.

He was going to be so happy.

THREE

1

He awoke to the sound of blasting.

At first, Bill thought it was part of his nightmare. He'd been battling creatures from an alien world, and when he heard the explosions, he thought they were merely a continuation of the dream. But Ginny was stirring next to him, and it was obvious that she'd heard the sounds, too.

She turned toward him, her eyes still half-closed. "What is it?"

"Blasting," he said.

"Blasting?" she said groggily. "Are they widening the highway or something? We would've heard about it if they were."

"No," Bill said. He pushed the covers off and rolled out of bed.

She shook her head. "What?"

"Nothing. Go back to sleep."

He slipped into his jogging suit as she silently snuggled back under the blankets. He knew what was happening, and it wasn't roadwork. There was only one major construction project in town this fall.

The Store.

His alarm wasn't set to ring for another fifteen minutes, so he turned it off on his way out of the bedroom. In the bathroom, he splashed water on his face to fully wake himself up, then went into the kitchen and downed a quick glass of orange juice before quietly sneaking out of the house.

Skipping his usual preliminary warm-up, he hurried down the drive to the road and started jogging.

Juniper seemed even more deserted than usual, and for once he found the lack of people oppressive rather than refreshing. He'd expected to see more lights in the houses, to see more people in the streets—hadn't anyone else heard the explosions?—but the town remained dark, dark and quiet, and he almost breathed a sigh of relief as he passed by the last of the downtown buildings and headed toward the highway.

Although the sun had not yet risen, there was a lightening of the sky behind the mountains as he approached his favorite stretch of highway. The forest was dark, the close-set trees still clinging to the blackness of night, but the open area ahead was clearly visible and bathed in a fading blue. He slowed down, not to savor the moment this time, but to see what was going on.

He stopped directly in front of the sign.

In the twenty-four hours since he'd last passed this spot, it had changed completely. The sign was still in place, but gone were the saplings and small bushes that had dotted the meadow. Gone was the meadow itself. The tall grass had been plowed under. Bare earth and surveyors' sticks marked the boundaries of the construction site. A portion of the hill had been blasted away, fallen timber and chunks of boulder fanning out onto the flat section of ground away from the remaining slope.

He stared at the scene, shocked. He'd seen pictures of rain forest destruction, the aftereffects of wanton slash-and-burn policies in underdeveloped countries, but even in his most pessimistic projections he had not expected to see anything like that here. Yet that was exactly what it looked like. The carefully planned and orderly executed clearing of the land that he would have thought a major chain like The Store would insist upon was nowhere in evidence. No trees had been saved, no effort had been made to preserve or protect the character of the area. The trees had been simply cut, the land gouged, the hillside blasted.

And they'd done it all in a day.

There was no sign of the workers, only the equipment—bulldozers, Caterpillars, shovels, cranes—parked side by side in the southeast corner of the site and set off by a chain-link fence. It had been only a half hour, maybe less, since he'd been awakened by the explosions, but the men who'd set off the blasts were nowhere to be seen. He looked carefully around, trying to spot someone, anyone, moving amidst the equipment. Nothing.

He frowned. Even if work was only performed at night, there was no way that there wouldn't be at least a few men still about—unless they'd detonated the explosives and then immediately vacated the site.

But he'd seen no cars on the highway, had met no vehicles on the road.

He jumped the small ditch adjoining the highway and walked past the sign onto the property, his jogging shoes sinking into the newly turned dirt. As he walked over rocks and ruts, around branches and boulders, his puzzlement over the workers reverted back to anger over the destruction of the meadow. How had this been allowed to happen? Where were the building inspectors? The code enforcement people? Juniper's zoning laws didn't allow builders to just decimate the landscape. The town's master plan specifically required all new businesses to "conform to the spirit and style of the existing community and its buildings, and to make a concerted effort to retain all geologic formations and as much natural vegetation as is feasible." The plan had been drafted in the early 1980s by the then-town council in an attempt to preserve the unique character of Juniper and its environs, and every council since had reinforced the town's commitment to controlled growth, making sure the builder of an apartment house incorporated an existing stand of ponderosas in his landscaping plans, withholding approval for a gas station until the company agreed to shift its building fifteen feet to the north in order to accommodate a huge house-sized boulder that had become a local landmark in the years it had sat on the undeveloped land.

Now, in one day, The Store had managed to circumvent that entire process and single-handedly destroy the most beautiful stretch of road within the town limits.

Well, that wouldn't last. As soon as it opened, he'd go directly to town hall and—

He stopped walking, his stomach sinking.

The perimeter of the site was littered with the carcasses of dead animals.

He took a deep breath as he stared at the scene before him. A wall of debris from the cleared meadow had been pushed back by bulldozers to the rear of the property and formed a semicircular barrier to the land beyond. He had seen only trees and bushes at first, logs and branches, but this close he could see that there were animal parts mixed in with the rest of the cleared brush, bodies lying on the ground in front of the debris. As his gaze moved slowly from left to right, he counted four deer, three wolves, six javelina, and over a dozen raccoons, squirrels, and chipmunks.

How had this many animals been killed?

And why?

The deer.

The deer had been an omen, a taste of things to come. He had thought it odd at the time, eerie even, but now the animal's death seemed downright malevolent. It was as if the deer had died as a result of the erected sign. And now these other animals had died because the land had been cleared.

Their deaths seemed to be the price of construction.

It was a trade.

That was stupid, he knew, but logical or not, something about the idea felt right to him, and goose bumps arose beneath the cooling sweat on his arms as he stared at the curved line of bodies.

He began walking forward. The first deer had not been shot or injured. Had these other animals died naturally?

He strode quickly across the unevenly graded ground. Two days ago, he would have laughed had anybody suggested anything as ludicrous as what he was thinking. This was a construction site. Local workers, people he probably knew, had been hired to clear a piece of land and build a building. There was nothing strange or unnatural about that.

Only there was. He didn't know how, didn't know why, but somehow within the last twenty-four hours everything had changed. The entire world seemed different. His unshakable faith in the rational and the material had been shaken, and while he wasn't ready to believe in ghosts and goblins and little green men, he wasn't quite the skeptic he had been. It was an unnerving feeling, and it didn't sit well with him, and once again he found himself wondering if it wasn't his personal connection with this area that was coloring his viewpoint.

Third Store Massacre in a Month.

Then again, maybe it wasn't.

He reached the first animal, a wolf. Like the deer, its stomach was distended. Also like the deer, there was no physical sign of violence. The wolf did not even appear to have been pushed here by a bulldozer. There wasn't a mark on it. It was as if it had walked or crawled to this spot of its own free will and died.

He looked past the dead animal to the wall of cleared debris immediately beyond.

And saw an arm protruding from the tangle of rocks and brush.

Bill's heart leaped in his chest. He took a hesitant step forward to verify that what he thought he was seeing was what he really *was* seeing.

Sticking out between the bare branches of a dead manzanita bush was a white hand and forearm, smeared with mud and blood.

He backed up, stumbled across the rutted remains of the meadow, and, as the sun rose over the mountains, ran down the highway as fast as he could toward the police station in town.

He returned with the police to the scene, answering questions and watching as they pulled the corpse out from the rubble. After the body had been loaded into an ambulance and taken away, he rode back to the station with Forest Everson. The detective took down an official statement, which Bill read and signed.

It was after ten when he was finally through with all of the forms and questions and reports. In the furor over finding the body, The Store's destruction of the meadow and its wanton disregard for local zoning ordinances had been pushed to the side, but though Bill was still disturbed by what he'd found, he had not been distracted from his original purpose, and he walked next door, to the town hall, and explained to the young acne-scarred clerk behind the counter that he wanted to talk to one of the building or code enforcement inspectors.

"Mr. Gilman's out for the week," the clerk said.

"And who is Mr. Gilman?"

"He's the code enforcement officer."

"Isn't there anyone else I could talk to?" Bill asked.

"Well, what exactly is the problem?"

"The problem is that whoever's in charge of clearing the land for The Store has totally ignored Juniper's zoning regulations. They cut down every tree on that property, they blasted a section of hillside—"

"You want to talk to Mr. Curtis. He's the Planning Director."

"Fine," Bill said. "Let me talk to him."

"Actually, he's not here right now. He's attending a seminar in Scottsdale. If you want, I can have him call you when he gets back. It's just a one-day thing. He should be in tomorrow."

"Look, all I want to do is let someone know what's happening so inspectors can be sent out there before any more damage is done."

The young man looked uneasy. "I, uh, think everything's been approved."

Bill stared at him. "What?"

"I think that was all okayed." He looked around the office, as though searching for someone higher up to help him out, but there was only a secretary seated at a desk against the far wall, typing on a computer and pointedly ignoring the exchange. "You'd have to talk to Mr. Curtis, but I think the Planning Commission gave The Store a waiver."

Bill was stunned. "How's that possible? I didn't hear anything about it."

The young man shifted his feet uncomfortably. "You'd have to talk to Mr. Curtis."

"Mr. Curtis? I want to talk to the mayor!"

"He's not in his office, but I could leave a message to have him call you."

"Is *anybody* in their office right now?"

"There's a town council meeting tonight. Six o'clock. You might bring it up in open discussion."

Yes, Bill thought. Open discussion. A public forum. That was exactly where this needed to be brought up. There was something fishy going on here. Decisions affecting the entire town had apparently been made by the Planning Commission in closed sessions, without any input from members of the public. He didn't know whether or not there had been any bribes involved, any promises made in exchange for cash or stock options or whatever, but something wasn't right, and it needed to be brought to the attention of the public.

He'd call Ben, make sure the editor put it in the paper.

"Thank you," Bill told the clerk. "I think I will bring it up in front of the council. What time does the meeting start?"

"Six o'clock. In the council chambers next door."

"I'll be there," Bill said.

Ginny called at lunch to find out how things had gone. He'd phoned her earlier, when he'd first run to the police station, to tell her that he'd found a dead body and wouldn't be home before she left for work. Now he filled in the details, explaining that they didn't know who the man was or how he'd died but that the body was being taken up to the county coroner's office in Flagstaff.

"Was he murdered?" she asked.

"I don't know," he said. "I guess we won't find out until they do an autopsy."

"That's so creepy."

You don't know the half of it, he thought. He was silent for a moment, considered telling her about the animals, but something kept him from it, and he switched the subject to The Store's desecration of the land.

"So that's what that blasting was," she said.

"They totally destroyed it. Drive by after work. You won't even recognize it."

"And that's how you found the body? When you were looking at the damage?"

"Yeah. I was walking onto the meadow—or what used to be the meadow—to check it out, and I saw an arm sticking out of the debris. I hauled back to the police station and told the cops." He leaned back in his chair, looked out the window at the forest. "There's not a tree left on that site, Gin. By the end of the week, the rocks and the hill and everything else will be gone, too. It'll just be a flat cleared space."

"What did you expect?"

"I don't know. I guess I figured they'd make a token effort to make the store blend in with the area, you know, not piss off the locals. But they just raped the place. Slash and burn. It looks like some Third-World construction site." He paused. "I'm going to the town council meeting tonight to talk about it. I think they violated the town's zoning ordinances, but when I talked to a guy at town hall, he made it sound like the Planning Commission granted them an exemption."

"Did you ask Ben if he knew anything about it?"

"No. I'm going to call him later."

"So what are you planning to do?"

"Nothing. Ask some questions, get some answers. I can't say I'll be completely surprised if our local leaders sold us down the river, but I want to make sure they're held accountable for it. You want to go with me tonight?"

"No."

"Come on."

"I have to work in this town. Those people you'll be butting heads with are my students' parents. I'm staying out of this."

"All right. I'll go with Ben."

"That's fine."

Ginny only had a half hour for lunch, and she said she had to hurry up and eat before recess ended, so he let her go, hung up, and walked into the kitchen to fix his own lunch—a can of ravioli.

Later that afternoon, he called Ben, and the newspaper editor told him that the body was that of a transient, a hitcher apparently passing through town on his way to Albuquerque. A preliminary examination indicated that the man had died from exposure, not from any injuries or inflicted wounds.

"I guess he was just lying there in the brush and got scooped up by a Cat or something while they were clearing the lot," Ben said. "It's kind of weird, but it's perfectly understandable."

"Is it?" Bill asked.

"What's that supposed to mean?"

"Nothing. You going to the council meeting tonight?"

"I always go. It's my job. Why?"

"I need someone to sit next to. Ginny doesn't want to go."

"Candy ass. I sit by myself every meeting."

"You're a he-man."

The editor snorted. "Why are you going?"

"To stop The Store from building here in Juniper."

Ben chuckled. "A little late for that, don't you think?"

"Probably. But have you seen what they've done to that land?"

"It's their land."

"There are zoning ordinances, building codes, rules, laws."

"And sometimes they get waived."

Bill was taken aback. "What have you heard?"

"I'm not a complete dunderhead. I ask questions when I see things that seem a little odd to me. I'm supposed to do that, you know. Being a reporter and all."

"And?"

"And, off the record, I was told that concessions had to be made if Juniper was going to get The Store. Otherwise, it was going to go to Randall. There was sort of a bidding war going on between our two fair towns, and whoever came up with the sweetest incentives would get the extra jobs, the added property tax revenue, and all those other wonderful perks that new businesses bring."

"Shit."

"You're going to be a lone ranger on this one. The

town's hurting. A lot of people here would peddle their own mama's ass if it would bring in new jobs. They're going to think bending a few cosmetic rules a small price to pay for economic security."

"What do you think?"

"What I think doesn't matter."

"But what do you think?"

Ben was silent for a moment. "Off the record?"

"Off the record."

"I'll deny I ever said this. I'm supposed to be impartial. My livelihood's involved here, too."

"Understood."

"I wouldn't've minded if The Store went to Randall."

Bill realized that he'd been holding his breath. He exhaled. "Why?" he asked.

"I don't know," the editor admitted.

"Come on. You can tell me."

"I'm being honest," he said. "I really don't know."

"But you don't like The Store."

"No," Ben said, and his voice was low, quiet, serious. "I don't like The Store."

2

They ate dinner early so he'd be able to get to the council meeting on time. Samantha offered to go with him, but he could tell that both of the girls were apprehensive about him speaking in front of the council, and he told her that it was okay, he was going with Ben.

Shannon was more direct. "Don't embarrass us, Dad."

He grinned. "Do I ever?"

"Constantly."

He and Ginny laughed.

The girls didn't.

After dinner, he drove to the town hall, glancing out the window at the empty storefronts and abandoned buildings as he drove. Downtown had been slowly dying ever since the lumber mill had closed in the late eighties. Blame had been placed by the locals on "environmentalists," a nebulous group that included not only the loose coalition of scientists, national ecological organizations, and ordinary Arizona citizens who had rallied to the defense of the endangered pine squirrel and had succeeded in getting the federal government to impose a moratorium on logging in this section of the Tonto, but also anyone who supported any sort of government regulation, be it health and safety standards or prohibitions against the dumping of toxic waste. The truth was that the pine squirrel had only hastened the inevitable, probably to the long-term advantage of the town. Logging could not have continued at its previous pace for more than another half decade before the entire supply of timber in the region would have been depleted. Trees were a renewable resource, and the logging companies had been pretty good about reseeding the land, but the fact remained that they were cutting a lot faster than the trees were growing.

Tourism had always been Juniper's second-biggest industry, and it would have disappeared had the area's scenery been marred by deforestation. No railroad ran through Juniper, no major thoroughfares passed through the town, it was neither convenient to reach nor strategically important to any company or corporation. The beauty of the pine country was Juniper's only selling point. The recession had hurt tourism, but the recession was ending, and despite the dying downtown, the region was realigning itself with the changing economy. Outside investors had bought land and built time-shares, and there was even talk about putting up a resort near Castle Creek.

Still, the high wages and steady employment of the lumber mill days were long gone, and the town council and chamber of commerce had been trying for some time now to lure corporate offices and software firms and other light industry to the area in order to bring jobs back to the region.

Now they'd landed The Store.

Bill pulled into the small, partially paved parking lot and swung his Jeep next to Ben's pickup. The editor had already staked out a seat in the front row of the council chambers, and Bill scooted in next to him. He glanced around the room. "Not very crowded."

"Never is. Here." Ben handed him a single sheet of paper with double-sided printing. "Council agenda."

"Anything exciting?"

The editor shook his head, grinning. "Nope. Looks like you're going to be the lead in my article. Give 'em hell."

The meeting commenced soon after. A local minister led the attendees in a prayer and the pledge of allegiance, there were some routine votes on procedural matters, then the mayor said, "We'll open the floor to comments from the public."

Ben nudged him. "That's you. Stand up and talk."

Bill stood, wiping his hands on his jeans. He was suddenly nervous, and he realized that he hadn't planned what he was going to say. He should've written it ahead of time and printed it out so he could read from a prepared text. Now he was going to bumble and stumble his way through a probably incoherent diatribe and forfeit any hope of credibility. His chances of effecting any sort of change were going to go straight into the toilet.

The mayor nodded at him. "Please step up to the podium and state your name and address for the record."

Bill walked up the side aisle to the front of the council chambers and stood at the speaker's podium. He adjusted the microphone in front of him and spoke into it. "My name is Bill Davis. I live at 121 Rock Springs Lane."

The mayor motioned for him to continue.

Bill glanced around the council chambers and cleared his throat nervously. "We all know that The Store is coming to Juniper, and I'm sure most of you have noticed by now that construction workers have decimated a stretch of land next to the highway just this side of the Acres. I jog by there every morning, so I saw it immediately. I understand that that's The Store's property, and I realize that they have to clear the land in order to put up the store and parking lot and everything, but I'm pretty sure that our local building codes are not being followed, and I know this goes against the town's Master Plan."

He paused, was about to continue, but the mayor spoke first. "We appreciate your concern, Mr. Davis, but The Store has proved in other towns to be a responsible and respected addition to the community. It's true that designs for The Store do not conform to Juniper's Master Plan and do differ in some respects from our local codes and ordinances, but compromises were required to lure The Store to our town, and we think the trade-offs were worth it. More jobs are going to be created, better goods will be provided to our citizens, everyone will be better off in the long run."

"I understand that," Bill said. "But why doesn't The Store have to follow the same rules everyone else has to follow? I don't think they should be exempt from the law, and I'll bet a lot of our local businessmen feel the same way."

"The Store is a national chain," the mayor said. "For obvious reasons, they have their own building designs and construction standards. They want all of their retail outlets, in every town, to look the same so they're easily recognizable. The corporation does not cave in to local pressures because it has a national agenda."

"It's like McDonald's or Burger King," Bill Reid, the councilman to the mayor's right, spoke up. "They all look the same. They have to. Otherwise, their national ads wouldn't work."

"I also have to point out," the mayor added, "that all of the towns that have a Store allow the corporation to dictate the terms of its construction. If we hadn't acceded to their wishes, Randall would have. And we would have lost The Store."

"I think we could have kept The Store and maintained our local standards, preserved the character of our town. I don't think it was necessary to totally decimate the property in order to put up a building. Hell, that's what those codes and ordinances are supposed to prevent. Our strongest selling point here is our natural beauty. I don't think we should let anyone take that away from us."

A burly, bearded, belligerent-looking man seated in the back of the council chambers stood up and strode angrily to the front of the room. Bill didn't know the man, but he'd seen him around town and he stood aside as the man stepped up to the podium and the microphone.

"State your name and address," the mayor said.

"Greg Hargrove," the man said. "1515 Aspen Road."

Bill wasn't sure if his turn was over and he was supposed to sit down, but he wasn't through talking, so he remained where he was.

Hargrove turned on him. "What's your problem, mister?"

Bill was taken aback. "What?"

"My company cleared that land. We followed the specs given to us by The Store, and we have all the proper permits. What the hell's your problem?"

"I have no problem with you," Bill said. "You were just doing your job. I have a problem with The Store's plans and with the fact that the Planning Commission and the council allowed the company to ignore our local ordinances and destroy one of the most scenic pieces of property in the area."

Hargrove shook his head disgustedly. "The Store will create jobs. Don't you understand that? All you tree-huggers care about is saving squirrels. You don't give a damn about people."

"You're wrong. I do care about people. I care about the people in this town. And I'm thinking of what's best for the long-term interest of all of Juniper, not just the short-term benefit to you and other construction workers."

"Bullshit!"

Hargrove was getting angry, really angry, and Bill stepped back, taking his hands out of his pockets and keeping them free—in case he needed to use them to defend himself.

"We will not have that sort of language in the council chambers," the mayor said.

"We moved to this town because of the area," Bill said evenly. "Believe it or not, the environment here—

the trees, the forest, the mountains—is the town's major selling point. People don't move here for city reasons or city jobs. That's why they move to Phoenix. Or Chicago. Or L.A. That's not why they move to Juniper."

"All you care about—"

"Maintaining jobs and protecting the environment are not mutually exclusive. You're thinking in old terms. You're thinking of the past. That's one of the great advantages of the Information Superhighway. With computers, you can now work for a company in New York or Los Angeles or, hell, even Paris or London, and have your office right here in Juniper. That's what I do. What I'm trying to say is that, yes, we need jobs here, but we can bring jobs to our area without sacrificing our quality of life."

"Well, I'm not a computer geek. I own a construction business. You can't do my work with a computer."

"I understand that—"

"You don't understand shit! All you environmentalists want to protect every square inch of land, but you don't give a damn how it affects businesses like mine. How much more do you want to protect? The government already owns all the land around here! The whole fucking county's practically BLM territory!"

"Mr. Hargrove!" the mayor said. "If you continue to use that sort of language, I will have you removed from the council chambers."

"Sorry, your honor." Hargrove looked embarrassed.

"Look," Bill said. "If Ted Turner or Bill Gates or some other billionaire bought exactly that same land, decided to protect it and put up a big fence around it, leaving it as is, you'd have no problem with it. Why is it okay for an individual to save land for himself but not okay for the government to save land for future generations? Two hundred years ago, there were only thirteen little colonies on the east coast of our country. Now we have chain stores in Juniper! If things continue at this rate, our great-grandchildren will be living in a world like *Soylent Green* or *Silent Running*!"

"*Soylent Green*." Hargrove grinned. "Good movie."

"That's not the point. We need to think about the future—"

"Mr. Davis," the mayor said. "I think we've had enough discussion on this subject. I appreciate your concern, but I think you're starting to get a little melodramatic. The world is not going to end because The Store is coming to Juniper. What will happen is that we'll have more jobs and a better place to shop. Period. I think you should both sit down." He looked out at the sparsely populated auditorium. "If anyone else has anything to add on this subject or has anything else to bring up, please step forward to the podium."

Bill walked back to his seat, slumped into the chair next to Ben.

"Game over," the editor said. "Davis zip. Store takes it in straight sets."

Bill looked over at his friend. "Thanks."

He drove home angry, feeling depressed. The mayor had been right. He *had* been melodramatic, and that asshole Hargrove had gotten him off on a tangent and his whole argument had gotten derailed. He thought again that he should've written everything out ahead of time and read it.

But it was too late now. The damage was done.

The front of the house was dark when he arrived home. He let himself in, checked on the girls. Sam was in her room, studying. Shannon was on the phone. He told them both to go to sleep early, it was a school night, then walked back to the master bedroom where Ginny was riding the exercise bike and watching TV.

"How'd it go?" she asked. "Did you stop construction and get The Store to rebuild the hillside and replant the trees?"

He sat down on the side of the bed, took off his shoes. "There's no reason to be sarcastic."

"Sorry." She stopped pedaling. "So what happened?"

"What do you think? Nothing. The council's bending and spreading 'em for The Store." He shook his head. "They're so shortsighted. They're willing to ruin a way of life for short-term economic gain."

"Then why don't you run for council?" Ginny said.

"Why don't you stop complaining to me and get out and do something about it?"

"I might do just that."

Ginny got off the bike, walked over to the bed, and sat down next to him. "It's not the end of the world, you know. Don't you think you're overreacting just a little bit?"

He smiled wryly. "That's just what our fair mayor said."

"Things change. Yes, The Store tore down trees and everything—and they shouldn't have done it—but I heard that they also bought that vacant lot next to the old Checker Auto and they're going to make it into a baseball diamond. They're trying to do something for the town."

"You're missing the point."

"What is the point?"

"Never mind."

"Never mind? You want to—"

"I'm all talked out," he said. "I've been talking all night. I just want to go to bed." He stood, took off his pants.

She watched him for a moment. "Fine," she said, and there was an angry tightness in her voice. "That's just fine."

They slept apart, not touching, on opposite sides of the bed.

He fell sleep almost instantly.

He dreamed of dead animals and dead bodies and the unending construction of a black building that reached miles into a polluted sky.

FOUR

1

Shannon sat at one of the tables outside George's Hamburgers, nursing a Coke and trying to read her history textbook. Jake was supposed to have met her here after school, but it had already been a half hour and he hadn't shown and she was starting to get restless.

She finally closed her book, giving up all pretext of studying. She stared across the street at the grassy lawn of the park and the dark pines of the forest beyond. Above the trees, the mountains were capped with irregular slices of white. The snow had not yet dropped below the timberline, but despite the sunny days of the past week, it had not melted off the peaks, and it was only a matter of time before winter arrived in full force.

The snow on the mountains reminded her of the Alps, and the Alps reminded her of *The Sound of Music,* and she found herself thinking of the oldest daughter and her boyfriend in the movie. The boyfriend was a mailman or something and he would pretend to deliver letters in order to secretly meet with the girl. Shannon had always found that relationship very romantic and very sexy. Especially when the daughter sang "Sixteen, Going On Seventeen." There was something sensual in the way she danced in the gazebo, in the sly expression on her face as she twirled for the boy, letting her dress fly up, letting him see her underwear. She seemed so much older than he did at that moment, so much more experienced.

She liked that.

She liked to think that was the sort of relationship she and Jake had, but she knew that wasn't the case. Jake had had several girlfriends before her, whereas he was the first boy she'd ever held hands with, ever kissed, ever . . . done anything with.

It worried her a little that he'd had other girlfriends. He'd assured her that nothing had gone beyond the hand-holding stage—and she chose to believe him about that—but he had no doubt told each of them that he loved them and that they'd be together forever.

The same things he told her.

Which meant that he could leave her the same way he'd left them.

If he found someone better.

That scared her. She'd seen him looking at her sister when he thought she wasn't watching, and though she told herself it didn't mean anything, was just a natural response, it still hurt. She knew that if he had been allowed to choose between the two of them, he would probably have taken Sam. Of course, who wouldn't prefer Sam? Her sister was prettier than she was, smarter. She'd be any boy's first choice.

She didn't blame Sam, though. If anything, she blamed Jake, although that was not something she'd ever admit to or bring up with him. But Shannon did not hate her sister. Sure, she was jealous sometimes, but she admired her sister more than resented her. She wished she herself was more like Sam, but she didn't blame her sister for that.

Some people just got lucky.

Some people didn't.

She herself had gotten a little bit lucky this time. She wasn't pregnant. Her period had come today during Algebra, and she'd never felt as relieved as she did when the cramps started.

Which was why she was so anxious for Jake to show up.

Where was he?

She glanced up and down the block, saw him come out of the grocery store across the street, eating a candy bar. He saw her, waved, but made no effort to hurry across the parking lot. She wanted to run over to him, tell him the good news, but something about his unhurried, nonchalant attitude annoyed her, and she remained at her table, sipping her Coke, until he arrived.

"So?" he said, sitting down on the rounded plastic bench across from her. "Any news?"

"I'm not pregnant."

"Thank God." He exhaled deeply, then took her hand across the table and smiled. "You had me going there for a while. I was trying to think if you should have the baby and we should get married, or find a place to get an abortion, and if we'd have to quit school, and where we'd get the money. We really lucked out on this one."

"We have to do something, though. Before we make love again. I don't want to go through all this every time."

His smile faded. "I'm not going to wear a rubber."

"Then I'll . . . get something."

"What?" he asked. "And where? And how?"

She looked at him. Was he stupid? Hadn't he learned anything from the close call they'd just had? It sounded like he was arguing against using any form of birth control, like he wanted her to have sex with him and just take her chances.

"Fine," she said. "We'll wait till we're married, then."

"You can't get pregnant with oral sex."

She stared at him in shock.

He nodded enthusiastically. "You could just suck me instead, and then we wouldn't have to worry about it."

She didn't know what to say or how to respond. They had never performed that act before, had never even talked about it, and though she knew about oral sex, she'd always planned on avoiding it. The idea of having sperm in her mouth disgusted her, especially after she'd seen how thick and sticky and snotlike it was, and she figured that if Jake really loved her, he would never ask her to do that.

"That way," he said, "we could still have sex, we wouldn't have to worry about a junior coming along, and I wouldn't have to wear a rubber."

"What's wrong with a condom?"

"I don't want to have anything between us."

So you'd rather just use my mouth as a sperm receptacle? she thought. You don't care about my feelings at all? A condom's uncomfortable, so you want me to give up having my orgasm and be grateful that I get to make you have one?

But she said nothing.

He squeezed her hand. "I think it's more romantic if there's nothing between us."

She forced herself to smile, though she felt sick inside. "Me, too," she said.

Her parents were asleep, and she had just finished chronicling the series of misadventures that had made up today and was hiding her journal beneath her mattress when Samantha walked into the room.

"Hey," Shannon said, looking up.

"Hey." Samantha sat down on the edge of the bed.

Something was wrong. Sam didn't just come into her room to hang out. When her sister dropped by it was always for a reason. She wanted to borrow something. Or she needed Shannon to help her lift something. Or she wanted to complain about the messiness of the bathroom.

She did not just come by to chat.

Samantha looked around the room. "Is there anything you want to talk about?" she asked.

Shannon frowned. "No. Why?"

Sam's face reddened. "I just thought . . . we're sisters, you know. You can talk to me if something's wrong."

No, I can't, Shannon thought, but she said nothing.

Sam took a deep breath. "We both share the same bathroom, you know. I can't help noticing if things . . . change."

Oh, God. She'd noticed that there were no maxi-pads in the wastepaper basket! Shannon felt a sinking in the pit of her stomach. "There's nothing wrong," she said.

Samantha's blush deepened. She almost stood, almost left, then changed her mind and started to say something, but only ended up clearing her throat. She looked away. "I know your period hasn't come," she said.

Shannon felt her own face grow hot. She didn't want to talk about this with her sister.

"Does Jake know? Have you told him?"

"There's nothing to tell," Shannon said. "I was just late. God, do I have to discuss every aspect of my body with you? Do you want me to tell you when I have to blow my nose? Do you want to know when I have diarrhea?"

"No!" Sam's face was now completely red. "I was worried, that's all."

"Well, worry about yourself! Don't worry about me!" Samantha stood, strode out of the room. "Sorry I was born!"

"So am I!" Shannon hurried after her sister and slammed the bedroom door shut behind her. She stood there for a moment, shaking, then sat back down on the bed, leaned her head against the pillow, and closed her eyes.

It was a long time before she fell sleep.

2

"Check."

Bill watched as Street McHenry moved his rook down the length of the board to steal Bill's bishop.

He thought for a moment, then picked up his knight, started moving it to capture the rook, but saw that that would leave his king undefended and allow Street's queen to take his king. Slowly, he moved his knight back into place.

Street shook his head. "What a pussy."

Bill grinned. "That's exactly what I said to your sister last night."

"Before she burst out laughing?"

"Laughing? She was gasping. In awe. My length is my strength."

"Just make your play," Ben said. "Christ, if you two spent as much time playing chess as you did flapping your gums, we might get out of here before midnight one of these evenings."

"Midnight?" Bill said. "It's only eight o'clock."

"Just play the damn game."

Four moves later, the game was over.

Street won.

As always.

Bill had won the computer match the night before.

As always.

"Record unbroken," Ben announced.

The three of them stood, stretched. Street finished off his beer, gathered up all of their cans and carried them to the kitchen.

Bill turned toward the editor. There'd been an article on The Store in today's paper, a fairly long feature describing the chain's history and plans for the Juniper store. The article had quoted Newman King, founder and CEO of The Store, extensively. "I read your Store article," he said. "You actually interviewed Newman King?"

The editor snorted. "Hell, no. They sent me a press release, quotes included, and I stole liberally from it."

"I was wondering. I thought he was like a Howard Hughes character, didn't like to appear in public and all that."

"Them's the rumors," Ben said. "To be honest, I did try to call corporate headquarters and get my own quotes, but if King ever did deign to speak with the press, it'd probably be to Barbara Walters or Jane Pauley, or Dan or Tom or Peter, not to a lowly podunk reporter like yours truly. I was told, politely but firmly, that King speaks to his customers through press releases and that those were the only quotes I'd be getting." He shrugged. "So I used them."

Bill nodded. "I should've known it was something like that."

Street put away the board, and the three of them walked out of the house and down the road to the café as they always did after these chess matches. The night was clear, the air cold and brisk. It felt good, and Bill exhaled as he walked, trying to blow smoke rings with the steam of his breath.

"Saw your article on Bill," Street said. "You made him sound almost articulate."

Ben grinned. "That's my job."

They laughed.

"I'm not too keen on The Store, either," Street admitted.

Bill shook his head. "That building'll totally fuck up the character of the town."

"Not just that, it's going to cut into my business. The Store sells electronic equipment. Stereos and radios and tools and wire and adapters. And they can probably sell it cheaper than I can. I'm not exactly rolling in dough as it is. I don't know how I'll be able to survive once they come in." He glanced over at Ben. "I was thinking maybe you could do some type of story on how The Store will affect local merchants, try to drum up some support for us. I know the town council and the construction companies are all gung ho for this, but none of us in the chamber of commerce are thrilled. A lot of us are just hanging on by a thread. The Store might finish us off."

"Sure," Ben said. "I don't know why I didn't think of it myself."

"I won't shop there," Bill said.

"You never shop in town anyway. You always go down to Phoenix."

"I shop at your place."

"That's true," Street conceded. "That's true."

"Maybe I'll start shopping here more."

"It's about time."

They reached the café, walked inside. A family was seated at one of the booths next to the window, a teenaged boy and girl at another. Buck Maitland and Vernon Thompson, the two old men who seemed to live at the café, were sitting on stools at the counter, full coffee cups and empty french fry dishes in front of them.

Street waved to Holly, the waitress behind the cash register, and the three of them sat down in the booth closest to the door. Holly stopped by, menus in hand, but they said they just wanted coffee, and with a look of annoyance she retreated behind the counter to pour their orders.

Street and Ben were already talking about something else, some suspense movie they'd both seen on cable, but Bill wasn't listening. It had taken him only a few seconds to determine that the two old men at the counter were talking about The Store, and he tried to tune out everything else and zero in on their conversation.

"Yeah," Buck was saying, "my son's working on that project."

"How's it coming?"

Buck shrugged. "Don't seem too happy."

"Why not?"

Buck took a sip of his coffee. "Don't rightly know. But it seems like a hard job. You know how some jobs just go smoothly? Everything kinda flows together? Well, this ain't like that."

"I heard there's been a lot of accidents," Vernon said. "My brother-in-law knows the blaster on that job. He's a powder monkey from way back, worked on Boulder and Glen Canyon, and he said the same thing. Said they've had more accidents on this job, which should've been a cakewalk, than they had on that stretch of highway they blasted through Pine Ridge. Said this is the toughest blast since the canyon."

"You heard about Greg Hargrove, didn't you?"

"Yeah," Vernon said. "The cliff road." He shook his head. "Guy was an asshole, but he didn't deserve to die that way."

"That's why I'm not real happy with my son there. Like you said, a lot of accidents."

Accidents.

Bill felt cold.

"Earth to Bill, Earth to Bill."

He turned to see both Ben and Street staring at him.

"Are you back on this plane?" the editor asked.

He laughed. "Sorry. I was thinking about something else."

"Everything all right?"

"Yeah," he said. "Yeah."

But he still felt cold.

3

Ginny stopped by the farmer's market after work. She did most of her shopping at Buy-and-Save, but the store's produce was consistently poor and she preferred to purchase her vegetables from the local growers who sold at the farmer's market. The prices were a little higher, but the quality was a hundred times better and she would rather her money go to local farmers than to some anonymous produce supplier.

She bought tomatoes and tomatillos, lettuce and onions, then drove home, where Shannon and Samantha were both lounging around the living room, watching TV. "Where's your father?" she asked as she dumped the sack of vegetables on the kitchen counter.

"Music store," Samantha said. "He told us to tell you he was bored and restless and needed some new tunes."

Ginny sighed. "He must be in the middle stretch. He always gets antsy when he's halfway through a manual. Did he say when he'd be back?"

"No."

"Well, we're having tacos for dinner. If he's not back by the time I finish chopping the vegetables and cooking the hamburger, he's on his own." She started unloading the produce sack.

Samantha sat up, then stood, walking over to the kitchen. "Need any help?"

"No. But change the channel. I want to hear the news. If you guys want to watch something else, do it in your rooms."

"Mom!" Shannon said, but she switched the station.

Samantha pulled out a stool, sitting down at the counter, watching her mother fold the sack and put it in the cupboard under the sink. "I think I'm going to go to ASU next year," she said.

"I thought you wanted to go to UC Brea or New Mexico State."

"Well, unless you or Dad win the lottery, chances of that look pretty slim."

Ginny laughed. "Glad you finally see it our way."

"The thing is, I'm going to need money. Even if I get a scholarship—and I probably will—my counselor said that'll only cover tuition. After that, there's books, room and board. I'll need transportation, too." She glanced out the window. "I figure if I start saving up now I'll be able to afford to afford a used car by the end of next summer."

Ginny nodded. "Your father goes to that car auction in Holbrook during the summer. Maybe you could find something there.'

Samantha nodded. "It's worth a try." She paused. "The thing is, I want to work at The Store—"

In the living room, Shannon laughed. "Dad'll love that."

Samantha looked at her mother. "That's why I was hoping you could sort of smooth the way for me. Maybe if you brought it up . . ."

Ginny held up her hands. "No. This is between you and your father."

"Come on, Mom. Please? You know his brain snaps on that subject. And if I bring it up he'll automatically say no and that'll be that. You can pave the way for me, get him used to the idea."

Ginny opened the top drawer, took out her chopping knife.

"Mom?"

"He's not going to want you to work at The Store."

"But you could hint around about it, soften him up."

"Why can't you work someplace else? George's? Or Buy-and-Save? Or KFC?"

"There aren't a lot of jobs in this town, in case you haven't noticed. Besides, I heard The Store pays better. Five bucks an hour, part-time."

"Wow," Shannon said. "That is pretty good." She walked up to the counter. "Maybe I can work there, too."

"If your grades don't improve, you're not working anywhere."

Shannon leaned across the counter, grabbed a piece of lettuce.

Ginny blinked, feigned shock. "Are you actually eating voluntarily?"

"Of course."

"Shannon Davis? This can't be true. Are your eating disorder days actually over?"

"They were never here. Except in your mind." Shannon stole another piece of lettuce and retreated back into the living room.

"So what do you say?"

Ginny looked at Samantha, sighed. "All right," she said. "I'll give it a shot. But I'm not promising anything."

"You're the most wonderful mom in the world."

Ginny laughed. "Just remember that when your father turns you down."

FIVE

1

There was a light layer of frost on the ground, but Bill awoke early as usual, put on his sweat suit, put on his gloves, put on an extra pair of socks, put on the knit ski cap Ginny called his "homeless hat," and went out for his morning jog just like he always did. He knew he was being a bit of a fanatic, but he'd made a promise to himself when he'd started exercising that, rain or shine, sleet or snow, he would jog at least three miles every day.

It was a promise he had kept.

He quickly sped through his stretching exercises, then ran down to the edge of the drive. He jogged up the dirt road, through the trees, down the hill, but when he reached the paved road and Godwin's meadow, he continued straight rather than turning into Main.

He had stopped jogging on the highway.

He ran past the trailer park into Juniper's residential area, careful not to slip on the frosty asphalt. He had not varied his jogging route in the ten years that they'd lived in Juniper—partly out of habit, partly out of intent. He was not the type of person to arbitrarily change his routine. Once he found something he liked, he stuck with it.

But he had changed his routine now.

He thought about the site of The store, the stretch of land that had been his favorite but was now the area he specifically avoided. There was something about the razed trees and flattened ground that did not sit well with him. It reminded him of Orange County, the place where he'd been born and raised, where he'd seen orange groves and strawberry patches give way to peach-colored condos and cookie-cutter shopping centers, and it depressed him to see the cleared earth, the demolished hillside, the chain-link fencing surrounding the heavy machinery. It upset him, angered him, and it ruined the mood of his morning jog.

But it wasn't just that, was it?

No, he had to admit. It wasn't.

It had been disconcerting at first to realize that he was not the calm, levelheaded rationalist he'd always believed himself to be, but he had made the adjustment to the new instinctual Bill Davis much more easily than he would have thought possible. It had been a basically painless transition, and he now found himself, without apology, looking for unseen and nonlinear connections between unrelated events in the same way he had previously searched for the logical reason behind every occurrence. It was strangely liberating, this reliance on gut feeling rather than hard fact, and in a way it required more intellectual acumen, more comparative analysis, more of the mental disciplines usually associated with the scientific method than did a strict adherence to a preconceived mind-set.

But that was intellectualizing.

The truth was that he was frightened of The Store. He might be able to come up with reasons for his feelings, but whether or not he could rationalize them, whether or not he could explain their existence, they were there, his natural reaction to the site, and that was why he had changed his jogging route.

The last time he'd been by, the previous Tuesday, when he'd had to drive up to Flagstaff with Ben to buy a water pump for the Suburban, he'd noticed the framework of the building already going up. They weren't wasting any time. Ordinarily, construction projects dragged on for months around here—the local contractors were notoriously slow—but The Store must have offered some sort of early completion bonus, because it had been less than a month since he'd found the body and already the ground had been graded, the unusually deep foundation dug, the cement poured.

There was something creepy about that.

He turned onto Granite, jogged down the street a mile or so to where the houses ended, then took Wilbert back up to Main. His cheeks were burning with the cold, the brisk air harsh in his lungs. The sun was rising but was little more than a bright spot in the uniform gray cloud cover that filled the sky.

Turning left onto Main, his back to the highway, Bill jogged up onto the sidewalk that ran the length of downtown. Instantly, he slowed his pace. Across the street, there was a banner hung in the window of the empty storefront between Yummy Ice Cream and the Video Barn: NOW ACCEPTING APPLICATIONS FOR THE STORE. Even in this weather, at this hour of the morning, a line of people stood on the sidewalk. Not just teenagers but adults. Well-dressed women and able-bodied men.

He stopped in front of the newspaper office, pretending to tie his shoe but glancing across the street instead. It looked like a recruiting office, he thought. There was something vaguely militaristic about the setup of the empty storefront, about the precise lineup of people and the stoic manner in which they were standing. He could see their breath in the cold air, but he could hear no voices, and he realized that no one was talking.

That was odd.

What made it even odder was that he recognized most of the people. Many of them were neighbors—hell, many of them were friends—but they were all grimly, uniformly silent, staring fixedly at the empty storefront, not even engaging in the polite, idle chitchat of strangers.

Paul Mitchell, the KFC manager, glanced across the street, caught his eye, and Bill straightened, smiled and waved, but the other man did not respond and refocused his attention on the banner.

Bill began jogging, heading quickly through downtown Juniper. The sweat was cold on his skin, and his heart was pounding. He was more unnerved by the waiting applicants than he wanted to admit, and he could not help noticing that there were large shadowed sections of the street, dark areas untouched by the dim, cloud-shrouded sunrise where night still held sway, and he did not relax until he had turned off Main and was heading past Godwin's meadow toward home.

2

Christmas was not the holiday it should have been.

Ginny surveyed the damage in the living room as Bill gathered up all the boxes and wrapping paper and carried them to the trash can outside. Christmas vacation had started late this year, and she hadn't had much time to go shopping for presents. They'd gotten up to Flagstaff but hadn't made it down to Phoenix, and they'd had to choose from what was available, making compromises on their gifts for just about everyone. Next year, she thought, it would be easier. She'd be able to shop in town, at The Store, and they wouldn't have to worry about traveling to a bigger city in order to buy presents.

Both Samantha and Shannon were in their rooms, listening to the new CDS they'd gotten, looking at or putting away their other presents. For the first time, none of their grandparents had been able to make it—Bill's parents spending the holiday with his sister in San Francisco, her parents visiting her brother in Denver—and both girls had obviously missed their presence. The mood this year had been subdued, and they'd all unwrapped their gifts rather perfunctorily, without the usual greedy gusto.

Bill hadn't been himself, either, but then he hadn't really been himself since he'd found the body of that transient. That was understandable, she supposed, although she didn't really understand this phobia he seemed to have in regard to The Store. Yes, the body had probably freaked him, and she understood his anger toward The Store for raping that beautiful piece of land, but she didn't understand this almost pathological grudge he seemed to have against the place.

She'd been feeling out of sorts herself lately, and although she put that down to the usual holiday pressures and Bill's one-note Store complaints, there was another, missing element as well, and she couldn't quite figure out what it was.

Bill returned, picked up his presents from the living room floor, and put them on the kitchen counter. He took her in his arms, kissed her, smiled at her. "Thanks for the presents," he said. "It was a wonderful Christmas."

It wasn't, and she knew it, but she smiled back, kissed him. "I love you," she told him.

"I love you, too."

Next year would be better, she thought. She'd make sure it was better.

SIX

1

There was something about The Store building that he didn't like.

Ted Malory stood up straight, wincing as his back unbent. He'd been up here for three days now, with his usual crew and a group of four pickup workers. He'd never landed a job this big before, and he'd been pretty damn excited when he'd gotten the contract. Every roofing company in Gila, Coconino, and Yavapai counties had bid on this one, and when he'd learned that The Store had awarded it to him, he'd been ecstatic. Not only would this mean big bucks, but if they pulled off this baby, he'd be able to parlay it into other, bigger jobs. He saw them roofing NAU buildings and Little America in Flagstaff, the El Tovar at the Grand Canyon.

Who knew where this might lead?

But it hadn't worked out the way he'd planned.

For one thing, he discovered, there wasn't as much money to be made as he'd originally thought. Or as much as the size of the job warranted. The Store had a take-it-or-leave-it standard contract and did not negotiate. They set the terms, and if he didn't like it, there were plenty of others who would jump at the opportunity to do the work.

So he'd taken it. He didn't like it, but he'd agreed to it.

Part of the deal was that he was responsible for all costs. The Store was paying a flat fee, and out of that, he had to pay labor expenses and purchase all materials for the job. He had no problem with that. His price quotes usually included supplies, and he got a good deal from his buddy Rod Hawkins in Mesa. But the terms of this agreement specified that he had to buy all material from The Store's wholesale supplier, and those prices were much higher than Rod's. The Store's representative also seriously undercalculated the time it would take to roof the building, considering the time of year and the total square footage of the project. They'd already lost two days because of snow.

The way he figured it, after this was all over, he'd barely be breaking even.

But that wasn't all.

That wasn't even half of it.

Ted looked over the raised edge of the roof toward the mountains. Snow still covered Hunter's Peak, and the other mountains closer in were also swathed in white. He took a deep breath, glancing over at the north-west corner of the roof and the black plastic garbage sack. He quickly looked away. Each morning when they'd arrived, there'd been dead birds on the roof. Crows. They hadn't been shot, they seemed to have no injuries, they'd just . . . died.

And fallen out of the sky onto the roof of The Store.

It was unsettling and a little creepy, but Joe Walking Horse thought it was more than that, and the second time it happened, he quit. On the spot. He'd simply turned and stepped back down the ladder the way he'd come up.

Joe was his best man, his most experienced worker and fastest shingler, but Ted had been so pissed off that he'd told the Indian that if he left now he'd never work for his company again. Joe had not even hesitated as he'd continued down the ladder. He'd simply called out to Ted that it had been a pleasure working with him and had walked across the open ground to his pickup, gotten in and driven off.

Ted regretted his behavior already, and he planned to apologize to Joe and offer him his old job back once The Store was finished. But Joe's dread seemed to have affected the rest of the men as well, and it had been an unusually somber few days. Hargus hadn't even brought his boom box to work, and Hargus brought his boom box everywhere.

Even he had felt uneasy, and though he'd tried to make sure they worked fast in order to finish this roof as quickly as possible, he also made sure they did the best job they could.

He didn't want to have to come back to fix mistakes.

He hadn't said word one to Charlinda, though. She still thought this job was a godsend, and he let her think so. She was superstitious enough as it was, what with all the astrology and tarot cards and crap, and the last thing he needed to do was tell her that Joe Walking Horse had walked and that they were all spooked by the place. That'd send her off the deep end.

He yelled out for everyone to take a ten-minute break, and he grabbed a beer out of the cooler and walked over to the edge of the roof, glancing down at the parking lot. It had just been given a layer of sealant the day before, and was scheduled to be painted tomorrow. The lot was massive, stretching all the way out to the edge of the highway, big enough to accommodate every vehicle in town with room to spare. Nine acres of asphalt.

It was a shame, really, because this had been such a nice meadow. With only minimal effort, it would have been possible to do what had been done with Buy-and-Save or KFC—construct the lot to fit the contours of the land and keep the biggest and best trees. But not only had the existing trees been cut down and hauled away, no new ones had been planted.

No shade.

In Arizona.

He shook his head. Oh, well. He supposed it would boost The Store's sale of windshield sunscreens come June.

Actually, he was a little surprised by the lack of landscaping. Even small businesses usually tried to make their places attractive and eye-pleasing. But The Store's exterior was strictly functional: tan cinder-block building, white sidewalk border, flat black parking lot. No plants, no trees, no decoration. It looked more like a prison than a retail outlet.

Below, a worker carrying a large metal pole was walking out of The Store to his truck, parked directly in front of the entrance.

Ted looked off into the distance. Hargrove's death hadn't even slowed down construction. The Store had simply brought in one of its own men, and work had continued, alternating shifts working twenty-four hours a day the last two weeks in order to meet the deadline for the bonus.

He'd heard from Frank Wilson, who'd worked with Hargrove on the project, that the building had a basement as deep as all get out, and that there were a couple of other construction quirks that The Store had insisted upon. No one knew why, but no one had dared ask, and The Store's plans had been followed to the letter.

Dead birds and secret basements.

It was all a little . . . spooky.

No, not a little.

A lot.

Shivering, he finished off his beer, dropped the can on the roof, and walked back to where he'd been working.

2

"Can I talk to you?"

Shannon looked up from the dirt to see Mindy Hargrove sitting on the weathered pine bench by the side of the road that served as a school bus stop. Mindy hadn't been to school much lately, had been acting, well, weird, since her dad died, but now she looked positively freaked. Her hair was uncombed, her jeans filthy, her once-white blouse half-unbuttoned. There was a wildness to her eyes and the cast of her features that Shannon had never seen before and that made her feel a little bit frightened. She wondered if Mindy was having some sort of nervous breakdown, if she'd gone crazy, and she quickly looked up and down the road, searching for signs of someone else, but there was no one here except Mindy and herself.

"Uh, I have to get going," Shannon said. "I'm late already, and my mom's waiting for me."

Mindy stood, walked toward her. "I know your dad doesn't like The Store. That's why I thought I could talk to you."

Shannon shifted her books from her left hand to her right. Mindy had been bad enough when she'd been a spoiled stuck-up bitch, but this new Mindy, this intense, emotionally disturbed Mindy who for some strange reason wanted to talk to her, even though they'd been bitter enemies since third grade, was even worse. She wanted to get out of here and away from her as quickly as she could, but she forced herself to remain pleasant and pretend that nothing out of the ordinary was going on. "It's not that he doesn't like The Store. It's more that he doesn't like where they're building it and the way they're building it."

Mindy glanced furtively around to make sure they weren't being spied upon. "It's built with blood," she said.

Shannon started backing away, keeping her eyes on the other girl. "Look, I've really gotta go."

"I'm serious. They put blood in the concrete. It was in the plans they gave my dad. Tell your dad. Maybe he can tell that guy from the newspaper and they can do something about it."

"Okay," Shannon said, humoring her. "I'll tell him."

"It's built with blood. That's why my dad was killed."

Your dad was killed because he was driving drunk, Shannon thought, but she smiled and nodded and continued backing away, finally quickening her pace, breaking into a jog. She looked behind her as she ran, but the road was empty, the bench was empty, and Mindy was gone.

3

Bill finished the GIS documentation on the last Saturday of January. He uploaded the completed manual, sent it off to the company, and celebrated the way he did at the end of every project: he opened his middle desk drawer, took out a Reese's Peanut Butter Cup, cranked up the radio, leaned back in his chair, and enjoyed.

He stared out the window as he ate. It had been raining for two days, the rain melting away the last of the snow, and it was still drizzling now, the trees outside little more than black silhouettes in the mist. He finished his Reese's, tossed the wrapper in the wastepaper basket. This was when he was really able to take advantage of the fact that he worked at home. Instead of sitting at his desk, finding papers to shuffle, pretending to look busy for the benefit of any supervisors who happened to pass by, he could watch TV, read a book, take a trip, do whatever he wanted until the next project came along. He was on salary, not an hourly wage, and as long as he did his work and met his deadlines, the company didn't care how he spent his extra hours.

In other words, his competence and efficiency were rewarded with spare time.

God bless technology.

He switched off his computer, stood, stretched, and walked out of his office and down the hall. The kitchen smelled of Campbell's tomato soup, and the insides of the windows were fogged with condensation. It seemed warm, cozy, and comfortable, and with the girls gone, it felt almost the way it had when they were newlyweds, when they were too poor to go anywhere or do anything and their chief form of entertainment had been sex.

Ginny was at the stove, stirring the soup, and he walked behind her, reached his hand between her legs, grabbed her. She yelled for him to knock it off and practically hit him with the spoon, a spattering of hot soup hitting his cheek.

"Jesus!" he said.

"That'll teach you not to sneak up on me like that."

He wiped the soup off his cheek. "What's the matter with you?"

"Nothing," she said. "I'm making lunch. I wasn't expecting to be molested."

"Who did you think it was? I'm the only one in the house."

"That's not the point."

"I used to do that all the time. You used to like it."

"Well, now I don't." She did not look at him but kept

her back to him as she continued stirring the soup. "Wash up," she said. "It's time to eat."

He sighed. "Look, let's not fight. I'm sorry I—"

She turned around, surprised. "Who's fighting?"

"I thought you were angry with me."

"No."

He grinned. "Then how about bending over the table so I can do my manly duty?"

She laughed. "How about washing your hands so we can eat lunch?"

"After lunch?"

She smiled. "We'll see."

They did make love after lunch, a quickie in the bedroom in case Samantha or Shannon came home early, and afterward he decided to get out of the house and take a walk. The rain had stopped sometime in the last hour, and he'd been cooped up inside for far too long and felt like getting outdoors. He asked Ginny to go with him, but she said she wasn't in the mood, and besides, she had some magazines to catch up on.

He walked into town alone, enjoying the smell of fresh rain on the roads and the sight of the clearing sky, the cracks of blue that were peeking out from between the parting grayness. He walked over to Street's store, said hello to his friend, shot the breeze a little, then stopped by Doane Kearns's music shop across the street, digging through the bins of used records against the far wall to see if he could find anything interesting, picking up a bootleg Jethro Tull and an old Steeleye Span album that he'd had in college but had lost somewhere along the way.

Before heading home, he walked into the café for a quick cup of coffee. As usual, Buck and Vernon were sitting at the counter, arguing. Today's bone of contention was country music.

"So sue me," Vernon was saying. "I like Garth Brooks."

"Garth Brooks is a pussy! Waylon Jennings. Now there's a real singer."

"Language!" Holly called from behind the counter.

"Sorry," Buck said.

Vernon grinned. "Is Waylon Jennings still alive?"

"You'll rot in hell for that one, son."

Bill sat down at the opposite end of the counter, nodding to the two men, who nodded back.

Holly stopped by, asked if he wanted a menu, but Bill said that all he was after was coffee, and she turned around, poured him a cup, and set it down in front of him.

"Bill."

He swiveled in his seat to see Williamson James, the owner of the café, walking out from the kitchen through the door next to the jukebox.

"How goes it?"

Bill shrugged. "Can't complain."

The café owner sat down on the stool next to him, motioned for Holly to pour him a cup of coffee as well. "Catch that game on Thursday?"

Bill shook his head.

"That's right. You don't go in much for football, do you?"

"Football, basketball, baseball, soccer, hockey. Don't watch any of 'em."

"You ever even play sports?"

"Nope."

"What about in school?"

"Well, yeah. PE. I had to. No choice. But not on my own."

"Why not?"

"Never liked 'em. Sports are for people who can't handle freedom."

"What?"

"They're for people who need to be told what to do with their free time, who can't think of things to do by themselves, who need rules and guidelines to follow. Like people who spend their free time going to Vegas, gambling. Same thing. Rules. You're told what to do. Other people decide for you how your time is to be spent. I guess for some people it takes the pressure off. They don't have to think on their own; everything's been set up for them already."

The old man thought on this for a moment, digested it. He nodded slowly. "I can see your point," he said.

Bill laughed. "You're the first person who has."

Williamson cleared his throat, leaned forward. "I'm putting the café up for sale," he said.

"What?"

"Shhh. Keep it down." The old man made a lowering gesture with his hands. "I haven't told anyone yet. Even Holly doesn't know."

"Why? What's the matter?"

"Nothing's the matter. It's just that . . ." He trailed off. "The Store's going to be opening pretty soon. It'll be putting a lot of us out of business."

Bill shook his head. "That won't affect the café."

"They're going to have their own coffee shop. Not just a snack bar. A coffee shop."

"Doesn't matter."

"I'm afraid it does."

"This café's a landmark. People aren't going to abandon this place in order to eat and drink inside a discount store. This place is a part of Juniper."

Williamson smiled sadly. "The fact is, no one cares about supporting us local businesses. Yeah, the café's a landmark, and when it's gone everyone'll miss it, and your friend Ben'll write a heartwarming story about the way things used to be. But the truth is that once The Store's coffee shop starts offering coffee for a nickel cheaper than mine, or fries for a quarter less, these guys'll be out of here so fast it'll make my head spin." He nodded toward Buck and Vernon. "Even those two."

Bill shook his head. "I don't think so. It's not the prices that bring people here, it's the atmosphere, it's . . . it's everything."

"You're wrong. You might not think it's price. But it is. Everything's economics. And once The Store starts buying big flashy ads in the paper, trumpeting their great bargains, everyone'll flock over there.

"I'm barely making it as it is," Williamson continued. "I can't afford to compete. I'd get my ass whupped in a price war. The Store can hold out forever. It can lowball me until I'm bankrupt." He sighed. "I can see the writing on the wall. That's why I want to unload this place before the shit hits the fan, while I can still get a decent price for it."

He was silent for a moment, looking around the café. "What I wanted to ask you about is advertising on that Internet thing. I figured if anybody'd know how to go about doing something like that it'd be you. I'm going to put an ad in the trades and all that, maybe even one with Ben, though I don't think any locals can afford to buy the place. But I thought I might send it out by computer, too. See if I get any response."

"Yeah," Bill said slowly. "I could help you do that."

"What if I write out what I want to say? Could you send that out on the Internet for me?"

"Sure, but do you really want to do that right now? Why don't you wait, try to stick it out, see what happens. The people of Juniper may surprise you. They might rally around the café. It could even be good for your business. Things might really pick up once everyone knows what's going on."

Williamson sighed. "Times have changed, son. Everyone today is so fragmented. This isn't a country anymore. It's a collection of tribes, all competing with each other for jobs, money, media attention. When I was young, we were all Americans. Back then, we did what we had to, or what we could, to make this a better nation. We did what was right, what was moral. Now people do what's expedient, what's 'economically feasible.' " He shook his head. "Used to be, we cared about our community. We were willing to do what it took to make this a better place to live. Now all anyone cares about is how much it costs." He met Bill's eyes. "No one gives a shit about preserving our town, our community, our way of life. All they care about is saving a few bucks so they can afford to buy their kids the latest name-brand tennis shoe. It's a nice thought, but no one's going to 'rally around' the café. That's just not going to happen."

He finished off the last of his coffee. "That's why I'm getting out now. While I still can."

4

Six inches of snow fell in a storm that hit on President's Day, and it was another twenty-four hours before the plow came by to clear the street. By the end of the week, however, it had all melted off, and they decided to drive to the Valley on Saturday to relax and do some shopping.

They left early, just after dawn, stopping around eight for a breakfast of Egg McMuffins in Show Low. Ginny stared out the window of the car as they traveled, watching as the passing scenery segued from pine to cactus country, the clean lines of the forested Mogollon Rim giving way to the wilder rockiness of the desert Mazatzals. Samantha and Shannon slept in the backseat while Bill drove happily and hummed along with the radio.

The vistas were spectacular, the canyons and mountains majestic, and, as always, Ginny felt awed and humbled. It was here, looking at the landscape, that she felt the presence of God. She had been born and raised a Catholic, had gone to mass twice a week from the time she was an infant until she went off to college, but she had never felt the inspiring exhilaration in church that she felt here, on the highway. The wondrousness and magnificence of God that she had heard about had been an intellectual abstraction for her until she had married Bill and moved to Arizona, and nothing in church had ever made her feel as religious, as profoundly touched by God, as the sight of her first desert sunrise on their honeymoon.

That was the problem she'd had with Catholicism, its smallness, its vanity, its emphasis on self. As a girl, she was led to believe that the world revolved around *her,* that if she ate meat on Friday or didn't give up something for Lent or had a mild sexual fantasy about David Cassidy, she'd be damned for eternity. God was watching her always, ever vigilant in His study of the minutiae of her life, and she'd felt constantly under pressure, as though her every thought and movement were being continuously scrutinized.

But as she'd gotten older, she'd discovered that she wasn't the focus of everything, she was not the fulcrum upon which the world and the church were balanced, and if she rubbed herself in the bathtub or called Theresa Robinson a bitch, Western civilization would not instantly come to an end. Indeed, she came to see herself as a minor character here on earth, barely worthy of God's attention, and she decided sometime during her high school years to simply be a good person, live a good life, and trust God to be smart enough to separate the good people from the bad once judgment day rolled around.

It had been the land here that had reawakened the religious feelings within her. She had seen in it the glory of God, had realized once again how small were her problems and concerns in the overall scheme of things— and how there was nothing wrong with that. It was as it should be.

She glanced over at Bill, singing along with an old Who song, and she found herself smiling. She was lucky. She had a good husband, good kids, a good life.

And she was happy.

Bill caught her smiling at him. "What?" he said.

She shook her head, still smiling. "Nothing."

They arrived in the Valley shortly after eleven and drove to Fiesta Mall in Mesa, separating once they were within the air-conditioned confines of the shopping center, the girls going off on their own to clothing and music stores, she and Bill heading to the multiplex to see a movie, all of them agreeing to meet at two o'clock in front of Sears.

The movie they watched was a romantic comedy, what Bill called a "cable movie," but everything was better on a big screen, and she was glad they'd gone to see it. Afterward, they hung out for a while at B. Dalton. She bought the latest *Vanity Fair,* and Bill picked up a new suspense novel by Phillip Emmons.

Sam and Shannon were already waiting on a bench in front of Sears when they walked up. Shannon had bought a cassette by a currently hot rock band, a band

Sam apparently hated, and the two girls were arguing loudly over musical taste.

"Break it up," Bill said in the gruff voice of a boxing referee. He sat down between the two. "You girls're starting to draw a crowd here. If we put you in bathing suits and a hot oil pit, we could start charging admission, make a little extra cash for the family."

"You're gross," Shannon said.

"Yeah, well, that's my job." He took both their arms and pulled them to their feet. "Come on, kiddos, let's hit the road."

They headed out, Ginny driving this time. The sun was setting by the time they reached Payson, and night had fallen before they hit Show Low. As usual, the girls were fast asleep in the backseat. Bill was dozing as well, his head slumped against the glass of the passenger window.

Ginny enjoyed the time to herself. There was something comforting about being surrounded by her family and at the same time being able to be alone with her thoughts. The highway was empty and had been since they left Show Low, and the scenery, so awe-inspiring in the daytime, was hidden completely by the black cover of night, only a narrow section of the road ahead illuminated by the car's bright headlights. Here and there, off to the side, the lights of individual cabins and ranches could be seen, lone beacons in the darkness of the landscape.

She was driving through the flat stretch of forest just before the long rise into Juniper when she noticed for the first time that they were not alone on the highway. In the rearview mirror, several miles behind, she could see the powerful headlight beams of an extraordinarily large vehicle, traveling fast, gaining quickly. Her heart rate immediately accelerated, and her first instinct was to wake up Bill, but she forced herself to remain calm and just continue driving. It was only a truck. Speeding. Not exactly a rare occurrence on an Arizona highway. But still, her initial reaction was one of fear and panic, and she understood how people living off by themselves, away from others, became jittery and frightened, ended

up seeing UFOs and believing in widespread government conspiracies. There was something unnerving
about contact in the wilderness, about the incongruity of
seeing something where you hadn't expected to see it.
Even on the highway.

Ginny glanced down at the speedometer. She was
going five miles over the speed limit, but the truck was
gaining on her quickly, cutting the distance between
them. She thought of *Duel*, checked in her rearview mirror. The mirror was tilted up for night driving, but still
the headlights behind her seemed impossibly bright, almost painfully so, and she saw as the lights grew closer
that there was not just one set of lights, not just one
truck.

Then the first truck passed her.

It was black, pure black, both the cab and the van
matching perfectly the surrounding darkness, even the
windows of the cab tinted. A shiver passed through her,
and she clutched the steering wheel tightly as the enormous vehicle cut in front of her and sped down the highway into the night, only its red taillights visible.

The next truck passed.

And still the brightness continued behind her.

Again, she thought of waking Bill, but something kept
her from it, and she slowed the car and pulled slightly
to the right as, one by one, ten speeding trucks passed
illegally over the double yellow line.

On the back door of the last truck, as it pulled in
front of her, her headlights illuminated two words, shiny
black against flat black: THE STORE.

Their car was once again alone on the highway, and
she exhaled deeply, realizing that she'd been holding her
breath. She tried to tell herself that there was nothing
unusual about the caravan, that the trucks were merely
bringing merchandise to The Store, that she was just
succumbing to Bill's paranoia.

She almost made herself believe it.

SEVEN

1

The entire town turned out for The Store's grand opening. Though it was a weekday, it was as if the town had declared a holiday. Several businesses were closed, construction had been suspended on more than one house, and it looked to Bill as though a lot of people had called in sick to work.

He drove slowly up and down the rows of the parking lot, looking for an open space.

"Just park out by the highway and we'll walk," Ginny said. "You're wasting your time. You're not going to find any spots."

"Yeah, Dad," Shannon echoed. "We're going to be the last ones in there."

"The Store's not going anywhere," he told them. "It'll be here all day."

Nevertheless, he drove to the far end of the lot and into one of two adjacent open parking spaces facing the highway. Samantha and Shannon immediately opened their doors, got out of the car, and hurried toward the flag-festooned building. "Later!" Shannon called.

"Don't leave without telling us!" Ginny called after them. She smiled at Bill as she got out of the car. "Exciting day."

"Yeah," he said.

He pushed down the lock button on the car door, slammed it shut, and turned toward The Store. He'd started jogging along the highway again during the past month. He seemed to have been cured of his physical aversion to the construction site, and he'd begun running past the area each morning, curious about the progress of The Store and unable to stay away. He found himself watching the stages of development with a sort of morbid fascination, the same sort he'd felt toward a decomposing dog he and his friends had discovered in a vacant lot near their junior high school. He was disgusted by what he saw but powerless to look away.

Even in *his* mind, though, The Store was already a part of the town. An unwelcome part, but a part nevertheless. It was difficult for him to remember exactly where the hill had been, what the outcropping of rock looked like. He could see only The Store now.

He wondered if someone somewhere had a photograph of the meadow the way it used to be.

Probably not.

The thought depressed him.

"Come on," Ginny said. "You can't put it off any longer." She moved around her side of the car, took his hand, and together the two of them walked up the row of parked vehicles to The Store.

The day was warm, unusually so for early spring, but the temperature cooled considerably as they stepped into the shadow of the building. Bill looked up as they approached. The structure was massive. He'd known it was big, but it had been impossible to get a true sense of scale from the highway.

Here, however, in front of the building, walking up to it, Bill was daunted by its sheer size. The Store's facade was the length of a football field and nearly three stories high. There were no windows, only several sets of tinted glass doors in the otherwise uniform tan of the giant block building. It looked like a high school gymnasium on steroids. Or a bunker for a race of giants.

Customers and curious browsers streamed from the parking lot, over the bordering sidewalk, through the automatic doors, and he and Ginny joined the crowd.

They walked into The Store.

Inside, the building was not intimidating at all. Rather, it was modern, friendly, and welcoming. The temperature was comfortable, the barely perceptible Muzak pleasant rather than cloying, and the silently circulating air smelled of cocoa and coffee and candy. The high white ceiling was lined with long wide light bars that clearly illuminated the entire store with a cheerful brightness that made the natural sunlight outside seem pale and faded in comparison, and the white tile floor gleamed between endless shelves fully stocked with an amazing array of products.

An old man Bill had seen around town but didn't know smiled at them, welcomed them to The Store, and offered them a shopping cart, which Ginny took. They walked forward slowly, looking around. A double row of cash register stations were lined up to their left, parallel to the exit doors. Already there were people pushing shopping carts through the checkout lines, taking out checkbooks and credit cards, requesting paper bags instead of plastic from the smiling, clean-cut clerks.

It was hard to believe that such an obviously well-stocked, state-of-the-art store would choose to build in Juniper. It was even harder to believe that such a store could make money. It seemed out of place here, incongruous, like a whale in a goldfish tank, and Bill had a tough time understanding why a large corporation like The Store would place an enormous retail outlet in a town this small. The local residents were, for the most part, poor, with little or no discretionary income, and even if The Store paid only minimum wage, the overhead for a place like this had to be at least double the most optimistic sales projections.

He didn't see how The Store could make a profit in Juniper.

"Hey, stranger."

He glanced over to see Ben, notebook in hand, camera slung over his shoulder.

The editor nodded to Ginny. "Hey, Gin."

She smiled. "Front page news, huh?"

"Don't knock it. No news is good news, as they say, and if we're fortunate enough to live in a place where a store opening is a major news event, we're pretty damn lucky."

Ginny touched Bill's arm. "I'm going to look at clothes. You take the cart."

"You don't want to be interviewed for the paper?" Ben said. "I need some reactions from local shoppers."

"Maybe later."

The editor turned toward Bill as she walked away. "Come on. How about you? You don't want to make me actually work, do you? I figured I could hit up friends for quotes and not have to annoy real people."

"Real people?"

"You know what I mean."

"If you really want a quote from me, I'll give you one. But I don't think it's what you want to hear."

"You think right. The Store's our biggest advertiser now, and word came down from on high that negativity would not be appreciated in Grand Opening coverage."

"Newtin's caving in?" Bill couldn't believe it. The publisher had always told Ben that the content of the paper was up to him, that he would not interfere with the presentation of the news or attempt to influence the paper's editorial slant.

Ben shrugged. "It's a new dawn."

Bill shook his head. "I never would've believed it."

"So you don't want to lie? Give me some fake words of praise and encouragement?"

"Sorry."

"I'd better find some other suckers, then." He nodded. "Later."

"Later." Bill pushed the shopping cart forward. He looked to the right, thought he saw Ginny's head above a blouse rack in the crowded women's clothing section but could not be sure. He continued forward down the center aisle, past rows of housewares, past shelves of cleaning supplies. He stopped by the book and magazine section. He was impressed by The Store's selection, he had to admit. The giant magazine rack contained not only *People, Newsweek, Time, Good Housekeeping, Vogue,* and the usual mainstream mass-market periodicals, but such obscure specialized publications as *The Paris Review, The New England Journal of Medicine,* and *Orchid World.* There were even copies of *Penthouse, Playboy,* and *Playgirl.* A first for this town. The bookshelves next to the magazine rack were stocked with works by King, Koontz, Grisham, and other best-sellers, as well as novels by Wallace Stegner, Rachel Ingalls, and Richard Ford.

Even the music selection was impressive. He moved on to the electronics department and glanced through the CDs, finding everything from currently hot rock and rap groups to such little-known contemporary classical artists as Meredith Monk and the Illustrious Theatre Orchestra.

He had been prepared to hate The Store—he *wanted* to hate The Store—and he was disappointed that there was really nothing he could find to criticize or disparage. Indeed, he found himself grudgingly, against his will, having fun, enjoying his exploratory trips down the endless aisles. It was not something he would ever admit to aloud, but he actually admired The Store for what it had done here.

He felt guilty for even entertaining such blasphemy.

He met up again with Ben in front of the crowded espresso bar near the automatic double doors that led out back to the nursery. The editor, sipping a café au lait, gestured expansively about him as Bill approached. "Quite a place, here," he said. "Quite a place."

Bill nodded. "Yeah," he said. "Quite a place."

Ginny walked slowly, looking around her in awe, filled with a pleasant feeling that was at once immediate and comfortably nostalgic. The Store was beautiful. It was like being back in California—only more so. Aisles stretched endlessly before her, stocked nearly to the ceiling with merchandise so new she wasn't even familiar with it.

She remembered the first mall she'd ever been to—Cerritos Mall—with Ian Emerson, her boyfriend at the time. That had been like this: the size, the scope, the wonderful impressive newness of it all. Cerritos at that time had been a small dairy farming community in the middle of the Southern California sprawl, but it had taken only a few years for an entirely new city to spring up around the mall. It had been like a catalyst for change, a magnet for houses and businesses and other stores, the hub around which everything revolved. Would this be like that? Would Juniper's population suddenly explode and a rash of development sweep through the town, obliterating their quaint, rural lifestyle? She hoped not.

But it might almost be worth it.

The Store was a godsend.

She touched a pair of Guess jeans hanging on a rack, fingered an Anne Klein blouse. She hadn't realized how much she missed having easy access to all this. Driving down to the Valley and shopping at Fiesta Mall or Metro Center had always been fun, something she enjoyed and looked forward to, but having contemporary fashions here in town, being able to try on nice clothes anytime she wanted to, without having to plan a trip and spend an entire day, was totally different. She felt as though she'd been holding her breath for a long period of time, conserving her oxygen, and now she'd been set down in a rich atmosphere and was able to breathe freely, deeply. She'd been depriving herself, doing without, and while she'd adjusted to such an extent that she hadn't even noticed what she was missing, now that it was again available she was grateful.

This was heaven.

They'd never have to go to Phoenix anymore.

Everything they needed was right here in Juniper.

The Store was wonderful.

Shannon wandered happily through the Juniors clothing department. The items here were as good as or better than those in any mall she'd ever been in. It was as if they'd taken all the best clothes from all the best shops and combined them in one store.

A discount store.

It was like a dream come true.

She pulled a skirt off a rack, held it up. There were fashions here that she'd only seen in magazines.

She put the skirt back, looked around for Samantha. Her sister was over by the shoe section, talking to Bernadine Weathers. Bernadine was a bore and a half, and Shannon didn't feel like listening to the older girl drone on in her usual monotone about what *she* thought of The Store, so she moved away, deeper into the clothes department, past mothers and their daughters, past old women and middle-aged housewives, until she found three of her own friends by the lingerie.

"So what do you think?" Diane asked as she walked up.

Shannon grinned. "Awesome."

"No kidding." Diane glanced around furtively, as though checking to make sure no one was eavesdropping. Ellie and Kim, next to her, giggled. She leaned forward. "Have you seen some of the stuff they have here?" She motioned toward the lingerie.

Shannon shook her head.

Diane glanced around again, then walked back a few steps into the nearest aisle. She surreptitiously lifted a red lace teddy from one of the hooks on the aisle partition. "Crotchless," she said. She shifted the garment, holding the crotch out, and Shannon saw a large slit that had been intentionally incorporated into the design.

"Maybe you should get one," Kim said.

Ellie giggled.

"I bet Jake would appreciate it."

Shannon reddened. "Yeah, right," she said.

But she stared at the teddy as Diane put it back and thought that Jake probably would like it.

And she would like to wear it for him.

2

Ky Malory looked straight ahead at the shelves of the toy department, his eyes widening. Firecrackers, cherry bombs, and M80s in a multitude of colors were arrayed in a beautiful display before him, and he reached out and tentatively touched one, shivering with excitement as he felt the cool rough paper covering.

Weren't fireworks illegal in Arizona? Or had he and

his friends been lied to about that? It wouldn't be the first time. Adults often seemed to lie or exaggerate when it came to things they thought were dangerous for kids to do.

"Ky?"

He looked up to see his dad standing next to him, smiling down at him. He quickly, guiltily, pulled his hand away from the shelf, stepped back, but the rebuke he expected did not materialize. Instead, his dad continued to smile at him.

His dad was too tall! He couldn't see the fireworks!

He smiled to himself. That made him happy; that made him feel special. Most stores arranged things for adults. Even the toys. But here was something just for kids like him, something specifically planned so that adults couldn't see it. It was obvious that the fireworks were put on a shelf this low so that parents wouldn't find out about them. Maybe they were illegal. Or maybe The Store just knew that parents didn't like fireworks. Either way, it was as if a pact had been made between him and The Store, and he vowed not to tell either his mom or his dad about it.

If he'd liked The Store before, he loved it now.

They were partners in this.

His dad's big hand clamped down on his shoulder. "I roofed this store, Ky. Did you know that? This entire store. From one side to the other. From front to back."

He nodded at his dad, pretended to be interested, but his attention remained focused on the fireworks. The cherry bombs, he saw, looked like real cherries, their bodies red, their fuses green, like stems.

He'd never seen anything so cool in his life.

And the best part, the most bitchen part, were the prices posted next to the bar codes on the small ledge below the shelf.

M80s: twenty-five cents.

Cherry bombs: fifteen cents.

Firecrackers: five cents.

Five cents apiece!

If he and his friends put their money together, they could buy tons of them. They could drop them in trash cans, put them in mailboxes, tie them to cats' tails. They could blow up the whole fucking town!

"So how do you like The Store?" his dad asked. "Isn't it nice?"

Ky grinned up at him. "It's great," he said. "I love it."

EIGHT

1

Bill had fully intended to boycott The Store, but to his own dismay he found himself going there quite often. He was offended by the way the corporation had bought off town officials, hated the way The Store had bull-dozed its way into Juniper, was suspicious of the unex-plainable strangeness surrounding its arrival, but he had to admit that The Store had an excellent selection of . . . well, almost everything.

And the fact was, it was much more convenient to shop here in town than drive up to Flagstaff or down to Phoenix.

Still, he always tried to buy whatever he needed at locally owned businesses first. If they didn't have what he was looking for, *then* he'd check The Store.

But the uneasiness he'd felt, that strange sense of dis-quiet that had remained with him since he'd seen the first dead deer, seemed to have vanished completely. It was hard to credit animal deaths and mysterious acci-dents when people were snacking on sushi and drinking espresso in a modern, well-lit, state-of-the-art retail store in which the newest books, CDs, video games, fashions, cosmetics, and household appliances were a mere aisle or two away.

Again, he felt like a traitor to his principles. But even that feeling faded as the days passed, and it was not long before going to The Store was like going to Buy-and-Save or going to Siddons Lumber, something he did eas-ily and naturally, without thinking.

That troubled him when he thought about it.

But he seemed to think about it less and less, and

when Ginny said to him one night that Sam wanted to apply for a part-time job at The Store, he did not say that she couldn't.

"You know," Ginny said, "she needs to save up some money for college. Even if she gets a scholarship, she'll still need money. And she wants to buy a car, too. She mentioned something about going with you to the auction in Holbrook."

Ginny had hinted around several times before that Sam wanted to work at The Store, and he'd thought of those people outside The Store's recruiting office, thought of all the weirdness that had been buzzing around the place since it had begun building in Juniper, and he'd automatically vetoed the idea. But it was hard now to maintain that sense of ominousness. What could happen to his daughter? Especially if she only worked part-time. Other people would always be around, both employees and customers, and it was virtually impossible for him to imagine all of them affected by some bizarre supernatural occurrence.

Supernatural?

Even the thought of it seemed ludicrous.

"The Store lets part-timers work flexible hours," Ginny added. "And they pay better than George's or KFC or any of the other places kids in town usually work."

He looked over at her. "We'll see," he said. "We'll see."

2

The Store was the talk of the school.

Ginny could not remember when one topic had so dominated all conversations. Local, state, and national elections, wars, international incidents—nothing had captured the interest of faculty, staff, and students the way The Store had.

It was a sad state of affairs when the opening of a discount retail outlet had more of an effect on people's lives than important world events.

Still, she found herself right in there with the rest of them, talking about the astonishingly new fashions and the amazingly low prices and the vast array of household products now available in town.

"I'm already in debt," Tracie Welles said at lunch one day when they were talking about how much they'd spent at The Store. "I'm maxed out on my MasterCard, and I had to put a couple of things on layaway."

For a brief second, Ginny thought of those black trucks traveling at night, thought about large segments of Juniper's population going into debt to The Store, and a quick chill passed through her.

Then it was gone, and she was laughing with the rest of the teachers in the lounge as they speculated about what their spouses would say when the credit card bills started rolling in.

What really surprised her was Bill's complete reversal on The Store. For months he'd been almost pathologically hostile toward anything even remotely connected to the business. Now, suddenly, all that negativism had disappeared. It was as if he'd been instantly converted. He'd gone to the grand opening, had seen that there was nothing strange or out of the ordinary, nothing evil or unusual, and all of his reservations had vanished. He went there, he shopped there, sometimes he even just browsed there.

And last night he'd pretty much agreed to let Sam work there.

Miracles never ceased.

After work, Ginny drove past the high school on her way home. It was a bad habit, she knew. And, as her friends told her, she should probably trust her daughters a little more. But she worked at a school; she knew what kids these days were like.

Besides, even good girls did bad things.

That's how Samantha had been conceived.

Ginny didn't regret it. She loved her daughter. But the fact remained that her life would probably have turned out far differently had she not gotten pregnant so young. She would have finished earning her master's degree, for one thing. Might even have gone for a Ph.D.

But the responsibilities of motherhood had been thrust upon her, and almost before she knew what had happened, she'd dropped out of college, she and Bill had gotten married, and her plans for the future had been radically redesigned.

She wanted better for her daughters. She wanted them both to finish their educations, to find themselves before they were forced to take on the roles that they would play for the rest of their lives. She did not want them to go straight from being a daughter to being a mother. They needed time to be adults themselves, to forge their own identities apart from parents or mates or children.

So, yes, perhaps she did keep too tight a rein on them sometimes. She didn't let them run around totally unsupervised. She checked up on them to make sure they were where they said they'd be. She and Bill both enforced strict curfew hours. Bizarre behavior by Juniper's redneck standards. But hopefully their daughters wouldn't end up like most of the other girls in town.

She stopped off at the farmer's market for vegetables, then picked up bread and milk at the Buy-and-Save before heading home. Bill was gone—at Street's, according to a note attached to the refrigerator—and she had the house to herself. For once.

Shannon arrived a half hour later while Ginny was chopping tomatoes for pasta sauce. She tossed schoolbooks on the table next to the door, plopped down on the couch, and immediately used the remote control to turn on the television.

"Silence is golden," Ginny said.

"Silence is boring," Shannon replied. "I hate coming home to a quiet house. It's creepy."

"I think it's nice," Ginny said, but her daughter was already flipping channels, trying to find the talk show with the most outrageous topic.

Samantha walked in a few minutes later. She smiled, said hello, went into her bedroom to drop off her books, then came back into the kitchen and got a can of Dr. Pepper out of the refrigerator. She sat down in the breakfast nook, across from where Ginny was chopping.

She sighed loudly, melodramatically.

Ginny tried not to smile, continued chopping.

"I need money," Samantha said.

"You could try getting a job."

"That's what I'm talking about." She leaned forward. "The Store's still hiring, but I don't know for how much longer. Those jobs are going fast. They need people to fill those positions."

"Then why don't you get an application?"

"Can I?"

"It's fine with me."

"I know it's fine with you. But what about Dad?"

Ginny stopped chopping, smiled. "Ask your father," she said. "I think it'll be okay."

"You talked to him?"

"What are mothers for?"

"Oh, thank you, Mom!" Samantha leaped up, ran around the counter, threw her arms about her mother and hugged.

"Puke," Shannon said from the couch. "I think I'm gonna barf."

Ginny laughed. "You could learn a little bit about the art of gratitude from your sister."

"Yeah, right."

Samantha remained in the kitchen, talking excitedly about how she'd juggle school and work, while Ginny finished making the sauce and then started to boil the pasta. She stopped talking when Bill came home, lapsing immediately into a nervous, expectant silence, and Shannon giggled at her from the living room.

Ginny silenced her younger daughter with a quick glance.

"Hi, Dad," Samantha said, moving out of the kitchen to greet him.

Bill frowned suspiciously, an expression that was only half put on. He looked from Samantha to Shannon to Ginny. "All right, what's going on? Who wrecked the car? Who broke my computer? Who had the nine-hundred-dollar phone bill?"

"Oh, Dad," Samantha said. "Can't I even say hello to you without you going overboard and reading something into it?"

"No," he said.

Shannon laughed.

Ginny saw an expression of understanding dawn in Bill's face. He glanced over at her, and she nodded almost imperceptibly, telling him with her eyes to keep his promise.

"Your mother tells me that you want to work part-time," he said.

Ginny looked at him gratefully.

Samantha nodded. "I'm going to need money for college next year."

"And you want to work where?"

"At The Store?" she said hopefully.

He sighed.

"I know you don't like The Store," she said quickly, "and I understand. But the pay's good, and it's only part-time. They'll also work my hours around my school schedule."

"You already talked to them?"

"No. I thought I should ask you first."

"Well, in that case . . ." He pretended to think for a moment. "Okay," he said.

"I can work there?"

He nodded grudgingly. "I suppose so."

"Thanks!" She gave her father a big hug. "You're the greatest dad in the world!"

"This is getting *really* pukey," Shannon said.

"He is!"

"Shut up, all of you," Ginny said, laughing. "And wash up. It's time for dinner."

3

Samantha looked up at the front of The Store, took a deep breath, wiped her sweaty palms on the back of her dress, and walked inside, running her tongue over her teeth to make sure no lipstick had smeared off.

She was nervous. She'd expected that job positions would automatically be given to the first applicants, but she'd heard at school that The Store was actually turning people down. According to Rita Daley, Tad Hood had applied for a box boy position, and they'd said thanks but no thanks. Apparently, they were looking for specific qualities in their potential employees and were not willing to settle for anything less.

In a way that was good. It meant that there were still job openings. But it also upped the pressure factor. Maybe she herself wasn't what they were looking for.

Maybe she wasn't good enough.

She thrust that thought out of her mind. She was the smartest girl in her class, bound to be valedictorian, probably prom queen as well. If she wasn't good enough, who was?

The cold air hit her the second she passed through the doorway, and she was grateful for it. Despite her attempt to be confident, despite her pep talk to herself, she was still anxious, still sweating, and she stood for moment just inside the door, letting the air conditioning cool her off.

An older man with a plastic smile on his face, wearing The Store's green vest over a white shirt, was standing near the shopping carts, and Samantha approached him. "Where would I pick up a job application?" she asked.

"Customer Service," he said, pointing.

"Thank you." She headed in the direction he'd indicated, and a second later spotted the words CUSTOMER SERVICE on the wall high above the electronics department.

Shannon's boyfriend, Jake, was at the Customer Service counter, getting his own application, and he smiled at her as she walked up. "Hi," he said.

She smiled back. "Hi."

She'd never really liked Jake, and she wondered what her sister saw in the boy. He'd been a brat and a wiseass when he was a little kid, and even now there was something Eddie Haskell-like about him, some obnoxious smarminess that set her teeth on edge and that she couldn't believe Shannon didn't see.

"What are you applying for?" he asked.

"Whatever's available."

Jake laughed. "Me, too." He looked at her in a way

that seemed far too personal, far too intimate, and made her feel more than a little uncomfortable.

"You going out with Shannon tonight?" she asked deliberately.

"Uh, yeah," he said.

"Well, have fun." Smiling sweetly, she turned away from him and faced the young woman behind the counter. "I'd like an application for a part-time job."

"Sales?" the woman asked.

"Yes."

The woman withdrew a form from a shelf beneath the counter. "You can take it home, fill it out, and bring it back when you're ready." She inserted the form into a square featureless machine that clicked loudly. "Deadline's a week."

"Is there an interview . . . ?"

"After your application is reviewed, then you may be invited back for an interview."

"Thank you." She smiled at the woman, took the application, and turned to leave. Jake was walking slowly down the center aisle of the electronics department, pretending to look at boom boxes, obviously waiting for her, but she quickly made a detour around the televisions, through the household appliances, and emerged near the checkout stands.

She glanced down at the application in her hand, quickly scanning some of the questions. She'd look good on paper, she knew. Once she filled in some of the biographical info, the clubs she belonged to, her GPA and extracurricular activities, she'd be in. There was no way they'd find someone better.

She felt good, she felt confident, and she decided to come back later, after she'd completed and turned in the application, to do a little shopping. It couldn't hurt to let her future employers know that she shopped here herself. Besides, she needed some new jeans.

She looked behind her, toward the electronics department, to make sure that Jake was nowhere in sight, then hurried past the checkout stands and through the exit doors to the parking lot outside.

4

"Every department, every aisle, every corner of The Store is equipped with hidden video cameras that are on twenty-four hours a day and record all activity within our boundaries."

Mr. Lamb walked through the stockroom. No, not walked. *Strode*. His bearing was that of a military man, his gait almost a march, and he moved purposefully past the warehouse shelves filled with crated merchandise toward a white door at the far end. Jake hurried behind him, trying to keep up. He'd heard bad things about The Store from July Bettencourt and some of the other kids who'd tried to get a job here and failed, but so far he'd had no problems. He'd turned in his application yesterday afternoon, and Mr. Lamb had called him this morning and told him to come in for an interview. The interview had been mercifully short, and now the personnel manager was taking him on a tour of the place and acting as though he'd gotten the job. He didn't know whether he had or hadn't.

And he was afraid to ask.

Mr. Lamb was an intimidating guy.

They reached the white door, Mr. Lamb pulled it open, and the two of them continued down a narrow white hallway that Jake estimated ran parallel to the hardware department, behind the tire wall.

"Here is our monitoring room," Mr. Lamb said, opening a door and stepping inside.

"Wow," Jake said.

Mr. Lamb smiled thinly. "Yes."

The walls of the room were covered with television screens, each showing a different area of the store. Ten or twelve men, none of whom Jake recognized, were seated in front of individual stations at a control console that wrapped around the room. Each man seemed to be responsible for keeping tabs on what was happening on a bank of six televisions that was three screens tall and two screens wide.

"This is our security team," Mr. Lamb said. "Right now, we're utilizing an interim crew from corporate headquarters. They're here to set up shop and assist with training. We hope to have a locally recruited team in place by the end of the month." He turned toward Jake. "You're our first recruit."

He *had* gotten the job.

Jake licked his lips, nervously cleared his throat. "I'm still going to school," he said. "I can only work part-time."

"We are well aware of your schedule, Mr. Lindley." The personnel manager's voice was cold. "We have three shifts. Yours would be swing—three in the afternoon until nine at night—if that is acceptable to you."

Jake nodded timidly.

"Very well." Mr. Lamb turned back toward the nearest wall. "As a security monitor, you will be responsible for observing customers on these video screens here and logging any inappropriate activity so that management can later determine whether it's feasible to prosecute or take other necessary action." He moved closer and pointed to a series of numbers on a digital readout below one of the screens. "As you can see, everything is taped. If an incident occurs, you will record the number corresponding to the tape location so that the incident can be easily referenced."

Jake nodded, not sure if he was supposed to be paying close attention, if this was part of his training, or simply an overview of information that would be repeated when his actual training began.

"Uh, when will I be starting?" he asked.

"When would you like to start?"

"Tomorrow?" he offered.

Mr. Lamb smiled. "That will be fine. There will be a two-day training session, before you begin monitoring the card department. If you are effective in this assignment, you may eventually move up to"—he paused dramatically—"the women's fitting rooms." His smile growing broader, he led the way across the room and pointed to a screen above the head of a young man with a blond crew cut.

On the screen, in a closed dressing room, Samantha Davis unbuckled her belt, unbuttoned, unzipped, and pulled down her jeans. The crew cut man turned a knob on the console, and the camera zoomed in on her crotch. Her panties had a hole in them, and through the small tear in the patterned cotton he could see blond pubic hair.

Jake was immediately aroused, and he casually moved his right hand in front of his crotch, surreptitiously trying to push down on his growing erection. He had often imagined what Shannon's sister looked like naked, and here she was in the flesh.

A natural blond.

She adjusted the panties, pulling them tight, clearly outlining the cleft between her legs, before trying on the jeans that she'd brought into the dressing room with her.

He dared not move, for fear that even that slight friction would set him off. He stared up at the screen in wonder. He could sit here and spy on the girls in town as they tried on clothes, see them in their underwear, and get paid for it? This was heaven.

Mr. Lamb grinned, put an uncomfortable arm around Jake's shoulder. "Sometimes," he said, "they don't even wear panties."

5

Bill stared at his computer screen.

Street had won the chess game.

It took a moment for him to realize what had happened. He hadn't expected this, hadn't been prepared for it, and he was mentally thrown off balance. When his brain finally did assimilate what had occurred, he leaned back in his chair, a shiver passing through him.

It was not an earth-shattering moment. Nothing important had occurred. Hell, by rights this was something that should have happened a long time ago. The surprising thing was that it hadn't occurred before now.

But after so many consecutive wins, this loss seemed somehow ominous, and he found himself reading into it an import that perhaps wasn't there.

Perhaps?

There was no "perhaps" about it. There *was* no larger meaning to the loss of a chess game; there was no significance to it at all.

So why did he feel . . . uneasy?

The phone rang. Street, no doubt. "I'll get it!" he called out. He picked up the cordless from his desk and pressed the "Talk" button. "Hello?"

It was Street, but he hadn't called to gloat, as Bill had expected. Instead, he seemed subdued. "I won," he said, and there was a superstitious hush to his voice, as though he had just broken a mirror and was waiting for the imminent arrival of seven years' bad luck. "I didn't think I'd win."

"I didn't either," Bill admitted.

There was a pause on the other end of the line. "Want to call Ben and come over for a board game?"

"Sure." Bill searched around his desktop, trying to find where he'd laid his watch. "What time is it?"

"Still early. Why don't you come on by?"

"Okay," Bill said. "See you in ten." He started to turn off the phone, then held it once again to his mouth and ear. "Oh, I almost forgot. Congratulations."

"Thanks," Street replied, but there was no joy in his voice.

Bill switched off the phone, switched off his PC, and emerged from his office, walking into the kitchen to get a glass of water.

"He does still live here," Shannon said loudly from the living room.

"Very funny." He made a face at her.

Ginny looked over at him from the couch. "You could spend a little more time with your family and a little less time hiding in your room with your computer."

"Yeah, Dad."

"You're with that computer all day. Do you have to do it at night, too?"

"Sorry." Bill grabbed a glass from the sideboard, rinsed it out, poured himself some water from the sink, and drank.

"So what's your plan now?" Ginny asked. "Are you

going to stay here with us for once, or are you going to
hang out with your cronies?"

"My cronies?"

"Your cronies." Ginny looked at him levelly.

"Well . . . I was going to go over to Street's house for
a quick game."

"Jesus. Don't you think for once you could do something with me instead of your friends?"

All lightness, all trace of bantering, had left her voice.
If it had ever been there. Shannon was on the floor,
moving closer to the television, trying to pretend she
couldn't hear what was going on.

Bill put his glass in the sink. "Fine," he said. "I'll stay
home. We'll have our match tomorrow."

"But you're going to be angry about it, aren't you?
You're going to be silent and pout all night."

"What's with you today?" He moved around the
counter, into the living room, sitting down on the couch
next to her. "That time of the month?"

"You're gross," Shannon said.

"Are your little hormones telling you to be angry with
me?" He pinched Ginny's side, tickling her, and against
her will she laughed. "You *are* gross," she said.

"But that's the way, uh-huh, uh-huh, you like it."

"Dad!"

"Okay, okay. Sorry." He gave Ginny a quick kiss.
"Just let me call Street and cancel."

"You sure you're not going to pout?"

"No," he said. And as he walked back down the hallway to his office, he realized that he hadn't been lying
to Ginny. He wasn't angry. In fact, he wasn't at all upset
that they wouldn't be playing chess tonight.

He was relieved.

"Thank you, Fred," Street said as he handed the customer his change.

The old man nodded, took his bag of adapters.
"Thanks."

Ben waited until the customer had left the store, then
turned toward Street. "Whatever happened to the words
'You're welcome'?"

"What?"

"It seems like every time I say 'Thank you' to some-one, they say 'Thank you' back to me. Everyone's thank-ing everybody these days. No one says, 'You're welcome' anymore."

"What is this crap? You trying to be Andy Rooney or something?"

"Like what just happened here. What are you sup-posed to say when someone buys something from you? Do you thank him for buying from you and patronizing your store? You do, right? Then he's supposed to say, 'You're welcome.' That's the correct response to 'Thank you.' But, instead, Fred said, 'Thanks.' Why? What's he thanking you for? Giving him his change?"

Street shook his head. "Give it a rest, will you? It's been a crappy day."

The editor looked over at Bill, changing the subject. "Well, maybe this'll start a new pattern. Now maybe he'll win all the computer games and you'll win all the board games."

"Street's right," Bill said. "Give it a rest."

He didn't feel like talking about the chess game. In fact, he didn't feel like playing chess ever again. He *had* won the board game in their little test, and that pattern reversal had shaken him far more than he cared to admit. It had not been a surprise—hell, he'd been ex-pecting it—but confirmation only made it that much worse.

Street, too, had avoided discussing the subject. Only Ben seemed to be unfazed by what had occurred, view-ing it dispassionately, talking about it as though he were a geologist who had just found some sort of interesting crystal formation.

The editor sighed. "Boy, you two are a barrel of laughs today. If you guys are just going to sit around and mope, I'm going back to the office."

Bill smiled. "And actually do some work?"

"He *is* still alive!"

"They're talking about raising the sales tax a quarter of a cent," Street said. "The city council. Either of you know anything about it?"

Bill shook his head.

Ben nodded. "I think it's done deal. That's the rumor."

Bill frowned. "Why? I never even heard about this."

Street snorted derisively. "Apparently, The Store wasn't required to pay for the traffic impact report, the easement fee, hookup fees, or anything else that the rest of us had to pay. They were given preferential treatment."

"Incentives," Ben concurred.

"Now the rest of us have to make up for those lost revenues."

"I imagine our local citizens are going to be pretty unhappy with that," Bill said.

"I hope so."

"It's only a quarter of a cent," Ben said. "A penny for every four bucks."

"People still won't like it."

"You know, that's something that always seemed ironic to me," Ben said. "It's the one who are so antitax-ation that are usually so gung ho about the military. They're willing to kill for their country but not pay for it."

Bill smiled. "You old hippie you."

"I admit it."

Street shook his head. "It's not that simple. These are the taxes that really hurt small businesses like mine. Someplace like The Store can afford to absorb the loss and not pass the tax on to the consumer. But the rest of us here are just making ends meet. My prices are going to jump. Not much, but maybe just enough to give The Store that extra edge."

"Besides," Bill said, "this is not providing better roads or better hospitals or things that will actually benefit people. This is subsidizing a successful business with tax-payer money. At the expense of our local merchants—"

"Damn straight," Street said.

"I know. I understand that. But what they're going to argue is that this is a small price to pay for so many extra jobs. And that, in the long run, The Store will bring in more revenue to the town than it's taking in these incentives."

Street snorted. "And you buy that load of horse pucky?"

"That's not what I said."

"Sounds like it."

"Look, I don't want to fight. Of course I'm against raising the sales tax to benefit The Store. But I just got through interviewing Rod Snopes and his militia buddies for a piece I'm writing, and I have to say that I'm pretty sick of this knee-jerk antigovernment, antitax shit."

Bill laughed. "And you call yourself an old hippie?"

"Reformed."

"You talk like a respected member of the status quo."

"Not really. It's just that a lot of these loonies like Rod are so worried about the federal government, and I never saw a government agency that worked worth a damn. These guys're so afraid of Big Brother and creeping totalitarianism, but our government's always seemed to me to be full of inept bunglers, not brilliantly organized master planners. Hell, they couldn't even pull off a third-rate burglary. It's the corporations we have to worry about, I think. They're the ones with the money. They're the ones who can afford to hire the best and the brightest, to competently carry out their plans. They're more efficient, better run, better organized. Shit, they can buy *off* politicians if they need a political favor."

"Like The Store," Street said.

"Exactly."

"Okay," Bill said. "I apologize. You're still a hippie."

"This isn't funny," Street said. "We're talking about my future here." He stared gloomily out the front window. "Or lack of it."

"You could always get a job at The Store," Ben suggested.

"Not funny." Street sighed heavily. "Not funny at all."

NINE

1

There were no windows in the room, nothing on the walls. It looked like a prison cell or a place where the police might conduct interrogations. There was only the one door, and a table and two opposing chairs underneath a bar of fluorescent light in the center of the ceiling.

Samantha shifted in the seat, adjusting her buttocks on the hard chair. She tried to remain calm and still, to maintain a pleasant expression on her face. They were probably watching her, she knew, studying her from behind a wall or through some hidden video monitor, and if she hoped to get the job she needed to make sure that she made a good impression.

Mr. Lamb walked in a moment later, looking down at a clipboard and what she assumed was her application. He sat down in the chair opposite her. "Sorry for the delay," he said.

"That's okay."

She watched as he read over her application and made small checks next to certain items with a red pen. There was something about the personnel manager that made her nervous, something in the implacability of his face: the coldness of his eyes, perhaps, or the hint of a smirk on his straight-lined mouth. She didn't like being alone with him, and she wished someone else was here, another manager or an assistant. Someone.

"First things first," he said. "We need you to take a short aptitude and placement test to determine your abilities and qualifications."

She nodded as he handed her two stapled pages and

a second clipboard he'd been hiding under the first. *Why didn't you give me this with my application?* she wanted to ask. *Why do I have to fill it out now?*

But she said nothing, merely took the pen he offered her and began answering the questions on the top sheet. He watched her silently as she completed the test. She could not see his face clearly, could only see him with her peripheral vision, but she had the impression that he stared at her without blinking, his eyes as still as the rest of his body, and that unnerved her.

She finished the test as quickly as possible, handing the clipboard back to him.

"Thank you." He gave the top page a cursory glance, then looked up at her. "As you may or may not know, The Store is a drug-free workplace and we have a policy of zero tolerance."

She smiled politely. "No problem."

"If you are going to work here, you will be required to take both a lie detector test and a drug test."

"Okay."

He stood. "I will bring in the polygraph."

Samantha was confused as she watched him leave the room once again. The woman on the phone had told her that she was being asked back for an interview, but Mr. Lamb hadn't asked her any questions. She'd expected to respond to queries regarding the answers on her application, to clarify any questions about her they might have, to basically sell herself as a potential employee. Instead, she'd taken an aptitude test and was about to take a lie detector test. Had she already gotten the job? It almost seemed like it—as though these were merely preliminary requirements, the red-tape steps she had to go through before being officially hired.

Mr. Lamb returned a moment later, wheeling in a peculiar-looking device on a two-tiered cart. The body of the machine was about the size of a small television set, but there were thin red and black wires spread across the cart top, and several cables that connected to what looked like a battery on the lower shelf.

He pushed the cart next to her, began untangling wires. "This is the polygraph," he said. "I will be admin-

istering the test, but the results will be recorded and
then evaluated at the corporate office since I am not
qualified to interpret them." He turned toward her.
"Please remove your blouse and your bra."

She blinked. "What?"

"The polygraph measures galvanic skin response. The
breast is the most sensitive and therefore the most telling
area. It prevents us from having to reperform the test."

Samantha licked her lips nervously. "I think I'd rather
do it twice if I have to."

"I'm sorry. It's policy. Multiple tests are too cost-pro-
hibitive. We only do it once. Please take off your blouse
and bra."

There was nothing keeping her here, no one forcing
her to submit to this. She could stand up and walk out
and not look back. She wouldn't get the job, but she
wouldn't have to expose herself to this creepy, slimy
man. And she could always get a job somewhere else.
Georges, maybe. Or Buy-and-Save. Or KFC.

She started unbuttoning her blouse.

Even as she did it, she didn't know why. But she me-
thodically went down the row of buttons, unhooking
them, pretending this was not unusual, not a problem,
that she was calm, adult, professional, and willing to do
what it took to secure this position.

She leaned forward, took off the blouse, laid it in her
lap. She reached around and unhooked her bra.

"Thank you." Mr. Lamb instantly began applying sensors to her skin: thin pieces of metal sheathed in plastic
and coated with some sort of clear gel that felt ice-cold
on her skin. He placed one in the middle of her chest,
just below her neck, one above her left breast, one above
her right.

"Raise your arms please."

She raised her arms, looked down as he applied a
sensor below each armpit. She had never felt so naked
and exposed in her life, not even when Todd Atkins had
burst into the girl's locker room on a dare in junior high
and had seen her and Jenny Newman naked and towel-
ing off. That had been embarrassing but essentially inno-

cent, probably just as scary for Todd as it had been for them, probably just as exciting for them as for Todd.

But this was different. Sitting here in this bare and empty room, stripped to the waist and being viewed so coldly, so clinically, so matter-of-factly, seemed at once more intimate and more degrading. All her flaws were accentuated, her inadequacies exaggerated. Her breasts looked too white compared to the rest of her body, the nipples too small. She looked down as he applied the thin sensors and could see the white powder of her deodorant under her arms, could see the beginnings of stubble beneath the deodorant. Her belly button looked dirty. She should've shaved last night instead of the night before. She should've washed better.

He placed a sensor directly on her right breast. His fingers remained a beat too long there, touched the nipple, then he was doing the same thing to her left breast.

This time two fingers touched her nipple.

She felt violated, humiliated, shamed. But something kept her from slapping his face and walking out. She didn't need the job. Not this badly. Not enough to degrade herself. But she refused to let him see any weakness, refused to give him the satisfaction of knowing that he had gotten to her, affected her. She pretended she hadn't noticed and remained staring straight ahead, expressionless, letting him think that she thought this was merely a routine formality, something she had acquiesced to many times before.

Mr. Lamb placed one final sensor on the slight bulge of her stomach, then moved around to the side of the cart and began turning dials and flipping switches. There was a slight jerk and a hum as the machine was turned on, then a series of small clicks.

Samantha continued to stare straight ahead, her focus on the opposite wall.

He moved the cart in front of her, faced her, smiled slightly.

"All right," he said. "We're ready to begin. Answer only the questions I ask, and answer them as accurately and succinctly as possible. For your protection, as well as the protection of The Store, this test will be audio recorded." He cleared his throat. "Application number two-eleven-A," he said. "Please state your name and age."

"My name is Samantha Davis. I'm eighteen years old."

"Do you attend school?"

"Yes."

"What is the name of your school?"

"Juniper High . . . uh, Juniper Union High School."

"Have you ever been convicted of shoplifting or stealing?"

"No."

"Are you a chronic drug user?"

"No."

"Have you ever used any illegal or nonprescription drugs?"

"No."

"Have you ever sold or been in the possession of any illegal or nonprescription drugs?"

"No." She took a deep breath. Despite the fact that she had never been involved in anything even remotely illegal, she felt nervous. Her heart rate had accelerated, and she could hear its pulse in her head. Would this affect the outcome of her test?

Mr. Lamb adjusted a knob on the polygraph, then looked up, meeting her eyes. "Have you ever performed fellatio?"

"Fellatio?"

"Oral sex with a male."

She stared at him, shocked.

"Have you?"

She shook her head.

"Please speak your answers aloud."

"No," she said, in a soft small, voice.

"Have you ever performed cunnilingus?"

"Cunnilingus?"

"Have you ever licked another female's vagina?"

"No," she said.

"Have you ever performed analingus?"

"No." She wasn't exactly sure what that was, but after the last question, she had a pretty good idea.

"Have you ever inflicted any fatal injury or intentionally caused harm to another human being?"

"No." Samantha looked away from Mr. Lamb, down at her chest, at the electrodes attached to her skin. What kinds of questions were these? Not only were they bizarre, but they seemed to have nothing to do with the job of being a sales clerk. She found herself wondering if these really were questions that The Store asked of its prospective employees or if Mr. Lamb was doing this on his own. Maybe he was some sort of pervert. Maybe he was taping this session—but for his own private use rather than as documentation for The Store.

That couldn't be the case, though. A secretary and several other people were in the personnel office right outside the door. And The Store had obviously provided Mr. Lamb with the lie detector and the recording equipment. He couldn't very well edit and doctor the results of this interview before turning them in.

No, The Store knew about all this.

"One last question," Mr. Lamb said. "Have you ever had a recurring dream in which you disemboweled a member of your family?"

"No!"

"Very good." Mr. Lamb flipped a switch, initiating a new series of clicks. "See? That wasn't so hard, was it?"

He started to walk around the cart to remove the polygraph sensors, but she wasn't about to let him touch her again, and she was already pulling them off her skin. By the time he reached her, she had removed all of them, and she handed the jumble of wires to him, quickly reaching for her bra and blouse.

"We're almost done here," Mr. Lamb said. He placed the tangled wires on the cart and pushed the cart to the bare wall on the opposite side of the room. From somewhere on the cart, he withdrew a glass bottle shaped like a wine carafe and carried it back. "We need you to give us a urine sample for the drug test." He held forth the bottle. "Fill this up."

She could feel the heat of embarrassment in her cheeks, and she knew that her face had to be bright red. "Where should I . . . ?"

"Here." He looked at her flatly.

She shook her head, not sure she had heard him right. "What?"

"If you take it into the bathroom, there's no way I could authenticate it. You'll have to do it right here."

"In front of you?"

He nodded. "In front of me."

Had the corners of his mouth crept up? Was he trying to hide a smile? She felt cold, not only deeply shamed but frightened.

Yet, again, no one was forcing her to do this. There was no one holding a gun to her head.

Not exactly.

But she didn't feel she could just get up and walk out. Something was keeping her here, whether it was psychological pressure or her own emotional inability to stand up for herself, and the thought occurred to her that she was being exploited, taken advantage of.

Sexually harassed.

She had never imagined being in this situation, but now that she was, now that it had crept up on her like this, she understood how victims could remain silent about what happened to them, how they could keep these things to themselves and not tell anyone.

Because . . . there wasn't really any need to tell anyone. She could deal with this, she could get past it, it wasn't going to scar her for life.

She could handle it.

"Please fill up the bottle," Mr. Lamb said.

She nodded, stood, took the bottle from him. She placed it on her chair, then reached up under her skirt and pulled down her panties, taking them off, one leg at a time, not letting him see beneath the skirt.

"The skirt as well, please."

She imagined him dead, imagined herself kicking his head as he lay on the ground. But she nodded, took off the skirt, placed it on the chair.

She was no longer cold. It was hot in here, outrageously humid, and she was sweating. She tried to imagine what her parents would say if they were in the room but couldn't.

Squatting, not looking at Mr. Lamb, she held the bottle between her legs.

Filled it.

Handed it to him.

Now he *was* smiling. "Thank you, Miss Davis. This concludes our interview. You may put your clothes back on. We will call you and let you know the results."

She nodded, put on her panties, put on her skirt.

She did not start crying until she was outside The Store and in the parking lot.

2

Another free day.

Bill woke up late, went for a jog, made himself breakfast, watched TV, signed on to Freelink and read today's headline news, then decided to take a shower and head into town. He didn't mind staying home all day when he was working, but when he was between assignments, the house made him feel claustrophobic, and he liked to get out as much as possible.

He stopped by Street's store, shot the breeze for a while, then walked over to Doane's to see if any new music had come in.

Doane was on the phone when he opened the door and stepped inside the small air-conditioned shop, so he merely waved hello and headed over to the New Releases bin, where he began sorting through the stacked CDs.

Although he'd always considered himself a rock fan, he had to admit that most of his recent purchases had been drawn from the Country section of the CD rack: Lyle Lovett, Mary Chapin Carpenter, Robert Earl Keen, Roseanne Cash, Bill Morrissey. He told himself that rock and roll was an attitude, not a specific musical style, and that if these artists had been around twenty-five years earlier, their records would have been placed in the Rock rack next to James Taylor and Carole King and Joni Mitchell, but the fact was that he was not really interested in most of the rock music being produced today. His tastes had changed over the years.

He wasn't sure he liked that.

Doane finished his conversation, hung up the phone, and Bill stopped looking through the CDs, glancing up. "How's business?" he asked.

The store owner shook his head. "Slow as hard-packed shit."

Bill started to laugh, but he realized almost instantly that Doane was dead serious. "The Store?" he said.

Doane nodded. "Bastards're lowballing me. They can *sell* CDs for less than I pay wholesale."

"They don't have your selection, though."

"Not the backlist, maybe, but they're stocking the Top Ten two weeks before my distributor can even ship the discs out to me. Teenagers are my bread and butter, man. I don't get those hot tunes in the store and on the shelves, the kids don't come in." He sighed. "Even if I do get the music on the shelves, they probably won't come in. I can't afford to even meet The Store's prices, much less beat them."

"You think you'll be able to survive?" Bill asked.

"I hope so, but I don't know. Maybe I'm being para-noid and have an exaggerated sense of my own impor-tance, but I really think The Store's trying to drive me out of business."

"And have a monopoly on music sales."

"Sure. Then they could jack up their prices and start making a profit instead of taking a loss." Doane smiled wryly. "If I'm touching your heart at all, feel free to buy something today."

"I will," Bill said. "I was planning to."

He ended up purchasing a CD of Cormac McCarthy's first album, a vinyl copy of Jerry Jeff Walker's "Viva Terlingua!" and a vinyl bootleg of a 1979 Tom Waits and Leon Redbone concert.

"Where do you get these bootlegs?" Bill asked as he wrote a check at the counter.

Doane grinned, tried to look mysterious. "I have my sources."

Bill walked out of the shop, carrying his purchases under his arm. The bootleg had cost a lot, and Ginny would probably get mad at him, but the album was rare and he considered it a true find, well worth the high price. Besides, he wanted to support Doane and help him out in any way he could. Digging through piles of used albums was one of his favorite hobbies, and he didn't know what he'd do if the record store closed. Shopping at The Store and looking at only new releases was not quite the same.

He walked slowly down the street, noticing for the first time the lack of foot traffic in downtown Juniper, and it brought home to him the fact that some of the businesses here might not survive. He'd known that intellectually, of course, but he had not understood it emotionally, and he now realized that any of these stories could disappear at any time. He'd never thought about it before, but he had expected Juniper to always remain as it was, and he was thrown surprisingly off balance by the knowledge that even in a small town, stability was not a guarantee and nothing was permanent. They had moved to Juniper precisely because it was a small town. They liked that atmosphere, that lifestyle. They wanted to raise their children in a community where neighbors talked to each other, where storekeepers knew their customers by name, and they had expected the town to remain that way throughout their lifetimes, for families that had put down roots here to stay and not move away, for businesses to remain open, for nothing to change.

Now everything seemed to be changing.

He stopped by the café for a quick cup of coffee and saw Ben seated at the counter, eating alone, a half-finished bowl of Williamson James's heartburn chili in front of him. He snuck up behind the editor, tapping him on the right shoulder then quickly sitting down on the stool to his left. "Hey, stranger," he said. "Long time no care."

"Asshole," Ben said.

"Language!" Holly called out.

Bill ordered coffee, and Holly poured a cup and brought it over immediately. He took a slow sip, then shook his head, sighed.

Ben took a bite of chili, wiped his mouth with a napkin. "What is it?"

Bill described his visit to the record shop. "I knew The Store would affect local businesses. I guess I just didn't think the effects would be felt this quickly."

"A lot of places are hurting already," Ben said. "Most mom-and-pop stores operate from month to month, and something like this has an immediate impact on them." He shook his head. "Steve Miller told me he's thinking of packing it in. That shop's been in his family since his grandfather started it . . . when? Sixty years ago?"

"Isn't there anything he can do?"

Ben shrugged. "Joe Modesto, down at First Western Bank, is setting up a new small-business loan program, to try to help our local merchants out, but I don't think he's going to have too many takers. I think most people here would rather cut their losses than go further into debt." He smiled wryly. "The ironic thing is that the paper's flush. The Store's been taking out full-page ads ever since it opened. As I'm sure you've noticed. They're even adding an insert this week, a two-page pullout with coupons. Our advertising revenue's way up."

"Well, I guess that's good," Bill said doubtfully.

"I'd rather have things back the way they were."

"Who wouldn't?"

On the way home, Bill passed by the new park, saw a clearly delineated baseball diamond with an oversized chain-link backstop and two three-tiered metal bleachers. A crew of workers was putting up a fence around a tennis court adjacent to the baseball field. Across an open expanse of grass was a fully installed playground complete with swings, slides, monkey bars, and teeter-totters. Next to that, more workers were pouring concrete for a public swimming pool.

The park was nice. New and clean and well planned. Like everything connected with The Store. But at the same time, there was something artificial about it, like a too-expensive present given by an acquaintance trying to buy instant friendship.

As nice as the new park was, he preferred the old park, with its low, sagging backstop made from rusted leftover pipe and torn chicken wire, its overgrown weed field, its tire swing, its primitive sandbox.

Did The Store have to change everything in Juniper?

The first thing he did when he arrived home was check his computer.

He'd received his new assignment: writing instructions for a new accounting package.

An accounting package being developed specifically for The Store.

Bill stared at the color monitor, not scrolling forward, not printing out the message, simply rereading the initial introductory paragraph the company had E-mailed to him. He felt weird, uncomfortable, uneasy. Automated Inferface was one of the biggest software firms in the country, and over the past several years he'd written documentation for programs that had been developed by their company for a host of major corporations: Fox Broadcasting, RJR Nabisco, General Motors, General Foods. But even though The Store was a national corporation, he had a local, personal connection to it, and it felt strange to know that he was helping to develop a product for its use.

He felt as though he was working for The Store.

In a sense, he *was* working for The Store, and he didn't like that. He knew now how all those old antiwar protesters felt when they ended up getting jobs at Rockwell and McDonnell Douglas and other aerospace defense firms. There was a moral dilemma here. He had rationalized shopping at The Store, had told himself that he wasn't betraying his principles by patronizing the establishment or by letting his daughter apply for a job there, and he felt comfortable with that. But this seemed different somehow, and he reread the message yet again before scrolling forward to check out the details of the project.

He knew he couldn't decline this assignment. He didn't have that luxury. If he refused to perform the job assigned to him, Automated Interface would simply let him go and hire another tech writer. So, in a sense, it was out of his hands, it was not his decision to make.

He felt guilty, though, felt as though he should do something to avoid contributing to the strength of The Store, and he was still sitting in front of the screen of his PC, rereading the assignment, when Ginny arrived home from work.

They went out for dinner that night. Chicken. He still called the place "Colonel Sanders,'" but the colonel was long dead, and he'd sold the franchise to some corporation years before that. These days, the bright red-and-white sign in front of the restaurant read KFC.

He wondered how many young kids knew that KFC stood for Kentucky Fried Chicken.

Not too many.

Their entire lives were run by corporations these days. Companies test-marketed names and logos and spokespeople, held conferences and meetings to determine how to best capture their target audience, based decisions on demographics. Chain outlets were given ethnic names or folksy appearances, attempts were made to disguise the individual tentacles of huge conglomerates by making them seem part of some other, smaller company. Actual small, locally owned businesses were becoming a thing of the past.

Shannon saw a group of her friends at one of the other tables and asked if she could stay and hang out with them, and Ginny said it was okay as long as she was home by ten. Sam was meeting two of her friends at the movie theater, so he and Ginny dropped her off on their way back.

"Looks like we have at least a couple of hours to ourselves," Ginny said, snuggling next to him in the car as they drove home.

"Looks that way," Bill agreed.

"You in the mood to make use of it?"

He grinned. "I'm always in the mood."

He wasn't exactly in the mood, though, and it took longer than they'd planned. They barely had time to get dressed and make the bed before Shannon arrived. Sam returned twenty minutes later, and both girls went immediately to their respective rooms, closing and locking the doors behind them.

Later, after they'd both showered, after they'd watched the late newscast from Phoenix, they lay in bed. Bill thought about Shannon's request tonight for her own charge card, and he cleared his throat. "Do you ever worry that the girls are too . . ." His voice trailed off.

"Materialistic?"

"Yeah."

She rolled over to face him. "Sometimes," she admitted.

"It's our job, you know, as parents, to instill values in them." He paused. "Sometimes I wonder if we've done our job or if we've completely failed."

"Society's self-correcting. Kids always rebel against their parents and that's why the pendulum always swings back."

"But I didn't think they'd be so . . . materialistic."

"You thought they'd be more like us."

"Well, yeah."

She sighed. "So did I."

They grew silent again. He thought about Shannon, about Sam, but it wasn't really the girls that were bothering him. It was his new assignment, it was Doane's business, it was The Store, it was . . . everything.

He fell asleep trying to think of ways to avoid writing instructions for The Store's new accounting system.

3

Samantha looked at the descending numbers above the elevator door. She was reminded of an old Dr. Seuss movie she'd seen when she was little, *The 5,000 Fingers of Dr. T.* In the film, there'd been a series of dungeon basements, and an elevator operator dressed like an executioner had sung out the gruesome specialties of each subterranean floor as the elevator went down.

Mr. Lamb wasn't dressed like an executioner, but the feeling here was pretty close to the one in the film.

The personnel manager had called her yesterday to tell her that she'd gotten the job. Her hands on the receiver had grown sweaty as she heard his voice, and she thought of the lie detector test, the urine sample. She wanted to tell him to go to hell, that she refused to work for The Store. But in a small scared voice she heard herself agree to go down to The Store the next morning an hour before it opened.

"There are a few formalities we have to get out of the way before you start," Mr. Lamb said. "Once they're out of the way, we'll begin training."

"I'll be there," Samantha said.

The employees' section of the parking lot had been full when she'd arrived this morning, but she had yet to see anyone other than Mr. Lamb. The interior of the building was dark, only dim security lights vaguely illuminating the cavernous room. Lights were on in Mr. Lamb's office, though, and it was here she was taken to sign tax forms and additional information forms and a secrecy oath.

"Secrecy oath?" she said, reading the paper in front of her.

"It's just a legality. An assurance to us that you will not use what you learn at The Store to assist one of our rivals in the retail business."

The entire idea rubbed her the wrong way, and the phrase "secrecy oath" put her in mind of clandestine organizations and secret societies, but she read through the document and could find nothing specifically offensive in it, and she signed and dated the paper at the bottom.

Mr. Lamb collected the forms. "Very good," he said. "We're almost done. Now all you have to do is run the gauntlet."

A chill washed over her. "The gauntlet?"

He looked at his watch. "We'd better hurry. They're waiting. And The Store opens in forty-five minutes. We need to get this done." He stood, walked around his desk, and she followed him out of his office and down a short hallway to an elevator.

Now she stood in the slowly moving elevator, staring up at the lighted numbers as they descended past the basement, past the first subbasement, to the second subbasement.

Why did The Store have two subbasements?

She wasn't sure she wanted to know.

The elevator doors opened, and as they walked out, she realized why she had not seen any of the other employees upstairs.

They were all down here.

A bare cement hallway stretched endlessly before her, looking much longer than the length of the building above, and it was lined along both sides with men and women dressed identically in green store uniforms. The sight would have been intimidating enough, but the employees were also completely silent, their faces serious, unsmiling.

"The gauntlet," Mr. Lamb said.

She wanted to turn around, wanted to go back upstairs and leave, and this time she would have done so, but the elevator doors had already slid shut behind her, and Mr. Lamb had placed a hand on her back and was guiding her forward, into the hallway.

Most of the faces before her were familiar, but they looked upon her as if they did not recognize her, and her heart rate accelerated. She tried to catch the eye of Marty Tyler, then May Brown, the first two people on either side of the hallway, but both stared at her blankly, and she quickly looked away.

What was she expected to do here? What was the point of this? She glanced over at Mr. Lamb, next to her.

"Strip," the personnel manager said. "Down to your underwear."

She shook her head. "I don't want to do this," she said, her voice sounding small and frightened. "I . . . I changed my mind. I don't want the job. I don't want to work here."

"It's too late to change your mind," Mr. Lamb said. "Strip."

She looked at the employees lining the hallway, but they were still silent. None of them had spoken or had as yet made a sound.

"Leave on your panties and bra," Mr. Lamb said. A hard smile touched the corners of his mouth. "If you're wearing a bra."

"I can't—"

"Strip!" he ordered. "The Store opens at eight! We don't have time for games!"

Frightened, she bent down to untie her tennis shoes. She looked up, expecting to see people laughing at her, giggling, but the faces remained unsmiling.

She took off her blouse, her pants.

She stood at the head of the hallway in her underwear, shivering with fear as much as cold. Her left arm was held over her bra, her right hand covered her pubic area. She turned toward Mr. Lamb. "What now?"

"You run the gauntlet. If you make it to the end, you will join our Store family. You will be one of us."

If?

She looked down the hallway, saw for the first time that many of the employees were holding objects in their hands. Objects that could be used as weapons.

"Run!" Mr. Lamb said.

She ran, felt a coat hanger hit her buttocks, felt a flyswatter slap her left breast. The pain was tremendous, and her eyes were teary, but she kept her focus on the far end of the hallway and maintained an even course between the two rows of employees, forcing her legs to run faster. A knitting needle was shoved into her upper arm, and she had to will herself not to scream.

"You're ugly!" someone yelled.

"You're flat!"

"You're worthless!"

"You have no ass!"

"You're a moron!"

"You can't do anything right!"

They were all people she knew, but she couldn't tell who was yelling what. It was all so disorienting, the jabs and the verbal abuse, and she could barely see for the tears, but she forced herself to keep moving forward. A cleat kicked against her shin, and now she was crying out loud, sobbing, but still she kept going.

"Loser!"

"White trash!"

"Bimbo!"

And then she was at the end of the hallway, facing a blank cement wall. She took a deep breath, wiped her eyes, then turned. She saw Mr. Lamb at the far end, nodding.

She'd made it.

It was over.

She was bruised and bloody, but they all gathered around her, the employees, hugging her. "We love you," they said in unison. "We love you, Samantha."

She was still crying, but the hugs felt good, and the warm words were welcome and she hugged her new co-workers back, kissing their cheeks, laughing through her tears.

"We love you," they said.

"I love you, too," she told them.

"Congratulations." Mr. Lamb walked up to her, smiling, handing her a folded green Store uniform and a copy of a black book identified by gold embossed letters as *The Employee's Bible.* "You're one of us."

TEN

1

They were supposed to go for a hike, she and Jake. It was a beautiful day for it, the temperature warm and pleasant, not too hot, the deep blue sky filled with huge white clouds, but Shannon sensed something wrong almost immediately. Jake was more subdued than usual, not himself, and he seemed not to care where they went. Ordinarily, he chose where they would hike, and if she made any suggestions he would invariably shoot them down. But today he acquiesced to everything she said, and that wasn't like him.

It worried her.

They hiked in silence, stopping only periodically to drink from their canteens. Usually, they walked together, hand in hand, meandering along the trails that led through the forest, talking intimately. Today, though, they walked single file, she in the lead, and it felt almost as though she was hiking alone. She had to keep sneaking surreptitious glances behind her to make sure that Jake was still there.

Shannon slowed. She'd never been this far along the trail before. Ahead, it wound down the side of a hill toward a small canyon below. A series of blue-green pools connected by a thin stream lined the bottom of the canyon to the right of the trail. To the left of the trail, at the bottom of the canyon, was a meadow.

She turned around, looked at Jake. "You want to go down?" she asked.

He shrugged.

She started walking.

Fifteen minutes later, they were at the bottom and she

was almost in tears. They'd walked close together, but they hadn't touched on the way down, hadn't even held hands. He hadn't helped her down the steep parts.

Something was definitely wrong.

She took a deep breath, turned, faced him. "What is it?" she asked. "What's the problem?"

"Nothing."

"Something." She stood there for a moment, looking at him. "Oh, Jake," she said. She moved forward to hug him, but he caught her wrists before she reached him and held her at arm's length. He would not meet her eyes, and she felt her stomach drop. She knew what was coming.

"I . . . don't think we should see each other anymore," he said.

Her mouth was dry, her vision suddenly blurry. "You don't . . . I thought . . ." She cleared her throat. "I love you," she said.

He still wouldn't look at her. "I think it's time we started dating other people."

"You found someone else! That's why—"

"No," he said. "That's not the reason."

"Then what is it?"

"My job."

She started to say something, then shook her head, not sure if she'd heard him correctly. "What?"

"I'm not allowed to date anyone outside The Store."

"Outside The Store? You mean you have to have all your dates—where?—at the snack bar? In the hardware department?"

"No. I can't date anyone who doesn't work for The Store."

"That's stupid! They can't do that!"

For the first time, he looked at her full on, and she saw nothing in his eyes, no sadness, no remorse, no regret. "I don't want to date someone who doesn't work for The Store," he said.

"I can get a job there. I can—"

"No."

She realized that she sounded desperate, but she couldn't help it. "I love you," she repeated.

He shook his head. "I'm afraid we have to stop seeing each other."

She wanted to remind him of everything they'd been through together, everything they'd done. They'd made out on this very trail, a half mile back. They'd gone to Winter Formal together, made love afterward. They'd eaten the same ice cream cone—he licking one side, she the other. They'd done everything couples were supposed to do. They'd even almost had a child together. Didn't any of that mean anything to him?

She wanted to say all that and more, but she could tell from the flat look in his eyes, the neutral expression on his face, that it would not get her anywhere. She would not be able to appeal to him on any sort of emotional level. He did not care.

For him, the relationship was already over.

She closed her eyes, trying not to cry. Why had he gone hiking with her? Why hadn't he told her at the outset that it was over? Why had he waited until they were out here in the middle of nowhere before springing this on her?

"Are you okay?" he asked.

"Fuck you!" she screamed.

She'd intended only to nod, to be dignified and pretend as though he meant nothing to her and this was no big deal.

But she'd loved him.

"Fuck you!"

He shrugged. "We'd better go back."

"I wouldn't walk back with you if you were the last person on earth! Go to hell, you son of a bitch! Walk back by yourself!"

"If that's the way you want it."

Through her tears, she watched him walk away, up the trail. Again, she thought of the *The Sound of Music,* when Rolf turns in the family at the end, betraying his love for the sake of the Party.

It was like Jake and The Store.

"Nazi!" she screamed. "You fucking Nazi!"

The echo of her cries sounded throughout the canyon. But Jake did not turn around.

2

Saturday. Samantha's first day of work.

Ginny awoke early to make Sam a special breakfast—her favorite Spanish omelette—but her daughter only picked at the food.

"This isn't a Shannon situation, is it?" Ginny teased. "You're not turning anorexic on us, are you?"

Samantha gave a perfunctory smile. "No, Mom." She made a big show of eating a few more bites of her omelette, but when she thought her mother was no longer watching, she put the fork down.

Ginny frowned, Three weeks ago, Sam had been ecstatic about the thought of getting a job at The Store, visibly excited by the prospect. But ever since her first interview, she'd seemed . . . different. Definitely not enthusiastic. For the past week, since she'd begun taking her nightly training classes, she'd seemed downright withdrawn.

It was as though working at The Store was something she was doing out of obligation, something to which she'd committed but had subsequently changed her mind about.

Ginny wanted to tell her daughter that she didn't have to go through with it if she didn't want to, she could get a job somewhere else.

But she said nothing.

"I have to get ready," Samantha said. "I can't be late on my first day." She pushed her chair away from the counter and walked into her bedroom to change into her uniform.

A few hours later, Ginny drove to The Store.

She went alone, not telling anyone, intending only to sneak a peek at her daughter. It was better this way. Bill, if he came along, would make a scene. Shannon would intentionally try to embarrass her sister. It would probably embarrass Sam to see her there, anyway, but it was her first daughter's first day at her first job, and she wanted to be there.

The funny thing was, Sam was the only person within their circle who'd actually gotten a job at The Store. Frieda Lindsborg had applied for a sales clerk position in Women's Clothing and Sondra Kelly's husband, Dar, had applied for a job in the Hardware department, but neither of them had been hired. Instead, Bob Franklin, who'd been a drunk and a bum and hadn't even been able to hold a trash-collecting job with his brother-in-law's company, had been hired as a "director," one of the employees who "directed" customers to the correct aisle when they were looking for a particular item. Ed Brooks, who wasn't much better, had been hired as a stock clerk. She'd seen both of those two in The Store, and she had to admit they looked cleaned up and competent, but she couldn't figure out why they'd been hired over Dar or Frieda or the other deserving applicants in town.

Which made her feel uneasy about Sam.

Ginny parked the car and walked into The Store. There was something smarmy about the young man who greeted her at the door and offered her a shopping cart, and as she walked through the building, several of the clerks and "directors" seemed equally off-putting to her. As she pushed the cart past Housewares, a uniformed clerk appeared at her side and asked if she needed any assistance. She said no, pushed on, and another clerk accosted her at Women's Shoes, offering to help her pick out footwear. She said that she was not shopping for shoes today.

She'd never liked salespeople, had always felt uncomfortable in stores where employees hovered around her, watching her every move. She liked to be left alone, to shop in peace. The Store had done that originally, but now it seemed that the pressure was being increased, that more time and energy were being expended spying on customers.

She didn't like that.

She thought of the convoy of black trucks she'd seen driving up to Juniper that night back in February. She'd never mentioned it to Bill, and she wasn't sure why. She hadn't forgotten about it—in fact, each time she'd gone to The Store or heard The Store mentioned, it had immediately come to the forefront of her mind. Yet she'd shopped here, let Sam apply for a job here, pretended that nothing was wrong.

Was there anything wrong?

She wasn't sure, and perhaps that was why she'd kept quiet. It had been an eerie feeling she'd had that night, a vague sense of unease, but that could have been the circumstances—the darkness, the solitude, the fact that the rest of her family had been asleep. Bill had been paranoid enough as it was at that time, and she hadn't wanted to contribute to his anti-Store obsession.

But he seemed to have gotten over all that, and now she wondered if that was healthy. There *was* something odd about The Store, something—

"Ginny!"

She turned at the sound of the voice. Meg Silva stood in the aisle to her right, holding in her hands a bolt of sewing fabric.

Ginny put on her best fake smile. Meg was about the last person in the world she wanted to see right now, but she nodded at the other teacher, walked over and said hello. Meg subjected her to ten minutes' worth of complaints about everything from the kids in her class this year to the quality of whole cloth made in Thailand, but Ginny was finally able to extricate herself, claiming that she had to hurry up and finish shopping because Bill needed the car.

"Well," Meg said, "I guess I'll see you Monday, then."

Ginny smiled. "Unless I win the lottery."

"That goes for both of us."

Ginny waved good-bye and pushed the cart toward the Toddlers' department, where Sam was supposed to be working.

As she passed by Linen and Bedding, she overheard a couple talking in the next aisle over.

"They have layaway," the man was saying. "We can get that TV now *and* the crib."

"I don't think it's a good idea to go into debt," the woman replied.

You're right, Ginny thought. But she said nothing, kept on walking.

Ahead, she saw Sam. Her daughter was facing another direction, talking to a woman who was looking at kiddie pajamas, and Ginny quickly maneuvered her shopping cart into a side aisle, intending to sneak around behind Sam and watch her surreptitiously. She reached the end of the aisle, turned left, and stopped in back of a series of tall shelves containing various strollers.

"Are these pajamas *fireproof* or fire-*resistant?*" she heard the woman ask.

"I don't know," Sam responded.

"Does it say anywhere on the label?"

"I don't know."

"Could you help me look?"

"No."

Ginny stood behind the shelf, shocked. Sam's attitude toward the customer was not only abrupt but rude, and it seemed totally out of character for her. Ordinarily, she was friendly, cheerful, happy. Especially around strangers. Of the two girls, she was the more even-tempered and easygoing. Shannon was the more abrasive.

"It's not my responsibility to fulfill your duties as a parent," Sam said. "I just work here. I'm a sales clerk."

Ginny frowned. What was going on here? What was wrong with Sam? She couldn't have been *told* to act this way, could she? Was that what they'd been teaching her in those nightly training classes she'd been attending the past week?

Possibly.

Now that Ginny thought about it, she had been treated rudely herself by several Store employees over the past few weeks. In fact, she'd never been treated normally here. Either the clerks had been unctuous and toadying, or rude and dismissive. They had never been simply polite or professional.

"I don't like your attitude, young lady." The woman was obviously a fighter, and she was not about to be treated this way. "I'm going to speak to your supervisor."

Ginny could almost hear the shrug in Sam's voice. "Go ahead."

The woman moved off with a rattling of her cart, and Ginny moved as well, backward, away from the Toddlers' section, troubled.

3

"So, dude, did you win, place, or show?"

"Took the Triple Crown, motherfucker!"

"Bullshit." Denny looked from Chuck to A. B. "You know he didn't even get to touch her hand, let alone anything else."

"Big words, cherry boy. Big words."

Denny shook his head. The three of them were sitting at a plastic table in The Store's snack bar, scarfing junk food, talking trash, and checking out the babes as they passed by. Chuck had gone out with Audra McKinley last night, and while half of him hoped that his friend had gone all the way with her so they could hear the intimate details, half of him hoped that she'd slapped his face if he so much as tried to touch her. He liked Audra himself, would give his left nut to go out with her, and the thought that she'd gone out with his friend instead of him made him feel more than a little jealous.

But Chuck was the brave one. He was the one who'd asked.

A. B. looked disgustedly at Chuck as he wolfed down the last bite of his snack bar hot dog. "You know, dude, you are what you eat."

Chuck grinned. "That can't be true. Otherwise, I'd be a pussy."

Denny laughed. "You are."

"No, he's not. He's a wienie."

Around them, other customers were eating sushi and quiche and that other trendy crap The Store was trying to force down everyone's throat. But the three of them had made a stand, saying that the snack bar had better start serving the same type of food as George's if it wanted *their* business, and The Store had caved in to their culinary demands, putting burgers and fries, hot dogs and shakes on the menu.

Now they hung out here all the time. In fact, the snack bar chow was so good that he couldn't even remember the last time they'd actually been to George's. Not that he cared. Downtown was dead, anyway. The Store was where all the action was.

And it was air-conditioned, besides.

Denny finished off his fries, dumped the last of the ice from his empty Coke cup into his mouth.

"Let's check out the games," A. B. said. "Maybe they have the new *Doom.*"

Chuck nodded. "Or the new *Mortal Kombat.*"

"Something."

Denny was still chewing his ice. He tried to say "Sure," but the word came out garbled, mushed.

"Don't talk with your mouth full," Chuck said. "Didn't your mama ever tell you that?"

Denny swallowed the ice. "Your mama did. But I couldn't understand her because I was filling up *her* mouth at the time."

"Dick."

"Exactly."

The three of them stood, moved away from the table, walked out of the snack bar area.

"May I direct you to the proper aisle?"

All of them jumped at the sound of the voice. Denny turned to see a tall, somewhat intimidating man in a Store uniform standing directly behind them. The man smiled, and Denny had to clear his suddenly clogged throat in order to speak. "We're looking for video games—"

"New games," A. B. said.

"Cool ones," Chuck added.

The man's smile broadened. "This way." He moved easily through the crowd of customers, past the checkout registers, past the displays of sale items. They hurried after him, up one row, down another, until they were in the electronics department.

Only . . .

Only Denny could not remember ever being in this aisle before.

He had spent a lot of time in this department—they all had—looking at games and videos, CDs and stereos and televisions, but he'd never seen the stuff they had here. He scanned the titles on the shelf in front of him: *White Power, White Rule; Sally's Three-Hole Fun Zone; Niggerkill.*

"Here you are, boys." The man gestured toward the shelves on either side of the aisle. "Hope you find what you're looking for." He nodded at them, strode away.

"Wow," A. B. said, looking at the titles.

Chuck grinned. "This is cool!"

Denny picked up a game box: *Raped and Snuffed.* He nodded, smiled. "Yeah," he said. "It is."

4

Frieda Lindsborg sat down in the center chair in Women's Shoes while the clerk went back into the stockroom to see if they had the sandals she wanted in black. She unlaced and took off her tennis shoes, then leaned back, closed her eyes. She was tired. She'd been shopping nonstop, running around town since she'd gotten off work, and she'd been on her feet since three o'clock this morning, when her shift at the bakery started. After she bought these shoes, she was going to rent a couple videos, go home, stretch out on the couch, and just watch movies for the rest of the afternoon.

A hand touched her ankle, began pulling down her sock, and she instantly opened her eyes, jerking her foot back.

"I found the sandals in black," the clerk said. "I was just going to help you try them on."

He was seated on a stool in front of her, an open shoe box containing the sandals on the floor next to him, and she immediately felt guilty for her little panic attack. She stretched her right foot out again, let him pull off the sock. "I'm sorry," she said. "It's been a long day."

"Nothing to be sorry about." The clerk dropped the

sock on the floor, lifted her foot, examined it. He turned it gently to the left, then to the right. One hand held on to the calf, while the other began to caress her sole. "Very nice," he said. "Very nice."

He still hadn't taken off her other sock, had not even taken one of the sandals out of the box. The attention he was paying to her foot seemed obsessive, and she felt more than a little uneasy as his finger lightly traced the outline of her toes, but . . . but there was something exciting about it, exciting and, well, sensual.

He placed the foot on his left knee, then picked up her other foot, carefully pulling off the sock, again rubbing and massaging the foot itself.

He looked up at her. "Can I smell your feet?" he whispered.

She grimaced in disgust and tried to pull her feet back, but he held tight to her left calf and continued to stroke it lightly, delicately. He stood, still holding her foot, and pushed aside the stool.

He knelt in front of her.

She did not try to pull her foot away this time. As much as she hated to admit it, she liked the subservient position he held, liked the fact that he had to look up at her while she looked down at him. It seemed sexy, and she found herself wishing that she'd worn a skirt instead of pants.

He said nothing, but looked up at her, smiled, put his mouth around her big toe and began to suck.

Frieda closed her eyes, leaned her head back, tried to give him more of her foot. She'd never felt anything like this. The sensation was exquisite, and she arched her back, trying to keep herself from moaning.

He sucked each and every toe.

On both feet.

Finally, she opened her eyes. She glanced around. There were people talking behind the row of pumps in front of her, other people with shopping carts passing by the main aisle, but she and the clerk were alone by the chairs and no one had seen them.

The clerk smiled slyly at her. "Would you like to try the sandals on now, ma'am?"

"Uh, no," she said, still breathing heavily. "That won't be necessary."

She stood in her bare feet, patted down her hair, smoothed out her pants.

"I'll take two pair," she said.

ELEVEN

1

Bill never would have expected it of himself, but he had become addicted to local politics. He went to all public meetings now—planning commission, sanitary district, town council. He'd never realized before how uninvolved most people were with their government. Theoretically, local politics was the arena in which people had the greatest voice. Its participants were most responsive to individual concerns because their constituencies were so small. Yet people were more familiar with national politicians—even national politicians from other parts of the country—than they were with their own locally elected officeholders.

They might have more control over local politics than national politics, but they were also a lot less interested in it.

Until recently, he himself had been one of the uninvolved. He'd voted in every election, but his votes had been based on general perceptions rather than specific knowledge. He'd been of the if-it-ain't-broke-don't-fix-it school, and if he hadn't heard anything bad about a town council member or a county supervisor, he had assumed that they were doing a good job.

He no longer made such assumptions. If he had learned anything from attending these meetings, it was that decisions were constantly being made that negatively impacted people's lives but that most people never learned about.

Which was one of the reasons he'd become such a fanatic meeting attendee.

That and the fact that he found it all so fascinating.

The town council meeting didn't start until six, but he was in his usual seat next to Ben by five forty-five. The editor was the only person in the council chambers and was busily circling items on the agenda that he could later expand into separate stories for the paper. A half-eaten tuna sandwich lay in an open baggie on his lap.

"You might find this interesting," Ben said, tapping a circled agenda item with his pen. "Apparently, The Store is not just building the new park, it's going to be responsible for park maintenance. The town's going to let one of its maintenance people go."

"Who?"

"Greg Lawrence."

"Don't know him."

Ben shook his head. "I guess we'll find out for sure tonight, but word is that Store employees are going to be assigned to clean up the park, trim trees, water and mow the grass, whatever."

Bill snorted. "Taking jobs everywhere they go."

"It's the American way."

The meeting was called to order fifteen minutes later. As usual, the council chambers were less than half full. There was only Ben, himself, a handful of retired people and local gadflies, and assorted individuals with items pending before the council.

After the pledge, the prayer, and the other opening formalities, the meeting got underway with the park maintenance issue. The agenda item was read, seconded, and as it was considered "old business," there was no opportunity for public discussion. The council unanimously agreed to accept what Councilman Bill Reid referred to as "The Store's gracious and generous offer" to provide all maintenance for the new park.

Greg Lawrence was laid off.

The mayor himself introduced the first item of "new business," the town's projected revenue shortfall for the next fiscal year. He read aloud a summary report from Juniper's financial manager stating that if the town's operating expenses remained at the current level, Juniper would run out of money before the fiscal year was half over.

"Obviously," the mayor said, "there's going to have to be some belt-tightening. As we all know, the county is having financial problems of its own and has appropriated a large chunk of the property tax revenue that used to go to the towns."

"That's *supposed* to go to the towns," Bill Reid said.

"Exactly," the mayor agreed. "And the result of this is that all we're really left with is our sales tax revenue. And with our tax base shifting, with our downtown businesses taking a hit because of Juniper's recent economic realignment, sales tax revenues are down considerably."

The mayor cleared his throat. "We also have a major unanticipated expense that we're going to have to encumber over to the next budget year. If you recall, as part of our incentive package to bring The Store to Juniper, we promised to ensure easy access for all vehicles entering The Store parking lot. They initially wanted an extra lane, a turn lane, constructed on the eastbound side of the highway, and we compromised by restriping that section of road and promising to constuct the lane if it proved to be necessary.

"Well, a representative of The Store has formally submitted a written request for the new lane, and our own traffic study has confirmed that the restriping is indeed inadequate for the flow of traffic generated by The Store." He cleared his throat again. "Which is a fancy way of saying that we are legally obligated to construct an access lane running from milepost 260 to The Store entrance."

"Where are we going to get the money for that?" Hunter Palmyra asked.

"Staff has proposed that we cut back on street maintenance, park and recreation programs, and other nonessential services. In addition, we should consider increasing building permit fees and dog licensing fees, charging for fire calls and police calls that don't result in action by safety officers—false alarms, basically—and we should look into contracting out specific services that are currently performed by town employees."

"I, for one, would like to see a breakdown of each proposed fee increase, and how much we would save from eliminating each program, service, or job position,"

Palmyra said. "I don't think any of us have enough information at our disposal right now to be able to intelligently address this issue, much less make any decisions."

"I make a motion that we postpone discussion of the revenue shortfall until our next meeting," Bill Reid offered, "and that staff provide us with the appropriate reports."

"Seconded," Palmyra said.

The mayor nodded. "Let's put it to a vote. All in favor?"

The hands of all five council members went up.

"All opposed?"

No hands.

"The motion has been carried unanimously."

Ben leaned over. "That means it'll be 'old business' next meeting," he whispered. "The public won't be able to comment. Pretty clever, huh?"

Bill did not respond. This whole meeting, the way it was being conducted, the subjects that were being discussed, none of it sat well with him. These five men—two of them real estate agents, one a developer who had only moved to Juniper three years ago, one a retired civil servant from back East, one a retired AT&T supervisor—were cutting jobs, laying off local workers, changing the entire face of the town in order to accommodate The Store. It wasn't right, it shouldn't be allowed to happen, and he wanted to stand up and make an impassioned speech on behalf of the local citizens and their rights and their concerns, but he didn't know what to say or how to say it, and he remained silently in his seat.

The mayor looked down at one of the papers in front of him. "Do I have a motion on the turn lane?" he asked.

Dick Wise nodded. "I make a motion that we accept the drafted resolution as is and encumber the funds to complete the highway construction contractually required of us, the contractor who will perform the work to be determined by the bid process."

"Seconded," Bill Reid said.

The motion was passed unanimously.

The mayor shuffled through the papers before him. "In a somewhat related matter, I have here a petition signed by downtown businesses and shopkeepers. All of the merchants on Main and Allen streets." He looked to his left, then right, at the other members of the council flanking him on the dais. "I trust you all have your copies?" Assenting nods. "Very well, then. The petition asks us to either lift our current sign ordinance or allow temporary exemptions to the ordinance. Specifically, we're being asked to allow banners to be placed in front of stores or business, on the building fronts or on light poles."

Bill looked around the council chambers. "How come none of the merchants are here?" he asked Ben. "Where's Street?"

"How come it's not on the agenda?" the editor replied. He shook his head. "They're trying to pull a fast one here. This'll be my top story. I'm going to nail their asses on this one."

The mayor glanced over at Ben. "Pursuant to Section Four, Paragraph Five of the Juniper Town Charter, I make a motion that the petition and its request for changes, exemptions, and/or variances to the sign ordinance be added to the agenda."

"Seconded."

Passed.

"We will open this matter for public discussion," the mayor said.

A quiet, nondescript man who'd been sitting unobtrusively at the back of the audience stood, walked to the podium.

"Please state your name and address," the mayor said.

"My name's Ralph Keyes. I'm here as a representative of The Store, located at 111 Highway 180." The man's voice was smooth, confident, with no discernible accent. "I would like to state for the record that we feel allowing exemptions to the existing sign ordinance would give preferential treatment to certain businesses and would constitute unfair competition. If such a course of action is taken by the council, we would be compelled to protest this matter and proceed to litigation. In our opinion, it is not the town's responsibility to promote or champion individual businesses." He spread his arms, smiled insincerely. "This is supposed to be a free country with a free market system. By its very nature, this means that some businesses will succeed and other businesses will fail. It is not government's responsibility to intercede on behalf of individual merchants merely because they are floundering in the marketplace." Keyes nodded respectfully. "Thank you, Mr. Mayor."

He returned to his seat in the back of the council chambers, and the mayor glanced over the sparse audience. "Does anyone else wish to speak on this matter?"

Bill stood, walked to the podium.

He didn't think about it, he just did it, and he was not even sure what he intended to say as he faced the council.

"My name is Bill Davis," he said into the microphone. "I live at 121 Rock Springs Lane. I heard what Mr. Keyes said, and I understand his position and the position of The Store, but I have to tell you that I disagree with him one hundred percent. By your own admission, the council provided incentives to The Store in order to lure it to Juniper. Rules were bent or ignored, exemptions were granted. I think all our local businesses are asking is that they be given the same latitude, that they be allowed to compete on a level playing field. I mean, you're building *roads* for The Store. The least you can do is let some of our local merchants hang signs in front of their shops so that people will know what they have, what they're offering, what's available. It's not an unreasonable request. And as for this idea of government intervention, you were elected by the people of Juniper to do what's best for the town of Juniper. I think that means you should extend a helping hand to our local businesses the same way you did to this national corporation. *That* would be in the best interests of your constituents. *That* was what you were elected to do."

The mayor nodded. "Thank you, Mr. Davis, I, too, wish to state my unequivocal support for our local merchants and businessmen. They are indeed the backbone of our town. Unfortunately, though, our Master Plan specifically prohibits the exhibition of signs and banners of the sort requested in this petition."

"The Store didn't have to follow *any* of the Master Plan!"

"No, that was a special case. We made an exception to the rule. But we are not going to change that rule simply because we did grant that one exception. And, I may add, The Store is now the largest employer in Juniper. I don't think I'm overstating the case when I say that our local economy hinges on how well The Store does. We knew that going in, and that was why we offered the incentives. To bolster the economic strength of our town."

"But you just said the town has less money, is going to have to cut programs and lay people off. Our local businesses are dying—"

"Your time is up, Mr. Davis. Thank you for your comments."

"I'm not through."

"Yes, you are."

"I'd like to be granted an extension."

"Denied. Please sit down, Mr. Davis, and allow others a chance to speak."

There were no others, and after a quick discussion among themselves, the members of the council voted to deny the request of the petitioning businesses.

Ben smiled cynically. "Democracy in action."

Bill shook his head. "Assholes."

He sat through the rest of the meeting—routine business that offended no one and affected no one and sped quickly by. Afterward, he quickly got up out of his chair and started toward the back seats. He wanted to talk to Keyes, the Store representative.

But though he had seen no one leave the chambers, though neither door had opened or closed, Keyes was nowhere to be seen. Bill hurried outside, scanning the small parking lot, but it was empty.

The man was gone.

2

Bill sat in front of his computer, brooding.

He stared at the page of instructions he'd just completed. The program for which he was writing documentation was going to put several people out of work. Hell, it might even eliminate a whole department. From what he could tell, this accounting system could probably be run by two people—a supervisor and a data entry operator—instead of however many individuals made up the current accounting staff at The Store's corporate headquarters.

It was something that had always been in his mind, the knowledge that his work was contributing to the "downsizing," "rightsizing," and "outsourcing" of America, that while he had a good life and a good job, they came at the expense of others. His company's systems were designed to replace people with computer programs, to decrease payroll costs and increase profit margins, to boost returns to stockholders without regard to the individuals who actually worked for a corporation.

But it was not something he had really focused on until now.

It was The Store connection that had really brought it home to him, that had made him realize how basically parasitic Automated Interface was. The ironic thing was that although he was indirectly helping to put people out of work, his job was pretty damn close to superfluous. Theoretically, documentation was necessary. Customers needed to be provided with instructions and descriptions of the software they purchased so that they could install it in their computers and use it. But the programs these days were pretty self-explanatory, the people who bought them were usually computer literate, and if users had problems they usually just called up the toll-free customer service number and asked questions of the support staff.

Most of the documentation he wrote sat in impressive-looking binders, untouched, on customers' shelves.

It was a depressing situation, and one he felt guilty about, but there was little he could do to change it. This was his job. He had a family to help support—they certainly couldn't survive on Ginny's salary alone—and he possessed no other skills, certainly none that could land him gainful employment in Juniper. At the very least, they'd have to move to a bigger city, someplace where he might be able to catch on at a large company. It was highly unlikely that another employer would allow him to telecommute and work out of his home.

Besides, he liked his job.

He felt guilty about that, too.

He wasn't in the mood to continue working on computer instructions, so he saved what he'd written on both the hard disk and a diskette, then toggled over to check his E-mail.

There was a message from Street, and he called it up:

> You are God, buddy! I heard about the council meeting, and I want you to know that all of us downtown are pretty damn impressed with the way you stood up for us. Especially for a guy who always did his shopping in Phoenix!
>
> Thanx for stating our case. Every little bit helps.
>
> Want to join the recall effort?
>
> How about chess tonight?

He smiled as he read the message. Maybe he wasn't such a traitor after all.

He sent Street a message agreeing to a computer game, then signed off. He stared at the blank screen and found himself wondering what would happen if Street lost his store. Would he be able to find a job here in town, or would he have to move? It wasn't just an idle question anymore. There'd been a seismic shift in the economics of Juniper, and the shift was permanent. The Store wasn't going anywhere, and whatever business couldn't coexist with it would be killed.

Street might survive, because his shop carried a broad range of seldom-needed electronic parts that it probably wouldn't be economically feasible for The Store to stock. But a lot of the local merchants carried a small selection of mainstream goods, and not only did The Store sell those items for a cheaper price, it offered a wider selection. Those businesses wouldn't make it.

The phone rang, and Bill answered.

It was Williamson James.

"Thank you," he said. "Thank you for posting my ad on the computer."

"What happened?"

"I found a buyer for the café."

"That's great. Who?"

"You're not going to believe this."

"Who?"

"The Store."

Bill was silent.

"Are you still there?" the café owner asked. "Bill?"

"I'm here," he said, and he tried not to let the emotions he was feeling into his voice.

"They're paying big bucks, too. I'm really lucky. Really *really* lucky."

Bill closed his eyes, held the receiver tightly. "Yeah," he said finally. "You are."

3

Ginny walked in from the bathroom, drying her hair, and glanced over at Bill on the bed. He was sitting up against the headboard, an open book in his lap, but his gaze was distant, far-off, not on the pages in front of him. She tossed the towel on top of the hamper. "Hey," she said, walking over. "What is it?"

Bill looked up at her. He shook his head, put his book facedown on the nightstand next to him. "Nothing."

"Something." She sat down on her side of the bed and picked up a container of moisturizer from the nightstand, opening it. "Tell me."

"It's not important."

"Suit yourself."

He smiled at her in his best adoring housewife manner. "So how was your day, dear?"

She started spreading the moisturizer on her face. "Except for the students and Meg, it was fine."

"That's nice."

She paused. "You know, it's weird. The past week or so, the kids have seemed completely different. Ever since Easter vacation. They were only out for a week, but it's like they were gone for a year. Now they all dress like gang members, with the big pants, the baggy clothes. . . ."

"Fads change. You know that." He chuckled. "So the MTV influence has finally penetrated our little town."

"It's not that. It's . . ." She shook her head. "I can't explain it, but something's changed. They don't just look different, they're acting different."

"Come on—"

"You don't know these kids. I do."

"I'm sorry."

"Their parents all bought them exactly the same clothes. Those clothes."

"If they shopped here in town, of course they're all going to buy the same clothes. There's not much of a selection."

"That's just it. These aren't Juniper, Arizona, clothes. These are New York clothes. South Central L.A. clothes. And it's not just a fad. It's more like they're wearing . . . a uniform. It's not like they want to dress this way, it's like they have to dress this way, like their parents and their friends and everything are forcing them into this, requiring it of them. The peer pressure factor's way up all of a sudden." She sighed, started again spreading the moisturizer on her face. "I don't like it."

Bill was silent for a moment. "We made a mistake," he said finally, and his voice was serious. "We never should've let Sam work at The Store."

She'd been thinking the same thing, but it felt strange hearing him say it, and she felt obligated to defend her daughter. "It's what she wants to do. Besides, she's eighteen. She's an adult. She has to live her own life."

"She may be eighteen," Bill said, "but she's not an adult. And as long as she lives in our house, under our roof, she's going to follow our rules."

"So you want her to quit?"

Bill looked at her. "Don't you?"

"I don't think it's my decision to make."

He sighed. "You're right." He leaned back against the headboard, looked up at the ceiling. "I don't know what to do."

Ginny put down the jar of moisturizer and scooted next to him on the bed. She put a hand on his leg. "Maybe we should both talk to her."

"No. She does need to earn money for college. Besides, if we forbid her to work, she'll just resent us for it. She might even do something . . . I don't know, drastic."

Ginny smiled. "Are you sure you don't have her confused with Shannon?"

"Sam's more like her every day."

So he'd noticed, too. Ginny thought of the way Sam had treated that customer at The Store, the almost surly attitude she'd had around the house lately. This behavior wasn't like their daughter, and it worried her. "Maybe she'll figure it out for herself," Ginny suggested. "Maybe she'll quit on her own."

"Maybe," Bill said doubtfully. "I hope so."

"I do, too," Ginny said, and a chill passed through her as she thought of the black convoy. She snuggled closer to Bill. "I do, too."

TWELVE

1

Aaron Jefcoat sat in his police cruiser, in the parking lot of Len's Donuts, finishing an apple fritter before beginning his midnight tour of the town. He'd had over a week to think about it, but he still wasn't sure how he felt about his wife working. He glanced over at the photo of Virginia he'd mounted in a clear plastic frame atop the dashboard. The picture had been taken a long time ago, before she'd had the boys, and she looked damn good in it. She still looked damn good, he thought, but the photo captured her in her prime, the way she'd looked when he'd married her, and it was a reminder, in case he ever forgot, of the way she had changed his life.

She'd had a job when they'd met. She'd been a carhop at Big Daddy's Diner, the old teenage hangout that had been torn down in the seventies to make room for KFC. But she'd quit working when they'd married to become a housewife, and she'd been responsible for taking care of the house, and later the kids, while he brought home the bacon.

It had been a fair division of labor, and it had worked now for over twenty-five years, but last week, all of a sudden, Virginia had decided that she wanted to go back to work. She wanted to get a job at The Store.

His initial reaction was to say no. He knew she'd been a little bored the past year, a little restless, and with the boys gone she didn't have as much to do, but he knew she'd get used to it. This was a transitional period, he told her. It would probably take a while to adjust.

She didn't want to adjust, she told him. She wanted to get a job.

He was against the idea, but he hadn't actually come out and forbidden her to work. Ten years ago, he would have. But women these days didn't act the way they used to. Times had changed. All he had to do was look at what had happened to his friend Ken. Ken's situation was almost identical to his own. A year or so ago, after his daughter had gone off to college, Ken's wife, suffering from the empty-nest syndrome, had wanted to get a job. He had forbidden her to do so, and there'd been nothing but headaches and heartaches for him after that. Finally, she'd threatened to leave him, and Ken had given in and let her go to work.

Aaron didn't want the same thing to happen with Virginia.

So he pretty much had to let her work.

And he still wasn't sure how he felt about that.

He finished his fritter, wiped his fingers on the napkin in his lap, and started up the cruiser.

Time for the tour.

When he'd first been assigned the graveyard shift, he'd hated it. On a purely physical level, his body had had a tough time coping with the change in sleep patterns, and he'd lain awake all day in his bed, while he was supposed to be sleeping, and dozed half the night in his patrol car, while he was supposed to be on duty. Not that it made much of a difference if he slept. Juniper rolled up its carpets at six and was for all intents and purposes dead to the world after dark. Len's Donuts was open all night, but he was usually the only customer, and it was a rare shift indeed when he saw even one other vehicle on the streets once the theater emptied at ten.

He supposed that was why he'd grown to like graveyard. He got paid more than he would if he worked day shift or swing, and there was a hell of a lot less to do. The way it worked out, he was able to spend more time with his family than he ever had before, and if that meant that he sometimes caught a few Z's during the early morning downtime, well, it didn't harm anyone.

Aaron took a slow, leisurely drive up and down the streets of Juniper. As usual, he saw no people, no cars, no movement. Everyone was asleep, snug in their beds, and he smiled to himself as he drove past his own house and thought of Virginia sacked out, snoring lightly in that cute little way she had. His eyes swept the street before him. Here and there, porch lights had been left on to ward off prowlers. Through an occasional curtain he could see the flickering blue light of a television that had not been turned off.

He felt protective of the town as he cruised its streets, as though he was a proud papa and all of the people were his children. It was a strangely comforting feeling, and at times like this he was glad he'd gone against his parents' wishes and become a police officer.

He drove down the dirt back roads at the east end of the town limits, then cut north through Creekside Acres in order to get to the highway. Turning left on the highway, he saw, through the driver's window of the cruiser, the square black bulk of The Store.

It was a shame, he thought, that they'd had to build The Store here. It seemed to him that it would've made more sense to build on that vacant lot next to the Tire Barn, maybe buy out and tear down some of those eyesore trailers set up there. But instead they'd built it in the meadow where he used to take his dates, back before he'd met Virginia. Even the hillside where he used to spread his picnic blanket had been blasted and flattened.

The next generation wouldn't know that the meadow had ever existed.

It was a damn shame.

And now Virginia wanted to work here.

He pulled into the Store parking lot, intending to take a quick spin around before continuing back toward Main.

Instantly, he slowed the car. The lights in the parking lot were off, but the moon was full and he could see small unmoving lumps on the asphalt: the forms of dead animals. He rode the brake as the cruiser slowly crept forward. He'd heard about this before, but he hadn't really believed it. Forest Everson had told him that there'd been a lot of croaked critters found on the property when The Store was being built—and Forest was the one who'd handled that dead transient case—but Aaron still hadn't put much stock in those tales. He figured it was like those full-moon stories, that crap about more crimes occurring when the moon was full. He knew that wasn't true.

But there was a full moon tonight.

And there were dead animals in the parking lot.

He drove the cruiser slowly through the lot, glancing through the window at the bodies. There was a possum, a dog, what looked like a baby javelina, two crows, a bobcat. It was an amazingly diverse group of animals, and they all appeared unharmed and untouched. It was like they'd simply crawled onto the parking lot to die.

Forest had told him that as well, and he'd dismissed it at the time, but he felt an unfamiliar tingle in the hairs at the nape of his neck as he stared at the dead animals.

Fear.

It was fear. Not the full-blown emotion generated by a life-threatening situation, more the mild sense of unease experienced by children when they heard strange noises in the dark, but it was fear nevertheless, and Aaron was both surprised at himself and ashamed.

He continued forward, toward the enormous black mass of the Store building, looking out the window at the individual animals. Another dog. A squirrel. A tabby cat.

A tabby cat.

He stopped the car.

Annabelle?

He opened the door of the vehicle and stepped out to examine the animal. It was Annabelle, all right. But how in the world had she gotten here? Their house was at least three miles away. Had she walked that far, or had somebody catnapped her and killed her and dumped her body? Neither explanation made sense, and with a sinking feeling in his stomach, he bent down and touched the cat's body.

Cold.

Virginia would be devastated. Hell, so would the boys. Annabelle had been a part of their family for the past seven years. She was almost like a little sister to them.

He didn't feel that hot himself, and there was a lump

in his throat as he looked into the cat's face. She appeared calm, peaceful, eyes and mouth shut. His fingers closed around her cold front paw.

And the lights in The Store flipped on.

Aaron jumped, nearly fell over backwards. He quickly scrambled to his feet, drawing his revolver. There were no windows in The Store, only sliding glass doors at the entrance, but in the gloom of night, the light was piercing. It shone through the building's entrance and into the parking lot like a white searchlight, illuminating a swath of asphalt all the way out to the highway, causing long shadows to spring up from the bodies of the dead animals, the previously bright moonlight fading into insignificance before its fluorescent power.

Aaron holstered his weapon, already embarrassed by his panicked first reaction, and hurried back to the cruiser, hopping in and slamming shut the door. He put the vehicle into gear and drove through the lot toward the entrance of the building. His heart was pounding, his nerves alive with an adrenaline rush. There was probably nothing out of the ordinary here. A nighttime cleaning crew or some other workers were no doubt performing the legitimate duties for which they'd been hired. But at this hour, in the middle of the night, after the animals—*Annabelle*—the sudden appearance of the lights was surprising.

No, not surprising.

Eerie.

Yes. As embarrassing as it was to admit, he was a little spooked by the lights, even here in his patrol car, with his two-way radio and his shotgun and his revolver. Not for any rational reason. Not even for any irrational reason he could point to or pin down. It was simply an instinctual reaction, one over which he had absolutely no control.

He forced himself to push that reaction aside, however, as he pulled the cruiser in front of the store entrance, slamming the transmission into Park. He took the oversize flashlight from underneath the dashboard and, leaving the engine running, stepped out of the vehicle. There was no need for the flashlight, really. Every inch of The Store appeared to be clearly illuminated. But the parking lot was still dark, and after midnight there was no such thing as too much light. Besides, the flashlight doubled as a club, and he was more than prepared to use it in that capacity if necessary.

He stepped up to the glass doors, looked inside. He saw nothing at first, only aisle after aisle of products and a bank of unmanned cash registers. Then he caught the blur of movement out of the corner of his eye, and he focused his attention on the right rear corner of The Store.

And saw figures.

Black-clad figures.

Aaron's grip on the flashlight tightened. They were fanning outward from the corner, walking up aisles, moving around racks. They couldn't be employees, he thought. There was no way these strangely garbed individuals were here to perform any sort of legitimate work. They wore hoods and hats and looked like a variation on the cinematic conception of a cat burglar. Which meant they were probably here to rob or vandalize the place, to commit some sort of crime. Which meant that he was going to have to confront them and prevent the crime from being committed.

There were a lot of them, though, and he would be perfectly justified in calling for backup. The problem was that, aside from himself, only Dirkson was on duty tonight, and it would take at least ten or fifteen minutes for him to rouse the other officers and dispatch them to The Store.

Ten or fifteen minutes was a long time.

In the night.

In the dark.

It was then that he saw the words THE STORE stenciled on the back of a shiny black—jacket? shirt?—it was hard to tell what it was, but one of the figures had turned around, and the words—black on black—were visible in the fluorescent light.

They *were* employees.

Aaron breathed gratefully, unaware until now that he'd been holding his breath. He watched through the closed doors as the figures separated, heading over to the various Store departments.

Figures.

Why did he keep thinking of them as "figures" instead of "people"?

Because they didn't look human.

It was true. There was something about the figures, their build, their appearance, their movements, that struck him as odd, that looked, to his eye, unnatural.

He stepped back, away from the entrance, trying to blend into the darkness, not wanting any of the figures to see him. From this vantage point, he watched them as they moved through the store. Beneath the black hoods and hats, their faces were white, skin the color of alabaster and possessed of an abnormal quality, an unidentifiable property that ordinary skin—*human skin*—did not have.

That wasn't possible, though. He was just being crazy. The animals had thrown him for a loop, and he'd been spooked ever since. There was nothing unusual here, nothing out of the ordinary. These were just people, people working the graveyard shift like himself, people who were trying to do their job.

Graveyard shift.

He was being stupid again.

But was he? What work were these figures performing? They were wandering through the store, but they didn't seem to be doing anything. They certainly weren't cleaning the floors or replacing lightbulbs. They weren't even taking inventory. They were just . . . walking through the building. That wasn't work—

A figure stepped in front of the door.

Aaron jumped, instantly retreating further back into the darkness of the night. The figure stood inside The Store, behind the glass, facing out. Its head moved from left to right, as if scanning the parking lot. Seen this closely, from this angle, its movements seemed even stranger even more unusual and unnatural, and the skin of its face seemed whiter than any skin could be.

Aaron's heart was thumping wildly in his chest, and his mouth was completely dry.

The figure's head suddenly snapped to the left. Its eyes locked onto his.

The surrounding night suddenly seemed much blacker.

The figure stared at him.

Grinned.

Beckoned.

Aaron ran around the patrol car to the driver's side and its welcome open door. He slammed the door shut, put the vehicle into gear, and took off. There was no crime being committed here, no reason for him to hang around. Technically, he was trespassing. He had no cause, no suspicions, nothing that would stand up in court if he attempted to explain why he was lurking outside The Store in the middle of the night.

He glanced in his rearview mirror at the black shape of the building as he swerved onto the highway. He could see a small square of light where the entrance was.

And a small black shape in the middle of the square.

That settled it. Fights or no fights, problems or no problems, Virginia was not going to work. Not at The Store. He'd get divorced before he let her apply for a job at that place.

He accelerated quickly, speeding down the highway toward Main, refusing to look in his mirror again until trees had blocked the view of The Store behind him.

He did not rest easy until the cruiser was once again parked in front of Len's, and the well-lighted donut shop and its jovial proprietor were all he could see through his windshield.

2

The polarities had reversed.

Bill had been unsure at first whether the change in their winning streaks meant that the outcome of the chess games would return to a normal randomness or whether it meant that the win-loss pattern would simply be transferred between him and Street.

Obviously the latter.

He'd grown to hate the game, but, as before, he felt

compelled to play, driven to follow this through to the end.

Yesterday, they'd played computer chess. Street had won.

He was winning today's board game.

No, he had won today's board game. "Check," he said, moving his bishop into place. "Mate."

Street examined the position of the pieces on the board, then with one sweep of his hand knocked them to the floor. "Shit."

"Two to two," Ben announced.

Street stood. "I need a beer. Anyone else want one?"

Both Bill's and Ben's hands went up.

"Buds all around." Street retreated to the kitchen, emerging a moment later with three cans. He tossed one to each of them, then popped open his own, taking a long draught. He sat back down, began picking up the chess pieces off the floor.

Bill stooped to help him.

"I can do it," Street said.

"I don't mind."

"If you really want to help . . ." Street's voice trailed off. He straightened, threw the pieces into the box, downed a long swig of beer. "Ah, fuck."

Bill frowned. "What is it?"

Street sighed. "You know I don't like to trade on friendship," he said. "I've never tried to make either of you feel obligated to buy equipment from me, I've never tried to force you or con you. But I'm asking you now: do you think you could use some electronic equipment?"

Ben's voice was quiet. "You're really hurting, huh?"

Street nodded. "The Store's killing me." He looked from Ben to Bill. "I'm not asking for charity, but check around your homes or your offices, see if there're any electronic items you legitimately need. I'd appreciate the business."

"Are . . ." Bill cleared his throat. "Do you think you can survive?"

Street shrugged, finished off the beer. "I hope so, but who knows? At least I don't have alimony payments anymore. And at least the house is paid off. I suppose, if worse comes to worst, I can always file for bankruptcy." He chuckled. "Then, after my electricity's shut off and I can't afford to buy food, I can catch squirrels and cook them in the fireplace."

Bill didn't laugh. "It's not that bad, is it?"

"Not yet."

They were silent after that. Street walked back into the kitchen, got himself another can of Budweiser. "So, gents," he said finally, "any plans for this evening?"

Ben looked at his watch. "Planning Commission. Actually, the meeting starts in fifteen minutes." He downed the rest of his beer. "I'd better start heading over there."

Street turned toward Bill. "What about you?"

"Same thing."

"What is this crap? I know why Ben goes to these things. It's his job. He has to. But you?"

"I like to know what's going on in my town."

Street snorted. "Since when?"

"Since I found out what an unreliable rag our friend here puts out."

"Hey!" Ben said. "I resent that!"

Street laughed. Too loudly.

"Why don't you come with us?"

"Pass." Street picked up his remote, turned on the TV. "I'm sure it'll be fascinating, but there's a one-star women's prison movie on cable. T and A wins out over civic responsibility every time."

"They'll be discussing The Store," Ben said.

"Yeah. That's just what I want to spend my night hearing about."

"I heard they'll be asking for rezoning and building approval. They want to sell groceries."

"They'll get their approval," Street said simply. "Fucking Planning Commission's in their fucking pocket, just like the council."

"Maybe you should speak out against it," Bill suggested. "It might help."

Street waved him away. "I'm no public speaker. Besides, just in case you haven't noticed, I'm feeling a little too happy right now. The last thing the local merchants need is a half-crocked electronics salesman talking for them." He pressed the volume button on his remote. "I'm going to watch my cable while I can still afford it."

Ben stood, patted him on the back. "Take it easy, then. I'll let you know what transpires. And I'll drop by the store tomorrow. The paper needs some surge protectors. Ours are getting old."

Bill stood as well, leaving his half-finished can on the table. "I still need to get that old turntable fixed. I'll bring it by and we can go over it."

Street nodded gratefully. "Thanks, guys."

"Hey," Ben said, "we're friends."

Bill grinned. "Half my beer's left, too. It's all yours if you don't mind the drool. I backwash."

"No problemo." Street reached across the table, grabbed the can, swallowed its contents in one gulp.

Bill grimaced. "You're gross."

"Thank you."

Outside, the night was warm. The moon was out but not yet up, hovering somewhere beneath the level of the ponderosas, its light diffused in the eastern sky. Ben had walked but Bill had driven, and neither of them spoke as they headed out to his Jeep across the loudly crunching gravel of the driveway.

"We really should try to help him out," Ben said once they were in the vehicle.

"Yeah," Bill agreed. "We should."

They drove the rest of the way in silence.

As predicted, The Store was the main topic of conversation at the meeting. There were only two people in the audience other than themselves, and though the Planning Commission met in the council chambers, it could have just as easily convened in a small conference room.

Fred Carpenter, the commission chairman, read aloud the text of the proposal to allow The Store to construct an addition to its existing structure in order to open a grocery department. The Store's property was currently zoned only to allow the selling of nonfood items, and the land would have to be rezoned to accommodate the proposed change in usage.

The chairman finished reading the proposal. "We will now open the subject up for discussion," he said.

Leander Jacobs raised his hand.

"The chair recognizes Commissioner Jacobs."

"I do not believe we should grant this rezoning request. Obviously, The Store intended to sell groceries all along. Decisions such as this are not made on the spur of the moment. They're made far in advance, back at the corporate office. The commission and the council should have been told of these intentions at the beginning. I feel that we were deliberately misled, and I do not think that we should rezone the property at this late date."

"That's all well and good," the chairman said. "But as you know, we've been given an ultimatum. If we don't rezone, The Store has threatened to leave town."

Bill's heart speeded up.

"Let 'em," Jacobs said.

The chairman looked at him. "Are you serious?"

"They won't leave. They have too much invested here. Call their bluff."

Yes, Bill thought. Show those bastards for what they are. He glanced over at Ben, caught the editor's eye. Ben was in his objective reporter's mode and looked noncommittal, but Bill felt unreasonably excited. For the first time, there was opposition to The Store by the powers that be, and he sensed an opportunity here. They might not be able to make The Store retreat, but maybe they could stop its progress.

Graham Graves raised his hand.

"The chair recognizes Commissioner Graves."

"I support the rezoning proposal. Allowing The Store to expand is in Juniper's best interest. This new grocery department will bring in fifteen new jobs. Five of them full-time."

Jacobs snorted. "And it'll take away thirty. Come on, Graham. You know as well as I do that it'll put Jed's market out of business. Buy-and-Save can't survive that kind of competition."

"Then he'll have to lower his prices. If his groceries are cheaper, people will shop at his store."

"First of all, you should excuse yourself from this vote. You've had it in for Jed ever since he broke up with Yolanda."

"That's a lie and you know it—"

"Gentlemen. Gentlemen!" The chairman banged his gavel. "We are not here to discuss prices or marketing strategies or personal affairs. We are here to address the question of whether or not The Store should be allowed to sell groceries."

Bud Harrison, the Planning Commission's quietest member, spoke up. "Can we look at the schematics for the addition?"

"I was just about to suggest that." The chairman stood and walked around the dais to where an overhead projector sat on a movable stand next to the wall. He wheeled the projector around, plugged it in, and motioned for Graves to dim the lights. A schematic drawing of The Store and its property was projected on the opposite wall.

Carpenter glanced around the council chambers as if searching for someone, and at that moment the door to the room opened. A young man dressed in an expensive three-piece suit strode down the main aisle of the chambers, nodded, smiling to the chairman, and pulled a pencil from his pocket. Carpenter returned to his seat, and the man, identified as "Mr. McBride, a representative of The Store," spent the next half-hour going over the schematic and explaining The Store's expansion plans.

"Thank you, Mr. McBride," Carpenter said when the Store representative had finished answering questions from the commission.

Mr. McBride nodded, bowed, and promptly walked out of the council chambers.

"Isn't he even going to stick around and see how it turns out?" Bill whispered.

"Weird," Ben admitted.

Carpenter looked at his fellow commissioners. "We've heard all the information we need; I suggest we put it to a vote."

Bill stood. "Aren't you going to open discussion to members of the public?"

The chairman stared at him. "I didn't think there'd be any discussion from members of the public."

"You thought wrong."

Carpenter's jaw tightened. He started to mouth a rebuke, then apparently thought better of it and nodded. "Very well, Mr. Davis. You have three minutes."

Bill glanced down at Ben, who shot him a look of encouragement. "From those plans," he said, "it appears as though the new grocery addition is going to be built behind the existing building."

"That is correct."

"I thought The Store backed up to national forest land."

"It does," Carpenter agreed. "But as part of the federal land exchange program, we traded forty acres of BLM-surrounded land we owned by Castle Creek for sixty acres adjacent to The Store's property."

"And now we're going to sell it to The Store?"

"No. In exchange for The Store's generous offer to provide park maintenance and to take over funding and organizing of the youth recreation programs, the town plans to donate the land to The Store corporation."

"This is outrageous!" Bill glanced around the room, looking for support. Ben was furiously writing in his notebook. The other two people in the audience were staring blankly at him. He once again faced the commissioners. "You mean to tell me that Juniper is deliberately helping The Store at the expense of Jed McGill and then telling Jed that he should lower his prices if he hopes to stay in business?"

"Not at all," Carpenter said.

"But you're giving The Store free land, you're going to rezone its property, and like Leander said, there're going to be no repercussions for keeping their plan secret and not telling you their intentions in the first place. Jed's been an honest local storeowner here for . . . for as long as I've lived in town, which is longer than most of you, and now you're going to give him the shaft."

Carpenter smiled indulgently. "Is there any valid point you wish to make, Mr. Davis? What specific legal objections do you have to the rezoning plan?"

"I don't think The Store should be given special privileges."

"The Store is threatening to leave Juniper—"

"Like Leander said, let them."

"—and The Store is our town's major employer. You are reacting out of personal bias, Mr. Davis. It is our job to examine our building codes and zoning ordinances and determine from that what is in the best interests of the entire town, not just a few specific individuals." He nodded at Bill. "Your time is up, Mr. Davis. Thank you for your input." He glanced around at his fellow commissioners. "Gentlemen, I suggest we put it to a vote."

By a vote of four to one, the Planning Commission agreed to rezone The Store's property to allow grocery sales.

"Big surprise," Ben said on the way out.

"I see an editorial here," Bill told him.

"There will be. But you know how well my editorials go over. People threaten to kick my ass and cancel their subscription." He grinned. "Luckily, we have a monopoly here."

"Have Laura write it."

"She's more popular than me?"

"Isn't she?"

"Yeah, but I hate to hear it."

"What about Newtin?"

"What about him?"

"He's not making you kiss The Store's ass anymore?"

"I think that still is our official policy, but I haven't been following it lately. And I think as long as the ad space keeps selling, he doesn't really give a damn what's in the articles."

Bill drove his friend home. "Doesn't all this just piss you off?" he asked as the editor got out of the Jeep.

"It not only pisses me off, it scares me," Ben said. He started up the path to his trailer. "Later!" he called, waving.

"Later."

Bill drove off.

It scares me.

It scared him, too, and he turned on the Jeep's radio

so he'd have noise instead of silence on the dark trip home.

In his dream, The Store was expanding its parking lot so that it covered the entire town. The forest was gone, the mountains and hills were bare, and there was not enough asphalt to pave over the cleared land, so an asphalt-maker, a machine that looked like an oversized thresher, was inching forward at the edge of the parking lot, a relay-line of uniformed Store employees passing forward the bodies of townspeople, throwing them into an open scoop on the machine, as a mixture of powdered bones and tar was excreted from a series of nozzles at its rear. He was standing on the highway, watching, horrified, when he saw Ginny being passed froward, the girls following her. Sam was still wearing her Store uniform, but that had not exempted her from her fate, and she was handed from one employee to another, toward the open mouth of the asphalt-maker.

Bill started running across the parking lot, toward the machine, but his feet became stuck on the gluey pavement.

Ginny was thrown into the scoop.

Shannon.

Sam.

Black bone-based asphalt emerged from the rear nozzles.

"No!" he cried.

And the machine continued on.

3

Jed McGill was awakened by the doorbell.

He sat up, then stumbled out of bed, aware that the doorbell had been ringing for a while but not sure for how long. The sound had been incorporated into his dream, and reality sounded like an echo to him as he groggily reached for his bathrobe. He glanced at the clock on his dresser.

Two a.m.

Who would be coming over at this hour?

Ring.

Yawning, his eyes still half-closed, he felt his way around the doorjamb, using the wall as his guide as he moved through the hallway toward the living room.

Ring.

He rubbed his eyes, opening them wider. There was something about the unhurried insistence of the ringer and the even intervals between the door chimes that set off his radar. Even in this sleep-numbed state, he recognized that whoever was outside had been there for quite some time, waiting far longer than any ordinary person would have, and was still at the door, patiently pressing the button every thirty seconds.

Ring.

He approached the door warily, feeling oddly nervous. Juniper wasn't exactly New York, with psychos and criminals and gangs prowling around at all hours of the night. And he wasn't a ninety-eight-pound weakling. He was six three, two hundred pounds, and he pumped iron. He was in good physical shape.

Still, he felt apprehensive, almost jumpy, as his hand touched the door handle. It was probably just someone whose car had broken down, someone wanting to use his telephone to call for a tow. He leaned against the door, peeked through the peephole.

It was a man in a three-piece suit.

That should have settled his nerves. It was not a thug or a loony but a businessman. For some reason, however, seeing his visitor made Jed even more uneasy. Why would a businessman be standing on his stoop and ringing the doorbell in the middle of the night? It made no sense. The man didn't look harried enough or annoyed enough for his car to have broken down, so that theory went out the window. But if he was here to talk business, it could have waited until morning. And he should have called first.

Something about this didn't feel right.

The man calmly pressed the button next to the door.

Ring.

Jed threw the dead bolt, unlocked the door, opened

it. The man stood on the stoop, smiling at him, and Jed didn't like that smile.

"Hello, Mr. McGill."

Jed stared at him dumbly.

The man pushed past him, uninvited, into the living room. "Nice place you've got here."

Get out, he wanted to say. Get out of my house. But he only turned and watched as the man maneuvered around the couch and the coffee table and sat down in the easy chair facing the television. The man was still smiling as he motioned for Jed to sit on the couch, and now Jed knew what he did not like about the smile. It was fake, yes, but that's not what unnerved him so. It was the hint of a threat behind the smile, the belligerence backing it.

He should not have opened the door, he realized. Whatever was going to happen was going to happen. It was too late to stop it.

Whatever was going to happen?

He looked at the smiling business-suited man on the couch.

Yes.

He wished he'd brought his shotgun out with him, but it was still in the bedroom, leaning in the corner by the dresser. His rifles were in the gun case.

"Have a seat," the man said.

Jed walked slowly forward, stopped in back of the couch. "What do you want?"

"I just want to talk, Jed. Is that all right with you?"

"Not at two o'clock in the morning it's not."

"I stopped by your store today. Buy-and-Save. Cute name. Cute store."

Jed stiffened. "I don't know who you are or what you're trying to do, but I'm not going to let you barge into my house in the middle of the night and make fun of my store—"

"Calm down, Jed. Calm down." The man's smile was wider. "I'm not criticizing your store. I liked it. It was a nice place." He paused. "While it lasted."

"What—"

"The Store is going to be selling groceries," the man said. "As of tonight, Buy-and-Save is out of business."

Jed walked around the couch, advancing on the man. "Listen to me," he said angrily. "I don't know what you think you're doing, but I can't be threatened and I can't be scared off. You get the hell out of my house right now or I won't be responsible for what happens."

The man stood, still smiling. "Jed, Jed, Jed . . ."

"Get the fuck out of my house!"

"I was afraid you'd take it this way."

There was a noise behind him, and Jed turned to see other men entering through the open front door. Tall men, pale men, dressed in shiny black leather, wearing jackboots. Their faces were blank, devoid of expression, and there was something inhuman about them. Vampires, was his first thought, but that didn't seem quite right.

It was in the ballpark, though. It was definitely in the ballpark.

The men continued filing into his house.

Six of them.

Eight.

Twelve.

He ran across the room, toward the gun case, but the black-garbed white-faced creatures were already there and in front of him. He whirled around. They were in back of him. To the sides.

He was surrounded.

"The Store is going to be selling groceries," the man repeated. "As of tonight, Buy-and-Save is out of business."

"The fuck it is!" Jed yelled at him.

The man pushed his way forward. His smile was now a full-fledged smirk, and the hostility was evident on his face. "The fuck it isn't," he said.

He faded into the background as the others closed in.

Jed did not even have a chance to scream.

4

Ginny awoke late.

She stretched, sat up, saw that Bill was not in bed and, hearing noise outside, peeked through the bedroom curtains. They'd talked last night before going to bed about cleaning out the garage, donating some of their old furniture and bric-a-brac to the Baptist rummage sale, throwing away the useless garbage that they'd accumulated over the years so they could actually walk into the garage, but they'd talked about the same thing a million times before and hadn't done it, and she hadn't expected them to follow through this time. Bill was already awake and dressed and outside, though, and when she peered through the window, she saw several boxes on the dirt drive and saw him carrying yet another one out of the garage. She tapped on the glass, and he waved at her, pointing to an imaginary watch on his wrist to indicate that she was late and should get out and help.

Ginny pulled on a pair of shorts and a T-shirt and walked out to the kitchen to pour herself a cup of coffee. Sam was already gone, at work, and Shannon was stretched out on the floor of the living room watching TV, an empty orange juice glass beside her.

"Why aren't you out helping your father?" Ginny said.

Her daughter did not even look up. "Why aren't you?"

"Smart-ass. I find anything of yours in the garage, I'm donating it."

Shannon sat up. "You better not!"

Ginny grinned.

"Dad!"

Laughing, Ginny walked outside. Bill was wiping the sweat from his forehead with the back of his hand. "About time," he said.

"I was getting my beauty rest," she told him.

He grinned. "Didn't work." He held up his hands to protect himself as she advanced toward him across the gravel. "You set yourself up for that one."

She punched him lightly on the arm. "Geek."

He drew himself up to his full height. "Computer nerd, if you don't mind."

Ginny glanced around at the array of boxes. "So what's going, what's staying? Have you found anything you're willing to part with?"

"Quite a bit, actually." He motioned toward a box

next to a manzanita bush. "There's some of your stuff in there. I didn't know what you wanted or what you didn't, so I figured I'd let you sort through it."

Ginny walked over, looked into the box, saw an old PTA plaque she'd gotten when Sam was in elementary school, a jewelry box Bill's mother had given her that she'd never liked, a folded red-and-white-checkered tablecloth. She squatted down and started sorting through the items, pushing things aside or moving them around but taking nothing out. Sandwiched between a Betty Crocker recipe book and a 1982 Sierra Club calendar, she found a single photograph, an old Polaroid shot. She pulled it out. "How did that get in here?"

The picture was of herself, as a teenager in the mid-seventies sometime, dressed in the absurd fashions of that era. She was at some sort of concert or rally, and her best friend, Stacy Morales, was next to her, posing in front of a bunch of other girls—

The ERA rally.

It all came back to her now. Spring, 1976. Her senior year in high school. She and Stacy and a bunch of other girls from Cortez had traveled in Stacy's mom's van to ASU, where the campus women's center was putting on a rally to support the Equal Rights Amendment. It had been her first exposure to college life, and the students, the campus, the ideas, the lifestyles had all made a huge impression on her. She'd left the rally feeling energized and empowered, as though she could do anything. It was as if a whole new world had opened up to her. She returned to her own school the next day feeling like an adult among kids, and her grades actually went up that last semester as she'd studied her hardest to make sure she'd be able to get into a good college.

As she stared at the photo now, she experienced more than a twinge of nostalgia. Behind Stacy was a female college student wearing a T-shirt bearing the partially obstructed slogan: A HARD MAN IS GOOD TO FIND. Next to her was a large-breasted young woman, shirt raised, flashing her tits at the camera and shouting joyfully. In those days, sex had been seen as liberating, and it had felt as though the dawn of a new era was upon them.

No longer were men going to be allowed to have domin-
ion over women's sexuality. The Pill had given them
freedom, had given them control over their own bodies,
and sex was going to be something in which women participated, not something to which they were subjected.

But those days were long gone. Today many of the
feminists were as bad as the old male chauvinists had
been. There was a prudishness in the women's movement now, a fear of sexuality that was more reactionary
and regressive than the attitudes of most modern men.
What had happened to the progress they had made back
then? What had happened to the concept of "libera-
tion"? Nowadays, women who called themselves feminists were advocating restrictions and censorship, trying
to inhibit freedom rather than expand it.

They'd become just like the people they were fighting.

Bill walked over, looked at the Polaroid. "What's
that?"

"Nothing," she said.

"There's another box for you over there."

She nodded. "I'll check it out in a minute."

She looked again at the photo, then slipped it into the
right front pocket of her shorts and followed Bill across
the gravel to the garage.

She had a hair appointment at one o'clock, but they
finished cleaning out the garage by midmorning, and she
accompanied Bill to both the Baptist church and the
dump before coming back to make lunch. They ate outside, on the deck, and afterward he did the dishes while
she took a quick shower and changed. Or, rather, he
had Shannon do the dishes. For when Ginny emerged
from the bathroom, he was back in his room, in front
of his computer, while Shannon was rinsing out the
kitchen sink.

"He gave me two bucks," Shannon explained.

"I've been working all morning!" he called from his
room.

"Next time," Ginny told her daughter, "I'll give you
three dollars if you make him do it himself."

"Three bucks for doing nothing?" Shannon laughed. "Deal."

"Four!" Bill called.

"Three bucks and no work beats four bucks and work!" Shannon called back. "Sorry, Dad!"

Ginny shook her head. "I'll see you two later," she said.

Ordinarily, Ginny enjoyed getting her hair done. She liked talking with the other women, catching up on all of the gossip that she missed out on at school. But the mood at Hair Today was grim. Although she had never known Rene to be anything less than cheerful, the hair-stylist seemed downright sullen this afternoon. She spoke hardly at all, and when she did her voice was curt, brusque.

Among the other women at the salon, rumors were flying. Kelli Finch, whose husband owned and operated Walt's Transmission and Tuneup, had heard that The Store was going to open an auto center and start performing repairs as well as selling parts. Maryanne Robertson, who worked part-time at The Quilting Bee, said there was a rumor that The Store was going to sell quilts on consignment.

Rene said nothing at first, but finally admitted that more than one customer had told her that a beauty salon would soon be opening inside The Store next to the espresso bar. "Pretty soon," she said sourly, "downtown'll be completely dead."

It was something that Ginny had noticed but had not consciously registered. Now that Rene mentioned it, though, Main Street did seem unusually quiet. Foot traffic was almost nonexistent, and only an occasional car drove past the front window. Even Hair Today seemed less crowded than usual, although that couldn't be attributed to The Store.

Not yet, at least.

"Maybe you should build a new salon across the highway from The Store," Maryanne suggested. "That way it would be convenient for people to go there. They wouldn't have to go out of their way."

Rene grimaced. "With what? I'm in debt as it is. How

am I supposed to get enough money to open a new shop?" She shook her head. "No, it's this or nothing."

"I'll still come here," Ginny promised.

The other women chimed in quickly, agreeing.

Conversation stalled for a moment. The only noise was the snipping of Rene's scissors and the hissing of Doreen's shampoo faucet as she rinsed Kelli's hair.

"You heard about Jed, didn't you?" Maryanne said. "Jed McGill?"

The other women—the ones who could—shook their heads.

"He's missing."

"Missing?" Ginny said.

"They think he's skipped town. No one's seen him for a week, and over at Buy-and-Save they're not sure they're going to be able to meet their payroll this month."

"What happens then?" Kelli asked.

"I don't know."

"Buy-and-Save can't close. There's nowhere else to buy groceries."

"Circle K." Rene suggested.

Maryanne snorted. "Yeah, right."

"Well, I hope The Store hurries up with its grocery department, then." Doreen led Kelli across the salon to the styling chair next to Ginny. "We have to have someplace to buy food."

"But would you really want to get your groceries from The Store?" Ginny asked.

"We have to have someplace to buy food," Doreen repeated.

Ginny waited a beat, but no one else answered. She thought of asking again, but she wasn't sure she wanted to hear the responses and she let the question die.

On the way home, she passed by the new park.

Twenty or thirty boys were lined up in rows on the field in front of the backstop. A table had been set up to the left of the bleachers, and a large blue banner strung between two posts behind the table read: SIGN UP NOW FOR STORE LEAGUE FAST PITCH!

She only got a quick look, but the kids all seemed to be wearing their baseball uniforms and the uniforms looked odd to her. Too dark. Vaguely militaristic. She thought they appeared out of place on boys so young. Wrong.

But then she was past the park and on the road to home and it was too late to slow down and take a longer look.

She'd have to tell Bill about the uniforms, though.

And the auto center.

And the salon.

And Jed McGill.

THIRTEEN

1

It rained for three days straight, the first major downpour of the spring. There'd been some low clouds and light mist during the preceding months, but it had been a dry season so far, and they desperately needed precipitation.

Just not this much of it.

The storm was a bad one—wind and lightning, not just rain—and sometime during the middle day there was hail, the pellets of ice ripping holes in established bushes, killing Ginny's newly sprouted vegetables in the garden, and blanketing their entire property, for an hour or so, with white.

By the beginning of the third day, Monday, the hard-packed drive had devolved into mud, and a section of the road to town had been washed away. School had been canceled, and although ordinarily the girls—and Ginny—would have been thrilled, they'd already been cooped up in the house too long and the phone call announcing the school closures seemed only to depress them.

"I'm supposed to work tonight," Samantha said. "How am I going to get there?"

"You're not," Bill told her.

"I have to."

"Explain the circumstances, trade with someone, call in sick. I don't care. You're not going in. Even the Jeep won't make it across that road in this rain."

"I can't call in sick."

"Yes, you can." Bill smiled slightly. "I used to do it all the time when I was your age."

"But I can't."

"Well, you have to do something, because you're not going to work tonight."

Samantha turned to her mother, and Bill saw the look that passed between them, but he chose to ignore it rather than turn the discussion into an argument.

He walked back to his office to check his E-mail and read this morning's online news. Radio reception for anything but the Juniper station was nonexistent, and he was about to pop in an old Rick Wakeman cassette when Ginny poked her head in the door.

"Bad news. The roof in the bathroom's leaking again."

He swiveled toward her. "I just fixed it last fall!"

"No, you tried to fix it. Obviously, you didn't. It's leaking."

"Shit." He pushed himself out of the chair and followed her down the hall to the bathroom. The ceiling above the toilet was darkened by a huge water stain. At three-second intervals, droplets fell into a pan that Ginny had placed on the floor next to the toilet.

Bill shook his head. "Couldn't it have been five inches to the left? Is that too much to ask?"

"That would be too easy. Besides, what's a leaky roof without pots and pans on the floor?" She pointed toward the wall behind the toilet. "That's wet, too. It's seeping down into the wall."

"I can't fix anything until the rain stops."

"But you can put a tarp up there or something, so it won't soak through the entire house."

Bill nodded, sighed. "I'll go down to Richardson's and get a tarp. I'll pick up some tar and some tar paper for when the rain ends." He turned away from the toilet. "Goddamn, I hate doing this every year."

"Maybe we should have the whole roof redone," she suggested. "Hire a real roofer."

"We can't afford that. Not right now." He pushed past her, walking across the hall into their bedroom, where he grabbed his wallet and keys from the top of the dresser. He put on his raincoat. "Check for any other leaks while I'm gone." He went back into his office, turned off the PC. "I'll be back in a half hour or so."

"Get enough to cover the whole roof."

"Don't worry."

The road was even worse than he'd expected, and he had to put the Jeep into four-wheel drive to make it through a couple of spots, but he lucked out and there was a temporary respite from the rain, then he was on pavement and heading down Granite toward the hardware store.

The only other vehicle in Richardson's small parking lot was the owner's own vehicle, parked near the side of the building. Bill pulled up directly in front of the door and ran quickly inside as another heavy downpour started. He stomped his boots on the doormat to dry them off so he wouldn't slip on the slick floor.

"Wet enough for you?" Richardson stood behind the cash register, grinning. On the counter in front of him was a huge sack of screws and nuts that he was separating into little piles.

"Not really," Bill said. "But I think my roof's had about enough of it." He looked around. "Where do you keep your plastic tarps?"

Richardson stared down at his screws. He cleared his throat, embarrassed. "Can't say as I carry any tarp," he said.

"What?"

"Well, if I could've predicted this storm, I would've ordered up a whole lot of stuff like that. But the truth of the matter is, Bill, I can't afford to stock much anymore. The Store's taking away most of my business, I'm strung out on credit as it is, and I only order what I know for certain'll move." He held up a nut. "Screws and nuts, bolts and nails. Mollies. Pipe and lumber."

Bill looked around, noticing for the first time that the shelves of many of the aisles were bare, the end displays empty.

"You don't have any kind of plastic sheets that I could use to cover my roof? No rolls of anything?"

"Nope." Richardson shifted uncomfortably from one foot to the other. "I wish I could help you, Bill. I honestly do. But times are tough." He gestured around the quiet store. "As you can see, the joint ain't exactly jumping."

"The Store doesn't sell hardware, though, does it?"

"They don't carry lumber, but they carry everything else. And they're lowballing me at every turn." He waved his hand dismissively. "I'm sure you've heard it all before."

Bill nodded. "That's the sad part. I have."

"I knew they might cut into my business, you know? I just didn't think it'd happen this fast. I mean, shit, I've been here since 1960. I've weathered a lot of trends." He shook his head, looked up. "And I thought people would be more loyal. I don't expect pity or charity, but I always considered my customers my friends, and I thought that would count for something. I didn't think they'd abandon me over a few pennies' price difference. It hurts, you know?"

They were silent for a moment, the only sound amplified rain on the tin roof.

"You don't have anything to help me with the leak?"

"I could order some tarps. Be here in half a week, maybe five days."

"I'd like to wait," Bill said. "But it's kind of an emergency. I need it now."

Richardson sighed. "Go ahead. Hit The Store. Everyone else does."

Bill thought for a moment. "You know what? I'll hold off on the tar and the tar paper. Why don't you order some for me. I don't need to fix the roof instantly, anyway. And I should wait until it dries out. I'll just get a cheapo tarp at The Store, keep the water out until the rain stops. It'll work temporarily."

"You're a stand-up guy," Richardson said gratefully.

Bill smiled. "No, but I can fake it."

The Store had quite a selection of tarps and plastic sheeting. There was even a Home Raincoat, a monstrous piece of waterproofed canvas that was specifically designed to fit over the roof of a house. But Bill bought four packages of the cheapest tarps he could find, did not take advantage of the two-for-one sale on rolls of tar paper, and quickly sped home, where he climbed up on the roof and spent the next two hours trying to weight down the tarps with rocks he salvaged from the forest behind the house.

His efforts paid off, however, and when he walked into the bathroom, the leak had stopped.

"Fixed!" he announced.

"For now," Ginny said.

"I've ordered some roofing supplies from Richardson. Once the rain stops, I'll patch it."

"I've heard that one before."

He slapped her rear end, making her jump, then, before she could hit him back, ran past her into the bedroom to change into some dry clothes.

Ginny and the girls spent the afternoon watching soap operas and talk shows in the living room, while he retired to his office and dialed up Freelink. There'd been a shooting at one of The Stores in Nevada last week, and he'd been keeping up with all of the current events surrounding the various Store shootings over the past six months, but even though he was writing documentation for a Store system, he'd never really bothered to check into the history of the company.

Until now.

He accessed Freelink's Business Information database, and downloaded everything about The Store that he could find.

He read it all.

According to articles from the *Wall Street Journal, Business Week, Forbes,* the *Houston Chronicle,* and *American Entrepreneur,* The Store began as a small mercantile in West Texas in the late 1950s. Newman King owned a single shop on a virtually untraveled dirt road, miles from the nearest town. Through word of mouth and, eventually, a series of billboards that he erected on major highways, The Store became something of a tourist spot, a must-see stop for easterners heading west on vacation. People were initially amused by the mercantile's humorously bland name and by the incongruity of its desolate location and up-to-the-minute stock, but they bought in droves. King kept his prices low and his selection large, and his combination of business acumen and self-promotion caused profits to shoot through the roof. Eventually he opened another store—also on a small back road.

By the mid-1960s, he owned a regional chain of discount retail outlets and had joined Texas's rank of self-made millionaires. There were scattered complaints from competitors of hardball tactics—bribes and intimidation, illegal business practices—but there was nothing provable and nothing stuck.

Taking his cue from Sam Walton and Wal-Mart, King began opening big, modern stores in towns that previously had only small, local markets. He would not go into a town that had a Wal-Mart or a Kmart, or even a Woolworth's or Newberry's, but in towns with only local competition, he would dazzle the locals with state-of-the-art products and contemporary fashions and items that had previously been available to them only through catalogs.

And they would buy.

Sometime within the next two decades, King dropped from sight. He had gradually become more reclusive over the years, the press conferences that had once been de rigueur before each and every Store opening dwindling to four, then two, then one a year.

There were accusations from former employees that The Store was more like a cult than a place of employment, that bizarre tests were required to get a job at The Store, that participation in strange rituals was mandatory for all management trainees, that any attempt to either quit or go public with nonflattering information was met with well-organized retaliation. King remained in hiding, would not publicly respond to any accusations, but no charges were ever filed, many of the accusers were discredited or disappeared, and after that brief flurry no complaints were ever brought up again by any subsequent employees.

In the mid-eighties, The Store's corporate headquarters moved from a nondescript series of offices in El Paso to a huge black twenty-story skyscraper in Dallas that was dubbed The Black Tower by friend and foe alike. Still, there was no attempt made to expand The Store's base, to move into larger cities or metropolitan areas.

King's reported eccentricity and mysterious private life—he was rumored to live alone in a concrete bunker under the desert, afraid of being exposed to ultraviolet rays because of the depleted ozone layer, afraid of breathing anything but specially filtered air—not only created an air of mystique but tapped into the public's never-flagging interest in the Howard Hughesian rich and strange. There was speculation on Wall Street that King was staging all of this in order to gain name recognition and from there move on into other ventures, but he continued his slow progress throughout the country, opening Stores only in small rural towns.

And now The Store had come to Juniper.

Bill stopped reading, rubbing his tired eyes. The articles were mostly from financial publications, focusing on the nuts-and-bolts of the business, so the emphasis was not on muckraking or human interest and there was nothing overtly negative about Newman King or The Store. But there was still enough between the lines to put him on guard.

Bribes, threats, and intimidation? A cult? If those aspects were even mentioned in articles focusing on the financial world, it meant that they were more than merely idle speculation or isolated charges. And combined with his own thoughts, feelings, and observations, they painted a rather frightening picture.

The phone rang and Bill picked it up. "Hello?"

It was Ben.

"Richardson's burned down," the editor said.

"What?"

"I just came back from taking pictures. The fire guys're still there. The rain's helping, but the lumber was covered and it went up like a tinderbox."

"Is—"

"Richardson's dead. He was trapped in the blaze."

"Jesus."

"By the time they got to him and pulled him out, he was gone."

"What caused it?" Bill asked. "Do they know?"

Ben didn't answer.

"Lightning?" he asked hopefully, though he'd neither heard thunder nor seen lightning all afternoon.

There was a pause. "No," Ben said finally, and there was a note in his voice that Bill recognized and didn't like. "Arson."

"It's taking over," Bill said, pacing up and down in front of the bed.

Ginny looked up from her magazine. "What is?"

"You know damn well what. The Store. Its competitors are disappearing. Or their businesses are burning down." He looked at her. "You don't think that might be just a wee bit on the suspicious side?"

"Don't yell at me."

"I'm not yelling!"

But he was, he knew. He was taking it out on her, although he wasn't mad at her at all. He was frightened. He'd been concerned before, angry, uneasy, but it was the physical presence of that blackened, still-smoking building that made him realize the death and destruction that The Store could cause.

The Store?

He was thinking of The Store as a single organism, a monolithic monster, but it wasn't that, was it? It was a corporation, a series of retail outlets scattered throughout the country and staffed by ordinary local people.

No, it was a structured organization created to follow the whims and carry out the wishes of Newman King.

That was how he thought of it.

But why? What was the point of it all? What was the purpose?

Those were questions he couldn't even hope to answer.

He thought for a moment, then opened the bedroom door and stepped out into the hall. "Samantha!"

Ginny hurried after him. "What are you doing?"

"Samantha!" He pushed open the door to his daughter's bedroom, walked in.

She'd obviously been sleeping, and she sat up groggily. "What?"

"You can't work at The Store anymore."

That woke her up.

"I can't—"

"—work at The Store," he finished for her.

"Well, I am."

"I'm afraid you're not."

"I'm eighteen," she said. "You can't tell me what to do."

"As long as you live in my house I can."

"Then I won't live in your house!"

Ginny stepped between them. "Come on," she said. "Let's not give any ultimatums or paint ourselves into any corners. Let's all calm down."

"You cannot work at The Store," Bill repeated.

"I like working there."

"You want to read what I read about The Store? You want to hear what I've heard?"

Sam shrugged in a way that was meant to be infuriating and was. "Not particularly."

He wanted to hit her, wanted to tell her to get the hell out of the house, then, and not come back. He was filled with an almost blinding rage, and it was his recognition of that emotion, his realization that he was overreacting in a way that was totally inappropriate, that brought him back down to earth.

He looked at Sam, who was staring at him, holding the covers under her chin. What was wrong with him? What was he thinking? He had never hit either of the girls. Ever. And he had never even been tempted to do so until now.

This was something he couldn't blame on The Store. Could he?

Shannon poked her head in the door. "What's happening?" she said. "What's all the craziness?"

"Go back to bed," Ginny told her.

"I just want to know."

"It's none of your business. Back to bed."

Embarrassed, Bill faced Samantha. "I'm sorry," he said.

"You should be."

"But I still don't want you to work there."

"It's my decision. I need the money, and I like my job."

"We'll talk about it in the morning," Ginny said. She ushered him out the door.

"It's my decision," Sam repeated.

"Like your mom said, we'll talk about it in the morning." Bill closed the door behind him and followed Ginny back to the bedroom.

2

Shannon walked into her sister's room after breakfast. Sam was still not up, but she was awake, and Shannon knew that she simply hadn't wanted to face their dad.

"So what was all that about last night?"

Samantha looked at her. "His brain snapped."

"But what was it about?"

"None of your business."

"Come on," Shannon said. "Don't you give me that, too."

"He doesn't want me to work."

"Why not?"

Sam shrugged. "Who knows?"

"It has to be something."

"Does it?" Sam looked at her. "Why am I even talking to you? Get out of my room."

"I was thinking of getting a job there, too, this summer."

"Yeah, right."

"I was."

"Didn't I tell you to get out of my room?"

"I thought you might want to talk—"

"With you?"

"Sorry. I forgot what a bitch you are. My fault." Shannon turned and walked out of the room, slamming the door behind her.

FOURTEEN

1

It had been a long time. Cash had died fifteen years ago this coming July, and she had not had a man since. She wasn't complaining. She had never wanted anyone else. Cash had been her husband, and as far as she was concerned, it would be unfaithful of her to make love with another man.

Still, sometimes she missed it.

Flo glanced up and down the store aisle to make sure no one was watching, then looked at the selection of massagers and vibrators on the shelf in front of her. There was one that strapped on to the user's hand, another that looked like a rubber ball on a wand, but she found herself focusing on the vibrator on the right, the one that looked like a man's penis.

"Excuse me, ma'am. May I help you?"

She jumped at the sound of the voice, turning in embarrassment to face a young man wearing a green Store uniform. She opened her mouth to say something, but no sound came out.

"These are nice models here," the young man said. He gestured toward the vibrators. "Top-of-the-line products. Discount prices."

"I—I wasn't looking at those," Flo said.

"Yes, you were." The young man smiled, but there was nothing snide or smirking or hurtful in his smile. Nothing lascivious.

Lascivious?

She was old enough to be his grandmother.

"I—" she began.

"You're looking for a vibrator." He picked up the

middle model, the wand. "This one is probably the best if you're going to be massaging your back muscles and those hard-to-reach places. On the other hand, if you're looking to sexually pleasure yourself—"

"I am not!" She was almost shouting, and she felt the heat of embarrassment flush her face. She quickly glanced around, but they were still alone in the aisle.

"It's none of our business if you are. And it's nothing to be ashamed of, ma'am. We're here to provide you with the products you need, not to pass judgment on your lifestyle. Our policy is to make sure that everyone finds what they want and that none of our customers are ashamed or embarrassed. If I've made you feel that way, I am truly sorry."

Flo took a deep breath. "No, I'm sorry. I over-reacted."

The young man placed a familiar hand on her shoulder. "Here at The Store, we have a confidential relationship with our customers. Like priests and lawyers, we do not divulge what is said to us in private. It remains between us and the customer. That is one of the cardinal rules listed in *The Employee's Bible,* and it is why we are able to provide such effective customer service."

Flo was silent.

"So anything you say is between me and you. Period." He replaced the wand vibrator and gestured toward the others on the shelf. "Now, if you're really looking for a muscle relaxer . . ."

"No," she said.

He smiled. "I didn't think so."

She looked at him. He was a nice young man, helpful, friendly, easy to talk to. She felt comfortable with him. She trusted him. "Maybe we should start over," she said. "From the beginning."

He nodded. "Very well." He walked down the aisle, turned, walked back, smiling at her. "May I help you, ma'am?"

"Yes," she said. "I'd like to buy a vibrator."

"As you can see, we have several different models for you to choose from."

"I already know which one I want."

"And which one is that, ma'am?"

"That one there," she said, pointing. "The one that looks like a cock."

2

Holly missed the café.

She wasn't the only one, either. A lot of the old regulars seemed to be lost, not knowing what to do with their time now that they didn't have a booth bench or a counter stool to park their butts on.

At least she had a job. As part of the purchase agreement, The Store had promised Williamson that all of the café's employees would be kept on. She'd assumed that that meant she'd keep her old position. But The Store had shut down the café and had transferred her, the cooks, and the other waitresses to the snack bars in The Store.

No, not snack bars.

Eating establishments.

It just wasn't the same. Aside from the froufrou food and the unfriendly coworkers, the space here was cramped, and she didn't feel comfortable, didn't feel she had room to move around. She also didn't like staring out at shoppers all day long.

And The Store didn't allow tipping.

That was her biggest gripe.

Vernon Thompson had followed her over from the café. The Store's espresso bar wasn't quite the same, and the old-timer complained about . . . well, just about everything. But she was there and he was there and at least that provided some sense of continuity, some feeling of home.

His buddy, though, was gone. The Store had done what nothing else could and had split up the friendship. From what she heard, Buck now spent his days on a barstool at the Watering Hole. She wasn't sure what had happened or why—and she didn't want to pry—but she knew that Vern missed his pal, and it was sad to see the old man moping alone on one of those tiny plastic chairs, trying to talk to other customers who were usually too rushed and busy to even give him the time of day.

She blamed Williamson. Why did that son of a bitch ever have to sell the café?

She patted Vern on the back as she poured him yet another in his endless refills of straight, plain, old-fashioned black coffee, started to pick up the oversized café au lait mugs from the empty table next to him, and looked up to see Buck, wearing a cowboy hat and an old longcoat, weaving down the center aisle toward the espresso bar.

She glanced over at Vern. He'd seen, too, and they both shared a glance. Neither of them were sure if this was good or bad, if Buck was coming here to hang out or cause problems, and they waited, unmoving, as he staggered toward them.

"Vernon!" Buck yelled. "You old peckerheaded son of a bitch! How's it hangin'?"

Shoppers across the aisle and customers in the espresso bar turned to look at him, but Buck paid them no heed.

Vern seemed to be unfazed. "Can't complain," he said. "Why don't you draw up a stool, have a sit down?"

"I will, I will." He turned toward Holly. "Holly! My favorite waitress! Ain't this just like old home week!"

"Sit down," she told him. "I'll get you some coffee, sober you up. On the house."

"Don't want no coffee!"

"Lower your voice. People're staring."

"Don't care!"

Holly looked at Vern for help.

"Come on," Vern told his friend. "Don't make a damn scene."

"I . . ." Buck blinked, looked confused, then quickly recovered. "I want to see the manager!" he announced.

Holly quickly looked around. "No, you don't, Buck. You're drunk. You either sit down and shut up, or you go home now."

"I demand to see the manager!"

"Is there a problem here?" The short, officious man

who suddenly appeared next to Holly looked quizzically at Buck. "Is there something I can do for you, sir?"

"Yeah, goddamn it. You can take me to the store manager."

"Certainly."

Holly licked her lips, suddenly feeling nervous. She had never met The Store's manager. As far as she knew, no one had. It was not something that was ever talked about or brought up, but by tacit agreement the manager was never mentioned.

She didn't know why.

Now the fact that Buck was going to be taken to him set off a feeling within her that was almost like panic. "He's drunk!" she said.

The short man turned to face her. She had never seen him before, but the name tag on his suit lapel read MR. WALKER. "I know," he said.

"I want to see the manager!" Buck demanded. "Now!"

"But the fact that he's drunk doesn't mean that he has no right to see the manager."

Buck grinned.

"This way, please. I will take you to Mr. Lamb. He will take you in to see the manager."

Holly watched, coffeepot still in hand, as Buck was led straight down the aisle to a door in the far wall. The door opened wide, she saw a stairway leading up, and then the door closed. High up on the wall, near the ceiling, she saw a series of one-way-mirrored windows that she'd never noticed before.

The manager's office.

She shivered.

"What's going to happen?" Vern asked. His voice was low, quiet, and she realized for the first time that he was scared, too.

That made her even more frightened.

"I don't know," she said.

"Could I have some service here?" a man behind her demanded.

Holly held up her hand. "Just a minute." She put down the coffeepot on Vern's table and, on impulse, started walking down the aisle toward the manager's office. Vern came with her.

They were nearly to the door when it opened and Mr. Walker emerged. He scurried away, into the hardware aisles.

Mr. Lamb, the personnel manager, came out seconds later. He quickly scanned the aisle before him, his gaze locking on Holly's. "Is that your friend who wanted to see the manager?"

She nodded dumbly.

His voice was serious, his words orders, but there seemed to be a trace of a smile at the corner of his mouth. "Call the paramedics," he said. "I think he's having a heart attack."

3

"Everybody's family's crazy," Diane said.

Shannon shook her head, sighing. "Not as crazy as mine."

The two of them were walking down the path that led through the forest from Granite Road to The Store parking lot. It was hot, felt like summer already, and Shannon wished they'd stopped off at George's to get a Coke or something before starting off on this trek. She was dying of thirst and the path seemed to be a lot longer than Diane had led her to believe.

But at least it gave them a chance to talk.

"My dad makes us say grace before every meal. Jo's a klepto, my brother's a doper, but my dad thinks that if we thank God for the meat loaf, it'll somehow make up for his poor parenting skills and we'll all turn out to be perfect people."

Shannon laughed.

"It's not funny."

"It's a little bit funny."

Diane smiled. "Well, maybe a little. But the point is, compared to me, you have nothing to complain about."

"I wouldn't say that."

"I would. So your dad's a little whacked-out about

The Store. Big deal. There're a lot worse things he could be."

Ahead, through the trees, they could see open space. Sunlight on car windshields. Black asphalt and brown brick. The Store.

"At last," Shannon said. "Civilization."

"Can you imagine what it must have been like in pioneer days? Traveling for months without seeing another human? Living on, like, a drop of canteen water a day?"

Shannon shook her head. "I don't even want to think about it."

They broke through the trees at the side of the parking lot and slid down a short dirt embankment to the asphalt. Diane leading the way, they wound their way through the rows of parked cars toward The Store entrance.

Suddenly Diane stopped short. "Oh, my God."

Shannon almost ran into her. "What is it?"

Diane pointed toward the row directly in front of them. "Mindy."

Mindy Hargrove, her hair disheveled, her clothes in disarray, was running toward them, away from The Store, crying uncontrollably. Shannon stood next to Diane, staring, not knowing what to do. She hadn't seen Mindy for a long time. The girl's attendance had been sporadic for most of this semester, and for the past month she hadn't been in school at all. The rumor was that she wasn't going to be promoted from eleventh grade, that she'd still be a junior next year. Everyone felt sorry for Mindy because of what had happened to her father, but at the same time, she'd always been a bitch and no one really felt *too* sorry for her.

For the first time since it had happened, Shannon thought of her encounter with Mindy on the road home after school.

It's built with blood.

The two of them had not spoken since then, although they'd seen each other a couple of times in the halls, and Shannon had sort of assumed that Mindy had been embarrassed by her outburst and had not wanted to be reminded of it. She'd stuck to her nervous breakdown theory and figured that Mindy had merely been looking for a scapegoat for her dad's death.

But for the first time, the thought flashed through her mind that maybe there *was* something wrong with The Store. Maybe her dad and Mindy weren't so far off.

She immediately dismissed that idea. It was stupid, childish.

Diane moved forward, stepping out from between the cars into the open row of the parking lot.

Mindy suddenly screamed at the top of her lungs and darted to the right, stopping next to the driver's door of an old Buick.

"What's she doing?" Diane said.

Shannon didn't answer. She watched as Mindy, still screaming, pulled a set of keys from her right front pocket and started sorting through them. Her unchecked cries had attracted the attention of a handful of other people in the parking lot and all were staring at her nervously.

"This is spooky," Diane said. "Let's get the hell out of here."

Shannon agreed, and they slipped between cars, moving around to the front of the building.

From behind them came the unmistakable sound of metal on metal, and they turned to see the Buick scrape the side of a Volkswagen as it sped through the parking lot away from them, heading toward the highway. A second later, it rounded the far end of the row and sped half the length of the lot, turning down the aisle directly in front of The Store's entrance and immediately accelerating.

"Oh, my God," Shannon said. "She's going to ram the building."

The car gained speed, its engine racing loudly as it shot toward the front doors. Mindy was screaming, her face red and contorted, and even from this far away, Shannon could see the expression of fanatic determination on her features.

The car hit hard with a noise that sounded like an explosion, a crunch that Shannon felt in her stomach and under her feet, like a sonic boom. The bumper and right front panel of the car smashed against the brick, crumpling instantly, but the rest of the car plowed into the doorway, glass shattering inward.

There were screams from all around, inside and outside the store, seemingly everywhere, and Shannon was suddenly aware of the fact that she was running toward the accident, Diane at her side. Mindy was slumped over the steering wheel, completely limp, held in by a shoulder harness, and it looked like she was dead, but with one convulsive jerk she was moving again, and the car, whose engine had never stopped running, lurched backward, tearing free from the building with an excruciating squeal and nearly plowing through the gathering crowd behind it.

From the side, Shannon saw Mindy's face, and it was covered with blood, but that look of crazed determination was still there, and she watched helplessly as the car backed up and then sped forward to make another run.

This time, Mindy missed the entrance entirely and the Buick smashed against the brick wall, bouncing back. It spun once and came to a stop, engine steaming, pieces of metal continuing to fall from underneath the vehicle as it stood there. The air seemed suddenly quiet after the crashes, the cries of the crowd muffled, and Shannon looked through the car's broken window to see if Mindy was still screaming, but she could not see Mindy's face, could only see the stem of the steering wheel that had been embedded there.

From somewhere came a policeman, a uniformed officer who pushed his way through the gathering onlookers and tried unsuccessfully to open the smashed driver's door of the Buick. Unable to budge either the driver's or passenger's doors, he pushed one burly hand through the glassless window, put a hand against Mindy's neck, feeling for a pulse. He looked back, shook his head.

"Is she—?" Diane began.

The policeman nodded. "She's dead."

FIFTEEN

1

He heard the saws when he awoke. The saws and the earthmovers.

The Store was expanding.

Bill got up, put on shorts and a T-shirt, went for his morning jog.

Construction had indeed begun on the recently approved addition, and an army of men and machinery were hard at work demolishing the stand of trees behind the building. These were obviously not local construction workers—the customized state-of-the-art equipment told him that much—but there was no site sign announcing the contractor's name. He jogged off the highway, into the empty parking lot, and as he drew closer to the side of the building, he could clearly see the logo on the side of a black bulldozer: a shopping cart filled with consumer products.

And the words beneath it: THE STORE CONSTRUCTION COMPANY. A DIVISION OF THE STORE, INC.

Ben was already at the site, behind the makeshift chain-link fence, taking photos for the paper. Bill saw the editor crouched next to a crane, camera pointed toward the rear of The Store.

"Hey!" Bill called.

Ben saw him, waved, and continued taking photos, moving around the crane to a tangle of fallen trees that were being cut into segments by ten or twelve men all armed with power saws. Bill stood outside the fence, watching, waiting. Finally, the editor finished his roll of film and walked past a tractor, through the gate, and out to the parking lot.

Bill walked over to meet him. He had to shout to be heard over the saws. "Why are you out here taking pictures this early? I thought you left that grunt work for your underlings."

"Grunt work? This is what passes for a glamour assignment here in Juniper. They'll cover this afternoon's Little League game and tonight's school board meeting. I get The Store."

"Dan Rather look out."

"Eat me."

Bill laughed, and the two of them headed slowly across the lot toward the front of The Store, where Ben had parked his car. Bill glanced to his right as they walked. The front entrance of the building had been repaired yesterday. By local workers, he had assumed at the time. Now he was not so sure. He gestured back toward the construction workers. "Are they the ones who fixed the front of the building?"

Ben nodded. "Yep."

"And they're doing the addition alone, with no help from any of our workers here?"

"You got it."

Bill shook his head. "The council could've at least insisted that they use local contractors. I mean, that's pretty crappy. Construction was the only business around here benefiting from The Store—"

"Except for the paper," Ben reminded him.

"Except for the paper," Bill conceded.

"So much for the providing-local-jobs theory, huh?"

"I'd say those people deserved it for being so naive and gullible—"

"Especially when you warned them, right?"

"—but the rest of us have to suffer the consequences as well." He looked at his friend. "Jerk."

"Come on, you don't think you're becoming just a little holier-than-thou on this subject?"

"You're not?"

"It's my job. I'm a journalist."

They reached Ben's car. "You want me to give you a ride home?" the editor asked, unlocking his door.

Bill shook his head. "That's okay. I need the exercise." He glanced back, saw only the edge of the construction fence behind the building on the south side. There was a loud crash as another ponderosa went down. "They're not going to be happy until every tree in Juniper is cut."

"Joni Mitchell called it. 'Big Yellow Taxi.' "

"Hippie."

"I've already admitted that."

They stood there for a moment, looking at each other over the roof of the car, listening to the sound of the saws.

"There's nothing we can do about any of this, is there?" Bill asked finally.

"It's progress. Hop on the bandwagon or get the fuck out of the way."

Bill stared up at the clear blue sky, ran a quick hand through his hair. "Any leads on Richardson's store?"

"What do you think?" Ben said.

"Just checking."

"Want my prediction?"

"On what?"

"The Buy-and-Save situation."

"Not really," Bill said, "but give it to me."

"I predict that its final demise will coincide with the completion of this food department here." He motioned toward the construction site. "It'll hold on till then." He looked over the car roof at Bill. "Want to give me odds?"

"I think not." Bill took a deep breath, waved goodbye, and started running. He wanted to be angry and outraged, he'd settle for scared, but he felt only tired and discouraged, and he jogged out of the parking lot and down the highway, heading toward home.

The sound of the saws followed him all the way.

2

Ginny usually spent recesses in the classroom—they were only ten minutes long, which didn't really give her a chance to do anything—but today she felt restless, antsy, and after leading her kids out to the playground, she hurried over to the staff lounge for a quick cup of coffee.

The lounge was empty save for Lorraine Hepperton, who was sitting on the couch, humming to herself.

Ginny smiled at the other teacher as she strode over to the coffee machine. "My, aren't we in a good mood today."

Lorraine smiled back. "Yes, we are."

Ginny laughed. She poured herself a cup of coffee, then walked over to the couch, sitting a cushion away from her friend. "So how're things going?" she asked.

"Here at school or in my real life?"

"Is there a difference?"

"There is now." Lorraine rummaged through the purse at her side. "Want to see what I bought?"

"Sure—" she started to say, but Lorraine had already found what she was looking for and held up a doll, an ugly, particularly nasty looking doll, an orange figure ostensibly human but with stiff bristle hair that extruded from the misshapen head in strange clumps and an off-center face comprised of black cloth dots connected by thread. The figure was nude, and an exaggerated vulva protruded from between its legs.

Ginny grimaced. "What is it?"

"A voodoo doll. I bought it at The Store."

"Why?"

"To try out. I figure it can't hurt." She chuckled. "I call it Meg."

Ginny was shocked. "You're joking!"

"No, I'm not." She glanced quickly toward the door to make sure there was no one else coming into the room, then withdrew a pincushion from her purse. She pulled out a pin, inserted it in the figure's left breast, pressing it all the way in.

She giggled.

A chill crept down Ginny's neck. She could not imagine any national chain store selling something like this, not even as a joke or gag gift, and she wondered where in The Store this creepy little doll was displayed.

Lorraine inserted another pin in the doll's stomach.

The black convoy.

Ginny stood, moved away from the couch, feeling cold. She turned around by the coffee machine. "You don't think that thing really works, do you? You don't believe that stuff?"

Lorraine turned the doll over, held out the tag. "Made in Haiti."

She still wasn't sure how serious the other teacher was. Lorraine's voice was pleasant, her tone light, but she did not sound the least bit jocular or facetious. It was as if this was a normal conversation, as if they were discussing the fabric quality of a new blouse.

Lorraine pulled out one more pin, pressed it directly into the oversized vulva, then put both the pincushion and the doll back inside her purse. A split second later, another teacher walked through the open doorway into the lounge.

"Hello, Meg," Lorraine said sweetly.

SIXTEEN

1

"The school year's almost over," Ginny said.

Bill glanced over at her. "Happy?"

"Yeah. I am. It's been a long year."

"Any more voodoo dolls lately?"

She shook her head.

"Witches' sabbaths? Satanic rituals?"

"Not funny," she said.

He sighed. "No. I guess it's not."

They were silent for a moment. The house was still, quiet. Both Sam and Shannon were gone, out with their respective friends, and the only noise was the muted hum of the refrigerator in the kitchen.

"She'll have to quit after summer," Ginny said. "Once she goes off to school."

"I wasn't even thinking about that."

"Bullshit."

"You're right." Bill leaned back on the couch, stared up at the ceiling. "Maybe she can get a summer job on campus, leave early."

"She hasn't even decided where she's going. She has to pick a college first."

"It depends on which one offers the best financial aid package."

They were quiet again, and Bill closed his eyes. He felt tired. He'd been tired a lot lately, though he wasn't sure why. He hadn't been getting any less sleep or doing any more work than usual. Stress, he supposed. He'd had a lot on his mind. Too much.

"We never sit outside anymore," Ginny said out of the blue.

He opened his eyes, turned his head toward her. "What?"

"We never sit outside anymore. Have you noticed that? We never sit on the porch together. You're always in front of your computer and I'm watching TV."

"We sit together. We're sitting together now."

"But not outside. We used to go outside after dinner, look up at the stars, talk. Remember that?"

"You're the one who doesn't like to go out at night. The bugs eat you alive."

"That's not the point." She moved closer, put an arm around his shoulder. "We don't spend as much time together as we used to."

She was right, he realized. He hadn't thought about it before, but despite the fact that he worked at home and she usually came home from school before four, the only quality time they seemed to spend together was in bed. It was as if they lived two separate existences under the same roof. It hadn't always been this way. Once upon a time, they'd spent every free moment together. As she'd pointed out, they'd sit on the porch, cuddle, talk about the past, plan for the future. It was partially the girls, he supposed. When they were around, it was pretty hard to be intimate.

But he couldn't blame everything on them.

"You're right," he said. "We should spend more time together."

"It's almost summer. It's warm enough to sit on the porch."

"You want to go outside? Look at stars?"

She kissed him. "There's hope for us yet."

"Did you ever doubt it?"

"No," she said slowly, and her voice was surprisingly serious. "I never did."

2

They all had to attend Sam's graduation.

As a family.

Shannon had wanted to sit with her friends, who were clustered in the right front corner of the bleachers, near the gate through which the graduates would walk, but her parents said this was a family event and the family was going to celebrate it together.

Her grandparents had come over for the occasion, and she sat between her two grandmothers on the hot metal bench. Her father was manning the video camera, and she had been given the Nikon and assigned to take still photographs. At least it gave her something to do. She loved her grandparents and all, was glad to see them, but it was kind of uncool to be hanging with them while her friends were on their own and had the run of the field.

She saw Diane hop over the rail of the bleachers and dash over to Zona Marsden, who was in the band, seated to the right of the empty folding chairs set up for the graduates. The two girls talked for a moment, heads huddled together, then both burst out laughing. Diane sped back across the athletic field and disappeared around the side of the bleachers.

Shannon thought of asking her dad if she could go with Diane, prepared to argue that she'd be able to get better pictures of Sam if she was down there with her, but at that moment, the band started up, playing some anonymous march, and red-jacketed ushers began leading teachers and school administrators to the first row of folding chairs.

"Make sure you get Sam when she steps onto the field!" her dad called, moving to the bleacher aisle and starting down the steps as he turned on the video camera.

"I will." Shannon stood, moved past her Grandma Jo and Grandpa Fred, and followed her father down the metal steps to the edge of the bleachers in order to get a better shot.

The adults were seated and the first graduates filed onto the field. They were doing it alphabetically, and the graduating class wasn't very big, so Sam would be near the beginning. Shannon took off the lens cap and adjusted the focus on the camera so she'd be able to just point and shoot when Samantha walked out.

"Here she comes!" her dad called.

Shannon snapped a photo as soon as Sam and her paired partner stepped through the gate, another as she approached the folding chairs, another as she sat down.

She'd be going through this herself next year. She wouldn't have the extra yellow tassel probably—her grades weren't as good as Sam's—but she'd be graduating. She glanced back at her grandparents. All four of them were smiling, and she knew they were happy, but the smiles seemed strained, as though they were in pain and had to force themselves to be cheerful. It suddenly hit her how old and frail her grandparents were, and the thought crossed her mind that they might not all be here for her graduation next year. She instantly pushed the horrible thought away, afraid to even think it, worried on some superstitious level that simply acknowledging the possibility might make it a reality.

She moved back to her seat for the remainder of the ceremony, putting warm hands on her grandmothers' cold, thin arms as prayers were said and speeches were read. Her dad remained in place, videotaping.

She went back down to the edge of the bleachers with her father when they started issuing diplomas, and she took a picture of Sam rising from her chair, another of her standing at the head of the line waiting to receive her diploma. When they announced the name Samantha Davis over the loudspeaker, she couldn't resist, and even as she snapped a photo of Sam accepting the diploma from the principal, she whooped loudly, screamed.

Quite a few other people screamed and clapped as well. Sam was one of the most popular seniors in school, and while Shannon often found herself somewhat annoyed by that, she experienced a surge of pride today, and she was proud to be the sister of Samantha Davis.

After the ceremony, they were taking pictures in front of the Juniper Union High School sign, Samantha posing with both sets of grandparents, when Diane, breathless, came running up. She waved to Sam, nodded to her parents, then stood directly in front of Shannon. "They need two people to work the punch bowl at Grad Night," she said. "You want to do it?"

"What?"

"Smith and Jimmy got caught trying to smuggle a bottle of scotch into the gym. I guess they were going to spike the punch. It's supposed to be a sober grad night, no alcohol, so they were automatically kicked out, and now they're looking for two replacements. Mr. Handy said it's ours if we want it."

Shannon looked hopefully at her mother.

"Go ahead," her mom said, smiling.

"Yes!" Diane pumped a fist in the air and grinned. "I'll tell them we're in." She started running back down the sloping grass toward the gymnasium.

"Where and when?" Shannon called.

Diane turned around, running backward. "Meet me at the gym when you're through here!"

"We're going out to eat!"

"Eight o'clock, then! The gym!"

Shannon nodded, waved, and Diane disappeared into the crowd of still-milling parents.

Dinner, Shannon thought, was somewhat depressing. They went to the Castle Creek Steakhouse, the closest thing to a decent restaurant in this area of the state, but so did half the graduating class. And although Sam spent most of the meal visiting with friends, talking to other kids, it was conspicuously obvious that she didn't have a boyfriend. Most of the other girls in the restaurant, except the losers, were eating out with their families and their boyfriends. Shannon knew for a fact that at least six boys had asked Sam to Grad Night—although she had decided to go stag—but it wasn't the same as having one special person to share this special night with.

She missed Jake.

That's what it came down to, really, and she found herself wondering if she would have a boyfriend by the time she graduated or if she would end up going out to dinner with just her parents and her sister and her grandparents.

Maybe not even all of her grandparents.

God, this was turning out to be a depressing night.

Things improved greatly after dinner, though. They all went home, she and Sam quickly changed into party clothes . . . and then changed again into party clothes that were acceptable to their parents, and their dad dropped them off at school.

After he drove away, Shannon shyly gave her sister a special graduation present she'd bought herself. She'd contributed to the PC and printer that the whole family had chipped in on, but she'd wanted to get Samantha something more personal, less practical. Something that was just from her. So she'd gone down to Ellen's Attic and, with the allowance and baby-sitting money she'd saved all year, bought her sister an antique brooch.

"I know you like those things," Shannon said. "And I thought it would be a good graduation present."

"It's a wonderful present!" Sam hugged her, awkwardly yet gratefully. "Thank you so much." She immediately pinned it to her blouse. "What do Mom and Dad think?"

"I didn't tell them. It's from me to you, so I wanted you to see it first."

Sam smiled. "It may not seem like it sometimes, but I really am glad you're my sister."

Shannon looked away, embarrassed. "Me, too," she said.

They split up after that, Sam walking over to where her friends were congregating for the last time at Senior Corner, Shannon heading straight to the gym, where Diane was already filling paper cups with red fruit punch.

"It's about time you got here," she said. "Help me fill these up before the rush starts."

Grad Night this year was sponsored by The Store, all of the decorations and refreshments, even the entertainment donated or paid for by The Store. A big banner strung above the doorway announced WELCOME TO THE STORE'S FIRST ANNUAL GRAD NIGHT CELEBRATION!

That was nice, Shannon supposed, but it also meant that they had to abide by rules and regulations imposed by The Store. Traditionally, Juniper's Grad Night parties lasted from dusk until dawn, with parent and teacher volunteers chaperoning the kids inside the gym and policemen monitoring the parking lot and the streets abutting the school in order to make sure there was no trouble. This year, however the chaperons had been scrapped. The Store had supplied its own security. And the police would probably have very little to do in the parking lot or on the street because once seniors entered the Grad Night party, they were not allowed to leave the gym.

This was all supposed to cut down on problems and troublemakers, but to Shannon it lent to the celebration an uneasy atmosphere. Teachers and administrators were still in attendance, but they were relegated to the sidelines: making lame announcements from the stage between songs, helping students serve refreshments. In contrast, stoic guards in green Store uniforms were conspicuously stationed around the gym to monitor the partiers' behavior and to block all exits. The guards were not people from town but part of the group of initial Store employees brought in from the corporate office. No one knew them, and they knew no one, and it made for an unsettling time. This was supposed to be a graduation party, a celebration of freedom from compulsory schooling, but it felt more like a dance at a prison, and long before midnight Shannon was sorry she'd agreed to help out. She felt like she was being watched all the time, monitored, and it was a feeling she didn't like.

Sam stopped by several times throughout the early evening, accompanied by different dance partners, but eventually Shannon lost track of her sister, and the next time she saw her, several hours later, Sam was huddled with a group of Store guards to the left of the bandstand.

During a break in the music, while Mr. Handy gave out joke awards that were supposed to be humorous but were merely embarrassing, Shannon made a quick trip to the bathroom. Sam was already in there with a bunch of other girls, and she put a hand on Shannon's shoulder. "I've been promoted," she said. "I'm going to be lead in Housewares this summer. They're letting me out of Infants. I guess they like me."

"What's a lead?"

"It's the lead salesperson. The department manager'll be over me, but I'm pretty much second in command. I'll be like the boss of all the Housewares part-timers."

"Who told you? One of those guys guarding the door?"

"Yeah. Ray."

Shannon smiled teasingly. "Ooh, first-name basis. Is there something going on here I should know about?"

"With Ray?" Sam laughed. "I don't think so."

"Well, I'm happy for you," Shannon said. "That's great."

But it wasn't that great, and she wondered why her sister seemed so proud and excited over such a trivial thing. Sam had always disdained those girls at their school who set their career sights no higher than being a waitress or a sales clerk. She was adamant about getting out of this town and getting an education and becoming part of what she called "the real world." It seemed completely out of character for her to feel honored because some security guard told her she'd gotten a minor promotion in her menial part-time job.

Shannon wondered if she should tell her parents what she thought but decided that it would only make her dad crazy. He had a bug up his butt about The Store, anyway, and this would only make him worse. So she said good-bye to Sam, pushed it out of her mind, and by the time she returned to the refreshment table she had completely forgotten it.

SEVENTEEN

1

The addition was finished.

The grand opening of The Store's new grocery department was tomorrow.

It was impossible to believe that it had been completed so quickly. Groundbreaking had been only a little over a month ago. By the time Ben's photos of that morning had appeared in the paper, they were already out of date. Construction had moved ahead so rapidly that, according to the town council, it was all Juniper's various inspectors could do to keep up.

Bill had jogged by there this morning, and already the banners had been strung, the helium balloons tied in place. A page of coupons had appeared in the paper on Saturday, offering such outrageously low-priced items as one-cent lettuce and twenty-five-cents-a-pound catfish fillet. The Store was bribing people to shop in its food department, and Bill knew the bribes were working, because he and Ginny were going to stock up on a bunch of groceries tomorrow—and if *they* could be bought, anyone could be bought.

He wished there was another place in town to buy foodstuffs. But Ben had been right. Buy-and-Save was scheduled to shut its doors next week—just after The Store's grocery department opened. Already, the place looked abandoned. He drove down Main, slowed as he passed the market. The windows were dirty and dark, and there were only two cars in the parking lot. Employees' cars, probably.

Once Buy-and-Save closed, there'd be only The Store. He wondered what had happened to Jed. Rumor had it that he'd skipped town, owing bills, but he didn't know anyone who actually bought that story. It was completely out of character for Jed, and Bill had the feeling that the truth was something far less ordinary and far less benign.

And connected to The Store.

He drove by the empty café. The windows were soaped up, whited out. As were the windows on an increasing number of storefronts in town.

It was Tuesday, benefits day, and up ahead the line in front of the unemployment office was long. Even longer than it had been after the lumber mill closed. It wound outside of the brown brick building and around the corner to the parking lot. At the end of the line he saw Frank Wilson, one of Hargrove's old cronies, and while a small mean part of him wanted to gloat because the man had gotten what he'd deserved, he couldn't really feel good about it.

Revenge was not always sweet.

There were quite a few construction workers in line, and underneath the metal letters euphemistically identifying the building as the Arizona Department of Economic Security, he saw Ted Malory. He waved, but Ted didn't see him, and he continued on, not wanting to honk and draw attention to himself.

According to Ted's wife, The Store had stiffed him on the roofing job he'd done, not paying the amount originally agreed upon, deducting money from the payment for imaginary errors and oversights. He hadn't had a job since, had had to lay off his whole crew, and Charlinda said they'd probably have to file for bankruptcy. To top it off, his son and a group of other boys had recently been caught dropping M80s down the toilets at school, and, along with the parents of the other boys, Ted and Charlinda were responsible for covering those damages as well.

Trouble came in waves, his grandfather used to say, and that sure as hell seemed to be true.

Especially these days.

Street's store was still in business, and he stopped by, bought a diamond needle for his turntable that he didn't need, then walked over to the record store.

Doane nodded a greeting as he stepped inside.

"Hey," Bill said.

"Hey, yourself."

"I probably shouldn't ask," Bill said, heading over to the used-CD rack, "but how're things today?"

"Well, you heard what happened to the radio station, didn't you?"

He shook his head. "No. What?"

"The Store bought it."

He stopped walking, turned to face the store owner. "Shit."

"Yep. They kept it quiet, but I guess the deal was finalized last week. The station switched over this morning." He smiled mirthlessly. "They even changed their call letters. The station is now called K-STOR."

"Why?"

Doane shrugged. "I guess they want to control what we hear as well as what we buy." He walked behind the counter, turned on his receiver, and the sounds of an obnoxious rap group blared through the speakers. "From what I can tell, they're only playing music they have in stock. You know that old saying, 'People don't know what they like, they like what they know'? Well, that's especially true in music. That's why there were all those payoff scandals years ago. It's a fact of life: if music gets played on the radio, if people hear it often enough, they start liking it." He turned off the receiver. "They'll have no problem moving their stock."

"But why did Ward and Robert sell? The station had to be making money."

"Rumor is, The Store made them an offer they couldn't refuse."

"What's that supposed to mean?"

Doane shrugged.

"You mean they were offered big bucks? Or they were threatened?"

"Maybe both." He held up a finger before Bill could respond. "I'm only repeating what I heard. I don't know any more than that."

Bill did not even feel like arguing. He should feel like ranting and raving. But he didn't. He felt drained, tried.

He recalled his dream about the asphalt machine. That's what The Store seemed like to him: an unstoppable force hell-bent on bulldozing its way over the livelihoods and lifestyles of the town.

"As you heard, they've switched formats already. They're playing top forty. Period. No country."

"No country?"

"Not anymore."

"People won't stand for that in this town."

"They'll have no choice. Besides, people are basically passive. They'll piss and moan for a while, but they'll get used to it. They'll adjust. It'll be more convenient for them to listen to the music they're being offered than to write a letter or make a phone call or do something to change it. It's human nature."

He was right, Bill knew. It was depressing but true. Human beings' capacity to adjust to almost anything was supposed to be one of their greatest virtues, but it was also one of their greatest weaknesses. It rendered them compliant, allowed them to be exploited.

Doane smiled weakly. "Promise me something. If you ever win the lottery, if you win, like, thirty million dollars in the Powerball or something, buy the station back and put on some decent music."

Bill forced himself to smile. "It's a deal."

There was nothing new in the store, and nothing that he really wanted or needed, but he bought a few CD versions of albums that he already had on vinyl. He'd probably spent more in Doane's store in the past three months than he had in the entire previous year, but Ginny seemed to understand why, and he didn't think she'd give him a hard time about today's purchases.

It was out of his way, but he drove past The Store on his trip home. In contrast to the deserted downtown streets, The Store's parking lot was crowded.

Even though it was a workday.

Even though it was the middle of the afternoon.

He drove by without slowing, glancing out the passenger window. All trace of the original meadow was gone. The contours and topography of the clearing had been changed completely, and the location now looked as though The Store had always been there.

He turned right down the road that led through Creekside Acres and drove down the dirt road toward home.

Where he spent the rest of the afternoon working on the documentation for The Store's accounting package.

2

Summer.

Shannon awoke late, ate a leisurely breakfast, and spent the rest of the morning lying on her bed, staring into space and listening to the radio. She hated summer, although she didn't know when that had started, when her feelings had flip-flopped. She used to love the season. As a child, there'd been nothing better than three months with no school, and the long days had been filled with limitless possibilities. She'd awakened early each morning, gone to bed late each night, and spent the sunny hours in between playing with her friends.

But she didn't play anymore, and now the days stretched endlessly before her, a massive block of time in which she had nothing to do.

It wouldn't have been so boring if her friends had been around, but this summer they all either had jobs or had gone on vacation with their relatives. Even Diane was working, spending the days behind the cash register at her father's gas station.

It would have been different if she'd had a boyfriend. Then she would've welcomed the freedom. She wouldn't even have minded the absence of her friends. She would have had plenty to do with her time.

Jake.

She still missed him. He'd been a jerk sometimes—a lot of the time—but she missed having someone to talk with, to walk with, to snuggle with, to just be with.

It was still hard to get used to the fact that someone who had meant everything to her, who'd claimed to love her, with whom she had shared intimate secrets, embarrassing fears, now didn't care if she lived or died. It was a hard thing to reconcile, a big adjustment to make, and she thought that this was what it must feel like when someone you love dies. The emotional withdrawal was the same.

She breathed deeply and with difficulty, stared out the window of her bedroom. It was one of those still summer days that were far too common in Arizona. Blue sky, no clouds. Heavy air: hot, no breeze. It might have been bearable if they had air conditioning, but they didn't, and the fan she'd set up on her dresser only created a weak warm current that died halfway across the room.

She thought of Sam, working in The Store. Air-conditioning. People. Music. Noise. Life. It suddenly sounded good to her and she decided at that moment that instead of wasting her summer vegging out and watching soap operas and television talk shows she'd get a job herself. There was nothing she really wanted to buy, no specific reason she needed to earn money, but she could take what she made this summer, put it in the bank, and get a head start on saving for her own college education.

Excited and newly energized, she bounded out of bed and hurried down the hall to her dad's office. The door was closed, but she opened it without knocking. "Daddy?"

He looked up from his computer. "What is it, daughter dearest?"

"Stop being a buffoon."

"That's why you invaded my privacy? To insult me?"

"No. I want to get a job."

The expression on his face shifted, hardened. "Where?"

"I was thinking of applying at The Store."

"I don't want you working there," he said grimly.

"Why? Everyone else does. Sam does."

"Sam's older." He paused. "Besides, I don't like her working there, either."

"Fine. I'll apply somewhere else, then. Although, just in case you haven't noticed, business is not exactly booming in Juniper."

"Why do you want to get a job anyway? It's summer. Enjoy it. You'll be working for the rest of your life. You might as well enjoy your summers while you're still a kid."

"Earth to Dad. I'm seventeen. I'm not a kid anymore."

He smiled sweetly. "You'll always be my little girl."

"Buffoon alert."

"You still haven't answered my question. Why do you want to get a job?"

"I'm bored. All my friends are either working or gone. There's nothing to do."

"There's always something to do—"

"I don't want an inspirational speech. I just want to find a job."

"Go ahead," he said. "With my blessing." He met her eyes. "Anywhere but The Store."

She nodded, started to close the door and turn away, then swiveled back to face him. "Can I take the car?"

"Your mom has the Jeep and Sam took the Toyota. But if you can find a third car in the garage, you're welcome to it."

"I forgot," she said sheepishly.

"Have a nice walk, and don't forget to close the door behind you."

She closed his office door, heading down the hallway to the kitchen, where she pulled a Dr Pepper out of the refrigerator. She considered scrapping the whole idea. Or at least waiting for another day. It was hot as blazes out there, and she'd be drenched with sweat by the time she walked all the way into town. The chance of anyone hiring a sweaty, smelly seventeen-year-old for any position was pretty slim.

But an endless afternoon stretched before her, and she'd already had enough of those the past few weeks to last her a lifetime. She needed to get out of the house, find something to do. Besides, no one was going to want to interview her today. She'd just pick up applications this afternoon, bring them home and fill them out, then return them tomorrow.

And she already knew where she really planned to apply.

The Store.

Any other place in town probably would give her an instant interview, a quick yes or no. The Store was the only employer big enough to be impersonal, and despite the promise she'd given her dad, it was the only place she wanted to work.

She knew her parents didn't like The Store for some reason, but she wasn't exactly sure why. Some of the rules for employees seemed to be weird—like that dating prohibition (wasn't it usually the other way around?)— and it still made her feel uncomfortable when she thought of the Store guards at the Grad Night party overseeing the rest of them as though they were cattle— and Mindy—but there didn't really seem to be anything about the place that would generate the sort of bizarre hatred her parents, and especially her dad, seemed to feel.

It was probably a political thing.

Her parents were big on that stuff.

She went into her bedroom and grabbed her purse, just in case she needed ID. "I'm going!" she called out.

"Good luck!" her dad yelled.

She let the screen door slam behind her and walked down the long drive to the road, where two of Mr. Sutton's horses were watching her forlornly from behind their fenced barricade. She ran across the dirt road, jumped the ditch, and gave them each a quick hug, murmuring reassuringly. If she'd seen them from the porch, she would've gotten some sugar cubes from the kitchen for them, but she didn't want to turn back now, and she patted each of the horses, promising to bring them a treat next time. The animals were hot, too, miserable in this windless weather and trying to stay in the shade. It was edging into the warmest part of the day, and though the horses obviously wanted company, she had to get going, and she gave them each a quick good-bye hug and jumped back over the ditch onto the road, heading toward town.

By the time she reached The Store, it looked like

she'd been running a marathon. Her blouse and shorts were sticking to her skin, her hair hung in wet clumps about her face. She couldn't ask for an application looking like this, so she bought a can of cold Coke from the newly installed machine next to the door and sat outside on the bench next to the building, staring out at the parking lot while she tried to cool off.

She looked around. This was the spot where Mindy had crashed into the wall, and though she hadn't thought of it in several weeks, she suddenly saw in her mind the stem of the car's steering wheel bloodily embedded in Mindy's face.

It's built with blood.

She took a deep breath, feeling a slight chill pass through her. Maybe her parents' feelings weren't quite so unfounded.

But then she looked out into the parking lot and saw a mother happily pushing a shopping cart toward the front entrance, a little boy singing loudly from his cart seat.

There was nothing weird here. This was a normal discount retail store. There'd been some bad luck, maybe, some negative coincidences, but that sort of thing happened everywhere, all the time.

The woman passed by her bench, and the little boy waved at Shannon. "Hi!" he said.

She smiled at him. "Hi."

A few minutes later, she was sufficiently cooled off, no longer sweating, and she walked into The Store, feeling a welcome burst of air-conditioning as she stepped through the doors into the building. A smiling director asked if she needed some assistance, she told him she wanted to get a job application, and he directed her to the Customer Service desk. The woman behind the counter, who Shannon remembered from Buy-and-Save, gave her an application and a pen and told her to move down to the end of the counter and fill in the requested information.

"We don't have many openings left," she said, "but you're in luck. There's a clerk position available in the Garden department."

"I'll take it," Shannon said.

The woman smiled. "Fill out the application, and we'll see."

Shannon did so, turned it in, then walked through The Store looking for Sam. She found her sister behind the register in the Housewares department, conspicuously yawning while an elderly woman lectured her for not being helpful.

Shannon pretended to look at dishes and silverware until the woman finally left, disgusted.

Samantha smiled. "We get all kinds." She looked down the aisle behind Shannon. "Mom and Dad here, too?"

Shannon shook her head. "Just me."

"To what do I owe the honor?"

"I'm applying for job here."

Sam's expression darkened.

"I thought you could help me," Shannon said quickly.

"You don't want to work here," Sam said.

"Yes, I do."

"No, you don't."

"Look, I was just asking you to put in a good word for me. But if that's too difficult for you, forget it. God, I didn't think you were going to turn it into a whole big thing."

"I'll tell Dad."

Shannon stared at her sister. "Thanks. Thanks a lot."

"I don't think you—"

"I already turned in the application. If you won't help me, fine. But I'm going to get a job here."

"You already turned it in?"

"Yeah."

Sam took a deep breath, and a look of—what? fear?—passed over her face. "Okay, I'll take care of it," she said.

"Take care of what?"

"There are tests and things you're supposed to go through before you get hired, but I'll see if I can get you out of it. I . . . think I can."

Shannon nodded. "Thanks," she said grudgingly.

Sam looked sick, almost physically ill. "Go home," she said. "They shouldn't see us together."

"Why?"

"Just go. I'll . . . talk to some people, and I'll tell you what happens tonight." She smiled, but her smile was forced, closer to a grimace, and once again, Shannon thought of Mindy.

It's built with blood.

She looked at her sister. "Thanks," she said again.

Sam nodded.

Shannon walked back through The Store toward the entrance, feeling uneasy but not knowing why.

Her mom was already home by the time she arrived back at the house. She was sorting through a pile of papers and mimeograph sheets on the coffee table in the living room, but she looked up as Shannon walked in. "Your father said you were out job-hunting."

"Yeah."

"Where did you apply?" her mom asked.

"Where didn't I apply?" she lied.

"Any luck?"

Shannon shrugged. "I don't know. There don't seem to be too many places looking for help right now."

"Summer school starts on Monday. I could use an aide."

Shannon snorted derisively.

"Ten bucks a week. And it'll look good on your résumé for college."

"We'll see. If I don't get a job, maybe I'll do it."

Samantha arrived home late. She walked directly into her sister's room and shut the door behind her. "You're hired," she said. "Report tomorrow. Ten o'clock. Mr. Lamb."

"Thanks."

Sam nodded.

She looked tired, Shannon thought. And pale. Sick. "Are you all right?" she asked

"I'm fine," Samantha snapped.

"Just asking."

"What are you going to tell Mom and Dad?"

"I'll think of something."

"Just leave me out of it."

"Okay." Shannon watched her sister turn and walk silently out of the room. A few moments later, she heard the shower running in the bathroom. She considered telling her parents that she'd gotten a job—she had to tell them, since she started work tomorrow—but she didn't know what to say and needed some time to come up with a plan.

They'd freak if they knew she'd be working at The Store.

Shannon lay on her bed, reading a magazine, and after Sam finished with her shower, she waited another ten minutes for the steam to clear out of the bathroom, then went in to take her own bath.

She pulled up the metal knob that plugged the drain and began running the water, testing it first with her fingers to make sure the temperature was okay. She undressed, opened the hamper to toss in her shirt and jeans, and saw Sam's panties lying on top of the other clothes. They were spotted with blood, and though at first Shannon thought nothing of it, she realized seconds later that her sister's period was not due for another few weeks.

Shannon paused. She thought of how worn out and sickly Sam had seemed tonight, and she considered asking her about it, seeing if anything was the matter, but she simply stared down at the bloody cotton underwear for a few moments, then threw in her own clothes, let the lid of the hamper fall, and stepped into the tub, sinking into the water.

She told her parents after her bath.

They were seated on the couch, watching TV, and she walked into the living room and stood before them. She'd considered just coming out and telling them the truth, considered easing them into the truth, but finally decided that the best course of action, the only course of action in this instance, was to lie.

"I got a job," she said.

Her mom smiled. "That's great. Where?"

"When did you find out?" her dad asked. His voice

was serious, not supportive, and she detected the beginnings of a frown on his face.

"Just now."

"How?"

"They called," she told him.

"I didn't hear the phone ring."

"It rang. I answered it. I got the job."

"Where?" her mom repeated.

"Yes," her dad said. "Where?"

Was that suspicion she saw on his features? She swallowed hard, tried to smile. "George's," she lied. "The hamburger stand."

Mr. Lamb was waiting for her the next morning by the Customer Service desk. She'd carpooled in with Sam, and she was a half hour early for her appointment, but Mr. Lamb was waiting for her anyway, and he smiled as he shook her hand. His skin was cool to the touch, his smile cold, and she wished Sam had stayed with her as the personnel manager began giving her a brief description of her duties. He paused in his prepared speech, as if reading her mind. "Yes," he said. "You're very lucky to have a sister like Samantha. She's quite a woman." His smile broadened. "Quite a woman."

Shannon felt chilled. She should've listened to Sam and her parents, she thought. She should not have applied for a job here.

This was a mistake.

Suddenly, a summer of lying on her bed, reading magazines and listening to the radio, seemed pleasant rather than boring, seemed like what she should be doing with her time, and for a brief second she considered turning down the job, quitting, getting out of here.

But Mr. Lamb was now leading her out of the Customer Service area, taking her on a tour of The Store, and it was too late. The chance had passed.

Too late?

Why was it too late?

She didn't know, but it was, and she followed him down the aisles, through the departments, as he explained the layout and operation of The Store.

Her panic passed, her uneasiness disappearing as quickly as it had come. Mr. Lamb showed her the break room, the locker room, took her through a stockroom, led her into a room lined with video screens in which Jake and his fellow security men monitored the building.

Jake, thank God, wasn't there.

She wondered what she'd do if she ran into Jake in the break room or something. How would she handle it? She tried to tell herself that the fact that Jake worked at The Store was another reason that she shouldn't have applied here, but she knew deep down that he was one of the reasons she had. Despite what she told people, despite what she pretended, somewhere in the back of her mind was the thought that they might get back together again.

Mr. Lamb was definitely a weirdo, but the initial chill she'd felt in his presence was gone, and the deeper into the building they went—Mr. Lamb introducing her to other, smiling employees along the way—the more comfortable she felt about The Store. She could work in this place. She could fit in here.

They took a small elevator downstairs, to a concrete-lined hallway that looked like a bunker, and he showed her a conference room and a training room and then stopped before an arched doorway with gilt-edged trim.

"Here," he said, "is the chapel."

Shannon glanced through the doorway, into the room. For a brief second, the coldness returned. Pews were arranged in rows, scented candles burned in twin alcoves in the side walls, but instead of a pulpit or altar at the front of the chapel there was a huge portrait of Newman King, lined with red velvet.

"This is where the department managers hold their meetings each morning. Before the store opens, they pray to Mr. King that we will have a profitable day."

Pray to Mr. King?

She'd seen The Store's founder on TV, on the news, and while he was obviously a rich and powerful man, he was not a god, and the idea that the man or woman she'd be working under came in here each morning and ritualistically prayed to the painting of a millionaire creeped her out.

Then they were moving on, back into the elevator, back onto what Mr. Lamb called The Floor, and shoppers and browsers were roaming the aisles, sitting in the sushi and espresso bars, and Shannon was thinking how lucky she was to have been hired by The Store.

"That's it for now," Mr. Lamb said. "There'll be a week's worth of training classes—how to work the cash registers, handle customers and the like—then there'll be a two-week probation period, then you'll be in." He handed her a photocopied schedule of training classes. "Your first class is tonight, in the downstairs training room. Be there or be square."

"Uh, thank you," she said.

He grinned. "Thank your sister." He looked her over, starting at her feet, moving up to her hair, then nodded, satisfied. "I think you'll be a model Store employee."

"I'll try," she said.

He started to walk back behind the Customer Service counter, then stopped and turned at the last minute. "A word of advice?" he said. "Lose the baby fat. You're a little chubby. We don't like to have fat bitches working for The Store. Not a good public image."

He smiled, waved, then stepped behind the counter and disappeared into an office.

Fat bitches?

She was shocked, not sure how to respond, not sure even what she felt. It had been said so offhandedly, so casually, that she was not even sure she'd heard him correctly.

No. She knew she had.

It was an unprofessional thing to say. That was her first response. A person in a position of authority shouldn't talk like that, shouldn't use words like that.

Her second response was to walk over to Women's Clothing and find a mirror.

Baby fat.

Chubby.

Was she really overweight? He'd zeroed in on that, offered it without being asked, practically ordered her to lose weight if she wanted to keep this job, so obviously it wasn't just a matter of her being paranoid, wasn't just a matter of perception. She had a problem.

She felt more defiant than hurt, more angry than embarrassed, but then she saw herself in the mirror, and all of those self-preservation instincts fled.

He was right.

She turned to the left, turned to the right, looked at her backside over her shoulder.

She'd have to stop eating so much. Her mom would throw a fit, give her that anorexia/bulimia lecture, but she'd stick to her guns this time.

It had been confirmed by a third party.

She was fat.

"May I be of assistance?"

She turned to see a trim middle-aged woman in a Store uniform smiling helpfully at her.

"No," she said. "Thanks."

She turned, walked down the main aisle toward the entrance.

That was it. She'd skip lunch today.

Maybe dinner.

She walked through the front doors.

Maybe she'd cut out breakfasts entirely.

EIGHTEEN

1

The town was broke.

For the first time since Bill had begun attending meetings, the council chambers were full, all of the seats taken. Ben had really played this up in the paper, had even sent Trudy out to interview Tyler Calhoun, the president of the chamber of commerce, and Leslie Jones, their county supervisor, about what would happen to the town and the county if Juniper was forced to declare bankruptcy. The articles had obviously stimulated quite a bit of interest among the townspeople and had spurred many of them into attending tonight's meeting.

Bill sat in his usual seat, next to Ben, who was grinning hugely. "Quite a turnout, huh?"

"You're taking credit for it?"

"Of course."

"It is pretty impressive," Bill admitted.

"Don't get your hopes up yet. I've been eavesdropping on the conversations behind me, and we've got some staunch Store supporters back there. They're not all disgruntled citizens."

"But they can't be happy with the idea of bankruptcy."

The meeting was called to order before Ben could respond, and Bill sat silently along with everyone else as the rote procedural requirements were met and the council debated and voted on a host of trivial issues.

Discussion of the town budget was the last item on the agenda, and the mayor had obviously hoped that the audience would thin out by that time, that at least some of the people would go home, but although it was now

after nine, not a soul had left the council chambers and
the townspeople sat expectantly, waiting to hear about
the state of Juniper's finances.

The mayor glanced around at his colleagues on the
council, then put his hand over the microphone in front
of him and whispered something to Bill Reid before addressing the chamber. "As you are all probably aware,
the council received an updated report this week from
Juniper's financial manager, and the prognosis for the
new fiscal year is not good. In fact, it is worse than we'd
feared. In an effort to lure The Store to Juniper, we
offered tax and other incentives to the corporation that
we are now contractually obligated to deliver. Most of
these involve the widening of streets and general rede-
velopment of the area immediately adjacent to The
Store. And while this greatly improves our bond rating
and the long-term economic outlook of the town, the
net result is that in the short run, despite our belt-
tightening, we are continuing to experience a revenue
shortfall."

He cleared his throat. "Simply stated, we're on the
verge of bankruptcy."

A murmur passed through the audience.

"Now, it's not as bad as the papers have been saying,"
the mayor promised. He glanced over at Ben. "No
offense."

Ben grinned. "None taken."

"The situation is serious. I won't kid you about that.
But it's not the end of the world. In fact, we've been
studying the situation all week, and it may even be a
blessing in disguise. I think we have the opportunity now
to reinvent our local government, to make it leaner and
meaner—"

"It can't get much meaner!" someone called out.

The council members laughed along with everyone
else. "Now, now," the mayor said, chuckling. "We're all
in this together. Let's not start pointing fingers. As I
said, we have a real opportunity here to not just alleviate
this temporary fiscal crisis but to correct the bedrock
structural problems that are at the root of it."

"Hold on to your hats," Ben whispered.

"We have already begun looking at outsourcing or privatizing nonessential programs and services. Our agreement with The Store in regard to park maintenance has turned out to be not only extremely successful but cost-effective, and I think it should serve as a model for our future endeavors. We have already raised certain user fees and have cut back on work hours, eliminating all overtime pay, but we still have a large shortfall to make up, and these baby steps are not going to do it. The town's largest single expense is personnel: salaries and benefits. I propose that we downgrade our full-time clerical and support staff to part-time or half-time, thus eliminating health insurance and retirement expenses. We should also look at the possibility of contracting out more than just nonessential services."

There was an angry undercurrent to the whispered reactions of the audience.

"Good solution," Ben said. "Put even more people out of work."

"Amen," a woman behind him added.

The mayor frowned. "We will be opening the floor to public comment in a moment. First, do any of the council members wish to address this issue?"

"I think it's an unfortunate but necessary step," Bill Reid said. "Desperate times call for desperate measures."

"We should also examine the option of using volunteers for some jobs," Dick Wise stated. "We have a wealth of unpooled talent in this town that we could take advantage of. And volunteerism is an American tradition. Our country was founded on the idea of a volunteer government."

The other two council members said nothing. Hunter Palmyra shook his head.

"Any other comments?" the mayor asked. He looked around at his fellow council members. "Very well. We will now open this matter for public discussion."

From the crowded seats in the middle of the chambers emerged a pale, nondescript man who stood, stepped into the aisle, and walked toward the podium, carrying a sheaf of papers. He looked familiar, but it took Bill a second to place him.

The man from The Store. The shill who'd spoken against waiving the banner ordinance for local businesses.

Bill glanced over at Ben, who raised his eyebrows, began writing in his notebook.

"Please state your name and address," the mayor said.

The man leaned into the microphone. "Ralph Keyes," he said. "Representative of The Store, located at 111 Highway 180." He placed his papers on the podium, shuffled through them. He cleared his throat. "The Store is not unaware of the town's current financial situation," he said. "And we would *like* to alleviate some of the financial burden by declining the offered tax breaks and paying for the various capital improvements to the adjacent highway. Legally, however, we are not allowed to do so. The Store can assist the town in other ways, though. We can offer Juniper our own incentives. Counter incentives, if you will."

He searched through his stack of papers. "I have here a proposal put together by The Store and drafted by our lawyers. In it, we detail how the town can effect a smooth transition to a privatized police force. The Store is offering to finance and maintain this force, to continue providing the full range of police services, and to absorb all incurred costs."

Arguments erupted in the chambers.

Quite a few people in the audience, it appeared, were policemen, firemen, and other municipal employees. But there were also Store employees present, and the two sides began loudly debating the merits of the proposal. The town employees angrily denounced the idea of privatization, and the Store supporters jumped in with their defenses of the plan.

"Order in the chambers!" the mayor announced. "Order! If you have anything to say, you can come up here and state your piece. But you cannot disrupt a speaker who has been recognized by the council."

Keyes waited calmly by the podium, a slight smile on his lips.

"We cannot have a private police department!" Aaron Jefcoat shouted. "The police are here to uphold laws and serve the public, not follow the orders of some company!"

Forest Everson faced the council. "We're a police force, not a private militia!"

"There would be no change in the department's structure or manpower," the mayor said. "The only difference would be on paper. Rather than the taxpayers funding the police department, The Store would provide the monies necessary." He looked toward Keyes. "Isn't that right?"

The Store's representative nodded.

"That's the way it should be!" said an overweight man Bill did not recognize. "Why should all of us have to pay for the police when not all of us commit crimes?"

"Because the police protect everyone!" Forest replied. "Including you!"

"We have to pay for protection? Who are you guys, the mafia?"

"Order!" the mayor announced.

After several more minutes of arguing and back-and-forth verbal volleys, the mayor finally succeeded in getting the audience quieted down. Keyes handed copies of the drafted proposal to each of the council members, then took his seat.

No one attacked him.

No one spoke to him.

Bill looked back at The Store representative, and the pale man met his eyes. Smiled.

Bill quickly turned away.

A host of speakers came up to the podium, most of them denouncing the privatization proposal, a few championing it. Bill thought of going up to speak, but all of the points he wanted to make had already been made, and there wasn't really anything fresh he could bring to the discussion. He was glad, though, that so many people were speaking out. It was about time the citizens of Juniper started getting involved in this, started taking some responsibility for what was happening to their community.

He expected the issue to be carried over to the next meeting. It was an important topic, a major decision. But an hour later, the mayor read aloud the proposal Keyes had submitted and without any further discussion said, "I make a motion that we accept the proposal as is."

"I think we should take some time to study this proposal," Palmyra said. "We should at least let the finance department and the police chief have a look at it and see if they have anything to add or amend."

The mayor ignored him. "Do I hear a second?"

"I second the motion," Bill Reid said.

"Let's vote."

The resolution passed, four to one, Councilman Palmyra voting no.

Bill sat, stunned. That was it? One quick vote and The Store was now in charge of the town's police department? That didn't seem possible. It didn't seem right. It didn't seem legal.

The reaction of the audience was subdued. "Stunned silence," Bill would have called it, but he was not sure how much of it was shock and how much was fear. This was a historic moment they were witnessing here tonight. The dismantling of local government, elected government, the transference of the mantle of power from the people to The Store.

He was not surprised when Keyes again approached the podium.

"Ralph Keyes," he said. "Representative of The Store, 111 Highway 180." The pale man shuffled once more through his papers. "By our calculations, the town could save additional money by contracting out the fire department as well. I have here a proposal by which The Store agrees to finance the Juniper Fire Department and take over all administrative duties while leaving the existing prevention and suppression programs intact . . ."

The debate this time was not as loud, not as long, and for a brief moment after the discussion in the audience had ended and Keyes had once again taken his seat, Bill was afraid no one would get up and speak against the new proposal.

Then Doane stood, walked to the podium.

He had not known that the music store owner was at the meeting, but Bill felt a surge of pride as he watched the long-haired man stride up to the front of the chambers. Doane had no fear, was more than willing to speak his mind and state his opinion on any issue, and he was perfectly capable of giving the council what for. Bill smiled as Doane tilted the microphone up to accommodate his height and brushed a wisp of hair from his eyes. This was one of his people, and he had never felt as much a part of the town as he did at this moment.

"My name is Doane Kearns," he said loudly and forcefully. "My address is Lot 22, Creekside Acres—"

"Creekside Acres is an unincorporated area," the mayor interrupted. "You do not live in Juniper and therefore cannot comment on town matters."

"I work in Juniper. I own a business in Juniper."

"I'm sorry. The rules clearly state—"

"Fuck the rules," Doane said.

There was silence in the council chambers.

"I have something to say, and I'm going to say it. Mr. Mayor—" He pointed. "You, sir, are selling this town down the river."

"You're out of line, Mr. Kearns."

"In fact, I think you'd peddle your own mama's ass to AIDS-infected convicts if The Store told you to."

The mayor's face grew red and strained, but his voice remained calm, even, only a slight hint of anger seeping through. "Jim?" He motioned toward the lone uniformed policeman stationed next to the door. "Please escort Mr. Kearns from the council chambers."

Doane's microphone had been cut off, but he continued to speak, raising his voice so it could be heard above the growing buzz of the audience. "You're letting them *buy* our government. I thought this was supposed to be a democracy. I thought the people were supposed to decide how money should be raised, how it should be spent, what the function of the town government is. . . ."

The policeman reached Doane, reluctantly motioned for him to leave.

"I'm going!" Doane cried. "But remember this! I was

silenced! The Store and their puppets silenced me and kept me from participating in participatory democracy!"

"I'll remember it," Ben said quietly, writing in his notebook.

The policeman led Doane out of the council chambers.

The mayor and the council did not even ask if there were any more speakers. The mayor made his motion, they voted on the proposal without discussion, and the fire department was contracted out to The Store.

"Meeting adjourned," the mayor said.

Discussions in the parking lot afterward were loud and probably would have become violent had there not been policemen present. Forest Everson stopped a fight between a Store custodian and an off-duty firefighter. Ken Shilts stepped between two women before they came to blows.

Bill walked with Ben out to his car. "How can anyone support The Store after this?"

The editor shrugged. "The Store's our major employer."

"So?"

"It's the old A-Rising-Tide-Lifts-All-Boats theory."

"Analogies." Bill shook his head. "I hate analogies. What if I don't buy the idea that the economy is analogous to a tide or that people are analogous to boats? What if I don't think those are valid comparisons? Or what if I concede the tide but think that people are more like shacks on the water's edge that are going to be destroyed by a rising tide?"

"You can't use logic. Analogies aren't logical. They fool simpletons into thinking they're logical, but the only thing they're good for is transforming complex ideas into easily understandable scenarios for dimwits."

They paused next to Ben's car. "So what happens next?"

"I don't know," the editor admitted. "In a big city, the police and fire associations would be on this like white on rice. They'd be filing motions and legal briefs from now till Tuesday, trying to get the courts to prevent this from happening. In Juniper, our combined police and fire department is—what?—twenty men? Not enough power. Not enough leverage."

"But all the other employees—"

"People only care about police and fire. They're the PR gold. Everyone else is expendable. And my hunch is that since The Store is saying right now that they're all going to keep their jobs, no one's going to want to rock the boat. They'll all be too afraid of losing their positions."

"It's a fucking Catch-22."

"Yeah," Ben said. "It is." He held up his notebook. "But there's still the power of the press. 'The pen is mightier than the sword' and all that good crap."

"You really believe that?"

The editor shook his head. "No. But we have to have something to pin our hopes on."

Ginny was asleep when he got home, but Bill turned the light on in the bedroom as he undressed, waking her up.

"What happened?" she asked groggily.

He told her.

"The council has their heads so far up The Store's ass that their necks are being constricted by Newman King's sphincter and it's cutting off oxygen to their brains," he said, snuggling next to her.

"So what's next?" she asked.

He kissed her cheek, put an arm around her. "I don't know," he said. "I don't know."

2

Not a single customer stopped by the shop.

All day.

Doane read the Phoenix paper, swept the floor, inventoried a shipment of new CDs, stood behind the counter staring into space, sorted his mail, read a magazine, played his guitar.

He wasn't going to be able to last much longer.

He was losing the battle.

He walked to the front of the shop, looked up and

down Main Street, saw no cars, no pedestrians. Catty-corner across the road, next to McHenry's electronics store, The Quilting Bee had finally given up the ghost, old Laura moving all of her stuff out yesterday. Word had it that she'd still be selling out of her house, but Doane wasn't sure. She seemed pretty burnt-out and bitter these days, angry at her old customers for not coming through when she needed them, still owing a month's rent, and he wouldn't be surprised if she just packed it all in permanently.

He knew how she felt.

All of the downtown merchants did. Members of the public always paid lip service to the idea of the small businessman and America's great entrepreneurial spirit. They bemoaned the loss of the corner store and complained about the impersonality of large corporations, the excesses of big business. But when push came to shove, they chose convenience over service, picked price over quality. There was no loyalty, no real sense of community among people anymore.

Now the town was siding with The Store, with Newman King and his multimillion-dollar corporation.

And turning their backs on local businessmen.

Like himself.

Those were the breaks, he knew. And if he was merely a consumer, he might do exactly the same. But he couldn't help feeling resentful over an attitude that he saw as shortsighted and self-serving.

Consumer.

He had never realized before what an aggressive word it was. In his mind, it conjured up an image of an insatiable monster, eating everything in its path, its only purpose, its only reason for existence, to consume whatever it could.

He stared out the window and found himself thinking of that old Randy Newman song, "It's Money That Matters." It *was* money that mattered, wasn't it? He shook his head. Times had changed. Twenty years ago—a decade ago, even—a rich man spending millions of dollars to get himself elected to public office would have been looked upon with suspicion and distrust. But in 1992, the town had voted overwhelmingly for Ross Perot, either buying completely into his "common man" persona and believing that the billionaire was more like them than were either of his two opponents, or else respecting and admiring his enormous wealth.

Doane suspected the latter.

The priorities of this fucking country were screwed up.

Hell, after the council meeting the other night, an angry old woman had accosted him in the parking lot of town hall and called him an obstructionist.

"It's people like you," she spat, "who are trying to stop progress and ruin this town!"

By progress, he assumed she meant the extinction of his business and the demolition of downtown Juniper.

Because that's what was going to happen.

He moved away from the window, went back behind the counter, and spent the next hour looking at a music catalog, reading through a list of upcoming CDs that he wouldn't be able to order, before going into the back room and heating up a Cup O' Noodles for his dinner.

The hours stated on the sign in his window were 10:00 to 10:00, but it was obvious to Doane by eight-thirty that he might as well close up shop. No one had stopped in during the previous ten hours, and it was pretty damn unlikely that they were going to do so now. Especially with the street as dark as it was.

He glanced out the window. All of the other shops were closed, and his was the only light visible on Main. The town never had gotten around to installing streetlights, and while that hadn't made much difference in the past, particularly when Buy-and-Save had been open, it now made Main look like a ghost town.

Sighing, Doane locked and double-locked the back door, put the register money in the safe, and switched off all lights except the small security bulb directly over the counter. He exited the store through the front, locking the door behind him.

And turned to see a line of tall men standing between him and his car.

His heart lurched in his chest, and there was a sudden feeling of cold dread in the pit of his stomach. He'd been jumped once by a gang in Chicago, saved only by the stiletto in his pocket and the provident arrival of two patrol cars, and the trapped feeling of fear he'd experienced when that gang surrounded him returned in a rush. The figures in the narrow parking lot before him weren't exactly threatening, weren't moving or making any overt noises or gestures, but there was something intimidating in their uniform stance, something aggressive about the way they were blocking access to his car.

He tried to ignore them but couldn't, thought of walking around them to reach his vehicle but didn't want to show his fear. They were wearing what looked like black raincoats—long jackets made of shiny jet material that was deeper than the night, darker than the shadows, but somehow reflective of both. He didn't know why they were wearing raincoats—it wasn't raining, wasn't even overcast, and their choice of garb seemed not only odd but menacing.

He took a step toward his car.

The figures took a step toward him.

"Hey," he said. "What do you think you're doing?"

There was no response.

No word, no grunt, no chuckle.

Only silence.

"Get out of my fucking way," he ordered.

None of them moved.

He considered going back inside, calling the cops, but he'd have to find his key on the key ring and then unlock the door, and he did not want to let these creatures out of his sight for a second.

Creatures?

He noticed for the first time that he could not see the faces of the figures. They looked like indistinct white blurs in the darkness.

Too white to be human.

Now he was just being stupid.

The figures started to advance.

"What do you want?" he demanded. He tried to make his voice angry, but it came out frightened.

There was no response. The figures—nine of them, he saw now—kept walking silently toward him.

He wanted to run. The silence, the raincoats, the white faces, everything seemed crazy, spooky. But he didn't want them to win, didn't want to give them that satisfaction, and he held his ground, reached in the pocket of his pants for his jacknife.

The figures pulled out weapons.

Knives.

Fuck it. He turned, started to run. In the diffused light, the posters in his window looked eerie. Jim Morrison. Jimi Hendrix. Kurt Cobain. He realized for the first time that all of the musicians in the window were dead men.

He dashed as quickly as he could toward the side of the building. If he could make it around back, there was a deep ditch abutting the trees that wasn't visible in the dark. He could jump it before the rest of them rounded the building and they wouldn't notice it and would fall in and break their fucking necks.

If he was lucky.

He was already panting, almost out of breath.

Who the hell were these guys and what the hell did they want from him?

Doane reached the corner of the building just as the figures reached him. He rounded the curve and was promptly shoved into the wall, the abrasive brick scraping open the skin of his face. A knife sliced into his right side, and he screamed as he fell onto the dirt.

He was still screaming as he looked up into the circle of blurred white faces and dull silver blades that surrounded him.

The figures crouched down, their knives beginning their work, and as the blood began to spurt, he suddenly realized why they were wearing raincoats.

They were going to get wet.

NINETEEN

1

There was an employee meeting a half hour before The Store opened, and Shannon barely made it. She was the last downstairs, the last to arrive, and she saw the look of disapproval Mr. Lamb gave her as, huffing and puffing, she took her place in line.

Still, she felt good. She'd lost three pounds the past five days and had not even aroused her mom's suspicions. She'd decided to take Mr. Lamb's advice, pull the scarf-and-barf routine instead of skipping meals, and it was working like a charm.

If things continued at this pace, she'd reach her desired weight by the end of the month.

All of the employees on duty this morning stood straight, hands clasped behind them, feet spread shoulder-width apart in the official Store stance, as Mr. Lamb informed them that a new outlet was opening in Hawk's Ridge, Wyoming, today. This placed the number of Stores in the United States at three hundred and five. And three hundred and five, he said, was a very powerful and spiritually significant number.

Here in the Juniper store, he told them, there was going to be a one-day sale on baked goods in the Grocery department as well as a weeklong promotion on coolant and antifreeze in the Automotive department.

He finished his talk and then came the part Shannon hated.

The chanting.

Mr. Lamb stood before them, looking from one to the next, all the way down the line, then pointed to May Brown, in the middle. The line parted at that point, May and everyone to the left of her stepping to the opposite side of the concrete room, Mr. Lamb remaining in the center between them.

"Okay," he said. "Repeat after me: My loyalty is to The Store."

"My loyalty is to The Store!"

"Before my family, before my friends, comes The Store."

"Before my family, before my friends, comes The Store!"

Shannon could see her sister standing across from her, on the other side of the room, three people down. Sam was chanting for all she was worth, caught up in the moment like a Holy Roller at a revival meeting, and the sight of her sister getting so caught up in all this made her a little uneasy. Shannon herself did not enjoy chanting, had her parents' disdain for any type of groupthink, and the fact that Sam so obviously responded to this coerced excitement, this forced camaraderie, made her uncomfortable.

They ended with the traditional "Long live The Store!" and then they ascended to the floor in groups of five to prepare for this morning's opening.

It happened just before noon.

They caught her.

In a way, it was a relief. She'd spent every hour that she'd worked on the floor worrying about whether her mom or dad would walk in and see her. It hadn't been so bad when she was in the stockroom or one of the non–public areas, but ever since her first day of work she'd been living with a dread born of certainty that her parents would find out that she'd gotten a job at The Store rather than George's.

Luckily, Sam was with her when it happened. Her sister had walked over to borrow a quarter for the Coke machine in the break room, and Shannon was just starting to dig through her purse for coins when she looked up and saw her parents striding purposefully up the aisle toward her.

All traces of saliva instantly evaporated from her mouth.

Her parents stopped in front of her register. Her dad's lips were flattened into a grim straight line. "You lied to us, Shannon."

She didn't know what to say, didn't know what to do. Her parents had never hit her, had seldom even punished her, but she stood in fear of them now, afraid to face them. Why had she done such a stupid thing? What could have possibly possessed her? She stared down at her hands, which were not shaking only because they were pressed flat against the register counter.

"Didn't we talk about this?" her dad said.

She looked up, nodded meekly, dumbly.

He met her eyes, held her gaze. "I want you to quit." He glanced over at her mom, who nodded. "We both want you to quit."

"She doesn't have to," Sam said.

"I say she does."

"Why don't you ask her what *she* says?"

Shannon stared again at her hands. She didn't want to stop working, but she didn't want to hurt her parents, either, and she could not reconcile the two. It was impossible. This was what it meant to grow up, she supposed, breaking away from your parents.

Before my family, before my friends, comes The Store.

"I like working here," she ventured.

This time her mom spoke up. "I don't like it," she said. "It's not a healthy place to work."

"It's evil," her dad said simply.

Shannon glanced around in embarrassment, making sure no one else had caught this exchange. "Jeez, Dad," she whispered. "Tone it down. You sound like a loony."

"Evil?" Sam laughed. "This is a discount store, not the First Church of Satan."

"You shouldn't be working here, either."

"Give me a break."

Shannon glanced uneasily from her father to her sister, not sure what to make of this exchange. It was Sam's militancy that was so surprising. She seemed to be taking all of this personally, and while Shannon was grateful for the support, she wanted to tell her sister to calm down, not take it so seriously. It was only a part-time job. If she had to, she'd find another one.

The behavior seemed out of character for Sam, Shannon thought, but now that she considered it, Sam had been acting a little odd ever since she'd started working for The Store. She'd always been such a goody-goody, never getting in trouble, never doing anything wrong, and now it seemed as though she was bound and determined to break that image.

The trouble was, she didn't seem happy about it. It didn't seem like something she wanted to do. It seemed like something she was *compelled* to do.

Now she was starting to think like her parents.

Before my family, before my friends, comes The Store.

"Look," she said, "I'm scheduled to work until five, and I'm working until five. Ground me, spank me, punish me, whatever. But I'm not going home until my shift's over. After that, we can talk about all this." She faced her father. "Okay?"

To her surprise, her parents agreed—although it was more her mom's doing than her dad's. He still seemed like he wanted to argue, wanted her to take off her uniform and follow him out of the store then and there, but he agreed to wait until tonight to discuss the situation, and he allowed himself to be led out of the building.

Shannon turned toward her sister. "Thanks," she said. "You really saved me."

"Yeah," Sam said. "Now how about my quarter?"

2

They confronted Shannon again that night.

She called shortly before five, explaining that the girl who was supposed to work the five-to-nine shift in her department had called in sick and that she had to sub for her. Bill was playing online chess with Street when she and Samantha arrived home, and by the time he signed off, got out of his chair, and made his way down the hallway to the living room, both girls were safely ensconced in the two bathrooms, bathing.

"Give them a little time," Ginny suggested. "Don't pounce on them the second they walk through the door."

"They've had all afternoon. We've put this off long enough. It's family discussion time."

Shannon went straight into her bedroom after her bath, closing the door behind her. They waited, gave her enough time to get dressed, but she did not come out again, and together they knocked on her door, then opened it.

She was in bed, lights off, pretending to sleep.

Bill flipped on the light switch.

Shannon pulled the covers over her head. "I'm tired," she complained.

"I don't care," Bill told her. "You're going to talk about this."

Sighing, she pulled the covers down, sat up. "What?"

"What do you mean, 'What?' You said you wanted to get a job this summer, and I said fine. The only stipulation was that you could not get a job at The Store. So what did you do? You got a job at The Store and lied to me about it."

"I didn't lie—"

"You told me that you were working at George's. That's not a lie?"

Shannon was silent.

"Why did you lie?" Ginny prodded.

She shrugged. "I don't know."

"You're not working at The Store anymore," Bill told her.

Shannon did not respond.

"I want you to quit. Tomorrow."

"I can't," she said quietly.

"You're going to."

"No, she's not."

Bill turned around to see Samantha standing in the bedroom doorway, legs spread, hands on hips, wearing only a white see-through negligee. "She's made a commitment. She's responsible for keeping it."

Bill tried not to stare at his daughter. His first instinct was to tell her to put some clothes on, but he didn't want her to know that he'd noticed. Her breasts and pubic hair were clearly visible through the sheer material, and he felt embarrassed. He was not aroused, but he could not help seeing her in a sexual light, and he did not know what to say or how to react.

Ginny was not so circumspect. "What the hell are you wearing?" she demanded.

"A nightie," Sam said defensively.

"You put on some pajamas. I will not have you wearing something like that in my house."

"I bought it with my own money."

"At The Store?" Bill said.

"I got a fifteen percent employee discount."

"You wear pajamas," Ginny told her. "Or you put on a bathrobe."

Bill turned back toward Shannon. "You're quitting."

"Mr. Lamb won't let her quit," Sam said.

"Who's Mr. Lamb?"

"The personnel manager," Shannon said.

"He won't let her quit," Sam repeated.

He won't let her quit.

Bill felt a small shiver of fear pass through him, but he pushed it away, would not let it gain a foothold.

"I'll talk to this Mr. Lamb," he said. "And I'm going to tell him that neither of you are working for The Store anymore."

He was at The Store when it opened the next morning.

Ginny had wanted to come, but he thought it would probably be better if he went alone and had a man-to-man talk with the personnel manager. After speaking with the girl behind the Customer Service desk, he learned that Mr. Lamb was not in yet, so he wandered around the store for a while while he waited.

He'd been avoiding The Store lately. Not staying away from it entirely, but only going when there was something specific he needed to buy. The aimless browsing and impulse shopping of the first few weeks was long gone, and now he came here only when necessary.

It had been over a month since he'd just wandered through The Store, and as he walked down the crowded aisles of the toy department, he saw products that made his blood run cold. Klicker-Klackers. Sooper Stuff. Balloon Makeums. Toys that were supposed to have been taken off the shelves decades ago. Toys that had been banned for sale to children in the United States.

Dangerous toys.

On a hunch, he hurried quickly through the rest of the store. In Infants, there were no fire-resistant or flame-retardant baby pajamas available. In Hardware, there were no warnings on packages of toxic chemicals. In Pharmacy, there were no medicines with childproof caps. In the Grocery department, all the health food seemed to have been removed from the shelves. There were no fat-free or cholesterol-free items. There was a sale on bacon and lard.

He walked down the row to the left of the soaps and detergents. Weren't the shampoos supposed to be here? He looked at the products on the shelf in front of him: embalming fluid, suture thread.

"May I help you, sir?"

He nearly jumped at the sound of the voice, turning to see a young director smiling mockingly at him.

"Where's the shampoo?" Bill asked.

"Right over here, sir." The smirking kid led him around the corner and down the next aisle, and there were the normal products: shampoo, mousse, conditioner, Grecian Formula.

"Next time, please ask for help," the young man said. "Sometimes it's dangerous if you try to do things on your own."

Dangerous?

He stared at the back of the green uniform as the young man strode away from him. The more he learned about The Store, the less he liked it. He walked back to the Customer Service counter to see if Mr. Lamb was in yet.

He was.

The personnel manager was a slimy, unctuous man who fit the cinematic stereotype of a used-car dealer to a T. Bill hated him on sight. He remained seated as Bill entered his office, smiling insincerely and motioning for Bill to take a seat across the desk from him. "What can I do for you, Mr. Davis?"

"I do not want my daughters working for The Store."

"And your daughters are?"

"Samantha and Shannon Davis."

"Ah, the Davis sisters." Mr. Lamb's smile grew broader in a sly way that Bill did not like.

"My daughters are no longer working for The Store."

Mr. Lamb spread his hands apologetically. "I'd like to help you, Mr. Davis. I really would. But both of your daughters are excellent employees and we have no cause to let them go. We are prohibited by company policy from terminating employees without justification."

"I'm not *asking* you to fire them. I'm *telling* you that they will no longer be working here."

"I'm afraid they will."

"No. They won't."

The personnel manager laughed. "Mr. Davis, this isn't nursery school. You didn't enroll your daughters here, and you cannot withdraw them whenever the whim suits you. Both Samantha and Shannon have an employment contract with The Store, and they are legally bound by the strictures of that contract."

"I'm their father. I know nothing about this so-called contract, and I did not give my consent."

"I understand that, Mr. Davis. But Samantha is eighteen. She is legally an adult. Shannon is not yet a legal adult, but she is protected under the umbrella of The Store from any attempt to infringe on her rights or civil liberties, whether that be from customers, coworkers, or her family."

Bill stood. "This is bullshit."

Mr. Lamb's eyes narrowed, grew hard. "No, Mr. Davis. It is business."

"I want to talk to the manager."

"I'm afraid that authority for all personnel-related matters rests with me."

"I still want to talk to someone above you."

"That won't be possible."

"And why not?"

"Our store manager has been transferred to another location and a replacement has not yet been assigned. Until we get a new manager, I am in charge of the day-to-day operation of this Store."

"Then I want to talk to your district manager."

"Very well." Mr. Lamb opened the top right drawer of his desk and withdrew a card. "This is Mr. Smith's business card. His telephone and fax numbers are listed on there." He paused. "But if you think that you can somehow bully or cajole Mr. Smith into releasing either Samantha or Shannon from their employment contracts, you are sadly mistaken. Like myself, Mr. Smith does not make the rules, he follows them. What I have stated to you is not my own personal decision. It is corporate policy." He smiled disingenuously. "If it was up to me, of course, I would not hesitate to release them from their obligations."

"Bullshit," Bill repeated. He started toward the door. "You'll hear from my lawyers. My daughters are not working here and that is that."

"That is *not* that, Mr. Davis." The personnel manager's voice was authoritative, edged with steel, and Bill stopped, turned around. "The contract we have with your daughters is legally binding."

"A court will determine that."

"A court *has* determined that. Ventura versus The Store, Inc. The case went all the way to the Supreme Court in 1994. We won in a five-two ruling." Mr. Lamb fixed him with a cold stare. "I can provide you with documentation if you wish."

"Yes," Bill said. "I wish." He believed Mr. Lamb, was sure the personnel manager was telling the truth, but he still wanted to cause that little prick as much inconvenience as possible, even if it only meant making him hunt up some Xeroxed copies of a legal brief.

Mr. Lamb opened another drawer, withdrew a sheaf of stapled pages, handed them across the desk.

Bill walked over, took them.

"Local law enforcement authorities have always been willing to uphold the law," the personnel manager said. "Simply stated, the police could make your daughters work. I don't think either of us want that, now, do we?"

Bill did not answer. If Juniper had had an autonomous police force, he would have told the man to fuck himself. But the fact was that with the police department privatized and The Store controlling the purse strings, the police probably would do whatever the hell The Store ordered them to do.

"I think our meeting is done," Mr. Lamb said, smiling again. "Thank you for taking the time to stop by. Have a nice day."

Bill looked it up online when he got home: Ventura versus The Store, Inc.

It had gone down exactly the way Lamb said it had.

He performed an online search for all court cases in which The Store was either plaintiff or defendant and came up with a whopping six hundred and fifty-four suits that had gone to trial.

No wonder the country's legal system was so backed up. The Store was hogging half of the available court time.

He did not have the time right now to read the details of each suit, so he simply called up a list of the cases that The Store had won.

The company had triumphed in all six hundred and fifty-four.

An asterisk next to the case numbers indicated that twelve others besides Ventura had gone all the way to the Supreme Court.

How could he hope to fight something like that? He exited Freelink, turned off his PC, and walked dejectedly out to the kitchen. Shannon was lying on the living room carpet, watching a talk show. She looked up. "Do I still have a job?" she asked meekly.

Bill nodded silently, not trusting himself to answer without going on the attack.

"Told you so," Sam said from the hallway entrance.

He looked over at her, wanting to hit her, wanting to slap her.

She smiled.

TWENTY

1

An hour before the council meeting, Bill and Ben stopped by Street's house.

They did not play chess this time, merely drank beer.

According to Street, Doane was MIA, hadn't been seen for nearly a week. And Kirby Allen, over at the Paperback Trader, was going to close his doors at the end of the month. Apparently, no one was interested in buying or trading used books anymore when they could get new books so cheaply at The Store.

"Whole fucking downtown's disappearing," he said.

"What about Doane?" Bill asked. "What do you make of that? It's not like him to just . . . vanish."

"Like Jed McGill?" Ben said softly.

All three of them were silent, the only sound the chirping of crickets somewhere outside.

Street started to say something, cleared his throat, then loudly slurped his beer, mumbling something incoherent.

"You think Doane's dead?" Bill asked.

Ben shrugged. "You think Jed's dead?"

"I don't know."

"What are we talking about here?" Street shook his head, slammed his beer can down on the coffee table. "You honestly think that in the United States of America, in the 1990s, workers at a discount store killed a grocer and a record shop owner so they could make a few more bucks?"

"That doesn't sound as implausible as you probably thought it would," Ben said.

"No," Street admitted. "It doesn't."

Bill turned toward him. "Have you been approached at all? Has anyone from The Store pressured you to quit or tried to put you out of business?"

"No."

"Not even any hints?"

"Maybe I'm just too dumb to get them."

"Your place might burn down," Ben said. "Like Richardson's."

"Thanks for the encouraging words."

They were quiet again.

"You realize what's happening?" Ben said finally.

"What?"

"For all intents and purposes, there's only one place to shop anymore. And I don't know if you've noticed, but our choices in products have been considerably narrowed since The Store's early days."

"I've noticed," Bill admitted.

"I call it corporate fascism." Ben stared into his beer can. "Juniper's turning into a company town, almost completely dependent on The Store, not only for food and merchandise, but jobs. We could shop somewhere else, we could drive to the Valley or Flagstaff or Prescott, but we're lazy and we don't. So we're forced to buy whatever The Store offers. The Store determines how we eat, how we dress, what we read, what we listen to, almost every aspect of our lives."

Bill shook his head. "It's not quite that bad."

"Isn't it?"

Street snorted. " 'Corporate fascism'? The Store's more like a corporate vampire. It's sucking this town dry and growing stronger from it."

Bill sighed. "So what are we going to do?"

Ben glanced at his watch, finished off his beer. "We're going to go to the council meeting." He turned toward Street. "You coming?"

Street nodded. "Yeah. Count me in."

"No," Bill said, "I mean what are we going to do about The Store?"

"What can we do?" Ben asked.

Street smiled wryly. "Pray?"

"Not funny," Bill said. "Not funny at all."

*   *   *

The council meeting was once again sparsely attended and, until the end, routine and uneventful. Then Hunter Palmyra, in a low, subdued delivery that was totally unlike his usual voice, made a motion to add an item to the agenda.

"I would like to make a motion that we add the following agenda item under 'new business,'" Palmyra said. He cleared his throat and read from a paper in his hand. "'The council hereby revokes Resolution 84-C, which grants an open-ended license to participating food growers to enable them to sell their goods at a so-called farmer's market. It has been found that said farmer's market violates county and local health regulations in regard to the sale of foodstuffs and does not legally constitute a business under Juniper definitions because of the absence of a single proprietor.'" Palmyra looked up at the mayor, nodded.

The councilman was unable to look toward the audience, Bill noticed. He was too embarrassed and ashamed to face the public.

"They can't get rid of the farmer's market," Street said, shocked.

"They can and they will," Ben told him.

"We shop there, too," Bill said. "That's where Ginny buys most of our vegetables. They can't expect us to buy everything at The Store. Their produce is even worse than Buy-and-Save's was."

The council voted to add the item to the agenda.

"They're trying to legislate away competition," Street said. "They're trying to outlaw small businesses in this town." He looked from Ben to Bill. "I'm going to go up there and give those assholes a piece of my mind."

"All right," the mayor said. "I don't think we need any discussion on this matter. Let's vote. A motion has been made to revoke the license for the so-called farmer's market. Do I hear a second?"

"Seconded."

Street stood. "Just a minute!" he called out.

The mayor faced him. "Sit down," he said coldly, "or I will have you ejected from these proceedings."

"There's supposed to be a chance for public comment."

"It was determined that there was no public comment," the mayor said. "You would know that if you had paid attention." He glanced to his left and right at his fellow council members. "Let's put it to a vote. In favor?"

All hands went up.

"Opposed?"

None.

"It is hereby proclaimed that local growers cannot sell their fruits and vegetables directly to the public at a farmer's market."

"I would like to add an addendum," Dick Wise announced.

The mayor nodded. "Yes?"

"Seeing as how this might create a financial hardship for some of our farmers and ranchers, I propose that we allow them to sell their products to a legitimately licensed business." He smiled broadly. "That way, the public could still have access to their delicious fruits and vegetables and they could continue to make a living."

"Seconded," Palmyra said.

They voted again, once more without allowing public comment.

The addendum passed.

"Very well," the mayor said. "It is hereby proclaimed that local growers cannot sell their fruits and vegetables directly to the public, but that they may sell their goods to The Store." He looked directly at Street, smiled mockingly. "I trust that makes us all happy."

"You trust wrong, asshole."

The smile remained on the mayor's face as he motioned for the policeman standing next to the door.

Street stood voluntarily. "I'm going," he said. "I don't want to spend another fucking second in this hypocrites' hideout."

The mayor turned toward Bill. "Friend of yours?" he asked.

"As a matter of fact," Bill said proudly, "he is."

The meeting ended a few minutes later, and they

walked outside to find Street pacing the parking lot, fuming. "Bastards," he said.

Ben grinned. "Welcome to the big, wide, wonderful world of local government."

"This can't be real," Street said. "They can't get rid of the farmer's market just like that, can they? By a quick vote?"

Ben snorted. "Oh, it's real, all right. And, yes, they can. They just did."

"People won't put up with it."

Ben put a condescending hand on his shoulder. "Yes, they will. You want to know what'll happen? I'll write about it in the paper and everyone'll read about it and shake their heads and say what a shame it is, and then they'll go back to eating their cornflakes."

Street was silent.

"He's right," Bill said. "I've seen it happen before."

"I say we wait for those fuckers. Wait for them to come out of those council chambers and beat the shit out of them right here in the parking lot. Teach 'em a lesson."

"I wouldn't advise that."

They turned to see a uniformed policeman standing behind them.

The cop motioned toward Street's car. "I suggest you all get out of here now and head on home. Show's over."

"What if we don't want to go?" Street asked belligerently.

"Then I'll cite you for loitering and haul your asses inside that building there and let you spend the night in jail. How does that grab you?"

"It doesn't," Ben said. He grabbed Street by the arm. "Come on. Let's go."

"All right," Street said, pulling out of the editor's grasp. He took out his keys and started toward the car. "All right."

The policeman smiled at them as they walked. "You all have a nice night now, you hear?"

None of them answered, and they could still hear the cop's mocking laughter as they got into the car and drove away.

2

Bill spent the morning working on documentation, but he was still restless, even after taking a break for lunch, and he decided to take a walk into town. He asked Ginny to go with him, but she was busy planting flowers on the side of the house, so he went alone.

Main Street was dead—no cars, no pedestrians—and as he walked along the dirty sidewalk toward the electronics store, he could not help thinking that if the town council had been made up primarily of merchants instead of real estate and construction people, the situation would be completely different.

A couple of merchants *had* run last time, he thought, but he was pretty sure he'd voted against them.

Why hadn't he gotten involved in politics earlier?

He reached the electronics store, walked in. Street was playing Tetris on a green-screened Gameboy, leaning against the register, facing the door. There were no customers, and Street looked up hopefully as Bill entered the shop. "Oh, it's you," he said, disappointed.

"Fooled you. You thought I was a real customer, didn't you?"

"Don't rub it in." Street finished his game, then put down the device. "On your way to the farmer's market?" he asked.

"Very funny."

"Just came down for a little shopping spree in beautiful downtown Juniper, then, huh?"

Bill walked around the counter, pulled out a folding chair, sat down. "Whatever happened to that recall effort?" he asked. "Weren't you guys going to get together and start circulating petitions?"

"Last I heard."

"What happened?"

"I don't know. Nothing ever came of it. Pete was supposed to be in charge, but then he decided to sell his place, and it all sort of fell apart."

"Maybe we should get it going again."

"I was thinking the same thing," Street admitted.

Street brought out a pen and notepad from the back room, and Bill began writing the text of a petition to recall the mayor and all four council members. They were on the second draft when the phone rang. Street went to answer it. "Hello? . . . It's Ben!" he announced.

Bill stopped writing.

"Bill's here . . . Yeah . . . Okay . . . See you in a minute." He hung up the receiver, looked at Bill with raised eyebrows. "He's coming right over. Important news, he says. Wouldn't tell me over the phone."

Bill stood, walked to the door, saw Ben hurrying across the street. "It must be important."

"Big news," Ben said, walking up.

"What is it?"

"The mayor's resigned."

Bill was stunned. He glanced over at Street, who shook his head in disbelief. "You're serious?"

Ben nodded. "The council, too. All of them."

"*All* of them?"

"What happened?" Street asked.

"No one knows. Or, rather, no one's talking. But it's effective immediately. We're without a local government at the moment." He chuckled. "Not that I'm complaining."

"So, is there going to be a special election?"

"Of course. But candidates have to file, the logistics have to be worked out. It'll be at least a month or so."

"Weird coincidence," Street said. "We were just working on a recall petition."

"Well, you won't need that puppy anymore. They're gone, they're out, they're history."

"I don't understand why they'd resign," Bill said. "Especially all of them at once."

"It's a strange world."

"You think pressure was put on them?"

"By The Store?"

"Who else?"

Ben thought for a moment. "I'd say that's a good possibility."

"But why? The council was a rubber stamp for everything The Store wanted."

"Maybe they didn't go far enough," Street suggested. "Maybe The Store wanted them to do even more."

It was a scary thought, and they were all silent, thinking about it.

"You think they'll run their own people?" Street asked.

"Probably," Ben said. "But this gives us a chance we didn't have before. We can run *our* own people. And the paper can get behind candidates who'll put the town's interests before those of The Store. I think we have a chance here to put this place back on track."

"We might have the paper," Bill said. "But they have the radio station."

"True enough. But I still think we have a fighting chance."

"They have more money."

"Money isn't everything."

"Isn't it?"

"Remember those television commercials in the seventies? Those beautiful scenes of wildlife and natural beauty that were sponsored by oil companies? We were supposed to think that the oil companies were not hurting the environment, but helping it. Nature was getting itself into all sorts of trouble and the oil companies were fixing it and cleaning it up. They spent millions of dollars on that ad campaign because they not only wanted us to buy their products, they wanted us to love them." He paused. "Did anyone buy into that crap? After all that money and propaganda and airtime, is there a human being in this country who thinks that drilling for oil is good for the environment?"

"And you think the same thing applies here?"

"Why not?"

"I guess you're not as cynical as you pretend."

Ben smiled. "It's all a facade. Underneath this gruff exterior, I'm Pollyanna."

Bill stared out the doorway. "The Store still has a lot of supporters, though. It did bring jobs to Juniper."

"And it took away just as many."

A pickup truck sped by, a dented red Ford filled with teenagers that burnt rubber as it zoomed toward Granite. "Fuck The Store!" a boy screamed at the top of his lungs, middle finger held high in the air.

Bill smiled. He turned back toward Ben. "Maybe you're right," he said.

He should've finished the documentation a week ago, but he'd been stretching it out. Ordinarily, he liked to complete his assignments as quickly as possible, but this time he intended to wait until his actual deadline.

He didn't want to help The Store any more than he had to.

Bill closed his eyes, leaned back in his chair. He had one humongous headache. He didn't know if he was actually getting sick or if it was simply stress, but for the past hour, he'd been concentrating more on the thumping in his head than on the work in front of him.

It was getting dark. The ponderosas outside his window had long since coalesced into a single jaggedly irregular wall of blackness, and the text on his screen had grown increasingly brighter as light drained out of the world around it. From the kitchen, he could hear Ginny taking plates out of the cupboard, and beyond that, the sound of the nightly news from the television in the living room.

He saved his afternoon's work on a diskette and was about to turn off his PC when the phone rang. The sharp sound of the ring intensified the pain in his forehead, and he closed his eyes against the noise, waiting for Ginny to answer the phone, hoping it wasn't for him.

"Bill!" she called a beat later.

Damn. He picked up the phone on his desk. "Hello?"

"It's me," Ben said.

"Yeah?"

"The mayor and the council. They're dead," Ben said. "All of them." There was a pause, and Bill could hear him exhale. "I've never seen anything like it."

"Back up. Where are you? What happened? Were they killed?"

"Suicide. I'm on the cell phone, and I'm looking at

them right now. You've got to come out here. You've gotta see this."

"Where are you?" Bill asked, though he was afraid he knew the answer.

"The parking lot of The Store," Ben said. "Better hurry. The ambulance just arrived."

He didn't want to go. Or part of him didn't. But another part of him had to see what had happened, and he grabbed his wallet and keys from the bedroom and told Ginny he was going out, he'd be back in a half hour or so.

"Where are you going?" she asked. "It's almost time to eat."

He didn't answer but dashed out the door, hopped in the Jeep, and took off.

He was at The Store five minutes later, and he sped across the parking lot toward the flashing blue and red police lights until he was stopped by a cop putting up yellow crime scene ribbon to cordon off the area.

Bill parked the Jeep, jumped out, and was almost stopped again by the same policeman, but Ben came to his rescue. "That's my reporter!" the editor yelled. "He's with me!"

The cop nodded, waved him through, and Bill followed his friend across the asphalt, between the ambulance and police cars.

To where the council lay.

He was not sure what he'd expected, but it had not been this. There was no blood, no guns, no weapons of any kind, only the nude bodies of the mayor and the other council members, lying faceup in a circle, holding hands. Their eyes were all open, staring upward, reflecting the light of the parking lot streetlamps.

For the first time in a long while, he thought about the deer, the animals, the transient.

He looked toward Ben. "Suicide?"

The editor shrugged. "What else could it be? Pills, I figure. Poison. They won't know for sure until they do the autopsies, though."

Bill shook his head. "I don't think it was pills. I don't think it was poison."

"Then what was it?"

He shivered. "I don't know."

Ben was silent for a moment. "It was suicide, though. This had to be intentional. Right?"

Bill looked at him. "I don't know."

On *20/20* that night, there was a report on Newman King and his growing Store empire. There were token references to the rash of shootings that had been plaguing The Store for the past year, but the report was basically a fluff piece and King was portrayed not as a whacked-out loon but as a down-to-earth self-made millionaire.

Or billionaire.

The exact numbers could not be substantiated.

King had not agreed to a sit-down interview, but he did allow *20/20's* cameras to follow him around on a "typical workday," and the reporter went with the CEO to a series of meetings in the black tower, a surprise inspection of a Store in Bottlebrush, Texas, a tour of a factory that was making generic Store products, and a negotiating session with a textile manufacturer.

Finally, at the end of the day, King went home, but the camera was not allowed to follow him to his house, and the last shot of the report was of King getting into a chauffeur-driven limousine in front of the black tower.

He waved good-bye as he smiled folksily at the camera. "God bless America," he said.

TWENTY-ONE

1

Doreen Hastings closed her eyes as she held Merilee to her breast. The baby suckled happily, and Doreen thought how different this felt than when Clete did it. Of course, that was a sex thing and this wasn't, but the physical act was basically the same. Now, however, there was milk flowing through her nipple, feeding her child, and somehow that bond made the entire act more intimate, more satisfying, more fulfilling. Sex seemed juvenile compared to this, like child's play, and she understood that her relationship with Clete, as great as it was, could never be as important to her or as emotionally gratifying as her relationship with this baby.

She would never be as close to Clete as she was to Merilee.

She opened her eyes. It was late, after midnight, and the hospital room was dark. Even the corridor outside was dark, the fluorescent lights dimmed so as not to disturb sleeping patients. She heard no sound, but neither was there silence. Instead, there was white noise, the hum of the hospital's twenty-four-hour activity: machines, nurses, patients, doctors.

She closed her eyes again, smiling as Merilee's little fingers pressed instinctively against the fatty flesh of her breast.

"Mrs. Hastings," a deep-voiced man said. "Room 120."

Doreen opened her eyes and looked toward the doorway.

Her heart lurched in her chest.

Outside, in the corridor, were five men dressed entirely in black, pale men who stared at her with blank, expressionless faces.

They were accompanied by Mr. Walker from The Store.

Mr. Walker smiled at her and strode into her room, flipping the light switch next to the door. The lights in the ceiling blinked on, but they did not appreciably illuminate the figures who followed the Customer Service manager toward her bed. Their garb was still blacker than black, their skin as pale as if they'd been dusted with flour. Mr. Walker himself continued to smile at her, but there was something in that smile that caused her to press the button on the side of her bed and call for the nurse.

She held Merilee tighter.

"Is that your new baby?" the Customer Service manager asked. He stopped next to her bed as the black-clad men kept circling around.

She continued to frantically press the call button with one hand while she clasped Merilee with the other.

Mr. Walker's fingers, strong and cold, pried hers away from the button. "No one's coming," he said. "The hospital knows why we're here."

"Why?" She looked around the ring of faces surrounding her bed, saw only blank expressions on snow-colored skin.

"Several months ago, you and your husband bought a microwave from The Store using our very generous layaway plan. You took possession of the microwave, but you did not make the last two monthly payments."

Her voice was high, squeaky. "Clete lost his job! We were having the baby—"

"We are taking the baby."

Her heart was pounding as though it was about to burst. It suddenly seemed impossible to breathe.

"The baby is ours."

She was finally able to suck in air. "No," she got out.

"Yes," Mr. Walker said.

"No!" She screamed it, screamed again: "No!"

"It was part of your agreement. You signed it." He withdrew from behind his back a copy of the layaway plan and pointed to a paragraph of fine print buried in the middle of the page. " 'In the event that payment is not made on time,' " he read, " 'the signee's first-born child will be accepted by The Store as payment of the unpaid portion of—' "

"No!" She struggled, tried to sit up, but the men in black were suddenly holding her arms, pressing down on her legs, restraining her from their positions surrounding the bed.

Mr. Walker reached for Merilee, took her.

"Help!" Doreen screamed, struggling against the restraining hands. "They're stealing my baby! They're kidnapping my baby! Nurse! Nurse!"

"It's a legally binding agreement," Mr. Walker said. "There's nothing any nurse can do about it." He passed the baby to one of the pale men.

"Clete!" she cried. Tears of anger and frustration were pooling in her eyes, overflowing onto her face, blurring her vision. "Don't let them take our baby!" She jerked her head toward the door as the men holding Merilee began walking away. Through her tears, she thought she saw white-robed doctors and nurses standing in the corridor, watching silently. "Take the microwave back!" she said. There was too much saliva in her mouth. She was spitting, her words slurring. "We don't want it! Take it back!"

"You should have made your payments."

"We'll send you the money! With interest! How much do you want?"

"We got what we want," Mr. Walker said. He nodded, motioned with his hand, and a doctor stepped in from the corridor. "She's hysterical," he told the doctor. "Sedate her."

"No!" Doreen cried, but she felt the sharp prick of a needle in her right upper arm, and her strength immediately began draining away.

The doctor stepped back, disappeared.

Her eyes were already closing, and she felt the pressure of the hands removed from her body. With her last bit of strength, she opened her eyes again, saw a blurry Mr. Walker follow the dark figures out of her room.

"Merilee!" she wanted to call, but she did not even have the strength to say her baby's name.

And then she was out.

2

Shannon walked up and down the aisles of the Garden department, intending to straighten the shelves before The Store opened. As always, many of the shelves were in disarray. She'd worked last night until closing and had straightened the mess before clocking out, but the cleaning people or someone must have come by afterward and moved things.

That really ticked her off.

She continued walking, then stopped. The cleaning people hadn't even done a decent job on the floors. There was a reddish brown splotch on the white tile next to the Italian flowerpots that hadn't been wiped up. It looked like . . .

Blood?

She frowned, bent down. The spot hadn't been there last night. She was positive of it. She'd been unwrapping a mint as she'd patrolled this aisle before closing, and the mint had slipped out of her fingers and fallen to the floor. She'd picked it up pretty close to where the spot was now, and she'd seen only clean white tile. It was possible, of course, that she hadn't seen the spot—*the blood*—because she hadn't been looking for it, but it was pretty noticeable, and if she saw it now, she should've seen it then.

It's built with blood.

She stood and walked quickly down the row to the fertilizers at the end, then up the seed aisle back toward the register. Even in the daytime, even with the lights on, even with other people in The Store, she could still spook herself back here.

She wondered what it would be like in this windowless corner of The Store after dark. When the lights were off. When the building was empty.

She shivered, sped back to the safety of the register.

She wasn't the only one who had questions about what went on in here after hours. Holly had told her yesterday that she'd heard that Jane in Lingerie had accidentally left her purse in her employee locker overnight and that when she'd come in the next morning the two tampons she kept in her purse in case of an emergency had been taken out of their wrappers and were soaked with blood.

Blood.

She'd also overheard two women talking in the break room once, one telling the other that she'd been the last employee to leave The Store the previous night and that she'd heard the sound of muffled screams coming from downstairs, through the closed elevator doors.

And, of course, there were the stories about the Night Managers.

The Night Managers.

It was a subject that was not discussed among the employees. Not in the open, at least. But she'd heard whispers, hints, rumors of the Night Managers since her first day of work.

Night Managers.

Even the name was scary, and though no one could claim to have seen them, the Night Managers had a reputation. Shannon was not even sure they really existed. There'd been no mention or acknowledgment of them from Mr. Lamb or Mr. Walker or any of the official sources. And, as far as she knew, only cleaning people worked after hours—why would The Store need managers when it was closed?

But employees whispered about them after work, made furtive mention of them in the parking lot on the way to their cars. The Night Managers were supposed to keep tabs on all stock clerks and directors and salespeople, to inspect work areas at night, to go over register receipts and make reports.

And if they didn't like what they found?

Goose bumps popped up on Shannon's arms. Word was that a kid in Sporting Goods had disappeared. She didn't know who it was or when it had happened, but rumor had it that the clerk had been asked to stay after closing and have a chat with the Night Managers.

And had never been seen again.

The next day, someone else had been hired for his position.

She didn't know if the story was true. No one did. But whether the Night Managers were fact or fiction, they were like Santa Claus or the boogeyman, a force to be reckoned with. They wielded power, even if they didn't exist, and everyone was afraid of them.

Shannon opened her register and began counting out her bills. She'd finished the fives, tens, and twenties and was halfway through the ones when Mr. Lamb strolled by, hands behind his back, smiling. He nodded at her. "Opening in five minutes," he said. "How're things in the Garden department? Everything neat and clean, everyone bright-eyed and bushy-tailed, ready for another successful day?"

Neat and clean?

She thought of the spot on the floor.

The blood.

She nodded, smiled at the personnel manager. "Everything's fine."

TWENTY-TWO

1

Bill drove to the Roundup, parked his Jeep in the dirt lot on the side of the dumpy, windowless building, and walked inside, stopping just within the doorway to give his eyes a chance to adjust to the dim interior.

Ben was at the bar, where he'd said he'd be, a full shot glass and a half a bottle of J & B scotch in front of him.

Bill walked around the crowded pool table and past the jukebox, where a pair of cowboys were arguing over what song to play. The saloon was one of the few businesses in town that wasn't hurting. Of course, now that he'd thought that, The Store would probably apply for a beer and wine license, open up a lounge next to the sushi bar, and suck away the Roundup's life.

A corporate vampire.

Ben had called him, fifteen minutes ago, already half-crocked, and said he wanted to meet at the saloon. Bill had asked why, but his friend wouldn't say, would tell him only that it was "important," and though Bill hadn't wanted to go, had wanted to continue watching TV with Ginny, he'd sensed the urgency in Ben's voice, and he'd forced himself to get off the couch, put on his socks and shoes, hunted up his wallet and keys, and driven to the Roundup.

Important. That could be good or it could be bad.

Bill was betting on bad.

He stepped up to the bar, sat down on the stool next to Ben, motioned to the bartender for a beer. "So what is it?" he asked. "What's the big news?"

"I've been fired," Ben said.

Bill blinked dumbly, not sure he'd heard correctly. "What?"

"I've been fired. Terminated. Let go. Newtin sold the paper." He smiled wryly. "Want to guess to whom?"

"The Store?"

Ben poured himself another shot. "Bingo."

"But why? There's only one paper in town. He had a monopoly. Everyone had to buy ads with him—"

Ben waved dismissively. "That doesn't matter. There's no real money to be made in Juniper. It's a break-even prospect at best. Newtin's been trying to unload it for several years now." He shook his head. "I guess he finally found a buyer."

"How did you find out?"

"Fax. You think he'd drive all the way up to Juniper just to tell me that he's sold the paper and my ass is fired? Hell, no. Besides, that pussy's too chickenshit to face me."

"And they fired you?"

"First thing. Laura was promoted to editor; I was told to hit the pavement. Herb and Trudy and Al and all the production people were kept on. Traitorous brown-nosers."

"You were fired? Not demoted?"

"Exactamente."

"Shit."

Ben drained his glass. "There goes the election."

"You think so?"

"As you said, they had the radio station, we had the newspaper. Now they have both."

"You think that's why they bought it?"

"No," Ben said sarcastically. His voice was becoming slurred. "They have no interest whatsoever in controlling the news and information in this town. They want to sponsor and subsidize the fourth estate out of the goodness of their corporate hearts."

The bartender set a glass of beer in front of Bill, who dug the money out of his pocket to pay him.

He took a sip, turned back toward Ben. "So what are you going to do?" he asked.

"Hell. My little trailer is paid off. I can live for a while."

"But what are you going to *do?*"

"Freelance." Ben looked around, lowered his voice. "I'm thinking of doing a Store exposé. I could probably sell it to the *Wall Street Journal* or *Time* or *Newsweek*. It's timely. It's of national interest. The Store's an up-and-coming corporation, Newman King's a big mystery man—and you know how the public is fascinated by that shit. I think it could be a really good article." He smiled grimly as he poured himself another shot. "Besides, I have scores to settle."

They sat there for a while, drinking, not talking, listening to the self-pitying songs the cowboys had chosen for the jukebox. Bill finished his beer, called for one more. Ben finished his bottle and plunked down bills for another.

"Take it easy," Bill suggested. "You're already two sheets to the wind."

"I'm going for five." Ben poured and polished off another glass. "We shoulda monkey-wrenched 'em," he said. "Shoulda spiked some trees, sabotaged some equipment, poured sugar in some gas tanks."

"The first construction workers were from Juniper," Bill pointed out.

"Fuck 'em. Besides, The Store woulda taken the financial hit, not our good ol' local boys." He closed his eyes, continued to talk. "Local boys. There were trees on that property that were old when their great-great-grandfathers were nothing more than ambitious sperm, you know that? That fucking hillock was probably millions of years old. And it was demolished by men born less than twenty-five years ago!"

"You're drunk," Bill said. "And you're getting loud."

"I don't care!"

"Come on. Let me drive you home."

"I don't want to go home."

The bartender walked over, confiscated his bottle and glass. "Your friend's driving you home. You've had enough."

Ben nodded docilely, got off his stool, almost fell,

then, concentrating hard, walked toward the door. Bill followed him, ready to offer support if necessary. He didn't feel entirely clearheaded himself, but he wasn't drunk, and he led Ben over to the Jeep, buckled him in, and drove him home, making sure that he was safely inside the trailer before driving off.

The movie they'd been watching had long since ended, and Ginny had turned off the lights in the front of the house and was in the bedroom riding the exercise bike. She told him to get ready for bed, but he wasn't tired and he said that he had some work to do.

He walked back to his office, sat down in front of his PC, and accessed Freelink. He thought for a moment, then called up a global bulletin board and typed in the heading: "The Store." In the space reserved for message text, he typed: "Is there anyone else out there who's had problems with the discount retail chain The Store?" He gave no name but left his E-mail address, then went out to the kitchen, heated up some old coffee, and sat back down.

He already had five messages waiting.

His heart began to race. He'd gotten the coffee because he thought it might help him stay awake, but now he didn't even need the caffeine, and he pushed the coffee cup aside and called up his E-mail.

The first message was from someone calling himself Big Bob, and it described efforts to get a simple refund for a sprinkler as a cross between *1984* and *Catch-22*. The second message was from an anonymous Hispanic woman who claimed that The Store discriminated against minorities and that not only had The Store refused to hire her, but it had banned her from shopping there. The reason she could not give her name or the name of her town, she explained, was because she had filed suit against The Store and she had reason to believe that her phone lines were tapped, that The Store was listening in on her phone conversations and reading what she wrote online.

A chill passed through Bill as he read the woman's story. Under other circumstances, he'd probably consider her tale the unfounded allegations of a raving paranoid. But he believed every word she wrote, and he found himself wondering if *his* phone lines were tapped, if The Store's security people were listening in on his conversations, reading his online messages. He looked around the room. His office seemed suddenly darker, filled with shadows, and he wished he'd turned on both lights instead of just the little desk lamp.

He called up the third message. This one was from a journalist, Keith Beck, who said that in his town The Store had not only economically decimated the area by killing off local businesses but had instigated feuds among local residents. The Store was a disruptive influence, Beck said, and was completely changing the character of the town. He added that The Store had constructed its building on an environmentally sensitive parcel of land, not waiting for the conclusion of an environmental impact report, buying the cooperation of elected officials.

It was Juniper's story exactly. Bill couldn't believe his good fortune. This was what he'd been looking for, and he wished that Ben was here to read this with him. He printed out a hard copy, then sent Beck a message directly, typing out a description of The Store's doings in Juniper. He left out the weird stuff—the deaths and disappearances—but he described the arson at Richardson's store, and he explained the problems he'd run into trying to extricate his daughters from The Store's clutches. He also told Beck about what had happened to Ben.

After sending off the message, he printed copies of the rest of the mail in his in box, now up to eight messages. All were horror stories of dealings with The Store that had led to business failures or firings or lawsuits or other sorts of personal hardship.

Bill printed the last message, then checked his in box again. Sure enough, Beck had already sent a reply.

He eagerly called it up. The journalist expressed sympathy for Juniper's problems, said he understood what was going on, but he was not particularly encouraging about efforts to combat The Store.

"We tried," he wrote, "in our own little way, to fight

The Store, but we were defeated. The outcome of our battle was a foregone conclusion. The Store is a powerful enemy."

Bill sent another message. "Any suggestions?" he typed.

The reply, when it arrived, was short and to the point: "Local, county, and state governments do not have the financial resources to fight The Store. The federal government *should* get involved, but interstate commerce regulations have been defanged over the past two decades and allocating resources to go after a major employer is not politically feasible in these antigovernment, pro-business times. You're on your own."

You're on your own.

The words jumped out at him, resonating in his brain. Beck had apparently tried going through the proper channels in his fight against The Store and had exhausted those possibilities, coming up a loser.

What was left? Using The Store's own tactics? Arson? Terrorism?

Bill stared for a moment at the screen. The journalist was obviously burnt-out and discouraged, but maybe there were other people out there, in other communities, with different backgrounds, who had ideas and suggestions.

He decided to try again, taking a different tack, posting another message on the bulletin board. "I am looking for information concerning activities and practices of the discount retail chain The Store," he typed. "Specifically, I am looking for ways to prevent The Store from completely taking over the town of Juniper, Arizona. If anybody has any ideas, please let me know."

He posted the message, the screen went blank for several seconds, then a one-line statement appeared: "This communication has been deleted."

What? He frowned. How could the message have been deleted? That made no sense.

He typed the words again, tried to post them on the bulletin board, and once more the statement "This communication has been deleted" appeared on his screen.

He thought of the Hispanic woman's claim that The

Store was eavesdropping on her computer conversations, and he quickly fired off a note to Keith Beck, asking the journalist if anything like this had ever happened to him.

A new message appeared onscreen: "This communication cannot be transmitted. It is in violation of Paragraph 4 of your Freelink online service agreement."

Online service agreement?

He searched through the shelf above his desk until he found the box containing the diskettes and instruction book for Freelink. He took out the book, opened it, and before he could even find Paragraph 4, saw on the inside of the front cover, in tiny letters, words he had never noticed but that now sent a chill through his heart.

He immediately turned off his PC.

Mouth dry, heart pounding, he reread the notice inside the book's front cover: "Freelink is a subsidiary of The Store, Inc."

In his dream The Store was alive and sentient, walking around with giant brick legs, leaning over as it walked, looking behind other buildings, looking behind hills.

Looking for him.

2

There was a board meeting on Tuesday afternoon at five, and though Ginny usually attended meetings only during salary negotiations, word had come down that the district was going to be in dire financial straits next school year—again—and that layoffs were being considered.

Bill had been cloistered all day in his office, working, and she popped her head in and told him that he and the girls were on their own for dinner, she was going to the meeting. He nodded absently, and she wasn't sure he'd understood what she said, but she assumed he'd figure it out when his stomach started to growl, and she grabbed her keys from the bedroom and yelled an unanswered "Good-bye!"

The district offices were located in a flat stretch of

weedy ground between the elementary school and the junior high. The small lot was already filled with other teachers' cars and trucks, so she parked in her usual spot at the elementary school and walked over.

The boardroom was crowded. All of the folding chairs were taken, and Eleanor Burrows and the other cafeteria and clerical workers were seated on too-small plastic chairs that had been brought in from some classroom and arranged along the side aisle against the wall.

There were a few baby chairs left, but Ginny preferred to stand, and she moved to the left of the door, where two male high school teachers were already leaning against the cheaply paneled wall.

The board wasted no time in getting down to it. Immediately after calling the meeting to order, Paul Fancher, the superintendent, announced that unless drastic steps were taken, there would have to be wholesale teacher layoffs from all three schools. "We simply cannot afford to continue on as is," the superintendent explained.

"There goes our raise," someone said.

Nervous laughter greeted the remark.

"Now, we have several options," Fancher said. "Everyone can take an across-the-board ten percent pay cut—"

A chorus of angry words erupted from the gathered employees.

"I know," the superintendent said loudly. "I don't think that's fair, either. But that's one option we're considering. Another option is reducing services. Eliminating bus service, for example, and forcing parents to provide their children's transportation. Or we could eliminate selective positions and double up the workload for senior employees—without overtime or additional compensation, of course." He paused. "Or we could privatize and contract out all non-teaching positions."

People were yelling at the board members now, all of whom were sitting in smug silence, watching and apparently enjoying the commotion caused by their plans.

Fancher raised his hands for silence. "These are hard choices we have to make for this coming school year," he said above the noise of the crowd. "That's why we're here today."

Ginny felt sick. She glanced over at Eleanor, who was in her late fifties and had been working for Juniper Elementary School since its inception. Most of the board members, Fancher included, were in their early thirties and had only moved to Juniper within the last five years. How dare they eliminate the jobs of people who had given the best years of their lives to Juniper's schoolchildren?

There was another man seated to the left of the board at the table in the front of the room, a youngish business-suited man who stared idly up at the ceiling, obviously bored. She did not know who he was, but there was a sinking feeling in the pit of her stomach, and she was pretty sure she knew whose interests the man represented.

Sure enough, after a heated discussion between Fancher, two other board members, and the most vocal employees in the audience, the superintendent called for order. He said a privatization proposal that should satisfy both sides had already been presented to the district by The Store.

Fancher introduced the man at the end of the table as Mr. Keyes, and Ginny watched as The Store representative stood, walked in front of the table, and addressed the assembled employees.

So this was the famous Mr. Keyes, she thought. This was the man Bill had ranted and railed against.

In a loud, clear voice, Keyes explained the privatization proposal. At this time, he said, only food and transportation services would be contracted out. And since The Store did not have any qualified employees of its own, it would keep on all existing school workers in their present positions. The only difference they would notice would be a technicality—their paychecks would now come from The Store rather than the district.

The angry tone of the crowd's noise subsided.

Should the financial crunch continue, The Store had contingency plans to fund all district operations. But, he emphasized, The Store would only provide funding and would not attempt to influence classroom subject matter or dictate curriculum.

Keyes smiled reassuringly, and Ginny wanted to throw a tomato right into the middle of his smug, duplicitous face.

"What about pensions?" Ginny couldn't see the woman speaking, but she recognized Meg's voice. "If The Store takes over, will you still contribute money toward our retirement? And will it be the same amount now contributed by the district?"

Keyes's smile remained constant. "I'm afraid there will be no more pension fund. Those monies will be absorbed into our operating costs. We encourage all of you to open your own individual retirement accounts."

Debate started up again. Ginny listened for a few moments, then slipped outside. This could go on for hours.

And it didn't make any difference.

The board had already reached its decision.

Back home, the girls were gone and Bill was making Rice-A-Roni.

"That's the last straw!" she said, slamming her purse down on the counter.

Bill looked up. "What is it?"

"The board's talking about letting it take over the district!"

"It?" he said, though he knew exactly what she meant.

"The Store!" She opened the refrigerator, grabbed a Diet Coke, popped open the tab, and took a long drink. "Elections are coming up, and they're supporting this tax cut, which'll gut the district, and in order to save money they're thinking of contracting out not only transportation and food services but clerical and teaching positions as well. The Store, of course, has graciously offered to provide funding for those services, no strings attached."

His jaw tightened. "How's it flying with the troops?"

"It's being presented as the only feasible option. It's a done deal."

"Goddamn it. Park maintenance . . . street maintenance . . . fire . . . police . . . schools. The Store owns this town." He shook his head. "That's it. I'm running for council."

Ginny's heart rate suddenly accelerated. "No," she said. "Don't run. Let Ben run. Or Street."

"Why?"

"I'm afraid."

He was silent, looking at her, and she realized that he was afraid, too.

"We can't let ourselves be intimidated," he said quietly.

She put her Diet Coke down on the counter, moved next to him, and hugged him tightly, burying her face in his shoulder. "I'm getting so tired of this," she said.

"Who isn't?"

"There just doesn't seem to be anything we can do."

"Maybe there isn't," he admitted. "But that doesn't mean we stop trying."

"We can't let them take control of education."

"We won't," he said.

It felt good, standing here like this, hugging him. It felt reassuring, and she reached behind him and turned down the burner on the stove so his dinner wouldn't burn.

They were still hugging when the girls returned home.

TWENTY-THREE

1

Ben tore the sign down from the telephone pole, ripping it in half before dumping it in the trash can in front of Street's shop.

That's what it came down to this time: pro-Store candidates and anti-Store candidates.

And most people seemed to be siding with The Store.

There'd been a sea change in American politics since the first time he'd run for council in the late seventies. He'd lost then, by a large margin, and that had kept him away ever since, but he'd lost to a man he respected, a man who had turned out to be a decent councilman and later a decent mayor.

Back then, people admired the citizen activist, were in favor of individuals getting involved with causes they believed in. But these days, that was looked upon with disfavor, considered an example of "special interest" politics, and the respect went to those who talked finances, not ideas.

Which was why The Store's candidates would probably win.

He couldn't understand why the prospect of having The Store control Juniper's government didn't scare people more. Sure, the corporation's big bankroll and the promises to cut taxes and fund programs with private rather than public funds sounded inviting on the surface, but even a casual examination of that revealed its flaws. Or at least it did to him. Because whoever controlled the money controlled the power. If services were financed with public funds, specific fees allocated for specific projects and decided upon by the people, the people were in charge. As they should be. But if The Store paid the bills, The Store got to call the shots.

That to him was truly frightening.

He was leery as well of this three-man council idea. The more diversity the better, he'd always felt. The more voices heard in a government—any government—the better the representation. But there'd been a town meeting at the high school last week, and by an overwhelming vote the attendees had decided to scale back the size of the council from five to three. At The Store's behest, the town charter had been amended for the first time in its history, and he did not see that as a good sign.

Ben stepped back onto the empty street and looked at the painted window of the electronics shop:

VOTE FOR A CHANGE!
ELECT ANDERSON, MCHENRY AND MALORY
TOWN COUNCIL

He smiled to himself. He'd come up with the slogan "Vote for a Change," amused by its double meaning, by its criticism of the town's apathy, and though Bill had not thought it wise to insult the voters they were trying to woo, Ben didn't think most of them would get it.

He still thought that.

Backing all the way to the sidewalk on the other side of the street, he continued to stare at the sign, trying to determine its efficacy. He walked from one end of the block to the other, glancing over his shoulder, pretending he was a driver in a car, then walked back across the street to the electronics shop. He was pretty happy with the way the job had turned out. The paint on the window was bright, and against the dull drabness of the dying downtown, the message stood out forcefully.

The cardboard signs they'd nailed up all over town and on the highway also looked good, but Ben knew from experience that that wouldn't be enough.

The Store had the radio.

And the newspaper.

Even thinking about the newspaper ticked him off.

He walked inside the shop.

"How's it look?" Street asked.

Ben gave a thumbs-up sign. "Excellent, if I do say so myself."

"Think it'll help?"

"No."

Ben walked over to the register counter, picked up his cup of coffee from where he'd left it, and finished off the dregs. When he and Street and Ted Malory had decided to run as a ticket, The Store had countered, offering an alternate slate. He wondered now if it had been a mistake to run together. Maybe they should have campaigned separately, as individuals, not tied their fates so closely to each other.

"Do you think we have a chance?" Street asked.

Ben shook his head.

"Maybe it'll go two-one, or one-two. Maybe we'll at least get one guy on there."

"I don't think so."

"So The Store'll own the council."

"Again."

"It'll be even worse this time. They won't have to buy anyone off. They won't need a middle man to do their dirty work. They'll be in charge themselves and they'll be legitimately elected."

Ben nodded. "I know." He looked at the back side of the painted window. "God help us all."

2

It was not going to be a victory party. They knew that going in. It was a defeat party, a commiseration session, a wake.

Still, the gym was more crowded than Bill had expected, and it kept alive a small spark of hope within him. Maybe more people than they'd thought had figured out what The Store was doing to Juniper. Maybe the citizens of the town were too smart to have been fooled by The Store's glitzy advertising and inflated promises.

He thought of the famous photo of Harry Truman holding up a newspaper with a banner headline reading: DEWEY WINS!

Sometimes the oddsmakers turned out to be wrong. Sometimes the underdog did triumph.

Sometimes.

He and Ginny walked into the gym holding hands, looking around. Whoever was in charge of the decorations definitely had a sense of humor. Black crepe paper hung from the bleachers and the blackboards, funereal wreaths of dead flowers were arranged in stands next to the appetizers and drink tables in the center court. There were quite a few people milling about: most of the downtown merchants and owners of the businesses that made up the chamber of commerce, displaced municipal workers, unemployed construction people. They were talkative, friendly, not particularly somber, but the overall mood seemed grim.

The other candidates were awaiting election returns and holding their party at The Store. No expense had been spared and the affair was being catered by The Store's in-house sushi and espresso bars, all-you-can-eat free food being offered to all supporters. The Store had closed at noon so that employees could set up the decorations and clear an area of the building for the celebration, and a live remote broadcast was planned for the radio station.

Ironically—and irritatingly—both Sam and Shannon were working the party. They hadn't volunteered, they'd been assigned, and Bill could not help thinking that that was intentional. The Store knew that, though he was not running for office himself, he was one of the architects of the opposition, and Lamb and his people no doubt wanted to rub his face in it.

He was still unable to understand why more people hadn't turned against The Store. It was obvious to even a casual observer that since The Store had arrived, downtown Juniper had become a virtual ghost town, unemployment had skyrocketed, and the jobs that were now available had sharply lower wages than their predecessors. The Store was sucking the town dry, yet far too many people either didn't notice or didn't care. Putting aside the mysterious occurrences that had accompanied its arrival, people should be rejecting The Store on a purely personal, selfish, economic level.

Yet they weren't.

And he could not figure out why.

Street wandered over. He had already been drinking heavily, and he gave Ginny a huge unwelcome hug and boozily clapped an arm around Bill's shoulder. "Mayday! Mayday! We're going down!"

"You don't seem too broken up about it," Bill said.

Street shrugged. "At some point, all you can do is laugh."

Ben, Ted, and Ted's wife, Charlinda, made their way through the throng toward them. They talked for a few moments, then Ginny and Charlinda moved off toward the hors d'oeuvres and the men stood alone.

"How badly do you think we're going to lose?" Bill asked.

"We'll get our asses kicked!" Street yelled.

Bill ignored him, turned toward Ted. "What's your feeling? You know a lot of people in this town. You're not a pariah like Ben or a clown like Street—"

"I resent that!" Street said.

Bill grinned. "What's your bead on the situation?"

"I don't know," Ted admitted. "All I hear is doom and gloom from you guys, but everyone I've talked to seems pretty supportive. There's a lot of resentment toward The Store out there. People might be afraid to admit it, but most of them don't like The Store. I may be crazy, but—knock on wood—I think we have a fighting chance."

Afraid to admit it.

Bill licked his lips. "Why would they be *afraid* to admit it?"

Ted shifted uncomfortably. "You know."

That was the problem. He did know. They all knew. And they faced each other, the knowledge in their eyes, until Street suggested that they all go over to the drink table and get something to wet their whistles.

The polls closed at eight, and counting began almost immediately. A team of election workers was at town hall, going through the ballots, and while tabulating results in big cities might take all night, the small number of voters in Juniper virtually assured that a count and recount would be concluded before ten.

The radio station had a live remote at town hall as well as at The Store party, and Street had hooked up a receiver to the gym's PA system so they could all hear the broadcast.

"How come there's no remote feed here?" Ben asked dryly, standing at the head of the drink table. "Aren't they interested in our reaction?"

Everyone laughed.

Bill listened only intermittently to the broadcast throughout the evening, but when it became clear that the counting was almost completed and that the winners would be announced shortly, he and Ginny gravitated with everyone else toward Street's receiver, which was sitting on an unadorned table next to the locker room entrance. There was no sound coming out of the receiver—it was issuing from speakers hidden high in the rafters of the gym—but symbolically this was the origin of the radio broadcast, and more and more people gathered around the black metal box and stared at the blue digital call numbers as announcement time approached.

Ben was describing for the hundredth time that evening, how different the outcome of this election would be if he was still editor of the paper, when people in the crowd began holding up their hands for silence, putting their fingers to their lips.

"Shhhh!"

"Shhhh!"

"Shhhh!"

Everyone leaned closer to the receiver, as though that would enable them to hear the results more clearly. Street turned up the volume. Bill winced as Ginny's hand tightened, viselike, on his.

"It's official," the radio announcer said. His voice echoed through the cavernous gym. "All of the ballots have been counted, and Mr. Lamb, personnel manager of The Store, is the top vote-getter and has been elected Juniper's new mayor. Mr. Walker, The Store's Customer Service manager, and Mr. Keyes, Store representative, have also been elected to the town council."

"Don't these assholes have first names?" Ben growled.

"Ben Anderson, Ted Malory, and Street McHenry have been soundly defeated," the announcer continued. "Final tally: Lamb, one thousand three hundred votes; Walker, one thousand one hundred and seventy-two votes; Keys, one thousand and sixty votes; Malory, nine hundred and ninety-nine votes; McHenry, nine hundred and eighty-seven votes: Anderson, eight hundred and fifty votes."

"Low turnout." Ginny nodded. "Interesting."

" 'Soundly defeated?' " Ted said. "I thought we did pretty well."

"Let's hear it for our side!" someone yelled. "Hip hip hooray!"

The rest of the crowd joined in: "Hip hip hooray! Hip hip hooray!"

On the radio, the feed switched instantly to the victory party at The Store. Even muffled by the gym's speaker system, the size and enthusiasm of The Store crowd was impressive. The cheers coming over the radio dwarfed the noise from their little chant and made their supporters sound tired and pitiful.

Sam's there, Bill thought. And Shannon.

People began wandering away, clapping sympathetic hands on the losers' backs, offering compassion and half-hearted promises to keep up the fight. Several supporters headed for the alcohol, but most were already making for the exit, ready to head home.

Bill and Ginny stood next to Ted and Charlinda, Ben and Street, as Mr. Lamb gave his acceptance speech over the radio. He began with an embarrassingly insincere acknowledgment of the commitment and good intentions of his well-meaning but misguided opponents, then heaped equally insincere praise on the gathered supporters.

Huge, inappropriate cheers greeted his every utterance.

"I think I'm gonna barf," Street said.

"It is sickening," Bill agreed.

"No. I think I'm gonna barf." Street made a mad dash for the boys' bathroom.

Mr. Lamb was already talking about some of his plans for Juniper after taking office.

"There have been complaints recently about the freshness of The Store's produce," the new mayor said. He chuckled. "I've heard rumors of it."

The crowd laughed.

"Our first order of business will be to pass a resolution requiring all local farmers and ranchers to tithe twenty percent of their produce and livestock to The Store. This will ensure the continued quality and freshness of The Store's product."

"I wish he would've said this shit before he got elected," Ted said. "We might've won."

"All town employees will now be required to wear a uniform to work. The Store has contracted with the manufacturer of *its* uniforms to provide special municipal employee attire."

Big cheers.

"There will also be an increase in Juniper's sales tax."

Groans.

"I know, I know," Mr. Lamb said cheerfully. "We promised a tax cut, and I wish we could deliver on that promise, but this sales tax is needed to adjust an existing inequity in the system. As it stands now, The Store is providing funding for most of Juniper's day-to-day operation as well as for upcoming projects. The Store is happy to do this. As a corporation, we feel it is our obligation to support the communities that support us, and it's good for local economies if we put money that we earn back into the towns that we take it from. However, it is unfair to expect The Store to shoulder the complete financial burden while other stores and businesses get off scot-free. Right now, the other businesses in Juniper are getting a free ride. We're paying their share, and we're getting punished for it. Therefore, the sales tax will be raised so that all local businesses can begin to contribute equally to the greatness of our fair town."

There was scattered applause, a few halfhearted cheers.

"The good news," Mr. Lamb said, "is that this increase will not apply to The Store. Since The Store is already shouldering most of the burden, it would be like taxing us twice if we participated in this revenue enhancement. Which is a fancy way of saying that other businesses may raise their prices, but The Store will continue to provide the highest quality products at the lowest possible prices!"

Cheers, clapping, ecstatic shouting.

Ben turned down the receiver's volume. "Propagandistic bullshit." He shook his head, sighed. "At least Ted almost made it."

Bill smiled. "And you have the honor of coming in last."

He shrugged. "Been there, done that. Nothing new."

"So what now?"

"What now? We stand idly by while more local businesses go belly-up and The Store takes over the entire goddamn town."

They were all silent.

Street came trudging up. "Did I miss anything important?"

"Only the final death knell of democracy and the legitimization of unchecked corporate power in Juniper."

Bill tried to smile. "You old hippie, you."

Ben met his gaze. "To quote the Jefferson Airplane, 'It's a new dawn.' "

•

TWENTY-FOUR

1

There were more vagrants on the streets of Juniper than there used to be. There'd always been a certain number of ragged, wildly bearded men in town—old prospectors come down from the mountains, bear hunters in for supplies—but there seemed to be more of them recently, and he wasn't sure that these were people who were purposely making a lifestyle choice.

Bill drove slowly down Granite toward the highway, saw an old man sleeping on a filthy blanket beneath a manzanita bush, saw a young man sitting in the doorway of an empty storefront.

Juniper was a small town, but he still didn't know everyone in it, and since there'd been a lot of business closing, going bankrupt in the wake of The Store's arrival, it was conceivable that these were merely jobless people who were hanging around town in order to look for work.

Conceivable—but not likely.

Most of them looked dirty and purposeless, and he suspected that they had no place to go.

Juniper had a homeless problem.

It was a weird thought. Homelessness was usually a big-city disease. Small towns had transients passing through, but they were essentially closed societies, where any change or deviation from the norm was noticed instantly. They were not anonymous enough to provide a place for America's marginalized.

There were no streets for street people to live on.

Yet here they were.

Bill reached the highway, stopped for a moment—

though there was no light or stop sign at the inter-
section—then turned right toward The Store. His muscles tensed, his grip on the steering wheel tightened.
He hadn't gone to The Store since the election, and
even driving this small section of the highway made
him feel as though he was entering an enemy camp
during wartime. Intellectually, he knew that it was
merely a discount retailer, the place where his daughters and half the town worked, and that the wide,
modern aisles would be filled with ordinary men,
women, and children doing their ordinary everyday
shopping. But he had so demonized The Store in his
mind that, emotionally, he felt like he was preparing
to enter hell.

It couldn't be helped, though.

He needed printer ribbon.

He'd finished the manual.

The actual deadline was day after tomorrow, and he
would be transmitting his work via modem to Automated Interface, but he liked to print out a hard copy
of his manuals first and then proof them. He seemed to
do a better job of copyediting if he worked off printed
pages instead of a screen.

He pulled into the parking lot and was lucky enough
to find a space near The Store's entrance. He'd known
this was coming, and he should've bought ribbons last
week when they'd driven down to Phoenix, but he
hadn't thought about it and now he was stuck. The
Store was the only place in town that sold printer
ribbons.

Bill got out of the Jeep, locked the door. He felt a
knot of dread in his stomach as he walked up the parking lot aisle toward the building. Neither Sam nor Shannon was working this morning, and for that he was glad.
He stared at the windowless expanse of wall before him
and could not help thinking that The Store saw him,
that it knew he was coming—and that it had something
planned for him.

He did not want his daughters to see that.

He walked inside, ignored the smirking director who
offered him assistance, and headed directly toward the

aisle containing computer, printer, and typewriter accessories. He glanced around the other rows as he walked. What had happened to all of the myriad choices The Store had offered? Where had all the products gone? The shelves were still filled with plenty of items, he noticed, but there was no variety. There were no nationally known names, no recognizable packaging.

There was only The Store brand.

For all items.

His feeling of dread intensified as he walked down the aisle where the printer ribbons were supposed to be.

Were *supposed* to be.

Instead, the shelves were packed with small boxes and plastic bottles. He looked carefully at the products facing him: Sneezing Powder, Itching Powder, Magic Toadstool Dust.

Comic book products.

Masturbation Lotion. Hot Love Oil. Breast-enlargement Gel. Penis-lengthening Creme.

He frowned. What the hell was all this?

"We're reorganizing."

He looked up to see the smirking director he'd bypassed on his way in.

"You'd know that if you'd accepted the help I offered you."

Was there belligerence in the director's voice? Was there a threat implied in his space-invading stance?

"You're looking for printer ribbon, right?"

How could he know that? Bill felt chilled, but he kept his face unreadable, met the young man's eyes. "No," he lied.

The director seemed surprised, caught off guard. "Then what are you looking for?"

"Oh, nothing." Bill smiled at him. "I'm just browsing."

Before the director could respond, Bill moved away. He did not know whether the young man was following him, but he would not give the bastard the satisfaction of seeing him check. He kept his eyes focused straight ahead, and when he reached the extra-wide middle aisle that dissected The Store and ran from the Automotive to the Lingerie departments, he hung a right and began walking purposefully toward the opposite end of the building.

In the center of The Store, where the two transverse aisles met, a booth had been set up, a flimsy, temporary counter with an overhead sign that reminded him of Lucy's psychiatrist stand in the old *Peanuts* cartoon strip.

JOIN STORE CLUB, the sign announced.

Two people he recognized, Luke McCann and Chuck Quint, were standing before the booth, and Bill slowed down as he approached them.

"Store Club?" Chuck asked the salesman manning the booth.

The salesman nodded. "If you become a member, you will be able to purchase goods at cost, without paying any sales tax. There are also numerous other benefits." His voice lowered. "Improved health, greater life expectancy, increased sex drive . . ."

Bill moved away, not wanting to hear any more.

He took the opportunity to glance surreptitiously behind him. The director was nowhere to be seen, and he relaxed, looking around, trying to figure out where they'd moved the printer supplies. A freestanding sign on the edge of the aisle touted EXCELLENT DEALS! NEW AUTOS AT FLEET PRICES! Beneath a picture of a red Saturn taking a mountain curve, the text said that The Store would be selling cars-to-order through a new catalogue, agreements with all of the major automakers allowing the vehicles to be sold at outrageously low prices and delivered directly to the buyers' houses.

There goes Chas Finney's Ford dealership, Bill thought.

He looked on the back of the sign, saw an offer for The Store's Discount Travel Bureau.

There went Elizabeth Richard's travel agency.

There was still no sign of printer supplies, but from a row halfway down the center aisle emerged a boy holding what looked like a mouse pad, and Bill immediately headed in that direction.

The row did indeed contain shelves and stacks of computer and typewriter accessories. He walked to the end of the section and scanned the packages of printer ribbons hanging from pegs on a recessed display. All were the generic Store brand, but there was an accompanying book attached by wire to the center of the display, and he cross-referenced his printer to find the ribbon that would be compatible.

"Do you have any naked-children videos?"

Bill looked up, shocked.

"Videos of children playing outdoors and having fun in the sun?"

The voice was coming from the next row over, and he quickly moved to the end of the row and peeked around the corner to see who the speaker was.

Reverend Smithee, the Baptist minister, was standing next to a Store clerk.

Smiling, the clerk shook his head and clucked disapprovingly. "Reverend. I'm surprised at you."

Smithee reddened but refused to back off. "I was told you did."

"Is that what you like?"

"No. I just—"

"Those videos are illegal, you know."

The reverend's face grew redder. "They shouldn't be. Everybody's naked under their clothes. It's natural. I've never understood why you can show people being killed, but you can't show a body without clothes. Killing's much worse."

"We have snuff videos, too," the clerk said.

Smithee licked his lips. "Snuff videos? Where?"

The clerk's smile broadened. "Right this way, Reverend."

"You're not . . . going to report me?"

"Our aim is to meet our customers' needs and keep them happy." The clerk walked forward, the reverend following. He smiled knowingly at Bill as they passed by, and Bill could not help thinking that The Store had *wanted* him to hear the exchange, that it had *wanted* him to see Reverend Smithee in this light, that it had arranged it all.

Feeling chilled, he found the right size of printer ribbon, picked up five of them, and hurried to the checkout stand at the front of the store.

TWENTY-FIVE

1

He usually enjoyed the free period between assignments, but this time Bill felt restless, stir-crazy, almost claustrophobic. Juniper seemed confining to him, and no matter where he went or what he did, it seemed that The Store was always there, looming in the background, monitoring his movements, watching him. Even hiking, alone, in the forest, in the canyons, on the hills, he felt the presence of The Store.

He needed to get away from Juniper.

The idea that his documentation was now winding its way through the channels from Automated Interface to The Store's corporate headquarters, and was about to be filtered down to individual Stores all over the United States, made him feel supremely uneasy. There was nothing he could have done, no way he could have avoided it, but the mere fact that he had been indirectly working for The Store, that he had even in a minuscule way contributed to the efficiency of its operation, galled him.

They were lying next to each other after they'd quietly finished making love long after the girls had fallen asleep one night, and the only noise in the house was the low murmuring of the bedroom television. He rolled onto his left side, looked at Ginny. "I think we should go on a vacation."

"A vacation? What brought this on?"

"I just think we need to get out of here, get away for a while. . . ."

"Get away from The Store?"

He nodded.

"Where do you want to go?"

"How about Carlsbad Caverns?"

"Sounds fine to me. But what about the girls?"

"They're going with us."

"Sam won't go. And at this point, I'm not sure we can make her."

"Shannon's going. I guarantee you we can make her."

Ginny was quiet.

"What is it?" he said.

"What if The Store won't let her go?"

Bill shook his head, sat up. "We've been too soft on all this. That's our problem. We should've put more pressure on her. Or, hell, maybe we should've just talked to her like an adult, told her what's really going on. I think we're still treating her—treating *both* of them—like they're little girls. We're still trying to protect them from things—"

"That's what parents do."

"I know. But what I'm saying is that we should've tried to convince them to quit on their own. The Store'll sue us and come after us if we try to force them to quit, but if they quit themselves it'll let them go."

She looked up at him. "You really believe that? After everything that's happened?"

"I don't know," he said. "But it's worth a try."

"Yes," Ginny agreed. "It is." She placed a soft hand on his stomach. "But Sam probably won't do it."

"Probably not."

"And if The Store won't let Shannon go?"

"We'll take her with us anyway."

"What do we do if The Store comes after us?"

He looked down at her. "We'll cross that bridge when we come to it."

They brought it up at breakfast.

Sam stated immediately and unequivocally that she had duties and responsibilities, that The Store put its trust in her and she could not let the company down. There was no way she could take any time off.

She walked out of the room without waiting for a

response. "I have to get ready for work," she informed them.

Bill turned toward Shannon, who was sipping her orange juice, trying to look invisible. "You, young lady, are coming with us."

"Da-ad!"

"Don't 'dad' me."

She put down her orange juice. "I can't. I'll lose my job."

"You have to quit anyway when school starts."

Shannon stared at him, shocked. "No, I don't!"

"Oh, yes, you do."

"You're part of this family," Ginny said, "and you're going to go on vacation with us."

"I don't want to!"

Bill leaned forward across the counter toward her. "I don't care if you want to or not. You're going."

"How come Sam gets to stay home?"

"Sam is a year older than you."

"So?"

"So, she's eighteen."

"Big fucking deal!"

Ginny hit her.

It wasn't a hard hit, not a punch, but it was loud, a slap across the face, and they were all stunned by it, Ginny most of all. She had never slapped either of her daughters before, and Bill could tell that she instantly regretted the action. Still, she did not perform the clichéd follow-up, did not immediately hug Shannon and tearfully apologize. She merely stood there, staring at her daughter, and it was Shannon who burst out crying and did the tearful hug, jumping off her chair, throwing her arms around her mother and apologizing. "I'm sorry! I'm sorry, Mom!"

Ginny gave her a quick hug in return, turned her about. "You should be apologizing to your father."

Shannon moved around the counter. "I'm sorry, Dad. I . . . I don't know why I said that."

Bill smiled. "I've heard the word before."

Shannon wiped her nose, laughed.

"But you're coming with us," he said. "We're all going on vacation. As a family."

This time Shannon nodded. "Okay," she said. "Okay."

2

Shannon approached Mr. Lamb with trepidation. She hadn't really spoken to the personnel manager alone, on a one-to-one basis, since she'd been hired, and she found herself somewhat frightened by the prospect. He was standing in front of the Customer Service counter, talking to a customer, and she waited for him to finish before approaching him, glancing nervously up at the wall clock above the counter as the minutes of her break ticked by.

She didn't want him to catch her taking a too-long break.

She watched the personnel manager as he talked to the woman. He had always seemed to her very intimidating, and he seemed even more so now, since he'd been elected mayor. He never mentioned his new office in meetings, and no one else did, either, but it was known and it was there, in the background, and it lent to him a power above and beyond what he already possessed.

At the party on election night, the victory party, The Store had provided free food and liquor, and more people had shown up for that reason than to celebrate the election results. She'd helped Holly pass out candy and mints, and the party had grown wilder and wilder as the night wore on, with Mrs. Comstock, the librarian, taking off her clothes and dancing naked in the Stationery aisle, Mr. Wilson, the postmaster, picking a fight with Sonny James in Boys' Wear, and a group of rowdy women puking on cue in Housewares. But Mr. Lamb had remained aloof and above it all, completely sober and in control, and Shannon's most vivid memory of that night was of loud, drunken, half-dressed men and women attacking each other while Mr. Lamb, smiling, looked on.

She hadn't told her parents what had happened that

night, but she'd talked to Diane about it, and her friend had suggested that she quit her job at The Store. "You're only there because you're bored," she said. "You don't really need the money. Why don't you just find something else to do?"

She'd seen Diane less and less this summer, and it wasn't just because of their conflicting schedules. Working for her dad, Diane had developed an anti-store attitude similar to her parents', and the same contrary impulse that had caused Shannon to defend The Store to her parents had made her do the same with her friend.

"I like working at The Store," she told Diane coldly. "I'd rather do what I'm doing than what you're doing."

Truth be told, she didn't like working at The Store. And she'd much rather be working for Diane's father than for Mr. Lamb. But for some dumb reason, she didn't seem to be able to admit that aloud. Not even to Sam, who had asked her point-blank about the subject more than once.

Which was why she and Diane were on the outs.

Which was why she'd fought with her parents about the vacation.

She looked up at the clock again, her hands sweaty with tension.

She wished she'd never applied for a job here.

Mr. Lamb finally finished with the customer, and as the woman walked away he turned, smiling, toward Shannon. "Shannon," he said. "You have exactly five and a half minutes left on your break. How may I help you?"

She'd practiced in her mind the words she would say, but all of her planned statements had suddenly fled. She could not remember what she wanted to say or think of how to ask him for time off. She stalled. "I, uh . . . could I . . . could we, uh, talk in your office?"

He looked her over and nodded. "Certainly. You still have four and a half minutes left."

Maybe she'd be lucky, she thought, as she followed him behind the Customer Service counter. Maybe Mr. Lamb would fire her.

Lucky? Would getting fired be lucky?

Yes, she thought, looking at the back of the personnel director's suit. Yes, it would.

He walked into the small room, sat down at his desk, motioned for her to take the chair opposite him. She did so.

The door to the office closed behind her, and she turned her head to see who had pulled it shut, but there was no one there.

"What is it?" Mr. Lamb asked. The patina of friendliness that had been in his voice outside, on the floor, was gone, and there was a hardness to both his words and his attitude as he faced her across the desk. She was not just nervous, she was afraid to ask what she'd come here to ask, and she suddenly wished she'd tried to do this some other place, at some other time.

She cleared her throat. "I know this is kind of short notice, Mr. Lamb, but my family's going on vacation to Carlsbad Caverns next week, and I was wondering if I could take three days off. We'll be gone for five days, but I don't work Monday, and Gina said she'd trade with me for Friday, so I'd only need Tuesday, Wednesday, and Thursday."

He smiled insincerely. "Oh, you're going to be going on a family vacation."

She nodded.

His smile disappeared. "You lazy bitch," he said. "You lazy fucking bitch. You think you can just waltz in and out every time you feel like it while all of The Store's hardworking *loyal* employees stay here and bust their asses to take up your slack?"

She was stunned, frightened, caught off guard as much by the vehemence of his delivery as the violence of his words. She shrank back in the chair, feeling deeply afraid as he leaned across the desk toward her.

"All of our rules and regulations, all of our work and responsibilities have to be altered and put on hold because one fucking little part-time slut can't do her damn job correctly. Is that what I'm hearing?"

Shannon shook her head meekly. "I . . . I'm sorry. I . . . didn't—"

"Quit your whining," Mr. Lamb ordered.

She shut up, and he leaned back in his chair, fingers pressed together, pretending to think. "The Store is not a charity," he said finally. "Give me one good reason why I should allow you to take off on a vacation, galavanting around the country when you're supposed to be working."

"There is no good reason," she said. "I'm sorry I asked. I didn't mean to disturb you—"

Mr. Lamb suddenly burst out laughing. He spun around in his swivel chair, pointed at her. "Gotcha!"

She blinked, confused. He was watching her, still laughing, and she tried to smile but was not sure why.

"I knew why you wanted to talk to me before we even came in here," he said. "It's all taken care of. Your shifts are covered for that time period. You may go on vacation with your family."

She shook her head. "How—"

"—did I know?" he finished for her. "Your sister stopped by before her shift and told me *all* about it."

"Sam?"

"Oh, yes," he said, and the playfulness was suddenly gone from his voice. He was still smiling, but there was a slyness to it now, something unpleasant that made her squirm in her seat. "Samantha and I had a nice long talk early this morning before The Store opened."

He pulled from his desk drawer a pair of panties.

A pair of panties stained with blood.

Sam's.

Shannon recognized the pattern, and she felt as though her guts had just been scooped out. Grandma Jo had sent each of them underwear last Christmas, identically patterned holiday panties with holly and teddy bear designs. She hadn't wanted to wear them, had been embarrassed to let Jake see her in anything so goofy, but Sam hadn't minded, and she'd taken all four pair.

Shannon stared at the reddish brown stain obscuring the festively dressed bear on the French-cut underpants.

Mr. Lamb played with the panties absently, stretching them between two fingers. "She's a very good sister to you," the personnel manager said. "Very caring, very supportive. You should consider yourself lucky."

Shannon nodded absently, unable to concentrate.

What had happened? And why? What had he done to her?

What had she allowed him to do to her?

No. Samantha would never allow this sleazebucket to touch even the toe of her boot.

Would she?

Shannon felt sick. Hurt and angry and afraid all at once. She stared with hatred across the desk at the personnel manager.

He put away the panties, closed the drawer. "You can go on vacation with your mommy and your daddy," he said in a mincing singsong voice. Abruptly, his tone grew serious, his smile cruel. "And you can thank your sister for it. Now get your worthless ass back to work. Your break's over."

3

They left early, before dawn. He'd packed everything the night before, loaded up the car, set the alarm for four. They'd given Sam an extra key to the Jeep, as well as a copy of their itinerary: the list of motels at which they would be staying, phone numbers, and approximate arrival times.

"Be good," Ginny told her.

Sam seemed almost sorry that she was not going with them, an expression of regret on her face as she held her bathrobe closed and waved from the doorway, and Bill took that as a promising sign.

There was hope yet.

They stopped by Len's before they pulled out of town, bought a sack of donuts for the road, coffee for him and Ginny, hot chocolate for Shannon.

Then they were off.

He marked out their route on a map ahead of time, sticking to the blue highways, the scenic roads, as much as possible. Shannon fell asleep immediately after finishing her hot chocolate, lulled by the rhythm of the wheels, but Ginny, as always, remained wide-awake, and she put her left hand on his right thigh and squeezed gently as they traveled east toward the dawn.

Juniper's radio station faded out an hour or so later, and Bill twirled the dial, searching in vain for music, but all he could get was a syndicated early morning talk show out of Flagstaff and a Navajo station from Chinle, so he popped in a tape.

He felt good. Gordon Lightfoot on the stereo, the sun coming up over the mountains. This was what it was supposed to be like, this was the life he should be living.

Shannon woke up, started to take the last doughnut out of the bag, then changed her mind and simply stared silently out the window.

They passed through towns that were recognized as such by mapmakers only—wide spots in the road consisting of little more than old broken windmills and dirty little gas stations. The forest segued to farmland, the farmland to desert. There were no strict dividing lines, the boundaries were fluid, and the shifting landscape along the narrow, seldom-driven secondary roads was both beautiful and continually surprising.

They talked as they drove, not discussing The Store but just about anything and everything else: music, movies, world events, feelings, thoughts, friends, family, the past, the future.

Shannon was quiet at first, subdued, almost withdrawn, but she seemed to relax and open up the farther away from Juniper they traveled, first jumping into the conversation at odd and irregular points, then finally being drawn in.

Bill smiled to himself as he drove. God, there was nothing better than traveling. He loved everything about it. Not only did he enjoy seeing new and uncharted country, but, as he'd told Ginny last night, taking vacations together strengthened the family bond. The enforced intimacy of an enclosed car mandated greater interaction. In real life, Shannon had enough space of her own, enough opportunity for physical movement, that the boundaries of their relationship could be voluntarily controlled. But here, they were stuck with each other, could not get away even if they wanted to, and the traditional teenage distance she'd kept from them the past few years was gradually broken down, worn away. It was like she was a little girl again, a fully integrated member of the family, and that nostalgic familiarity felt good.

"How far are we from the border?" Shannon asked.

"A hundred miles or so."

"I've never been to New Mexico before."

He smiled. "That'll only be true for another hour and a half."

The smile faded on his face even before he'd finished the sentence. Ahead, on the desert hillside, he could see the clustered clinging buildings of Rio Verde and, dominating the landscape of the town, The Store. It stood amidst the older structures like a rocket among biplanes, drawing attention to itself, its recently constructed windowless facade and bright shiny sign looking exactly like its Juniper counterpart, calling to him, mocking him.

He said nothing, did not point it out or mention it, but Ginny and Shannon could not help but notice the building, and they were silent as they drove through the town, not speaking until they had gone some miles beyond it and the low mesas of New Mexico were in sight on the cloud-crowded horizon.

Sometime after two, they stopped for a late lunch in Socorro, eating at McDonald's, a mile or two from the Rio Grande.

Socorro didn't have a Store, but Las Palmas, the next town, did—a huge, conspicuously expensive building situated between poor adobe farmhouses. The town could not have had a population of more than a few hundred, but the gigantic Store parking lot was filled. All of the vehicles, he saw as they drove by, were old and dusty, and the men and women trudging into The Store looked discouraged, whipped, beaten.

Like a conquered people, he thought.

But he said nothing, kept driving.

He'd made reservations for the night at a Holiday Inn in Encantada, based on a favorable description in the *AAA TourBook*. Encantada turned out to be a one-street town on a flat plain at the edge of a massive oil field. Following the speed limit signs, he slowed the car to thirty-five miles an hour as they entered the town limits.

Immediately, the hair began prickling on his arms and the back of his neck.

Shannon was asleep in the rear, but Ginny was wide-awake and she looked over at him, fear in her eyes. "Bill," she said quietly.

He didn't have to be told. He could see it for himself. Everyone on the street was dressed in The Store uniform.

The men, the women, the boys, the girls.

"My God," Ginny said. "Oh, my God."

Bill said nothing, slowed to thirty. In the window of the town's lone gas station, the attendant was wearing a Store uniform. An oil truck driver, jumping down from his cab, was wearing a Store uniform as well, as were the diners at the café to which the trucker was headed.

At the far end of town, just past the Holiday Inn, was the intimidating bulk of The Store itself.

"We can't stay here," Ginny said. "We have to stay somewhere else."

Shannon awoke in the backseat. "What is it?" she asked groggily. She sat up, looked around. "Oh," she said, and was silent.

"We have reservations here," Bill said weakly. "They'll charge us even if we don't stay."

"Let them."

He thought of arguing, then got out his map. "I guess we can go on to the next town, see if they have any place to stay."

"And we'll go to the next town if we have to. And the next. We'll keep driving until we find a motel." She looked at him. "You've been driving all day. We'll switch off. I'll drive for a while."

He looked at the dashboard. "We need to get gas, though. We're almost out."

Ginny nodded. "Fine," she said. "Let's get it and go."

But the Store-suited attendant at the station informed him that the tanks were empty and the truck hadn't been by yet. A shipment was supposed to have been delivered this morning, but there'd been some sort of mix-up near Albuquerque and the driver had radioed that he wouldn't be in until late.

"How late?" Bill asked.

The attendant shrugged. "Ten, maybe. Midnight."

"We're screwed," he told Ginny, walking back to the car. He explained the situation, and after a brief discussion, they agreed to stay that night in the Holiday Inn.

The motel itself was nice. There was cable TV, a heated pool, a Jacuzzi, and there was nothing sinister or threatening about any of it. But every window in the place had a view of The Store, and even the maids and desk clerks were wearing Store uniforms.

They locked themselves in their room, pulled the drapes, and had a dinner comprised of the snacks they'd brought along with them: Coke and potato chips, apples and pretzels. Ginny lay on one bed, Shannon on the other, and he sat in a chair next to the curtained window as they watched a New Mexico newscast, the national news, and a syndicated tabloid show.

They didn't talk about The Store or the town, commented only on the stories broadcast on television. Shannon went to take a shower, and Bill moved next to Ginny on the bed. She snuggled next to him. "I'm scared," she said.

"I know," he told her. He was scared, too, although he told himself logically that there was no real reason to be.

He changed the station when Shannon emerged from the bathroom, switching to a movie channel, and they watched a bad John Candy movie and then part of an even worse Chevy Chase flick.

Shannon had already crawled under the covers of her bed, and Ginny was about to go into the bathroom and take a shower herself, when Bill made a big show of standing, stretching, and looking at the clock.

"I'm going to go get some gas," he said. "I'll be back in a few minutes."

Ginny stopped cold, whirled to face him. "What?"

"I'm going to get some gas."

"You're not going out after dark," she told him.

Shannon pretended not to listen, kept her attention on the movie, and he walked over to where Ginny was standing. "What if there is no gas in the morning?" he said. "Are we going to stay here another day? The truck's supposed to come tonight. I'll fill up the tank and be right back."

"I don't like it."

He pointed out that the gas station was half a block away, between a Burger King and a 7-Eleven, in the opposite direction of The Store. "There won't be any problem," he said.

She looked at him, took a deep breath. "Make it quick."

He drove directly to The Store.

He'd been wanting to drive by ever since they'd arrived in Encantada, ever since he'd seen the uniformed populace, but he knew that Ginny would be against it and he hadn't even mentioned the idea to her. Now he drove into the huge parking lot and toward the entrance of The Store.

It was eerie, seeing the familiar building in these unfamiliar surroundings. He understood the corporate desire for uniformity, but there was something about the deliberately induced déjà vu he experienced while driving through a parking lot he knew toward a store that he knew in a town that he'd never been in or seen before that was not only disorienting but disturbing.

It was after ten and The Store was closed. He'd expected to see a few stragglers, the cars of some late-working employees in the parking lot, but everyone must have bailed instantly because his was the only vehicle on the wide expanse of asphalt.

He slowed the car as he drove toward the glass doors of the entrance. Inside, the building was fully lit, a lengthening parallelogram of light spilling onto the empty parking lot. Despite the absence of other vehicles, he thought he could see movement inside The Store, the silhouettes of several figures, and though the night and the darkness and The Store and the town all conspired to send a chill down his spine, he continued forward slowly.

This close, he could see a figure through the glass, standing on the other side of the door, waving at him.

The figure looked familiar, and at first he couldn't place why.

Then he turned the car slightly to the left and his headlights illuminated the face of the form.

Jed McGill.

He sucked in his breath, terror blooming full-fledged within him.

In his lights, the figure grinned.

Jed McGill.

It couldn't be.

But he didn't want to know for sure, and he sped by, turned around, drove back out onto the highway and to the gas station, where he filled up the tank.

He was still shaking when he arrived back at their room, but Ginny was in the shower and Shannon was asleep, and he quickly locked the door, turned off the lights, took off his clothes, and crawled into bed.

They left early the next morning, well before dawn, and while he tried not to think about what he'd seen last night, tried not to think about The Store at all, they had to pass it on their way out of town, and as the buildings gave way to desert, his headlights played across a series of billboards posted by the side of the road:

THE STORE WANTS YOU
NEW MEXICO IS STORE COUNTRY
ASK NOT WHAT THE STORE CAN DO FOR YOU
BUT WHAT YOU CAN DO FOR THE STORE

None of them mentioned the billboards. Or The Store. They drove through the predawn desert in silence.

That night and the next were spent at a Best Western in White's City, near the entrance of the national park. They took all the tours, went on all the trails, but even with a day between Encantada and Carlsbad, he could not enjoy the caverns. None of them could. The caves were beautiful, spectacular, truly a natural wonder, but

The Store remained in his mind, and he could not keep from thinking, irrationally, that everyone in Juniper would be wearing Store uniforms when they returned.

They skipped the scenic route home the next day, took major highways, and arrived in Juniper long after dark, tired and hungry.

"We'll unpack tomorrow," he said, getting out of the car. "Just leave it."

The house lights were all off, so Sam was either out or asleep, and Bill took out his house key as he trudged across the dirt up to the front door. There was a piece of paper attached to the door, but he couldn't read it in the dark and he opened the door and flipped on both the living room and porch lights.

It was a note.

Written on The Store's letterhead.

Heart thumping, he pulled out the tack holding up the paper and read:

NOTICE:

Shannon Davis, you have been transferred out of The Store's Garden department and are hereby ordered to report for duty in Housewares at 6:00 A.M. Tuesday morning. By order of The Store, your vacation is officially over.

It was signed by Samantha M. Davis, Assistant Manager.

"Look's like Sam's been promoted," Ginny said.

Bill didn't respond. Neither did Shannon.

They walked into the house, closing the door behind them.

TWENTY-SIX

1

Monday morning. Shannon was up before they were, waiting for them in silence on the couch in the living room, no stereo on, no radio, no TV.

"Mom?" she said. "Dad?"

Ginny looked over at Bill. He hadn't slept well, and it showed. His face was wan, his eyes red and puffy. He met her gaze, nodded, and they sat down on the love seat across from the couch.

"What is it?" Ginny asked softly.

Shannon wouldn't meet their eyes, would only look at her hands, which were twisting an already shredded Kleenex in her lap. "I don't want to work at The Store anymore."

Ginny was filled with a powerful sense of relief.

"Thank God," Bill said.

"But I don't know how to quit." She looked up at them for the first time. "I'm afraid to quit."

"There's nothing to be afraid of—" Bill began.

"Yes, there is," Shannon said. "We all know there is."

"What I mean is that I'll go in with you, if you want. We'll both go in and tell them that you're quitting."

"I have a better idea," Ginny said.

They both turned to look at her.

"We let Sam do it for you."

Bill was already shaking his head.

"She's assistant manager now."

Shannon was nodding excitedly. "She got me the job. Now she can get me out of it. She's the one who wrote the notice, anyway."

"Let me talk to her," Ginny told Bill.

Samantha had come home late last night, after they'd gone to bed, and she was still locked in her room, sleeping.

"I'll wake her up," Bill offered.

"No," Ginny said. "Let her sleep."

His jaw grew tense. "I'm not going to tiptoe around my own house, kowtowing to my daughter because she works for The Store. We're still the parents in this household. They're still the children."

"I know that," Ginny said patiently. "We all know that. And if you'd gotten a decent night's sleep, you'd know it, too. But since Sam is in a position to help her sister, I think it would be a good idea if we talk to her when she's in a positive mood."

"Fine," Bill sighed. He turned toward Shannon. "But if it's a no-go, I'll still go down with you to talk to that Mr. Lamb. If you need moral support, I'll be there."

"Thanks, Dad."

He got up, walked over to the couch, kissed her on the forehead. "And I'm happy you decided to quit," he said. "You make me proud."

Ginny decided to talk to Sam without Bill present. He'd only get angry, aggravate the situation, cause problems. She told him that, and he agreed—reluctantly—so she waited until he was safely ensconced in his office, playing with his computer, before collaring Samantha.

Shannon was in her bedroom, waiting, and Ginny gathered both girls together in the living room, sitting them down on the couch.

She came right out and said it: "Sam, your sister wants to quit. She doesn't want to work at The Store anymore."

Samantha's face tightened, her expression hardening. "She can't quit. She starts in Housewares tomorrow morning. I got her that job."

Shannon would not look at her sister. "I don't want it," she said quietly.

"Well, you've got it. I pulled a lot of strings to get it for you."

Ginny watched Shannon's face, saw an expression

there she had never seen before and couldn't decipher. "You can't force your sister to work if she doesn't want to," she told Samantha.

"She was hired to work through October."

"I changed my mind!" Shannon said.

"The Store can terminate that contract. You cannot. For better or worse, you are a member of The Store Corps. Live it, love it."

A rush of anger coursed through Ginny. "Knock this off," she told Samantha. "Now."

"Knock what off?"

"Your sister is quitting, and that's it. Period."

"It's not my decision." Sam's voice had taken on a defensive edge. "I'd let her quit if it was up to me, but it's not. I'm just following policy."

"Then Shannon and your father will just have to have a talk with the store manager."

"They can't," Sam said quickly.

"We'll see about that."

"What if I just never show up again?" Shannon asked. "They'll fire me, right?"

Sam did not answer.

"Right?"

"Will they fire her?" Ginny asked.

Sam's voice was quiet. "No. They won't fire her. They'll come after her. They'll find her. They'll *make* her work."

Ginny shivered. A chill passed through her, and she looked over at her younger daughter, who had suddenly turned very pale.

"You can't fight it," Sam said.

"It's okay," Shannon said shakily. "I'll work."

"You don't have to—"

"I want to." She stood, hurried off, into her bedroom.

"Sam?" Ginny said.

Samantha stood, would not look at her. "I have to work," she said. "It's going to be a busy day."

"So how did it go?" Bill asked.

"It didn't."

"Then we'll force them to quit. Or at least we'll force Shannon."

They'll come after her. They'll find her. They'll make her work.

Ginny shook her head. "I don't think it's a good idea," she said quietly.

"Why not?"

She told him about what Sam had said, the implied threat.

"So unless we're planning to move somewhere else, I think it's safer to let them work there. It's not causing any real problems. They work at cash registers, sell things, pick up their paychecks. But if they pulled out . . ." She let the thought trail off.

"There'd be trouble," he finished for her.

She nodded.

"I thought Shannon wanted to quit."

"She changed her mind."

He laughed harshly. "Jesus. Employment by intimidation. What's this world coming to?"

She put an arm around his shoulder, rested her chin on the top of his head. "I don't know," she said. "I really don't know."

2

Sam dropped the bombshell after dinner.

"I'm not going to college," she said.

Bill looked over at Ginny. It was obvious that this was the first time she'd heard these words as well, and he could see the anger settle upon her face. "What do you mean, you're not going to college?" she demanded.

"I'm in the management program now. They're sending me off to the corporate headquarters in Dallas for training. It's a two-week program, and after that, I'll be back in Juniper. The Store already found me a house over on Elm, and it's rent-free. They pay for everything. I can move in this weekend."

They were all stunned. Even Shannon was silent, and they looked dumbly at each other while Samantha smiled brightly.

"I know I was planning to go to college, but this is a great opportunity."

Ginny was the first to find her voice. "A great opportunity? Assistant manager of a discount store in Juniper? You can be anything you want. With your grades and your brains, if you graduate with even a bachelor's degree, you can write your own ticket. You can get a job anywhere, with any company. You can get a job like your father's, work at home."

Bill heard the hurt in her voice. Neither of them had ever imagined that their daughters would not go to college. It had never even been considered an option. Ginny, in particular, had had high hopes for both Sam and Shannon, and he could see from the expression on her features that she felt betrayed.

"College is a great experience," Ginny continued gamely. "Not just a learning experience but . . . a social experience. It's where you get a chance to grow, to learn things about yourself, to find out who you really are and what you want from life."

"But there's no reason for me to go," Sam said. "I don't need to 'find myself,' and I already know what I want from life. I want to be on The Store's management team."

Silence again. Shannon shifted uncomfortably in her seat, would not meet anyone's eyes. She stared down at her plate, pushing her rice with a fork.

Ginny looked to Bill for help.

"The Store will always be here," he said. "And you can always come back to it. But this is your only chance to go to college. These are the only scholarships you'll get."

"I know."

"And once you get caught up in the rat race, you won't go back to school. You might tell yourself that college will always be there and you can enroll later if you want to, but the truth is that that very seldom happens. If you don't go now, you won't go."

"I don't need to go."

"We didn't raise you to be a dummy."

"I'm not a dummy," Sam said defensively.

"Then prove it. Go to school."

"I don't need to."

"Everyone needs to."

Sam stood. "The fact is, Dad, college *will* always be there. I *can* go anytime I want. But this position won't stay open forever. If I don't take it, someone else may get it. And they may stay until they retire. This is a once-in-a-lifetime chance. And if I don't like it or it doesn't work out"— she shrugged.—"I'll go to college."

"So you want to move out?"

Samantha nodded, barely able to hide her excitement or keep the smile off her face.

"Over my dead body," he said.

Her smile faltered. "Dad—"

"Yes," he said. "I'm your dad. And I'm telling you that you can't do this."

"I'm eighteen, and I can do what I want."

"Bill," Ginny warned.

He ignored her. "Once you move out, you can't move back. Even if they fire you."

Ginny stood, threw down her napkin. "Bill!"

"What?"

"You are over the line!"

"It is a little harsh, Dad," Shannon said.

Sam was smiling again. She looked around the table, beamed at them. "It may take a little getting used to," she said. "But don't worry. It'll be great."

She looked like a fucking Moonie, he thought. Like some brainwashed bimbo who'd been captured by a cult.

He turned away from her, unable to look at his daughter and contain his rage. He had always considered himself a pacifist, had never really harbored or entertained any violent thoughts or desires—not even in regard to his enemies—but his feelings toward The Store and its minions were invariably revenge fantasies, tinged with violence. And never more so than now. He imagined beating the shit out of Mr. Lamb and Mr. Keyes, physically injuring them, and the aggressiveness of his thoughts disturbed him. He wasn't sure where these thoughts had come from, or why he was stooping to The

Store's base level of discourse, but he wanted to hurt those sons of bitches.

Especially for what they'd done to his daughter.

His daughters?

He glanced toward Shannon. No, he thought thankfully.

At least not yet.

He did not help Sam move out of the house. Ginny did, Shannon did, Sam's friends did, but he remained in his office, in front of his computer, pretending to work, as they carried the furniture and boxes out of her bedroom. He knew how he was behaving—and he hated himself for it—but he could think of no other way of demonstrating to her the depth of his disapproval.

It was ironic, really. He had always felt nothing but disgust for those hard-hearted fathers who kicked their children out of the house for some minor transgression, who disowned their own children and refused to see them or talk to them. He'd always thought those fathers stupid and shortsighted. What disagreement could possibly be so serious that it was worth jeopardizing the relationship between a parent and a child?

Yet here he was, acting the same way, doing the same thing. Not wanting to, but not being able to avoid it. Ginny had been as angry as he was, and even more hurt, but she was better able to adjust, to roll with the flow, to accommodate change.

He could not do that.

He wished he could.

But he couldn't.

And he stood alone in his office, in the silence, listening to the fading motors of the pickup trucks as his oldest daughter moved out of his house.

3

The mood of the town seemed different, Ginny thought as she drove to the salon. Either something in Juniper had changed during their absence, or her perceptions had been altered by what they'd seen on the trip.

The Store.

It was the last thing they'd seen as they'd left town and the first thing they'd seen on their return.

And it had taken Sam.

If before she had felt that The Store was an intruder in her town, now she felt like the intruder. A transformation had occurred while they'd been on their trip, and now Juniper no longer seemed like her town. It seemed like The Store's town. And she was the unwelcome guest.

She drove down Main. The library, she'd heard, was being privatized. County funds had been slashed at the last board of supervisors meeting, and since Juniper's library was the smallest and least frequented in the county, the decision had been made to close it. But once again—of course—the heroic Store had ridden to the rescue and offered to underwrite the entire operation— a proposal that had been gratefully accepted.

The Store now controlled the police department, fire department, all town services, the school district, and the library.

And Sam.

Ginny gripped the steering wheel more tightly. She shared Bill's anger and frustration, but she still saw their daughter as a victim, not an accomplice, and though her gut reaction was to slap the girl and ground her for a month, she realized that Sam was at the age where she had to make her own mistakes.

And learn from them.

She had enough basic faith in her daughter to believe that that would occur.

And she did not want to alienate her and push her away at a time when Sam might need her mother the most.

For things were getting rough out there. She herself was avoided, ostracized, whispered about. Ignored by her friends. The recipient of cold stares from coworkers and giggling derision from old students.

This must be what it felt like to have been a Japanese-American during World War II, she thought, to have been a civil rights activist in Mississippi in the sixties.

She was treated not merely as a stranger or an outsider, but as a traitor living among them, as an enemy.

Because she was not a Store sympathizer.

There were plenty of people who weren't, she knew. The displaced workers, the unemployed, all of the people who'd voted against the current council. But they'd been marginalized, shunted off to the side, and they didn't dare express their true feelings. It was as if, overnight, everything had changed, and all of their allies had either gone into hiding or disappeared.

The Store was now organizing Neighborhood Watch groups. Juniper's crime rate over the past two decades had been nearly nonexistent, but suddenly everyone was concerned about drugs and robberies, gang activity and sexual assaults. Now people in one part of town were reporting people from other parts of town who were seen innocently walking through their neighborhoods.

And the police were responding to the calls.

The town was becoming fractured, fragmented, the larger community breaking off into smaller, potentially adversarial groups.

And The Store was reaping the benefits.

Yesterday's issue of the newspaper had a full-page ad for a weekend sale of home security devices.

Ginny pulled into one of the empty parking spaces on the street in front of Hair Today. A bearded, obviously homeless man, wearing torn jeans and a filthy flannel shirt, walked directly in front of her car, and she pretended to look through her purse, waiting until he had gone before getting out of the vehicle.

She was a little intimidated by the vagrants. Most of them simply sat in empty doorways or on raggedy blankets under trees, but the bolder ones staked out specific spots in order to ask passersby for money. She knew she should be more understanding, and in an abstract, intellectual way, she sympathized with their plight, but on an emotional, personal level, she was slightly afraid of these people. She did not like seeing them, was uncomfortable around them, and she did not know how she was supposed to act.

So she tried to avoid them as much as possible.

She was the only customer in the salon, and Rene was the only stylist, and the two of them coexisted in uncomfortable silence while Ginny's hair was washed, then cut and permed. She would have liked to have talked—about anything—but Rene was obviously in a bad mood, and Ginny let her be.

Afterward, she left an extra-large tip of ten dollars.

Rene smiled for the first time, touched her hand as she placed the bill on the counter. "Thank you," she said. "For everything."

Ginny nodded, smiled back.

On the way home, she saw Sam on the sidewalk, heading away from her new house and toward the highway and The Store. She stopped to offer her daughter a ride, but Sam looked at her and gave her a cold smile. "I don't accept rides from strangers," she said dismissively.

She kept walking.

"Sam?" Ginny called out the car window. She thought at first that it was some sort of joke, but when her daughter would not look back, continued on at the same even pace, she knew that it was not. "Samantha!" she called.

No answer.

Ginny moved the car forward, pulling next to her. "Honey? What's the matter?"

Sam kept walking.

"Get in the car. I don't know what the problem is here, but obviously we need to work it out."

Sam stopped. "There's nothing to work out. Fuck off, Mom."

"What?"

"Fuck. Off."

Another car drove by, and Samantha flagged down the driver. It was a man, someone Ginny didn't know, and before she could call out, before she could say anything, Sam was in the car and off to The Store.

She thought of following, did for a few blocks, but then she thought better of it and turned back toward home as the other car turned onto the highway.

She made it all the way into the drive before bursting into tears.

4

Shannon stood against the wall with the rest of the employees, legs spread to shoulder width, hands clasped behind her back in the official Store stance. Mr. Lamb walked slowly back and forth in front of them. "The new uniforms have arrived," he said. His voice was low and seductive. "They are beautiful."

Shannon felt uneasy. She thought of the trip, of Encantada, of the people in that town all wearing Store uniforms.

Mr. Lamb smiled at her, and she thought of—

Sam's bloody panties.

She looked quickly away, feeling cold and sick.

"You are all going to wear your beautiful new uniforms today. You will wear them proudly. For you are the elite, you are the chosen."

He walked into the dark doorway of the small stockroom to the left of the elevator and emerged with one of the new uniforms on a hanger. It was leather, black leather, and shiny. Holding the hanger with his left hand, he used his right to pull off and display the uniform's top, a strange-looking article of clothing that to Shannon resembled a straitjacket. Next, he held up the pants. "They're tight in the crotch," he said. "You'll love them."

There were a few nervous giggles from some of the employees.

There was a cap as well, a leather beret with a silver-studded insignia, and matching leather underwear: a codpiece for the males, French-cut panties for the females.

"And you all get boots," he said. "Knee-high storm troopers. They're perfect."

He stood there, bouncing a little on the balls of his feet, looking up and down the line, grinning at them. Neither Shannon nor anyone else seemed to know what came next—what they were supposed to do or say, how they were supposed to react—and they stood there dumbly, looking at each other, looking at Mr. Lamb.

"All right," the personnel manager said finally. "What are we waiting for? Strip!"

Shannon sucked in her breath, not sure that she'd heard correctly, praying to God that she hadn't.

Mr. Lamb clapped his hands. "Come on! Hop to! Take off your clothes! All of them! Now!"

Joad Comstock was next to her on the right, Francine Dormand to her left, and she didn't want either of them to see her naked. She had a big red pimple on the left cheek of her buttocks, and more pimples on her shoulders. Her breasts were too small, much smaller than Francine's, and despite all the dieting her stomach was still too big. She hadn't shaved her legs, either, not for over a week, and the stubble looked really gross.

She didn't want *anyone* to see her naked.

Around her, the other employees were perfunctorily taking off their clothes: removing their shoes, unbuckling their belts, unbuttoning their tops.

"Throw your old uniforms into the center of the corridor," Mr. Lamb ordered.

No one was balking, no one was complaining, no one was talking. There were no jokes cracked, and even the youngest employees did not giggle as their coworkers stripped.

Jake was somewhere in line, Shannon thought.

"Shannon Davis," Mr. Lamb said loudly, warningly, staring at her.

She began unbuttoning her top.

"These are *our* uniforms," Mr. Lamb stated. "They are the uniforms of The Store and they will not leave this building. You will keep them in your lockers, and you will put them on when you arrive and take them off before you leave. You will wear your uniforms only within the confines of The Store." He paused. "If you wear your uniform outside of this building, you will be terminated." He paused again. "If you are scheduled to work and do not wear your uniform, you will be terminated."

A wave of cold passed through Shannon as she pulled down her panties. Mr. Lamb's peculiar emphasis of the word "terminated" was extremely unsettling. She knew that was intentional, knew he wanted them to pick up on the double meaning of the word, but that did not make it any less upsetting.

Following Mr. Lamb's directions, they filed naked into the small, dark stockroom. They'd lined up alphabetically, and boxed uniforms with name tags attached were piled in the same order, illuminated by a single recessed bulb in the ceiling. Shannon kept her attention focused on Joad's head in front of her, not wanting to see his exposed back or legs or hairy buttocks, not wanting to see any part of any of her coworkers' bodies.

She hoped Francine was doing the same behind her.

Picking up the box with her name tag attached, Shannon carried it out to the assembly corridor.

No one was yet putting on the new uniforms. They all stood, holding their boxes, at attention. Somehow, in the few brief moments it had taken her to walk into the stockroom and out again, all of their discarded clothes had been piled in the center of the corridor.

"It is time," Mr. Lamb said, when the last employee emerged from the stockroom.

They burned their old uniforms—and their underwear and their shoes and socks—in a ceremonial fire. Mr. Lamb made them walk around the flames, holding hands, singing The Store's irritating commercial jingle.

Or, as Mr. Lamb referred to it, "The Store's Official Anthem."

Still naked, they were herded into the chapel, where one by one they were each required to kneel down before the massive painting of Newman King. Shannon's body was covered with goose bumps, the chilled flesh of fear, not cold, and she watched the employees before her kneel down on the red carpet, bow their heads and give thanks to Newman King for allowing them to graduate to this new level. There was no way any of them could not know that this was wrong, crazy—*evil*—yet none of the other employees seemed fazed. They were quiet, a little more subdued than usual, perhaps, but there was no opposition to what they were doing, no recognition that this was something an employer should not be able to demand, or even request, from an employee.

Shannon knew it was wrong, but she walked forward just like the others, knelt, gave thanks, afraid to voice her disapproval, not brave enough to refuse to participate.

She stood, walked out of the chapel. All of the shifts would go through this, she realized. All of The Store's workers.

Sam would go through this—if she hadn't already.

"Okay!" Mr. Lamb said, clapping his hands, when the last employee had given thanks. "To the lockers! Put on your uniforms and be on the floor in five!" He glanced over at Shannon, smiled, and a hot flush of shame passed through her as she saw where his eyes were looking. "The Store opens in ten minutes! Be there or be square!"

TWENTY-SEVEN

1

He had stopped jogging entirely.

The streets were getting too scary.

It was not something Bill had ever expected to happen in Juniper. A year ago—six months ago, even—such an idea would have been unthinkable. But things were different now. The Store had recruited its own security force to augment the police department, and though ostensibly the reason was to combat the increased crime in town, the truth was that The Store merely wanted to increase its hold, to flaunt its power, to make sure that everyone knew that it was now in charge of Juniper.

Besides, although he could not prove anything, most of the crime, in Bill's mind, seemed to be committed by this new security force.

And the victims always seemed to be people who were opposed to The Store.

Which was why he no longer jogged.

He had not yet received a new assignment, his days were still free, and he now spent most of them hanging around Street's place. Ben hung there, too, and it had the feeling of one of those cinematic barbershops where a group of crotchety old man sat around, day after day, critiquing the world that passed by the windows.

Only there was no world passing by the windows.

There were only occasional cars driving past on their way to The Store.

Bill pulled up in front of the electronics shop and hopped out of his Jeep. There was something different about the street today, and it took him a moment to figure out what it was.

Multicolored flyers had been posted on the trees, telephone poles, and abandoned storefronts downtown.

He walked up to the closest telephone pole. No, not flyers. Announcements:

BY THE ORDER OF THE STORE, NO CITIZEN MAY BE OUTSIDE HIS OR HER HOME AFTER 10 P.M. UNLESS ENGAGED IN STORE BUSINESS. THIS CURFEW WILL BE STRICTLY ENFORCED.

"Do you believe this shit?" Street walked outside onto the sidewalk, Ben following. "A fucking discount store making laws and setting policy, telling me when I can and can't walk around my own town? How the fuck did this happen?"

"How did we let it happen?" Ben said quietly.

"Good point," Street said. He walked up to the wooden pole, pulled off the pink sign, crumpled it up, grimacing disgustedly.

"When did these go up?" Bill asked.

"Last night, this morning. They had kids from church running around putting up this crap."

"Church?" Bill said.

"Oh, yes." Ben nodded. "Most of our local clergy are big Store supporters."

"How is that possible?"

"Donations to their coffers, perhaps?"

Street laughed harshly. "I guess if The Store's on God's side, then God's on The Store's side. Kind of a you-scratch-my-back-I'll-scratch-yours deal."

They walked into the shop. "That's what I've always hated about the religion/politics connection," Ben said. "These clergymen tell their followers who to vote for, what legislation to support, because this is what God wants them to do." He shook his head. "The hubris, man. Don't any of them pick up on that? They think they know the mind of God? Them claiming to know how God would vote is like an amoeba claiming to know what car I'm going to buy."

"So much for 'rendering to Caesar,' huh?"

Street tossed the crumpled announcement in a wastepaper basket and walked into the back room, returning a moment later with three beers. He tossed one can to Bill, one to Ben, popping open the tab on his own.

"During business hours?" Bill said.

Street shrugged. "What business?"

Ben was on a roll. "What really ticks me off about these religious assholes is that they always claim they're for less government, and they are—when it comes to economics. But they're all for letting government regulate our social lives, our bedroom behavior, what movies we can see, what pictures we can look at, what books we can read."

Street took a long swig. "They want to tell me where I can and can't put my dick."

"Because they can't even use theirs," Ben said. "Those cows they're married to won't let 'em."

Bill burst out laughing. A second later, Ben and Street started laughing as well.

None of them went to church on a regular basis. Street used to go every Sunday, when he was married, but he hadn't gone since. Ben considered himself an agnostic and hadn't attended since Catholic school. In the fuzzy, evasive neuterspeak of today, he himself had what was called "a personal relationship with God." Which meant that his religious beliefs were privately held and were not sanctioned or reinforced by any church or organized religion. He'd always considered suspect the faith of people who had to go to church every Sunday. As an old college friend of his had said, once you got the Word, you got it. There was no reason to reinforce it every seven days unless you were so damn stupid that after a week you forgot everything you'd learned and needed to be reminded again of the basic tenets of your faith.

Street shook his head. "It's wrong using kids, though. If churches are going to get involved, let the adults do it. Keep the kids out of it."

"Amen," Ben said.

"So what are we going to do about this?" Bill walked over to the door, pointed through the glass at the multi-colored announcements dotting the downtown. "You know damn well that people in Juniper, *most* people, aren't in favor of a curfew. Adults don't want to be treated like children. And what about the bar? The video store? Circle K? There are a whole bunch of businesses that depend on people being out at night."

"Petition," Street said. "We start one to rescind this ordinance."

"Not a bad idea," Ben admitted. "People'd be in favor of this idea. It might give us an opening, a little chink in the armor we could exploit. I think we'd get quite a few signatures."

"If people weren't afraid to sign."

"If people weren't afraid to sign," Ben agreed.

Street finished off his beer, grinned. He moved around the back of the register counter. "Start thinking, boys. I'll get some paper and pens."

An hour later, Bill was at the park, pen, clipboard, and petition in hand. They'd hashed it out quickly, he and Ben, then he'd rushed home, typed it on his PC, and printed it out, making multiple copies. Ginny had been in her garden, killing tomato worms, and he'd shown her the petition and left her a few copies. "Just in case any of your friends come by," he said.

He dropped more off at the electronics shop, Street promising to hit up anyone he saw on Main, Ben vowing to take it to the source and camp out in The Store's parking lot "until they kick me out."

Bill brought his petitions to the park.

There were quite a few people here. Little League kids practicing, mostly. Some old men. Mothers and small children. A couple playing tennis.

He approached the tennis couple first, explaining what the petition said and what they were trying to do, and the man seemed close to signing at one point. But he was wary of being the first signee, and his wife pulled him quickly away, frightened, nearly panicked. "It's a trap!" she said. "Don't do it. They're trying to trap you."

The couple hurried off, and he walked around the tennis court to the row of benches where several of the old men were sitting.

None of them would even hear him out.

The only signature he received was from a middle-aged woman watching her young daughter play on the swing set. She was nodding even before he'd finished explaining what the petition was meant to do.

"One of those announcements was nailed to our front door," she said. She seemed nervous, kept glancing at her daughter on the swing as if to make sure that the little girl was still there.

"We need to put a stop to this," he told her. "And we need your help."

"They're enforcing the curfew already."

"I didn't know that," he said, surprised. "In fact, I only learned about the ordinance this morning."

She glanced suspiciously around. "They're out after dark," she whispered. "I saw them."

"Who?"

"The men in black. The Night Managers."

The men in black.

He thought of Encantada. Of Jed McGill.

Once again, the woman quickly looked around. Before he could say anything else, she grabbed the pen from his hand, scrawled a quick, indecipherable signature, and hurried away, grabbing her daughter.

"Thanks!" he called after her.

She did not acknowledge him, and he watched as she and her daughter practically ran to their car.

Jed McGill. He wondered sometimes if he'd really seen what he thought he'd seen. He'd been in such a hurry to get away, so desperate not to know, that even in his own mind there was no clear confirmation of the figure's identity. Even now, he still wasn't sure whether he wanted to know. It made absolutely no sense whatsoever, was so bizarre as to be incomprehensible, and the questions that it raised terrified him.

The men in black.

The Night Managers.

He tried to concentrate on the task before him, to think only about getting signatures for his petition.

On the street, in back of the woman's departing vehicle, a police car pulled up, cruised to a stop, and Forest Everson got out. Even before the policeman began walking across the grass toward him, Bill knew why he was here.

He stood his ground.

Forest looked embarrassed as he walked up to where Bill was standing. "I'm sorry, Mr. Davis, but you're going to have to stop with that petition."

Bill faced him. "Why?"

"It's against the law."

"It's against the law to get people to sign a petition? Since when?"

"Since last night. The town council convened in a special meeting, and they passed a new ordinance making it illegal to circulate a petition of any sort within a five-mile radius of The Store. I guess they consider it a restriction of commerce because they feel it impinges on The Store's ability to do business."

"Jesus."

"It's not my decision," Forest said. "I don't make the laws. I don't even agree with all of them. But I'm paid to enforce them, and that's what I do."

Bill was still trying to sort out the order of events. The council created the ordinance last night? He and his friends had only thought of the petition this morning. The council knew what they were going to do before *they* did?

"This can't be constitutional," he said. "This is America, damn it. We still have freedom of speech here."

The policeman smiled wryly. "Not in Juniper."

"So I can't do this anywhere in town? I can't even have people sign petitions on my own property?"

Forest shook his head. "Not within a five-mile radius of The Store."

"The damn town's only two and a half miles long. That means there can't be any petitions anywhere in Juniper."

The policeman nodded.

"I'm not giving you my petition."

"I'm not asking you for it. Although the new chief'd have my ass if he knew that. He'd want the name and address of everyone on there. And he'd want you in jail." Forest sighed. "Go home. Take your petition with you. Lay low."

"Ben's at The Store, trying to get signatures."

"I'll try to head him off before anyone else does."

"This is wrong," Bill said.

"I know." Forest nodded. "But for now it's the law, and until things change, it's my job to enforce it." He started back across the grass toward his car.

"Thanks," Bill said. "You're a good man."

"And these are bad times. Go home. Stay out of trouble. Stay away from The Store."

He and Ginny were waiting for Shannon when she came home from work.

They let her go to the bathroom, get something to drink, eat a snack, then called her over to the living room.

She knew something was up, and she sat down across from them, sighing. "What is it now?"

"The Night Managers," Bill said.

She paled. "Where did you hear about them?"

"I have my sources." He smiled, tried to keep his tone light, but was aware that he failed miserably. He gave it up, addressed her seriously. "Who are they?"

"More like *what* are they," she said quietly.

His mouth suddenly felt dry. "All right, then. *What* are they?"

"I . . . I don't really know," Shannon admitted. "I don't think anyone does. But . . . they're not good." She took a deep breath. "No one talks about them. Everyone's afraid to."

"But there are rumors."

She nodded. "There are rumors."

"Like what?"

She licked her lips. "That they kill people."

"Do you believe it?" Ginny asked.

She nodded.

Bill looked at her. "Someone said that they're the ones enforcing the curfew. She said she saw them."

"I don't think so," Shannon said.

"Why not?"

"Because no one's ever seen them. And I don't think anyone outside The Store has even heard of them. I think . . . I don't think they ever leave The Store."

"They never leave The Store?" Ginny said.

"I don't think so."

Bill nodded thoughtfully. "They never leave The Store. Maybe we can use that."

"How?" Ginny asked.

"I don't know," he said. "Not yet. But every little bit helps. Knowledge is power, and we have our own little spy within the organization."

"Me?" Shannon said.

"You."

"What . . . what am I supposed to do?"

"Just keep your eyes and ears open," he said. "And look for weaknesses."

TWENTY-EIGHT

1

They were on to him.

Ben didn't know how they'd found out, but The Store's officials knew that he was working on an exposé.

And they were after him.

He'd called earlier to get a standard party-line quote from The Store's manager, and had talked instead to Lamb. He'd explained to the personnel manager that he was a freelance journalist, working on a feature article for a national magazine, but the man had cut him off. *"Feature* article, Mr. Anderson?" The personnel manager's voice was snide. "You're writing a muckraking piece, a sensationalistic piece of shit, you cocksucking son of a bitch."

Ben had been shocked into silence.

"We know who our friends are. And we know our enemies."

There'd been a click after that, the hum of a dial tone, and though Ben had been a reporter for the past twenty-five years, had dealt with confrontation many times over, his hands were shaking, his heart pounding.

Something about those Store people spooked him.

But he'd been given a break. Someone within The Store's organization had reached out to him, provided him with a tip, given him a lead. And it had been confirmed by Bill and Shannon.

There were people within the organization who were unhappy and dissatisfied.

That was a good sign.

That was a very good sign.

The Night Managers.

He didn't know who they were, but it sounded promising. The concept itself was pretty damn creepy, but it also seemed unethical, immoral, illegal. And in a spectacular, media-friendly way. This was what editors liked to buy and readers liked to read. This was what brought down giants. This was the stuff of journalistic wet dreams.

Even without the Night Managers, it was going to be one hell of an article. He'd talked to Jack Pyle, an old buddy of his in Denver, who'd promised to send him a ton of info. Jack had been working on a similar story, inspired by his son's recent involvement with The Store, but he'd chickened out at the end, afraid that The Store would retaliate against his boy if the piece got published.

"It's a cult," he said. "And if one of their own breaks ranks, breaks that wall of silence . . . God help them."

"You have documentation?" Ben had asked.

He could almost hear Jack nodding over the phone. "Oh, yes," he said. "Oh, yes."

Another week of waiting and researching, a week of writing after that, and this puppy was ready to be sent out and shopped around.

But he needed another angle, some personal involvement between reporter and story. That was the trend these days. That's what people liked. Hard research and solid quotes were fine, but the news-hungry public now wanted more than that. They wanted an element of danger. They wanted a tale of intrigue and infiltration.

Which was why he was going to spend an entire night in The Store.

And see the Night Managers for himself.

He'd been planning the stunt for the past three days, and he was pretty sure he could pull it off. Just before closing, he would go into the rest room, hide in one of the stalls, crouching on top of the toilet so his feet could not be seen in the gap beneath the stall door, and wait until everyone had gone.

It was a risky plan, of course. For all he knew, The Store might make its employees conduct a thorough search of every nook and cranny within the building. The door of each toilet stall might be individually opened and checked. But he was betting that on Friday, at the end of an ordinary, uneventful week, such precautions, even if in effect, would not be followed to the letter.

Besides, he had a head start going in. Despite the appalling number of security cameras all over The Store, there were no cameras trained on the men's room door.

It was something he had checked, double-checked, and rechecked.

The Store did not keep track of who entered and exited the men's rest room.

Of course, the perverts had a video camera inside, on the wall opposite the urinals. But he'd come up with a way to take that camera out without being noticed and without making it seem suspicious.

There was an element of danger to this. He knew that going in, and he didn't want to involve anyone else. But he needed help. He needed someone to drop him off at The Store and act as lookout while he secured his hiding place.

Bill was the logical choice. He'd hated The Store since the beginning—since *before* the beginning—and he was both reliable and trustworthy. But he also had a family. And his daughters worked for The Store. Bill himself worked for a corporation that was supplying computer software for the chain, and Ben didn't want his friend to lose his job if they got caught.

Lose his job?

The Store would do worse than that to them if they were caught.

No, he thought. Bill had too much to lose. Street was the better choice in this instance.

He started to call Street, then put down the receiver and drove to his house instead.

Never could tell. The phone lines might be bugged.

Probably were.

Street wasn't too thrilled with the idea. He agreed to go along with it, had no problem playing his part, but he didn't think there was any need to spend the night in The Store. "It's stupid," he said. "It's a fucking Hardy Boys plan. Something Tom Sawyer and Huck Finn would do. Not the way a respectable journalist would get his story."

Ben laughed. "Since when have I been a respectable journalist?"

"Good point."

But Street remained troubled, and Ben had to admit that his friend's reservations were valid. He began having second thoughts himself. But even as he inwardly debated whether or not he should go through with this, they were doing what they were supposed to do, taking the actions they'd planned and coordinated, and before they knew it, they were in the empty men's room, Street locking the door and pretending to take a piss while Ben used his cover to sneak under the video camera and, with the help of some handy-dandy tools, disconnect the video feed.

"What time do you have?" Ben asked, walking over to the sink to check his appearance in the mirror.

"Almost ten."

"They'll be closing," Ben said. "You'd better hit the road."

"In a minute."

"Now."

"I really do have to take a leak," Street told him.

Ben laughed. "Sorry." He leaned over, pretended to peek. "Wow! You have a big dick!"

Street grinned. "But of course."

There was a knock on the rest room door, and they both froze.

"Is anyone in there?" someone called.

"I'll be out in a minute!" Street answered. He flushed the urinal and ran the sink tap. Covered by the noise, Ben locked himself in the far stall, crouching on the toilet seat.

"I owe you," he whispered.

"Check in with me when you're finished. I want to know that you're safe."

"Will do."

Street unlocked the door, stepped out, and Ben heard a Store employee say, "Is there anyone else in there?"

"Just me and my diarrhea," Street announced cheerfully.

"That door's supposed to remain unlocked during business hours."

"Sorry," Street said. "I just don't like people to hear me making disgusting noises."

The door closed, and it did not reopen. Ben waited. Fifteen minutes. a half hour. An hour. The lights did not switch off, but no one returned, and when he checked his watch and saw that it was nearly midnight, he realized that they'd gotten away with it.

Carefully, quietly, he stepped down from the toilet, nearly falling from the sudden shift of weight on his cramped, weakened muscles. He stood in place for a moment, stretching, then walked across the tiled floor and pushed open the door to peek into The Store proper.

The building was silent.

All of the lights were still on, but The Store appeared to be empty.

He walked out carefully, practically tiptoeing, listening for noise but hearing nothing. Even the air conditioner had been shut off. There might be a security person around somewhere, maybe someone monitoring the other video cameras, but there was no one else around. No one could be this quiet unless they were asleep.

The other video cameras. He'd forgotten about them. He should've brought a mask to wear, something to hide his features so they wouldn't be able to identify him on videotape—

There was the sound of an elevator door opening.

Ben's blood began racing, his adrenaline pumping. He ducked quickly behind a shelf of CD players and adjusted his angle so he could peer through the stacked merchandise to the source of the sound.

They emerged from the elevator and the stairwell next to it, one after the other, a line of whey-faced men dressed entirely in black: black shoes, black pants, black shirts, black jackets. They moved silently, and there was something about the absence of sound that bespoke danger.

The Night Managers.

The elevator and stairwell were only a few yards down from the rest rooms, and he realized that if he had waited a few moments longer, if he had spent even another minute stretching his cramped muscles, they would have caught him.

But what would they have done to him?

He didn't want to find out. There was something terrifyingly unnatural about the appearance of those blank white faces, and he suddenly wished that he had heeded Street's advice and given up on this whole infiltration idea.

Of course, now that he was here . . .

He checked the miniature tape recorder in his shirt pocket, took out the tiny camera with which he planned to surreptitiously photograph the Night Managers.

The lights in the building winked off.

He jumped, startled, and nearly fell, almost knocking over a CD player. He caught himself before anything happened, and the only sound was a slight click as his hand steadied the stereo component, but even that noise seemed outrageously loud in the stillness, and he remained tensed, unmoving, waiting to see if he'd been caught.

The lights came back on.

He was safe. The Night Managers were walking up and down various aisles, robotically, in groups of three, not looking around, not stopping, not slowing, simply pressing onward, like unstoppable windup toys. They did not even know he was here.

He moved away from the CD players, saw three Night Managers moving down an aisle away from him, and he quickly snapped a picture of their retreating backs. To his left, two rows over, three others were passing by, not looking to the left, not looking to the right, facing straight ahead, and he took a profile photo.

The lights went off again.

He didn't panic this time, simply waited. This was obviously part of some standard chain of events, some sequence that happened nightly, and he stood in place until the lights came back on.

A hand fell on his shoulder, gripping him tightly.

He dropped his camera, startled, and turned to see one of the Night Managers.

Grinning at him.

They'd known he was here all along.

They'd been playing with him.

No, he thought. Not playing. The Night Managers of The Store did not play.

The others surrounded him, their trips up and down aisles all ending at precisely the spot where he was standing.

"I can explain . . ." he began. He trailed off, expecting to hear a "Shut up," or a "There's nothing to explain," or some other such order, but there was nothing, no noise, only silence, only those grinning white faces surrounding him, and it was the absence of noise that scared him more than anything else.

He tried to break away, tried to run.

The grip on his shoulder kept him from moving.

"Help!" he screamed at the top of his lungs. "Help!"

A cold white hand clamped around his mouth. Over the white knuckles that covered half his face, he saw the other Night Managers all withdrawing knives from somewhere on their persons. Long, shiny knives with sharp, straight edges.

He tried to squirm away, tried to kick, tried to lash out, but he realized that all of his limbs were now being held, and then he was lifted into the air and then he was dropped flat on his back on the floor.

Something snapped in his spine, and suddenly he couldn't move, and the hand was still over his mouth as the knives began carefully entering his flesh, cutting his skin.

He prayed for unconsciousness from the depths of his screaming agonized mind, and when he finally felt himself slipping away, he was flooded with an overwhelming sense of relief, grateful that the end had come.

But it was not the end. He regained consciousness sometime later, in a dark room in one of the basements, and he learned that it was nowhere near the end.

It was only the beginning.

2

From the first, there seemed something wrong with the deal. Night Managers or not, there was no reason for Ben to sneak into The Store and spend the night. It was not necessary for the article and, as far as Street was concerned, it was unnecessarily dangerous.

He told this to Ben. Several times on the way over. But Ben was in his Woodward-and-Bernstein mode and nothing could dissuade him from what he perceived to be his higher calling, his mission to uncover The Truth.

Ben told him to hit the road after leaving him in the men's room, to get out of there, and The Store director who caught him coming out of the bathroom had been a pretty good impetus to do exactly that, but he couldn't simply abandon his friend, and he left The Store lot and parked along the edge of the highway instead, waiting.

He waited for nearly an hour, but then the lights in the parking lot went out, and when they turned on again a few seconds later, they were pointing not down at the parking lot but out toward him, trained on his truck like searchlights, and he quickly turned on the ignition, put the truck into gear, and took off.

Maybe they'd gotten Ben.

He didn't want to think about it.

Arriving home, he was still shaken. He picked up his phone, tried to dial Bill, but the line was dead, no dial tone even, and he immediately turned on his PC to check whether it was the phone or the line.

His monitor brightened into existence, but the screen, instead of displaying his usual menu, showed row after row of the same sentence, the same four words, moving up from the bottom of the screen and disappearing at the top:

THE STORE IS COMING

He closed his eyes, hoping this was just some sort of hallucination, a panic attack, but when he opened his eyes and looked at his monitor the words were still there, scrolling faster than ever:

THE STORE IS COMING THE STORE IS COMING THE STORE IS COMING THE STORE IS COMING

Suddenly the scrolling stopped. The last appearance of the sentence remained at the top of the screen, followed, halfway down, by two new words:

FOR YOU

They knew! They'd captured Ben and now they were after him! His thoughts were racing a mile a minute, his mind filled with conflicting options and contingency plans, but his body was listening to some rational, logical section of his brain, and even as he tried to figure out what to do, he was turning off the PC, unplugging it, rolling up the cables and power cords.

He had to escape, he had to leave, he had to get out of Juniper.

After that, he could figure out what action to take.

He picked up his PC and, struggling mightily, ran with it out to the truck.

3

Street was gone.

Bill had wanted to meet with him and hash out what they could piece together about Ben's disappearance, but the shop was closed, and when he arrived at Street's house, the truck was not there, the front door was open, and his friend was nowhere in sight.

And Ben's car was in the driveway.

He walked slowly through the empty house. There was no sign of a struggle, no indication that anyone had broken in, and it was Bill's gut feeling that Street had simply panicked and fled.

But why?

Because he'd seen what had happened to Ben?

He walked into Street's bedroom. This was Juniper and not New York, so even though the door to the house was wide-open, nothing had been stolen or vandalized, but in a way that made it seem even more disturbing. He moved on to the guest room. Ben's disappearance, like most of the others recently, seemed to him a legitimate missing person case. But Street's truck was gone, and that said to him that Street had taken off on his own. Someone may have been after him, but he'd hightailed it out of here before they could catch him.

It was still strange that Street hadn't made even a token effort to get in touch, though. That was the only thing that worried him. Of course, he hadn't bothered to take his clothes or personal belongings, either, so maybe he simply hadn't had time.

Maybe they'd captured him and taken him away in his own truck.

He didn't want to think about that.

Not yet.

He walked into Street's den, and the first thing he noticed was that the computer was gone. And the modem.

That made Bill feel better. Those were Street's priorities. He might not have had time to pack clothes or family photos, but he'd taken his computer.

Bill stared at the empty space on the desk for a moment, then turned around, walked out of the house, and headed over to the police station to file a missing persons report.

"Do you think we'll ever find out what happened to them?" Ginny asked quietly.

Bill shook his head, closing his eyes against the headache that had kicked the asses of four aspirin tablets and had been with him all afternoon.

"What about the police?" she said.

"What about them?"

"Aren't they supposed to be investigating this?"

He nodded. *"Supposed* to be. And I'm sure they're going through the motions, filing all the paperwork, dotting every *i* and crossing every *t*. But, let's face it—they're working for The Store."

"Can't we go above their heads? Talk to . . . I don't know, the FBI or something?"

He sighed tiredly. "I don't know."

She sat down on the couch next to him. "There's going to be no one left in this town pretty soon."

"Except Store employees."

She did not respond.

"Maybe we should move," he said. "Get out while we can."

She was silent for a moment. "Maybe we should," she said finally.

After dinner, while Ginny did the dishes, he snuck back into his office and checked his E-mail.

There was a message from Street.

It was what he'd been hoping for, and he excitedly called it up.

A message appeared in the center of the screen: "Pages 1 and 2 of this message have been deleted."

Shit!

He scrolled forward, to the end, saw only half a page of text: ". . . So that's what happened. I know The Store owns this shitty little online service. So I'm not sure if they'll even let this through. But I had to contact you and tell you what went down. I won't be able to do it again, and it may be some time before I see you, so I just wanted to tell you to keep fighting the good fight. I'll miss you, good buddy. You're one of the true. To quote the mighty C. W. McCall, 'We gone. Bye bye.' "

He stared at the screen, unmoving, and it was not until Ginny came into the office, calling his name, that he realized he was crying.

TWENTY-NINE

1

Shannon arrived early for work. She walked into the locker room to change into her uniform and saw on the bulletin board a new notice:

KEEP OUR STREETS CLEAN!
VOLUNTEER CREWS NEEDED
FOR SATURDAY MORNING SWEEPS.
PARTICIPATION MANDATORY.
SIGN UP IN PERSONNEL.

She stared at the sign as she pulled down her pants and slipped off her panties. Above the row of lockers, she heard the click-hum of the security camera as it adjusted to her movements. She quickly put on the leather Store underwear, covering what she could. She pulled on the tight pants of her uniform, sucking in her stomach so she could fasten the snap.

She wondered if Jake was the one monitoring the cameras that videotaped her dressing.

She wondered if he was the one who monitored the cameras in the bathroom.

As quickly as she could, she took off her blouse and bra and slipped on the leather Store bra and uniform top. She glanced again at the notice on the bulletin board as she sat on the bench and pulled on her boots.

Morning sweeps.

She didn't like the sound of that. And the fact that participation was mandatory for a "volunteer" crew didn't set well with her, either. Of course, it could be totally innocent. Maybe The Store was promoting environmentalism. Maybe these cleanup crews would simply walk along the highway and the roads, picking up the trash and debris that ignorant drivers tossed out of their vehicles.

Maybe the vigilante overtones she was reading into the notice weren't really there.

Maybe.

But she didn't think so.

Putting on her Store hat, she walked out of the locker room and onto the floor.

Shannon showed up early for the sweep. Holly was there already. So was Francine. And Ed Robbins. The three of them stood in the parking lot at the designated meeting place, trying to keep warm. Summer was winding down, and the mornings and evenings had started to get chilly, a foreshadowing of fall.

"Should've made us some coffee," Holly said. She smiled at Shannon. "Or hot chocolate."

"And brought some doughnuts," Ed said.

Francine rubbed her arms. "Anything sounds good to me."

They kept their conversation light, trivial, purposely avoiding the reason they were gathered here this morning.

It was exactly what Shannon had feared. They'd had training on Wednesday evening, from a policeman, and he'd shown them how to work in teams of two to subdue a person, how to load a recalcitrant subject into a police van, how to manacle an individual if necessary.

They would be "sweeping" Juniper of the homeless.

They would be keeping the streets "clean" by removing people who were unemployed, whom The Store had rendered jobless.

"We got a lot of them with the curfew," the policeman had told them. "But there are still quite a few out there. Hopefully, you'll be able to clean them up."

Clean them up.

She hadn't told her parents about the sweeps, although

she wasn't sure why. Embarrassment, she supposed. Shame at taking part in anything this inhumane—even if her involvement was coerced.

More people were arriving now, and soon there were a dozen of them waiting for their sweep leader.

Jake.

She didn't know until he announced it that he would be in charge of the sweep, didn't know until she saw him that he would even be here.

Her heart was pounding in her chest as she stood next to Holly, watching him. Even after all this time, he still had an effect on her. She didn't often see him in The Store—like most of Security, he remained in the monitoring room, invisible—but she was always aware of his presence, he was always there in the back of her mind.

She wasn't sure if she hated him or still loved him, but he definitely provoked an emotional response within her. Her hands were sweaty, her heart pounding, and she felt nervous even being this close to him.

His eyes met hers, and she quickly looked away.

"Okay!" Jake announced. "Teams!"

He read off a list of pairings and told each team where they were to conduct their sweeps. Shannon was to work with Ed, and the two of them were supposed to round up derelicts at the park. They would be provided with batons and handcuffs, if necessary.

Shannon talked with Ed for a moment. She didn't want to do this, and she made that clear to him, but he was a gung ho member of The Store Corps, and he considered her attitude treasonous.

"But it don't matter," he said proudly. "I don't need your help anyway. I can do it by myself."

"Whatever," she said.

They were driven into town in three vans and dropped off at their assigned locations. The vans were parked equidistantly from each team, providing easy access.

Shannon and Ed walked slowly onto the grass of the park. Behind them came a loud scream, and Shannon turned to see one of the other teams—Rob and Arn—

beat a homeless man across the back with their batons
and force him into the van behind them.

She felt sick. It was not the same as it had been at
the training session. It was nothing like that. The man
was neither hostile nor belligerent. Instead, he seemed
confused, hurt, and though he was not uncooperative,
they hit him anyway, intentionally hurting him, inflicting
pain, and he cried out as he stumbled into the back of
the van.

"There's one," Ed said excitedly.

She followed his pointing finger, saw a bearded man
in a long coat who looked like the guy on one of her
dad's old Jethro Tull albums.

"He's mine," Ed announced.

She stood, watching, as he ran across the lawn and
tackled the man. He had no baton, but he began beating
the surprised derelict with his fists, shouting joyfully
while the man bellowed in pain and vainly tried to ward
off blows.

This was wrong. She didn't know whether or not it
was legal, but it was wrong, morally and ethically over
the line, and she felt queasy as Ed stood, hauled the
man up by the collar of his coat, and she saw the bright
red blood streaming down his face.

Grinning hugely, victoriously, Ed dragged the man
toward her.

"Stay away," she warned him.

"You're supposed to be helping me, Shannon. You're
not much help so far."

"Knock it off, Ed."

He was close to her now, and he pushed the bloody
man in her direction. She ran. She heard Ed laughing
raucously behind her, and then she was at the edge of
the park, panting, feeling nauseous, feeling faint.

She bent over, gulped air, and promptly threw up into
a bush.

Then Jake was there, leaning over her, and there was
malicious glee in both his voice and his expression. "Get
back in there, Davis."

She wiped her mouth, hand shaking. "I . . . I can't do
it, Jake. I can't—"

"How the fuck did I ever go out with you?" He straightened, moved away. "Get busy," he ordered. "You have a quota to meet. And you'll be out here until you reach it."

Behind her, Ed continued to laugh. "Yeah!" he yelled.

Shannon closed her eyes, tried to stand straight, tried to walk away, but almost immediately she saw the derelict's gashed and bleeding face, and she doubled over again, heaving into the bush until there was nothing left in her stomach to throw up.

2

There were no vagrants on the street.

Ginny noticed it for the first time, although she had the feeling that that had been the case for a while and she simply had not registered the fact. She looked up Granite as she pumped gas into the tank of the car. She had not liked seeing the homeless people, but there was something even more ominous about their absence. The streets and sidewalks looked clean, even the empty buildings appeared freshly restored, and she found herself thinking of *The Stepford Wives.*

That was it exactly. There was something artificial here. Clean and wholesome, yes. But not in a good way. In a creepy way, an unnatural way.

The pump stopped at nine dollars and eighty-nine cents, the tank full, but she topped it off until the counter read ten dollars, then walked into the office of the gas station to pay.

Barry Twain was working this afternoon, and he smiled at her. "Hey there, Ginny. How goes it?"

"Could be better."

"But it could be worse." He squinted at the fuel monitoring box next to the cash register. "That'll be ten dollars."

She handed him a twenty, and he gave her back two fives.

"How are things with you?" she asked.

"Not good. I heard The Store's going to start selling gasoline."

She stared at him, shocked. "What?"

Barry laughed wheezingly, pointing at her. "Gotcha!" he cried. "Gotcha good that time!"

Against her will, she broke into a smile. "That you did."

"You bought it! Hook, line, and sinker!"

"It's not that far-fetched."

Barry's smile faded a little. "You're right."

"I'm sorry," she said quickly. "I didn't mean to—"

He waved her apology away. "Don't worry about it. Gasoline's one thing that can't be sold inside a store. And even if they do build that auto center and eventually decide to sell gas, I'm not worried about it. I've built up a lot of customer loyalty over the years. And I have a lot of friends in this town. Like you."

She smiled at him. "Barry, I'd still keep coming here even if your gas was two dollars higher than theirs."

He cackled. "Hell, maybe they *should* come up against me. Then I'll be justified when I jack up my prices, and I'll make a fortune."

"I'll go to Texaco," she said.

"Traitor!"

She laughed, waved, walked out the door. "Later, Barry!"

"See you, Ginny!"

On the way home, she did see a homeless man. A big, burly, bearded guy in a dirty fringed jacket.

He was being shoved by a group of uniformed Store employees into a black Store van.

She drove past quickly, not wanting to see the faces of the Store people, not wanting to discover that her daughters were among them.

She told Bill about it when she arrived home, describing what she'd seen, and he nodded, admitting that he'd witnessed a similar scene the other day.

"But these homeless people," she said. "Where are they taking them? What are they doing with them?"

He shrugged tiredly. "I don't know."

"Our daughters are involved in this."

"How does it feel to have members of the Hitler Youth in your own family?"

"This isn't funny."

"I'm not joking."

They looked at each other.

"Doesn't it feel a little Red Guardish?" he asked. "What if we do something that ticks Sam off? Is she going to turn us in? Is The Store's gestapo going to come after us and load us into vans?"

"Stop it," she said. "You're scaring me."

"I'm scaring myself."

She confronted Shannon about it later, after dinner that evening, and the girl burst into tears, running from the room. Ginny told Bill to stay out in the front, and she followed her daughter back into her bedroom.

"I'm sorry," Shannon sobbed, throwing her arms around her mother as she sat down on the bed. "I'm sorry."

Ginny held her. "Sorry for what?"

"There was nothing I could do. They made me go on the sweep."

"What happened?"

"I didn't help. I just stood there. I just watched. But I . . . I didn't do anything to stop it. I just stood there. I just watched."

"What happened?" Ginny repeated.

"They . . . beat them up. The homeless. They beat them up and put them in vans and . . . drove them somewhere."

Ginny felt cold. "Where?"

"I don't know. They didn't tell us." She started sobbing again. "Oh, Mom, it was awful!"

"It's okay." Ginny held her tightly. "It's all right."

"There was nothing I could do!"

"It's all right," Ginny said again.

"I wanted to make them stop it, but I didn't! I couldn't!"

"It's all right." Ginny hugged her even harder, a tear squeezing out of the corner of her own eye. "It's all right. It's all right."

3

Ginny emerged from Shannon's bedroom a half hour later.

"So?" Bill said.

"She was there, but she was just a witness. She refused to help."

"Help with what?"

"She doesn't know much more than we do. Apparently, The Store's forcing its employees to volunteer for what they call morning sweeps. They're trained by a cop, and they're sent out to, quote unquote, clean up the streets. When Shannon went out, that meant that they beat the homeless men with fists and batons, and threw them into vans. The vans were driven away and none of the homeless men have been seen since."

Bill pounded his fist against the counter. "God*damn* it!"

Ginny put a hand on his arm. "She wants out."

"And we want her out. But what the hell can we do about it?"

The pipes shuddered as Shannon started the shower in the bathroom.

"She has something she wants to show you," Ginny said. "She's going to bring it out after she takes a shower."

"What is it?"

"I'm not supposed to say. She wants to show you herself."

"Come on."

"All right. Don't tell her I told you. It's *The Employee's Bible.*"

"The Employee's Bible?"

"She had to smuggle it out of The Store and she's really nervous about it. I guess it's a book they're given when they get hired. It's forbidden for outsiders to see it."

Bill felt a rush of excitement. "It probably explains all about The Store," he said.

Ginny nodded.

"This may give us some info we can use."

Shannon came into the living room after finishing her shower, dry-eyed and wearing a bathrobe. She handed him a black-bound book and sat on the couch. She wouldn't meet his eyes, would only look at her hands, which were twisting and bunching the robe in her lap. "We're not supposed to show this to anyone. It's for Store employees only. But I thought you'd want to see it."

The Employee's Bible.

Bill flipped through the pages, scanning the subheadings: THE STORE IS YOUR HOME. BECOMING ONE OF US. DEALING WITH TRAITORS. DEATH BEFORE DISHONOR. TERMINATION PROCEDURES.

Shannon nervously twisted the robe material. "I'm not supposed to bring that home. It's not supposed to leave The Store."

He continued looking through the book. It was appalling, frightening, both its words and the accompanying drawings making his skin crawl. But he'd been hoping for more. Weaknesses. Trade secrets. Achilles' heels. It seemed to be mostly propaganda, ham-handed attempts at intimidation, and there was not really anything that could be used against The Store. Even the references to what he knew were illegal acts were couched in careful language, carrying another, more innocent, meaning.

"I work tomorrow," she said. "I have to bring it back."

He nodded, turned to the index, scanned the entries. "School's going to be starting in a few weeks. What's going to happen then? Are they going to let you quit?"

"They're cutting down my hours. But I can't quit. My work contract runs through October. The end of October."

"That's only two more months," Ginny offered.

"Two more months of sweeps? Two more months of . . ." She shook her head. "Forget it."

"Maybe there's something in here," Bill said. "Some loophole we could exploit. Maybe we can get you out of there."

"They're smarter than we are," Shannon said dejectedly. "There aren't going to be any loopholes."

She was right. If there were any, he couldn't find them, but he scanned as many of the book's pages as he could into his PC before giving it back to her. He'd study it more carefully tomorrow, see if he couldn't come up with something.

He wished Ben was here. And Street. Three heads were always better than one.

Both Shannon and Ginny went to bed early, but he wasn't tired, couldn't sleep, was too wound up, and after kissing Ginny good night, he remained in his office until well after midnight, faxing and E-mailing messages to Arizona's two senators, to their local assemblyman, to the county Board of Supervisors, to the Better Business Bureau, to the Federal Trade Commission, to the FBI, to the Commerce Department, to anyone he could think of. He even sent a fax to The Store's corporate office in Dallas, addressing it to Newman King himself, detailing his complaints and suspicions, his problems with The Store, demanding that his daughter be released from the involuntary servitude in which The Store illegally and unconstitutionally held her.

Ginny was asleep and snoring when he finally crawled into bed, and he put his arm around her and cupped her breast. She stirred, moaned, backed against his hardening penis. He wanted to make love to her. It had been over a week since they'd done it, but he restrained himself, moved his hand down to her belly, closed his eyes, and concentrated on falling asleep. He wanted to do it, but they couldn't. They had no protection. He had no condoms, and she was out of spermicide for her diaphragm.

They'd have to go to The Store tomorrow and buy some.

THIRTY

1

There was a faculty meeting the week before school started, and Ginny called up various friends on the staff to see if any of them needed a ride.

None of them wanted to go with her.

She'd been afraid of that—it was the real reason she'd called, to gauge the mood of her coworkers—but instead of intimidating her, making her nervous about showing up, it angered her, fortified her, and she was determined not to cave in to any sort of pressure.

She drove alone to Juniper Elementary, took a seat at the front of the assembly room. The other teachers filed in, took their seats, talking among themselves, but there remained a circle of empty seats around her, an artificial barrier that none of the other faculty would cross.

Until Meg sat down next to her.

Ginny had never been more grateful to anyone in her life, and though she had never really liked Meg, though "coworker" had always been a more accurate description of their relationship even than "acquaintance," she reached out and spontaneously hugged the other teacher.

The older woman smiled. "I guess we misfits have to stick together."

Ginny smiled back. "So where are you shopping these days?"

Meg burst out laughing.

"So what happened here?" Ginny asked. "Why did they all jump ship?"

"I don't know. I've never been privy to their thoughts,

never shared their confidences. You were always closer
to the rest of the staff than I was."

"Until I suddenly became a leper."

"You have standards," Meg said. "You have integrity.
You and I may have totally different teaching techniques. We may disagree on almost everything. But one
thing we have in common is that we stand up for what
we believe in. And we don't back down in the face of
adversity. I've always admired that about you."

Ginny was genuinely touched. "Thank you."

"The rest of our fellow teachers are easily corrupt-
ible sheep."

"And so are the kids and their parents," Ginny said.

Meg nodded. "It's going to be a long year."

The principal came out then, walking to the front of
the assembly room, and those teachers who were standing took their seats, everyone growing quiet.

"There are going to be some changes this year at Juniper Elementary," the principal said after making a few
introductory remarks. "And I'm very excited about
them. I hope you will be, too." He explained that the
teachers' union, the district, and The Store had just finished hammering out an agreement by which Juniper's
elementary, junior high, and high schools would be privately rather than publicly funded, on a trial basis, for
this school year, The Store volunteering to foot the
town's educational bill in exchange for a few small
concessions.

"Firstly," he said, "there will be new textbooks. As
we all know, our current books are embarrassingly out
of date and woefully inadequate. The Store will be providing us with new texts that we will be required to use."
He held up a hand, anticipating objections. "I know that
teachers are usually involved in the selection process for
classroom materials, but your union leadership agreed
to this arrangement because of the last-minute nature of
the talks. As I said, the final agreement has only just
been worked out, so I assume you will all be voting on
it later. Let me just assure you that The Store has started
similar programs in other towns in Texas and Arkansas
and New Mexico and Oklahoma, and that a panel of

nationally recognized educators was chosen to evaluate and select texts for each grade level. Teachers at the other districts all seem to be very satisfied with the provided materials.

"The Store will also be giving us free computers," he continued. "With appropriate educational software and access to FOLS, the Freelink Online Learning Service."

The principal cleared his throat. "The other big change involves class schedules. There will be no adjustments to the number of hours that you will work each day, but we will be adopting the same format as the junior high and high school. Which is to say that students will no longer remain in one class all day long but will have seven periods throughout the day."

"What?" Meg said angrily.

He ignored her. "The periods will not be divided by subject, as is traditionally the case with the upper grades, so teaching specifics will have to be worked out between you in regard to the individual children."

Meg stood, refusing to be ignored. "What is the point of this?"

"The students need flexible hours."

"Why?"

"To accommodate their work schedules."

Work schedules? Ginny glanced around the assembly room. A few of the teachers were talking among themselves, a few looked unhappy, but the majority of them sat unmoving in their seats, listening to the principal.

"The Store is donating money and materials to help educate these children. The least the students can do is donate an hour or so of their time each day to help The Store."

Now Ginny stood. "What does that mean?"

"It means, Mrs. Davis, that they will be sweeping, picking up trash, doing the type of work that I used to do as a child. It will foster responsibility and make them feel as if they are part of the community. They'll be contributing to their town and learning about the importance of the work ethic at the same time."

Sweeping?

"It's called child labor," Ginny said. "There are laws against it."

"It's called volunteerism and the school supports the concept fully."

"Elementary school children do not learn as well with their day broken into separate periods with separate teachers," Meg said. "It's been proven. They need the stability of a single class with a single teacher and a set group of classmates."

"That is the way we *used* to do it," the principal said, giving her a withering glance. "This is the way we will be doing it now."

Ginny and Meg continued to argue with the principal for the next half hour or so, but none of the other teachers joined them, and eventually their objections were cut off and they were told to sit down.

"Why don't you retire?" Lorraine said to Meg as they all walked out the door after the meeting. She held up her voodoo doll and stuck a pin in its face.

Ginny grabbed the doll and threw it on the ground. "Bitch."

"I can get one for you, too," Lorraine said.

"Go ahead."

"Maybe I will retire," Meg said as they walked out to the parking lot. "I don't exactly see myself fitting in with the new order."

"You can't retire," Ginny told her. "The school needs you."

The older teacher smiled. "Who'd've thought that you would be asking me not to retire and saying that the school needs me?"

"Politics make strange bedfellows," Ginny said.

"I guess it does. I guess it does."

"Besides, I found out that you were right."

"About what?"

"Those Douglas kids are all troublemakers."

Meg looked puzzled for a moment, then she started to laugh.

They were both laughing as they walked out to their cars.

2

Shannon sat alone in the break room, eating a rubbery pastry she'd bought from one of the vending machines. School was starting next week and her hours would be cut, so to make up for it The Store had scheduled her to work every day this week, from opening until closing, thirteen hours a day.

She shifted uncomfortably on the hard seat, her inner thighs chapped from the tight pants and rough leather underwear.

Sam was supposed to meet her here for break, but her sister had canceled out on her the past three times they'd arranged to get together, and her absence wasn't a big surprise. Shannon glanced up at the wall. Ten more minutes to go.

Sam wasn't going to make it.

She missed her sister. They'd never been particularly close, weren't best friends or anything, but obviously they'd been closer than she'd thought, because she longed to talk with Sam the way they used to, longed to have one of their stupid arguments over a meaningless matter. They still talked, she and Sam, but there was distance between them now, a barrier, and it wasn't quite the same.

Her sister had never even invited her to the house The Store had given her, and while Shannon told herself she didn't care, it didn't matter, she did care and it did matter.

With five minutes left to go on her break, Sam finally showed up. Smiling, she walked quickly over to where Shannon was sitting. She even looked good in the ridiculous Store uniform, and Shannon couldn't help wondering how many of her fellow employees had come on to her.

The bloody panties.

Shannon felt guilty for even briefly entertaining jealous thoughts about her sister, and she smiled and nodded as Sam sat down. "Hey," she said.

"Sorry I'm late, but there was trouble in your old

department. Kirk was letting himself be berated by a disgruntled customer, and I had to go over there and set things straight."

"What if you couldn't set it straight?" Shannon asked. "Would the manager have to take care of it?"

"I suppose so," Sam said.

"Have you ever seen the manager?"

Sam shook her head, and for a brief fraction of a second, she looked troubled, "No," she said. "I never have."

"Has Mr. Lamb?"

"Oh, I'm sure he has."

"So Mr. Lamb's above you?"

"No one's above me except the manager. I'm second in command. I'm assistant manager." Sam laughed. "Why the third degree?"

Shannon shook her head. "Nothing," she said. "No reason."

"So how're Mom and Dad?"

Shannon shrugged. "The same, I guess."

"Dad still on the warpath?"

"Always."

Sam laughed. She was about to say something else when three chimes sounded over The Store's PA system. "Three rings," she said. "That means all nonessential personnel." She looked over at Shannon. "Is someone covering for you right now?"

"Mike."

"Come on, then. Let's go."

Shannon followed her sister out of the break room and down a short hallway to stairs that led to the basements.

Mr. Lamb was waiting for them at the bottom of the steps. "You're just in time."

"What is it?" Sam asked.

"We caught Jake Lindley stealing. From The Store. Apparently, he was on his break, and he decided to pilfer a Snickers bar from the check stand display next to Francine Dormand, with whom he was having a one-way conversation." Mr. Lamb smiled dryly. "Francine turned him in."

The personnel manager's attention shifted to Shannon. He eyed her intently. "You used to date him did you not?"

She felt nervous, frightened, but Sam stood up for her. "Yes, she did. And Jake broke it off, although I fail to see what bearing that has on this case, Mr. Lamb."

"Quite right," he said, bowing obsequiously. "Quite right."

"So what is the penalty?" Sam asked.

"As per the rules spelled out in *The Employee's Bible,* he shall be taken to the Hall of Punishment and the appropriate disciplinary action will be there decided."

Sam paled. "The Hall of Punishment?"

Mr. Lamb smiled. "The Hall of Punishment." He motioned toward an open door halfway down the corridor. "Come. The others are waiting."

Sam shook her head. "I can't oversee something like that."

Mr. Lamb's smile never faltered. "I'm afraid you have no choice, Ms. Davis. It is the manager's day off, and you are in charge during his absence."

"Then we should call him—"

"To again reference *The Employee's Bible,* the manager is not to make any decisions or oversee any disciplinary actions on his day off. Those responsibilities automatically and irrevocably devolve to the assistant manager." He took her hand, led her toward the door. "Come."

Ignored by the personnel manager, forgotten about by her sister, Shannon nevertheless followed them down the corridor and through the door, down a short flight of steps and into another basement.

She had never been here before, and she stopped, looking around, feeling frightened. The walls were black. As was the ceiling. As was the floor. Wrought-iron Gothic chandeliers with red flame-shaped bulbs offered what little illumination there was.

Ten or twelve employees were lined up in the usual double row in the center of the high-ceilinged room. In this light, she thought, in this place, with their stylized leather uniforms, they looked like medieval torturers. Members of the Inquisition.

Sam and Mr. Lamb walked between the two rows to the head of the room.

The Hall of Punishment.

A rack of gleaming metal instruments, tools she did not recognize and had never seen before, was wheeled out by two tall exceptionally pale men wearing shiny black coats. They immediately retreated back through the side door from which they'd entered, and Mr. Lamb lovingly touched what looked like some sort of knife.

They were going to hurt Jake, she realized.

Kill him?

No. Even The Store wouldn't go that far. It couldn't. Such a thing was illegal. They might beat him, yes. Humiliate him. Punish him. But they wouldn't *kill* him.

Would they?

She stood just inside the doorway, watching the scene unfold, feeling not only nervous and anxious and terrified but . . . something else. Something more personal. This was Jake they were talking about. Her Jake. He was a jerk and an asshole, and she had no doubt that he had ripped off a candy bar while he was trying to pick up on a big-titted babe, but that didn't mean that he deserved to die. Stupidity was not a capital offense.

And The Store had no right to act as judge, jury, and executioner.

Die? Capital Offense? Executioner?

She realized that those words came naturally to her, that they did not seem at all far-fetched or out of place in this hellish black room.

But this was still America. Laws still applied. To The Store as well as to individuals. The Store might be able to fire Jake, might be able to press charges and go after him in court if he'd done something illegal, but they could not physically harm him.

She stared at the twin rows of leather-clad employees, at her sister and Mr. Lamb standing beneath the flickering glow of the red-lighted chandelier.

No, that was not true.

They *could* harm him.

And they would.

And no one could stop them.

She felt sick. Even after everything, even after what had happened at the sweep, maybe, somewhere deep down, she did still love him.

Sam looked over, meeting her eyes. "Maybe you'd better go back to work," she said. Her voice, authoritative and powerful, carried clearly across the Hall.

Shannon shook her head, her mouth dry, unable to speak.

"It's not a suggestion," her sister said. "It's an order." There was hardness in her voice, a tone of command, but there was also concern, a caring intent hidden from all but herself that told her she had better leave. Next to Sam, Mr. Lamb stood grinning.

Shannon looked away.

"Leave," Sam said. "Or I will have someone escort you back to your post."

She wanted to stay, wanted to fight, wanted to protest whatever they were going to do and protect Jake from The Store's punishment, but she nodded, acquiesced, and turned to walk out.

From somewhere far away, in another room, another basement, she heard Jake. He was screaming. She recognized his voice, and her heart sank within her, but she did not stop, did not turn around. Instead, she increased her pace, trying to get away from the horrible sound. She actually felt relieved when she was once again among customers and merchandise on the floor.

Sam came over to her register an hour later. Shannon was helping a customer, and she wanted that customer to remain forever; she did not want to be alone with her sister, did not want to know what had happened, but the customer paid for his purchase, thanked her, and left.

Shannon pretended to fiddle with some receipts and void forms, then finally gathered her courage and looked up. "What happened?" she asked. "To Jake?"

"He's been . . . reassigned."

Shannon felt cold. "What does that mean?"

Sam met her gaze, and the expression on her face was one of muted horror and stunned disbelief. "He's a Night Manager," she said softly.

3

The alarm woke her up at five, as it always did, and Samantha rolled out of bed. She missed living at home. It had been exciting at first to have her own place, and The Store had given her a decorating allowance, letting her choose items from the Furniture department to furnish the house. But even though this cottage was all hers, it wasn't home. Home was where Shannon and her parents lived.

And she missed it.

She missed a lot of things. And there were times that she wished The Store had never come to Juniper. She'd be starting school right now if she hadn't gone to work for The Store, beginning her first semester in college, surrounded by guys and girls her age, meeting interesting people, learning new things.

Instead, she'd met—

Mr. Lamb.

She shuddered, pushed the thought out of her mind.

There were a few negatives, but overall she liked The Store. She had an aptitude for the retail business, and she'd risen quickly through the ranks. The Store had been good to her. The Store recognized and made use of her abilities. The Store rewarded her hard work.

Still, sometimes, when she was alone, she wished that things had turned out differently. The scariest thing was how easily she'd adjusted to Store life, how comfortable the fit felt. Intellectually, she knew she should be shocked and horrified by some of the things that went on. She should be outraged and refuse to participate. But the truth was that she really had no emotional response to most of what happened. She understood the necessity of it all, and none of it provoked any feelings within her.

Almost none of it.

Mr. Lamb.

She would not think of him.

She took a quick shower, masturbated with the shower massage, ate a piece of toast, drank a glass of orange juice, and drove in her new Miata to The Store.

Mr. Lamb was waiting for her in her office, sitting in her chair, his feet up on her desk. "The manager wants to see you," he said.

Her heart skipped a beat. "Me?"

He nodded. "You."

There was a hard knot of fear in the pit of her stomach. She had never seen the manager, and she never wanted to. She'd heard stories about him ever since he'd come to Juniper, rumors, horrible rumors, and if even a fraction of what she'd heard was true, she knew that meeting him was the last thing she wanted to do.

Nevertheless, he was her boss, the person to whom she was theoretically supposed to report, and she tried to put on a brave face, tried to pretend she wasn't frightened. "When?" she asked.

"Now." Mr. Lamb swung his feet off the desk, stood. "Come on. I'll go with you."

He walked around her, and she followed him out the door, down the hall, and onto the floor. The lights in The Store were all on, but the Muzak was turned off, none of the rest of the staff had yet arrived, and the place seemed eerily silent and empty.

"Do you know why he wants to see me?" she asked.

"Yes." Mr. Lamb continued walking, not elaborating, and she knew enough not to press further. The knot in her stomach tightened.

They walked up the main cross aisle, away from the espresso bar, to the manager's door on the far opposite wall. Mr. Lamb rapped loudly three times, the door swung open, and the two of them stepped inside. There was a stairway leading up, and with a flourish, the personnel manager indicated that she was to proceed first.

He just wants to look at my ass, she thought. But she walked ahead, up the stairs, concentrating on the black door at the top of the steps.

The door opened when she stepped onto the landing. And she beheld the manager.

He was nothing like she'd expected, neither an intimidating thug nor a hideous monster. He was a cowed and frightened old man, hiding behind a too-large desk and watching her with scared eyes.

"No!" he said.

"Yes," Mr. Lamb responded from behind her. The door slammed shut loudly, and the personnel manager moved around her, into the center of the room. He turned around, and in his open hands lay a dagger. He held it out, offering it to her.

"What's this?" she asked. "What's going on here?"

"Kill him," Mr. Lamb said.

"No!" the manager cried.

"Kill him and The Store is yours."

Samantha shook her head, backing away. "No. I can't."

"Mr. King wants you to."

That threw her. She shook her head, as if to clear her thoughts. "Newman King?"

Mr. Lamb smiled, nodded. "He's been watching the tapes. He's very impressed with you."

The man behind the desk tried to sound strong, failed. "I'm still the manager here!"

"No, you're not!" Mr. Lamb snapped at him. "You're out!" He held forth the dagger, smiled at Samantha. "Take it."

"I can't."

"Do what you have to do."

She backed against the closed door, shook her head. "It's . . . it's murder."

"It's business. And if you don't do it, someone else will. Why should they get the job you deserve?"

"I . . . can't kill anyone."

"I'll call the police!" the manager cried.

"Shut up!" Mr. Lamb roared at him.

"I . . ."

"You can," Mr. Lamb said. "You must."

"It's wrong," she said. "It's murder."

He took her hand, put the dagger in it. "You can," he said.

4

There was a Kmart in Flagstaff, and a Wal-Mart, but the city did not have The Store, and for that Bill was grateful. Newman King had taken Sam Walton's approach and pushed it to its limit, opening stores in small towns in which there were only locally owned businesses, but The Store would not build in a town that was host to another chain.

King hated competition.

Bill needed to remember that. It might be something he'd be able to use.

They stopped at Target, bought toilet paper and cleanser and detergent and other household items, then stocked up on groceries at Fry's. It felt strange shopping at regular stores after all this time. There was no pressure, no tension, no threatening employees, no bizarre products, only a relaxed, pleasant atmosphere and an extensive selection of goods. This was what shopping was supposed to be like, he thought. Fun. Not the horrible ordeal it had become in Juniper.

He had not really realized until now just how deeply The Store had affected their lives. He'd known intellectually, of course, but he hadn't really understood, emotionally, the depth of it, had not fully grasped all of the peripherals. It took this exposure to normalcy to enable him to recognize how strange and skewed everything had become.

Shannon came with them, and though they didn't talk about it, he knew that she, too, noticed the difference.

They returned to Juniper after dark, and the phone started ringing the second they stepped through the door. All three of them were loaded down with grocery sacks, so he quickly flipped on the lights, put his sacks down on the kitchen counter, and grabbed the phone. "Hello?"

It was Sam.

She wanted to tell them the good news.

She'd been appointed manager of The Store.

THIRTY-ONE

1

They received a gold StoreCard in the mail the next day, along with a photocopied form letter, signed by their daughter, that explained the benefits of belonging to the Store Club.

Bill called Samantha for the first time since she'd moved out, thanking her for the card. He was not at all sure that he ever wanted to shop at The Store again—the drive to Flagstaff seemed infinitely preferable—but with Sam in charge now, there was an opening, an opportunity, and he made a concerted effort to take a more conciliatory stance.

Their conversation yesterday had been brief. He hadn't known how to take her announcement, and while she was obviously proud of her news and wanted to share it with the family, he could not be proud of her or happy for her, and after awkwardly insincere congratulations, he had handed the phone to Ginny.

He was better today. He'd had time to get used to the news, and he even managed to sound supportive.

At the very least, the breach between them had been healed.

But when he asked her to release Shannon from her contract and allow her to quit, Sam grew rigid, formal, toed the party line, said it was not her decision to make, that even though she was manager, she was still required to follow corporate policy.

He didn't fight with her, didn't try to force her to let her sister go, but he didn't tell her that he understood, either. He didn't make her feel that her decision was all right with him. He was not going to put any pressure on her, but he would make it clear that he didn't approve, and he'd let that work on her for a while.

Maybe she'd come around.

Then he'd ask her about Ben and the others.

The important stuff.

They talked for a little while longer, but she was on break and he had to get back to work as well, and she promised to come over for dinner later in the week.

He walked back into his office, checked his fax tray and E-mail to see if there was any news from the company or on the off chance that Street had finally decided to send him another message, but as usual there was nothing. He quickly fired off his daily complaint letters to various business regulatory agencies and to The Store's corporate headquarters, then got busy with his documentation.

He'd gotten another assignment last week, this time a human resources package for a midsize Southern California city, and the deadline was just around the corner. Someone somewhere had screwed up, and he'd gotten involved in the project at a very late date, had not been involved in the development or testing phases at all, and now he was expected to crank out a set of instructions, with almost no lead time, on a system he didn't really understand.

He was going to earn his pay on this one.

He wrote until midafternoon, then Ginny finally persuaded him to take a break and have something to eat, and he walked out to the kitchen and wolfed down a peanut butter and jelly sandwich and a glass of milk.

The fax was waiting in the tray when he returned to the office.

He read it.

Read it again.

Read it again.

Ginny poked her head in the door. "Hey—" she began, but she stopped as soon as she saw the look on his face. "What is it?" she asked, walking up to him.

He held up the fax. "Looks like I finally got a response," he said dryly.

Ginny looked at him, already a little frightened.

"It's from The Store's corporate headquarters. From Newman King himself. He's invited me to Dallas. He wants to talk to me."

They'd debated whether or not to tell the girls and had decided to do so but to downplay it. Now, in bed, they were alone, and the false nonchalance they'd been feigning was gone. The spin they'd put on the situation had not fooled Shannon, but she'd pretended it had, and for that Bill was grateful. Honesty was nice and communication was important, but sometimes events were too big to be digested at once, and he was glad that she hadn't forced him to talk in detail about this, that she'd allowed him to sidestep the issue. She was a good girl, more sensitive than he gave her credit for, and he was thankful that she'd understood the situation without him having to explain it to her.

He'd pay her back somehow, make it up to her.

If he ever got the chance.

He looked over at Ginny. She'd finished putting on her moisturizer and was fluffing up her pillow before turning off the light.

She sighed, looked over at him. "Why does he want to talk to you? That's what I don't get. He probably gets a thousand complaint letters a day. Why does he want to see you?"

"Because I'm a persistent pain in the ass?"

She kicked his leg under the covers.

"I don't know," he answered seriously.

"It frightens me."

They were both silent for a moment.

"Sam thinks its an honor. I think she has renewed respect for you now."

"Didn't realize what a bigwig her daddy really is, huh?"

Ginny laughed, but it was a forced laugh and it died too soon. "Do you think that's all he wants to do?" she asked. "Talk?"

"I don't know."

"Maybe you shouldn't go."

"Maybe that's what he wants. Maybe he's just trying to frighten me and cow me into submission."

Ginny's voice was quiet. "Maybe he wants to do more than frighten you."

"That's a chance I have to take."

"I don't want you to go."

"I don't want to go, either. But I have to."

"Why?"

"Because if I don't, that means he's won. Ben's gone, Street's gone, everyone else has either died, disappeared, or been intimidated into silence."

"Not me."

"You weren't invited."

She kicked him again.

"It sounds paranoid and egotistical and everything else, but it's true."

"I know," she said quietly.

"That's why I have to go."

They made love after that, the first time in several weeks, and though it should have been great, for some reason it wasn't. It was good, though, and they both came, and afterward fell instantly asleep.

In his dream, he flew to Dallas, was picked up by a limo at the airport and driven to The Store's corporate offices, where he was led past desks of secretaries and assistants before finally entering the CEO's office.

There was no one there.

"What—?" he started to say. Then he realized the truth. Newman King was a fictional figurehead, a made-up character. There was no CEO. There was no president. There was no leader. There was only the company. It ran itself, and the bureaucracy maintained it, and there was no way on earth to stop it.

Ginny dropped him off at Sky Harbor in Phoenix the next day. Arrangements had been made online, through King's secretary, and he'd been assured that everything was taken care of, but he still wasn't sure what to expect. He assumed there'd be tickets—coach, probably—waiting for him at the counter where he was supposed to check in, but instead a tall, straight-backed blond man in a black leather Store uniform met him at the desk and escorted him through a series of doors and hallways until they were outside the terminal and on the tarmac, where a black Lear jet was waiting. Ginny was not allowed to go any farther than the terminal exit, and she pulled him aside, hugged him. "Be careful," she said.

"Always."

"I still don't think you should do this."

"We've been through all that."

She hugged him again. "I'm scared."

He hugged her back, held her. He was scared, too, but it would do no good to tell her that, would only make her worry more, and he said nothing.

The blond man cleared his throat. "We have to go, Mr. Davis. Our flight has been cleared."

He kissed Ginny. "I love you."

She was already crying. "I love you, too."

It felt too much like permanent parting, a final goodbye, and he was creeped out by it. He wanted to postpone it, wanted to linger, wanted to somehow shake off this feeling of dread that had crept up on him, but instead he waved to her, blew her another kiss, then hurried across the tarmac to the loading ramp of the jet.

The flight itself was uneventful. He was the only passenger, and he had the entire center section of the jet to himself. There were couches, a bar and small refrigerator, a television and VCR. The pilot assured him over the loudspeaker that he was free to use any of the luxuries and partake of any food or beverage provided. He was not hungry, but he was thirsty, and he opened a can of Coke. He was nervous, antsy, and was not in the mood to watch TV, despite the impressive selection of videos offered. He was tempted to use the cellular phone to call Ginny, but he knew the conversation would be bugged, and what he wanted to tell his wife was not something he intended to share with officials of The Store. Besides, she'd still be driving back to Juniper.

So he sat on one of the couches for most of the two-hour flight, staring out the small porthole window at the passing desert below.

They were over Dallas when the pilot finally spoke again. "The Tower's off to your right," he announced over the loudspeaker, and Bill looked out the window to see a black skyscraper situated several blocks from the other downtown high-rises. It probably didn't look that strange from the ground, but from this perspective it appeared that the Black Tower was being ostracized by the other buildings, and the visual symbolism was not lost on him.

He fastened his safety belt, the jet touched down smoothly, and a moment later the hatch was being opened, the same Aryan employee offering to help him down the steps.

Bill declined, disembarking on his own, and he glanced around as his feet touched the tarmac. He was sweating already, the heat unbearable, and he looked up, thinking idiotically of how similar the blue Texas sky was to that of Arizona.

"Over here, sir."

He turned toward the voice, and the hairs prickled on the back of his neck as he saw The Store employee standing next to a long black limousine.

The limo from his dream.

He made no effort to move.

"Sir?" the employee said. "Your ride is here."

Bill nodded dumbly.

A pause. "Mr. King is waiting."

"I'm coming," he said. "I'm coming."

He moved forward, put one foot in front of the other, and it was a cold sweat that dripped down his face as he walked across the tarmac and forced himself to get in the car.

2

He was dropped off directly in front of the Black Tower.

It was like nothing he had ever seen.

The Stores themselves bespoke average American sophistication—up-to-date, but in a way the ordinary swap meet shopper could relate to. They were impressive not so much for what they were but for the context in which they appeared.

The Black Tower was just plain impressive.

Under any circumstances.

He got out of the limo, looked up. The building was not catering to rubes or yokels or the average joe. There was no attempt here to feign modesty or mediocrity. This was the true Store, the real Store, the home of Newman King, and though it possessed superficially the attributes of the average downtown Dallas skyscraper, within those confines it asserted its independence and its supremacy. The Black Tower stood alone, the artistry of its design and the quality of its construction marking it as the property of an extremely powerful, important, and influential man.

Newman King.

The smoked-glass front door of the tower opened, and the same blond employee who'd met him at the airport in Phoenix and the airport here in Dallas strode down the marble walkway toward him.

Bill frowned. This wasn't possible.

The employee drew closer, and now that he looked more carefully, he realized that it was not the same employee after all. The one in Phoenix probably hadn't been the one at the Dallas airport, either. They just looked the same.

He found that disturbing.

"Mr. King's waiting for you," the blond man said with a smile. "I'll take you to him."

Bill nodded. He didn't know what he was going to do, what he was going to say, how he was going to act when he met the CEO. He thought of Ben, and part of him wished he'd brought a gun or a bomb or some type of weapon, but he knew that even if they didn't search him, he'd probably have to go through some type of metal detector.

The two of them walked through the front door into an enormous lobby with a two-story-high ceiling. The floors were marble, the walls were marble, there were palms and cacti, modern sculptural fountains with running water. Behind a gigantic desk, under The Store logo, sat a single receptionist, a pretty blond woman wearing black leather.

He was led past the receptionist, ushered into a glass elevator, and he and his escort rode to the top of the Tower.

The metal doors slid open. Before them was a huge boardroom with windowed walls that overlooked the skyline of the city.

The CEO's office from his dream.

A chill passed through him as he glanced around and saw familiar furniture in familiar places, a scene through the windows he had seen before.

In front of him, fifteen or twenty business-suited men were seated around a gigantic black marble table.

But the only one who mattered was the one at the table's head.

Newman King.

There was something inherently frightening about the CEO, something unnatural and disturbing in his too-pale face, his too-dark eyes, his too-red lips. Taken individually, his features were not that unusual, but they had come together in a way that seemed grotesque, both aberrant and abhorrent. It was not something that translated, not something that could be seen in photographs or on television. There was intelligence evident in his face and an all-American sort of ruthless business acumen, along with an aw-shucks, one-of-the-guys demeanor that could be highlighted or shut off at will, emphasized or de-emphasized according to need. Those things translated.

But that inner wildness, that horrible, undefinable inhumanity—that could only be experienced in person. Even this far away, across the boardroom, with all of those other people present, it was a powerful thing to behold. Bill's instinctual reaction was to run, to get as far away from King as he could, as quickly as possible. He felt shaky, his bowels and bladder ready to give at any second, but he stepped out of the elevator and into the boardroom, facing the CEO.

King smiled, and though his teeth were all white and even and straight, there was a sharklike malevolence to the gesture, a vampiric quality about it. "Mr. Davis, I presume?"

His voice was smooth, strong, carefully modulated, with none of the twangy folksiness he used in public, but again, there was something about it that seemed unnatural.

Bill nodded.

"Welcome. Have a seat." He motioned toward a series of black chairs to the left of the conference table.

"No, thank you."

King's smile widened. "Brave man." He held up a hand and was suddenly holding a sheaf of papers, though Bill could have sworn that both of his hands had been empty a moment before. "Do you know what these are?" He did not wait for an answer. "Your faxes, your E-mail."

Turning on the charm, the CEO began walking around the table toward Bill. The other board members remained seated, unmoving, staring across the huge table at each other. "If I didn't know better," King said, "I would say you were not a supporter of our organization. If I didn't know better and I was a cruder sort of person than I am, I would say that you're an anti-American agitator. But of course, that can't be the case. You're a Store Club member, your youngest daughter works as a Store sales clerk and your oldest daughter has been appointed temporary manager of the Juniper, Arizona, Store."

"Temporary manager?" Bill said.

"She cannot become a full-fledged manager unless she completes our two-week training course."

"I thought she had."

"No."

Newman King was next to him now, and this close he seemed even stranger, even more monstrous. Not only was his skin pale, it seemed to be fake, made out of rubber or some sort of malleable plastic. His too-perfect teeth also looked artificial. The only parts of him that seemed real were his dark, deep-set eyes, and they burned with a cruel animal ferocity.

The CEO held up the handful of papers, shook them. "So what do you want me to do?" he asked. "I've been reading your missives, and I can't quite figure out what you want. Do you want me to close the Juniper Store?"

Bill was more frightened than he had ever been in his life, but he ignored his quaking legs and gathered his courage and, in the strongest voice he could muster, said, "Yes."

King was smiling. "What would that accomplish? It would put a lot of people out of work, that's all. It wouldn't bring back all of those other businesses." His smile grew. "It wouldn't bring back your Buy-and-Save market." The smile stretched into grotesquerie. "It wouldn't even bring back Street's electronics shop."

Bill's heart was pounding crazily. "You know about them?"

"I know everything that affects The Store."

"You drove them out of business."

"So?"

"You killed people. Or you had them killed. Or your people did. All those missing—"

"Casualties of war," King said.

Bill stared at him. If he'd only smuggled in a tape recorder . . .

"Tape recorders don't always record me correctly," King said. He turned away, began walking back up to the head of the table.

Lucky guess, Bill thought, hoped, told himself. Hands shaky, legs wobbly, he started after the CEO, not sure if he planned to jump on him or punch him in the back or simply yell at him. Everything he'd ever thought about The Store, the worst of it, was true, and though he was more terrified than he'd ever been before, he was angrier than he'd ever been before, as well, and he focused on the anger, used it to give him strength.

King suddenly whirled around, and the air between them seemed to shift in a way that emulated but did not quite replicate wind. Bill instinctively moved back.

"You were about to ask me about Store policy," the

CEO said. "You wanted to know why we do what we do."

"Why do you?"

King smiled, not answering.

He faced the CEO. "Why did you bring The Store to Juniper?"

"It was an open market."

"But what's your goal? What do you hope to accomplish? You're not just in it for the money. You had that from the beginning. You didn't have to . . ." He shook his head. "You get people dependent on your store, then you switch products on them, force them to buy . . . bizarre items. Why? What's the point?"

King smiled. "I don't force people to buy anything. It's a free country. They can buy what they want."

"Bullshit." Bill stared at him. "What are you after?"

"We've just about conquered all the hick, hillbilly, Podunk, redneck, backwater, dipshit towns in America. It's time to move onward and upward, to expand our base, to drive Kmart and Wal-Mart and Target and all of the rest of those losers into the fucking ground." He pointed to a map of the United States on the wall next to him that was dotted with blinking red and yellow lights.

"That's what you're after?"

"Partially."

"And what else?"

King shook his head. "You wouldn't understand."

"What do you mean, I wouldn't understand?"

"You're not capable."

"Try me."

For a brief fraction of a second, there was a look on King's face that he could not interpret, an unfamiliar, unreadable expression that made him appear even more alien than he already did. Then, as quickly as it had come, it was gone. "Believe me," King said. "My motives are not even in your vocabulary."

Bill suddenly felt cold. King was right, he realized. He probably *wouldn't* understand.

And that knowledge frightened him.

"Why did you invite me here?" Bill asked.

"To talk."

"About what?"

"The future."

"What the hell is that supposed to mean?"

King chuckled. "You're a good man, a smart man, a fine chess player, a worthy adversary. I admire that."

"So?"

"So I asked you what you wanted—"

"And I said I wanted you to get The Store out of Juniper."

"And what I tried to tell you was that progress can't be undone. The world can't go backward. It can *not* go forward, it can stay where it is, but it cannot go backward. The Store is in Juniper. That's a done deal. But I'm offering you the next best thing."

"What's that?"

"As I said, you're a good man. I admire you." He paused. "I'd like you on my team."

Bill started to respond, then shut his mouth as what King was saying sunk in.

The man was . . . offering him a job?

"Your own store." The voice was soft and seductive, the deep-set eyes piercing and hypnotizing in the pale-skinned face. "You pick the town. You run things the way you want. Juniper's available if you'd like it."

"I—"

The CEO held up a hand. "Don't say anything. Not yet. Don't make up your mind, don't say yes or no." His voice was smooth, mesmerizing. "This is a once-in-a-lifetime opportunity. And I'm only going to offer it to you this one time. You turn it down, and you're out of this building and on your way back to Arizona within the hour."

"Why?" Bill said.

King smiled. "I've always found that my worst enemies, my most bitter critics, those who put up the greatest fight against me, invariably turn out to be the best managers. They're thinkers, they're doers. They're not sheep. They can handle power and they know how to use it when it's given to them. You'd make a great manager."

"Why would I want to?"

King's voice dropped, and he closed his long fingers into a fist. "You can *own* that town. You can decide what people eat, what they wear, what they listen to, what they watch. You can control everything from their brand of underwear to their type of toothpaste. You can experiment. You can mix and match." He leaned forward. "That's what The Store can give you. Power." He held up the papers. "What I read here in these faxes and messages is that you're not happy with the way things are; you want to change them. Well, I'm giving you the chance to do exactly that. You can rebuild that town in your own image, and it'll be exactly the community you always wanted."

"What I don't like is The Store. That's what I want to change."

"And here's your chance. You can do it from the inside." King dropped the papers on the table. "The dirty deeds are done. That's all over with. You don't have to be a part of that. What we have now is a level playing field. And what I'm offering you is one of the pieces." He grinned. "Now give me your response. Now tell me if you'll accept the challenge."

"Okay."

He surprised even himself with the answer. He'd been planning to ask more questions before eventually saying no, but the word was out of his mouth before he had time to think about it, and he found that he did not want to take it back.

King was laughing and shaking his hand, clapping him on the back, congratulating him, and the board members around the table were smiling and nodding their support. He wasn't sure why he'd agreed, and wasn't being allowed to think about it, wasn't being given the time to examine his motives. He hated The Store and wanted it destroyed, and he saw the opportunity here to infiltrate the enemy, to do damage from within.

But . . .

But there was something to what King had said, and he was not entirely immune to it. The Store offered power. And power was neither good nor bad. It was a tool, only as good or bad as the person using it. He could do a lot of good as manager of the Juniper Store. He would be in a position to call the shots, he could force the town council to roll back the ordinances it had passed, use it to pass better, more beneficial laws.

"One thing," Bill said. "I want my daughters out of The Store. Now. Today. Fire them, release them from their contracts, do whatever you have to do, but get them away."

King nodded. "Done."

"They're out? No strings?"

"If they want to be."

"What if they don't?"

The CEO shrugged. "I can't live their lives for them."

Shannon wanted out, he thought. She'd quit. Sam wouldn't, but Shannon would.

It was a start.

And when he was manager, he could fire Samantha.

"So what do I do? Where do I sign? What happens next?"

"Call your wife. Tell her good-bye. You have two weeks of training ahead of you. You won't be seeing her until you're done."

"Is there a phone I can use?"

"On the wall behind you."

He didn't want to talk in front of all these people, but he called Ginny anyway. She'd just arrived home, and he explained briefly what was happening, told her not to worry, told her he'd be back in two weeks.

"They kidnapped you!" she screamed. "They're forcing you to say this!"

"No," he said.

"Then what's happening? Why—?"

"I can't explain right now. I'll tell you all about it when I get back."

"They'll kill you!"

"It's nothing like that," he promised. "It's a good thing. But I can't talk now."

They went through this for several more minutes before he finally got her calmed down and convinced that it was on the level. They hung up, exchanging *I love you*'s.

If he were her, he wouldn't believe it either, he

thought. He had come to Dallas this morning ready to rip Newman King a new asshole, and now he was going to work for The Store? It didn't make any sense.

It *didn't* make any sense.

So why was he doing it?

He still wasn't sure.

Two guards had entered the boardroom behind him, and he started as they drew even with him and grabbed his arms. "What the . . . ?" he said, looking around at them, then over at Newman King.

"It's training time," the CEO said. "They're here to escort you to our training facilities."

Bill squirmed out of the guards' grasp. "They don't have to treat me like I'm a prisoner."

"Quite right," King said. He made a motion with his hand, and the guards stepped back. "Sorry. Habit."

Bill took a deep breath. What had he gotten himself into here? And how was he going to get out of it?

He suddenly wished he had not taken King up on the offer to come to Dallas.

No. That wasn't true.

The CEO walked over to him. "We're happy you've decided to join The Store family," he said. "You will be a welcome and valuable asset to our team." He shook Bill's hand once again, and his grip was cold. "Please follow the guards. They will take you to our training facilities." Grinning, he motioned toward the elevator door. "And have a nice day."

3

Shannon was called into Mr. Lamb's office, not during her break but almost immediately after starting her shift. Another employee, a new employee, came by to tell her the news and man the register for her.

There was something wrong.

She was ushered immediately into his office, and he looked up as she entered. There was no preamble, no small talk; he did not offer her a seat. Mr. Lamb stared at her from across the desk with barely disguised contempt and said simply, "You're fired. Turn in your uniform and your *Bible*."

She blinked, not sure she'd heard right. "Excuse me?"

"Clear the fuck out." The personnel manager stood. "You're through, you're fired, The Store no longer wants you, you stupid fat cow. Get off our property. Now."

She was stunned into silence.

"Now!"

She turned tail and ran. She didn't know what was happening or why, but she was smart enough not to question it. Never look a gift horse in the mouth, as Grandpa Fred always said. She quickly hurried away from the office, excited and angry at the same time. Excited that she was finally able to get out of here and away, to escape The Store's clutches, but angry at the way she was being treated. The anger was an instinctive reaction, though, an emotionally defensive response, and she knew enough not to act on it. She kept it controlled and sped downstairs to the locker room, where she took off her Store uniform while the camera videotaped her for the last time.

This was too good to be true, and she wanted to get off the premises before Mr. Lamb changed his mind.

She wondered, as she put on her street clothes, why it was that Mr. Lamb could fire her but Sam could not, then decided that Sam had probably arranged this, had probably figured out a way to get her out.

Or her dad had talked to Newman King in Dallas and King himself had arranged this.

No. It wouldn't have happened this fast.

She left her uniform and her *Employee's Bible* in the locker, went back out onto the floor, stopped by the Customer Service desk to find out about her last paycheck, was told to leave The Store immediately, and then she was outside, in the parking lot, and she was free.

Free!

She almost felt like dancing.

She didn't know what to do. She didn't want to go home yet, and she got in the car and drove aimlessly and happily around town, finally pulling up in front of Diane's house.

She sat in the car for a moment, not sure she was brave enough to go up and knock on the door, but before she could make any sort of decision, Diane opened the front door and started up the walk toward her.

Shannon tried to read her friend's face, couldn't.

"Hey," she said.

Diane smiled shyly. "Hey."

She blurted it out. "I just got fired from The Store."

"They fired you?" Diane was up to the car now, leaning in the passenger window.

Shannon nodded. "Thank God."

Her friend laughed. The awkwardness that had existed between them for most of the summer seemed to have disappeared, and Shannon was glad she'd come by.

"So what are your plans?"

"Don't have any."

"Want to come in?"

Shannon thought for a moment, shook her head. "Want to cruise around?"

Diane nodded. "Okay. Let me tell my mom." She ran back inside the house, emerging a moment later with her purse. She opened the passenger door, hopped into the car.

"Still friends?" Shannon said.

Diane smiled. "Always."

"It would've been a long senior year without you."

"Tell me about it." Diane looked at her. "I'm glad you're back."

Shannon smiled. "I am, too," she said, starting the car.

She put the vehicle into gear and burned rubber toward Main Street.

THIRTY-TWO

1

For the first three days, Bill was kept alone in a completely dark room. Solitary confinement. There was no light, no sound, no furniture, only padded floors and walls, rounded corners. No one opened the door to feed him, but there were sacks of potato chips, bagels, and fruit against one wall, plastic bottles of water and soft drinks next to them. There was a toilet in one corner, a trash can in another.

This was supposed to be training?

He should have expected something like this from The Store.

He couldn't help thinking that he was being watched, observed, videotaped with an infrared camera, and even in the pitch-dark he felt acutely self-conscious about his movements and behavior and facial expressions. He could not relax, could not get comfortable, was always performing for an audience that might or might not be there, and when he was finally let out, blinking and flinching from the light in the training facility's main corridor, his muscles were knotted, tense, both his neck and back hurting.

He'd been allowed to keep his clothes on in the dark room, but now he was stripped and placed naked in a glass cage in the center of a crowded office, pointed to and laughed at by secretaries and executives. He was left there for twenty-four hours, forced to defecate in front of staring strangers, since the office never closed and workers were at the desks night and day.

What in God's name had possessed him to agree to this? If he'd said no, he would be back in Juniper now, with Ginny and Shannon, and Samantha would be overseeing The Store.

Maybe.

He had only Newman King's word that he could have refused with no repercussions.

The truth was that they could all be dead now if he had refused. King could have had them all killed.

He would not put it past the man.

Or whatever he was.

They might be dead anyway, his wife and daughters. There was no way to know, no way to check, and it was the uncertainty of the fate of his family more than his own discomfort and embarrassment that consumed him.

He was let out of the cage by two guards, a collar looped around his neck, and led naked and filthy through the office of giggling secretaries, down a long corridor, to an all-white room, where a huge blond man sat on a white bench.

"Good morning, Mr. Davis. I am your instructor."

Bill licked his cracked lips, trying to wet them. He hadn't eaten since he'd left the dark room more than a day ago. "I thought this was supposed to be management training."

The instructor smiled coldly. "It is."

"But what's the point of . . . all this?"

"Humiliation is the key to cooperation. That is why we turn out such effective and efficient managers here."

Bill licked his lips again. "Can I get something to drink?"

"In a moment." The instructor stood, and Bill saw that behind the huge man was a freestanding black rectangle with several handles poking out from a hole in its top. Even from here, he could see the shimmering air of heat waves radiating from the object.

The guards pushed Bill forward. They tied him naked to the bench, bending him over, buttocks up.

"You will now receive The Store brand," the instructor told him.

Behind him, he heard sizzling. He craned his neck, twisting to see the instructor holding a red-hot branding iron that he'd taken from the black rectangle.

"No!" Bill screamed.

"This is going to hurt," the instructor said.

The hot metal seared the flesh of his buttocks, and he passed out.

When he came to, he was strapped to a chair in a darkened cell, facing a gigantic television on which Newman King paced back and forth in a featureless white room, talking to himself. The pain was tremendous, unbearable, and he passed out again almost instantly, but he awoke sometime later in the same position, and Newman King was still on the TV screen, talking.

"Greed. It's the impulse that drives us. Not sex, not love, not the desire to help others, but the desire to acquire, the need to own. It is from this impulse that love and sex spring. Relationships are a form of ownership . . ."

He passed in and out of consciousness, in and out of sleep, and always, whether his eyes were open or closed, he heard the melodious voice of Newman King.

". . . If people don't want it, we make them want it. We make sure that everyone around them has it and they feel left out if they don't. We use peer pressure to our advantage. We exploit their . . ."

Hours went by.

Days.

Sometime during the week—he'd lost track of time—the television was turned off. He was released from his bonds by a man dressed in a doctor's white smock, was given an injection in his arm and was allowed to stand and walk around the room.

The pain in his buttocks had completely disappeared.

He was fed a sumptuous meal of deliciously unhealthy junk food brought in on a cart by a gorgeous, bikini-clad young woman. As he ate the meal, the instructor returned with a portable chalkboard, and using lectures and drawings he explained the duties of a manager, went through the organization of The Store. He read extensively from both *The Employee's Bible* and *The Manager's Concordance,* and Bill was allowed to stop him at any time and ask questions.

The lecture continued after he had finished his food and the woman had taken the table away. Bill was so grateful to be able to talk to someone, to be able to again communicate, so thankful for any sort of human response, that he paid close attention to what the instructor said and asked as many questions as possible.

That evening, he was brought by elevator to what appeared to be a huge, expensive hotel suite, complete with a walk-in closet filled with fine clothes, a king-sized bed, and a whirlpool bath. It was, without a doubt, the most luxurious place in which he had ever stayed, and after the deprivation of the past several days, it seemed to him like paradise.

There was a phone, but he could not dial out, could only call for room service, and there was a television, but he could watch no network or news stations, could only watch cable movie channels or view videotapes of recent blockbusters. He was still in the Black Tower, he knew, but aside from those small reminders, the illusion was perfect, and through the huge windows in the bedroom he watched the sunset dying over the desert.

After the orange ball of the sun had disappeared beyond the horizon, he looked through the leather-bound menu, called room service, and ordered lobster and filet mignon, with wine. The meal was again delivered by a gorgeous woman, this one in an evening gown. She offered to remain with him, to bathe him and give him a massage after dinner, but he told her that he wanted to be alone, and she left.

She returned a half hour later to take away the empty plates, and he locked the door to the suite and went into the bathroom where he soaked for a long time in the whirlpool, letting hot jets of water massage his muscles. His head resting on an inflatable pillow, he watched a Tom Hanks movie on the bathroom television set.

This was nice, he thought. He could get used to this.

He put on the robe that had been provided, walked out into the bedroom. He fell asleep almost immediately after crawling into the soft bed, but his sleep-bound imagination was not at all influenced by his surroundings.

He had nightmares.

There were several, but in the only one he could re-member, Newman King showed up in class with the in-structor. The CEO seemed even stranger and more frightening than before, and Bill could not look at him at first, was forced to focus his attention on the instruc-tor, the chalkboard, the bare walls of the room.

"This will be a short test," King said. "I just want to see how you're progressing." He smiled. "As a Store manager, you may be called upon to do things that are personally repugnant to you. But it is your duty and your obligation to put the welfare of The Store before any of your own personal concerns. As an example, I will let you watch the termination of one of our employ-ees who has not performed to expectations."

A black-raincoated man brought out Samantha.

Bill's heart lurched in his chest. "No!"

"Yes."

His daughter was squirming and crying, her eyes filled with terror. The man held her firmly while another Store employee in an identical black raincoat carried in a stunned-looking middle-aged man, walked up to the front of the room, and stood on the opposite side of the CEO.

King smiled. "Now, here's the test. One of these two must be terminated. Which one should it be?"

Bill shook his head. "No. I'm not falling for that. I'm not playing this game."

"Come on. It's your decision."

"No."

"Choose."

"I can't do it."

King nodded to the other manager, held out a knife. "Kill her."

"No!" Bill screamed, jumping up. Hands grabbed him from behind, forced him back down into the chair.

King's smile broadened. "Very good, Mr. Davis. You've made your first decision. You'll make a manager yet." He turned toward Sam, handing her the knife. "Kill him."

The man in the raincoat let her go; she grabbed the

knife and moved past the CEO. She pushed back the other manager's forehead and drew the blade across his throat.

Blood spurted onto her face, onto her clothes, splashed onto the raincoats of the other Store employees. She fell to the floor, dropping the knife, laughing or crying, Bill could not tell which. He wanted to rush to her and hug her, wanted to scream at her and hit her, but he could do nothing, could only sit there, with the strong hands on his shoulders holding him down, and watch as Sam was led out of the room.

King patted Bill on the head on his way out. "See? That wasn't so hard, was it?"

He was provided with a wake-up call the next morning, and after he finished his breakfast, he was brought back to yesterday's classroom, where his lessons continued.

The real training was nothing like his dream. Despite his prejudice against The Store, despite his animosity toward Newman King, he had to admit that a lot of what he was being taught made sense. There seemed to be a lot of merit in The Store's approach to everything from retail strategies to labor relations, and he found himself understanding and agreeing with a lot of what he was being taught. The knowledge seemed useful to him, the ideas effective. Power might have been misused in the past, but it was not intrinsically bad, and even King could not have total control over everything that went on beneath him. On the surface, at least, King's methods seemed far less extreme than those of his protégés, and while he had absolute power in regard to his empire, he delegated authority and gave each manager complete autonomy over The Store to which he or she was assigned. The CEO wasn't necessarily aware of and didn't necessarily approve of everything that was perpetrated in his name.

As taught by the instructors, King's managerial theories and entrepreneurial goals seemed sound.

Maybe King wasn't the threat after all, Bill thought. Maybe it was the petty bureaucrats under him, the overzealous managers who misused the power they were granted.

The training went on for several days. In addition to lectures from three separate instructors, he was given readings and worksheets that reinforced the lessons he'd been taught verbally, and tests that measured his retention of that knowledge. He memorized the standard Store layout and the hierarchy of positions within each retail outlet. Eventually, he was brought into another classroom with other management trainees and they all participated in a roundtable discussion of general Store management techniques and addressed specific problems and incidents that were bound to come up during the course of their work. His fellow trainees proved not to be incipient monsters or tyrants in training but merely ordinary men like himself who were trying to make the best of their situation.

He even became friendly with several of them.

Each evening, he was rewarded for a good day's work with a generous present, always accompanied by a humorous card signed by Newman King. One night it was a palm-sized camcorder and a large-screen television, one night it was keys to a new Lexus, one night it was a gift certificate for free ski lessons and a week's stay for him and his family at The Store's executive condo in Aspen, Colorado.

Each evening he was also offered a bath and a massage by the parade of beautiful women who delivered his dinners, and though he always declined the bath, he accepted the massage his second night. His muscles were aching, and the woman said that she was a certified masseuse. The idea of having trained hands relieve the pain and tension in his muscles sounded wonderful. Following her instructions, he undressed in the bathroom, came out with a towel wrapped around his waist, and lay down on the bed. She did his back first, and the massage was indeed fantastic. All pain fled beneath the ministrations of her expert fingers. She rolled him over and started working on his thigh muscles, and against his will he became aroused. She noticed, slid her hands under the towel and touched him there, but he pushed her away, feeling guilty and embarrassed. Smiling, she continued with the massage.

The ritual was repeated each night.

He began to take all of this luxury for granted. It was not a hard thing to get used to, and he started to feel that he deserved to be pampered after his long day of lessons. Restraint, denial, and asceticism were worthy and noble, all well and good, but there was something to be said for the high life.

As King wrote in *The Manager's Concordance,* rejection of and disdain for the material world were merely ways for the have-nots to make themselves feel morally superior to the haves.

"And in retail," he wrote, "we are only concerned with the haves."

The man was on to something, Bill thought that night as he sipped champagne and received his massage. The man knew what he was talking about.

He closed his eyes, let the beautiful masseuse do her work.

2

Training ended with a daylong practice session in which he acted as manager over a group of employees in a huge Store mock-up.

The week had been building up to this, with an increasing number of tests and quizzes focusing on appropriate reactions to specific in-store situations. King's rules were harsh, but within his broad boundaries he provided a lot of leeway for individual managers to assert their own personalities, and it was clear that today Bill was supposed to show King and his corporation the stuff he was made of.

There were no other trainees in the classroom today, only himself, and he was issued a black leather uniform and told to put it on. He did so, and was taken by elevator to a gigantic room that was an exact double for the Juniper Store. For all Stores. He walked slowly up the main aisle, marveling at the thoroughness of the illusion, the extent of the make-believe. There were employees and customers, fully stocked shelves, and piped-in Muzak. Everything, down to the last detail, was perfect. This was all located somewhere within the Black Tower, but it was indistinguishable from a real Store.

He was led by the instructor to the manager's office, was given a Xeroxed sheet that described a short history of the "problems" facing this particular Store, and was left alone to perform his managerial duties.

He loved it.

The power felt good, and he was comfortable exercising it. He found that he liked having authority over people, liked having them answer to him, liked making decisions, and he easily and quickly addressed the problems that had been created for him. He held a meeting with the department managers, went over sales figures, approved exchanges and refunds. While performing his rounds of the departments, he caught a teenaged boy shoplifting, and a feeling of satisfaction coursed through him as he ordered security to detain the boy and call the police. On a monitor in the Security room, he caught something none of the observers did—a female clerk smoking marijuana in one of the rest room stalls. He fired the girl and was gratified to see her cry.

He was on his feet all day. The experience was tiring but exhilarating, and back in the classroom that evening he was handed a printout that critiqued his performance.

He had received an almost perfect score.

The instructor smiled at him, shook his hand, handed him a diploma.

"Congratulations," the instructor said. "You have successfully completed The Store's manager training course."

"That's it?"

The instructor laughed. "That's it. You've graduated. You are now qualified to run your own Store."

He was exhausted but happy as he returned to his luxury suite. A three-course dinner was waiting for him, still steaming hot, and he ate it gratefully, sorting through the new pile of videotapes that had been provided for him. There was no woman tonight, but he wasn't in the mood for a massage anyway, and he didn't bother to call for one. Instead, like the first night, he soaked in the whirlpool bath and watched a movie before crawling into bed and instantly falling asleep.

He awoke in the middle of the night with a woman straddling him.

The room was dark, lights off, doors and drapes all closed, and he could not tell how she had gotten into his suite. He had locked the door before going to bed, thrown the dead bolt, but of course he had always known in the back of his mind that if King wanted someone to be able to enter his room, that person would be able to do so.

He felt soft thighs gripping his midsection, pubic hair touching his stomach.

He was quickly kissed by sweet feminine lips, a warm tongue was lightly flicking against his own, and a few seconds later the pressure on his midsection disappeared.

Then she was kissing him between his legs. Her mouth began working on him and it was the most exquisite thing he had ever experienced. There was no hesitation, no sloppiness, no scraping of teeth, no awkward tongue, only smooth velvety lips and an unfailingly even rhythm that made him hard almost instantly.

He wanted to push her off, wanted to tell her to stop, but he lay there unmoving, saying nothing, letting her continue. He felt guilty, horribly, tremendously guilty, absolutely reprehensible, but, God help him, he did not want it to stop. It was wrong, it was immoral, it was a violation of his marriage vows and everything he had ever stood for.

But it was also the best sex he'd ever had.

Tonight's present, he thought. His reward for today.

Courtesy of Newman King.

He told himself he shouldn't do this, couldn't do this, had to put a stop to it, but in his mind he was already rationalizing the experience. The sex had been forced on him, he'd been sleepy, too tired and confused to react; he hadn't known what was happening, and by the time he did figure it out too was too late. He'd been tricked, coerced, raped.

He had never cheated on Ginny before, had never even considered it, but he was cheating now and it was too late to turn back and what difference did it make if he finished? The damage had been done.

Besides, there was no way she'd ever know.

The woman's lips slid to the bottom of his penis, taking in all of him, and he came in her mouth, an explosion that never seemed to stop. She did not pull away as Ginny so often did, did not gag and spit out his semen, but continued to hold him between her tightly closed lips, waiting until he had completely finished before licking the final drop off the tip with her expert tongue.

He lay there for a moment panting, trying to catch his breath. He wondered which of the massage women had been sent to reward him, and he wanted to turn on the light, but then she was squatting over his face, obviously expecting him to reciprocate. He could feel the wiriness of her pubic hair against his face, could feel the soft flesh of her sex against his mouth, could smell the muskiness of her arousal in his nose, and he began licking her, his tongue working between her vaginal lips and into her ready opening.

She was quiet, did not moan, and though he usually liked to hear a verbal reaction to lovemaking, there was something sexy about the silence. It allowed him to hear the noises of their bodies more clearly, the harsh raggedness of their breathing, the wet sounds of his tongue lapping between her legs.

She took him in her mouth again and miraculously breathed life back into him. Soon he was hard once again, and she moved off his face and straddled him, taking him deep within her, moving carefully up and down in such a way that he could not even feel the weight of her body atop him. He grabbed her buttocks to help, and then he was coming again, the soft muscular walls of her vagina contracting and expanding, contracting and expanding, pumping out every last drop until his penis was sore and spent.

She rolled over next to him, held him close, hugged

him, and he hugged her back, tears silently escaping
from his eyes and rolling down the side of his face as
the enormity of what he had done sunk in, thinking in
the darkness, *Ginny Ginny Ginny* . . .

The woman was gone when he awoke the next morning, and a moment later the phone rang, an old lady's
voice informing him that there would be no breakfast
today, that he was to get dressed immediately and then
report to Newman King.

The walk-in closet was empty save for the black
leather suit he had worn yesterday to the simulation,
and he put it on and walked out of the suite. A blond
man in an almost identical uniform was waiting for him
in the hall, and he was led over to the elevator and back
up to the top of the Tower, back to the boardroom. King
was alone this time, there were no other men seated
around the table, and the guard who had escorted him
this far moved back into the elevator. The doors closed,
and for the first time he was alone with Newman King.

Even after all that had happened, even after all he'd
been through, the physical presence of the CEO still
seemed frightening. There was nothing rational, logical,
or intellectual about it. This was animal fear, pure and
instinctual, and with every fiber of his being he wanted
to recall that elevator and run out of this room as
quickly as possible, but he maintained a calm exterior
and stood unmoving as King walked slowly toward him.

As always, the mouth was smiling, but there was a
dark wildness in the eyes. King reached him, stood before him, grinned. "Congratulations. You are our top
managerial graduate this year. It's time to celebrate your
accomplishment." He made a wide sweep with his hand,
taking in the map on the wall. "You can have a Store
anywhere you want!" he said. "Pick a spot!"

"Juniper," Bill said. His voice sounded weak, uncertain.

The CEO laughed heartily. "Where else? Ordinarily,
when we have a new manager, we move the entire family
and have them set up in their new home by the time
the manager's training is completed. But this time, we
had an opening at the Juniper outlet, and since you'd

already indicated that that was where you preferred to be assigned, I gave it to you."

He beamed broadly, and Bill had to look away from his pale, creepy face.

Again, as if pulled out of thin air, there was a sheaf of documents in King's hand, and he laid out a series of pages on the table in front of him. "How did you enjoy your little celebration last night?" he asked. He raised his eyebrows conspiratorily.

Bill felt sick.

"Don't worry. These little perks are only for managers and we don't like to let anyone else know about them." He chuckled, nudged Bill with an elbow. "I won't tell if you won't, eh?"

Bill nodded.

King withdrew a pen from somewhere and handed it to him. "Now if you'll just sign these contracts, we'll be all set."

Bill wanted to read each document before signing, but he felt uncomfortable being alone with King, being this close to him, and after giving each page a cursory glance to make sure there was nothing obviously tricky or unusual there, he scrawled his signature on the appropriate lines and handed the pages to the CEO.

King clapped him on the back. "You're one of us!" he said. "You're now part of The Store!"

The elevator door opened, and a group of business-suited yes-men, wearing happy smiles and party hats, streamed into the boardroom and congratulated Bill, shaking his hand and patting him on the back before taking their places around the table. The elevator doors opened again, and a phalanx of bikini-clad women pushed steaming food carts into the room.

King beamed. "Breakfast time!" he announced. "Eat up! We have a full day ahead of us!"

He held up a glass of orange juice. "A toast to Bill Davis, our newest Store manager!"

An hour later, they were in the black jet, on their way back to Phoenix. He and King and an entourage of the yes-men. King chatted amiably on the two-hour flight, talking of the future, expansion, the day when any city he flew over, anywhere in the country, would be home to The Store. He sat gracefully on an elegantly designed chair, dressed impeccably, but he looked as though he was trying to be something he wasn't, and his strange features and unnatural skin seemed even more obvious and noticeable against the mundane background of the airplane interior.

It was a monologue, not a dialogue, and for the most part Bill listened without speaking. He found himself rerunning the events of last night over and over again in his mind. How could he possibly face Ginny after what he had done? He had failed her; he had betrayed her. He'd been corrupted by The Store. He had gone to Dallas to fight it and had become part of it. He had been contaminated and infected and he'd defected to the enemy.

No, that wasn't true. He had the opportunity now to do a lot of good for Juniper. He could reverse the damage that had been done to the town, could implement new policies, could overturn the destructive, divisive decisions that had left the community in the state that it was today. He was working within the system now instead of outside it, and that would enable him to accomplish a hell of a lot more than he would otherwise be able to do. He had made the right decision. He had not sold out.

But he had still betrayed Ginny.

No rationalization that he was working for the greater good could ever excuse that.

The end did not justify the means.

He thought of her lying in bed, alone, asleep, waiting for him, praying that he returned safely, blindly trusting him.

What would he say to her? What could he do to make it up to her? How would he ever deserve her again?

He realized that he was crying only when King leaned over and whispered, "Knock it off. You're acting like a pussy."

He stared at the CEO, wiped his eyes and nodded, looking out the window.

"Be a man," King said. "Act like a manager."

It was midmorning when they landed at Sky Harbor, and they took a limo from Phoenix to Juniper. He pretended to sleep on the ride over, not wanting to talk, but the CEO either knew he was faking or didn't care, and he continued to chatter nonstop all the way there.

Juniper.

It had changed in his absence. Not really changed, not physically, but there was a difference now. It no longer seemed like a dying town, like a lost cause. He no longer felt powerless to stop its decline. He had power now, and rather than looking like a shell of its former self, he saw the town as a blank canvas, a place that could not only equal but surpass what it had been before.

He wanted to go home first, to see Ginny and Shannon, make sure they were all right—

alive

—but the limo drove them straight to The Store. King smiled to himself as they passed the abandoned Ford dealership, chuckled as they drove past an empty feed-and-grain wholesaler.

It was just as well, Bill thought. He didn't know if he was ready to face Ginny yet, anyway. He needed more time to prepare himself, to figure out what he was going to say and what he was going to do and how he was going to act.

King's coming had obviously been announced in advance, and The Store was closed, the parking lot empty and closed off. Two uniformed guards pulled open a barricade to let the limo pass, and the long car moved slowly between twin rows of employees lined up in a path to the front entrance. The employees were holding balloons and signs, throwing confetti, cheering wildly. This was a big event, and seemingly every employee who worked for The Store was there. Bill looked carefully through the window at the passing faces, and his muscles grew tense as he saw no sign of his daughters.

"I had Shannon fired," King said, as if reading his thoughts. "I thought that would make you happy."

"What about Sam?"

"I've transferred her to the corporate office. She's too valuable to lose."

The limo pulled to a stop in front of the entrance, and Bill slid across the seat and opened the door, getting out of the car.

King got out on the opposite side, the side facing The Store, and a huge cheer went up as employees gathered around him, fawning over him, asking for his autograph, trying to touch him. He smiled graciously, magnanimously, and he motioned for Bill to join him as he walked toward the open doors of the building.

Bill felt exhilarated as the adulation expanded to include him. He liked the warm greetings, the cheers, the slavishly obsequious behavior of his new underlings. It felt good to be adored, the object of attention, and he smiled and waved at the rejoicing employees. In the back of his mind was the thought that these were the same employees who had so disdained him and his wife, who had made their lives a living hell, and the fact that he was now their lord and master gratified him immensely.

The celebration stopped the second they walked into The Store. As if on cue, employees placed their banners and balloons and confetti into a lidded bin just inside the door and scurried off to their assigned positions in their individual departments. The change was too abrupt, too complete. Perhaps the employees were just trying to demonstrate their efficiency. Perhaps they really had been excited to see them and were now just as intent on proving what good workers they were, but Bill could not help wondering how much of it was genuine and how much of it had been staged by Mr. Lamb.

Mr. Lamb.

The personnel manager stood nervously off to the side, flanked by Walker and Keyes, waiting for an acknowledgment from Newman King.

King ignored all of them.

He walked slowly up the main aisle, an arm clasped around Bill's shoulder. There were strong muscles in that arm—Bill could feel them—and beneath the muscles, in unusual places, in places they should not have been, were bones. Too many bones.

But it felt good to be walking with King, good to return triumphant to the site of his defeat, and he found that he was proud to walk beside the CEO.

"You will have complete autonomy," King said. "You can hire and fire whomever you want." He stopped walking, paused, smiled. "You can *terminate* whomever you want."

They were walking again, faster this time. The yes-men from the plane, who'd driven to Juniper in a series of cars behind them, were following Bill. Lamb, Walker, and Keyes were following them.

King stopped before a door in the wall. "The manager's office," he said. "*Your* office." He frowned, looking over Bill's head. "What are you three doing here? Did I ask you to tag along with us?"

Bill turned around, saw Mr. Lamb shaking his head nervously. "No, sir. I just thought—"

"Don't think. It's not your strong suit." He pointed toward the Customer Service counter at the far end of The Store. "Back to your offices. Back to work. Now."

All three men were bowing. "Yes, sir," they said in unison. "Yes, sir."

"Fuck off!" King yelled.

They ran, scattering, and King laughed. "I love to do that," he confided. "You can do it, too. Try it sometime."

He would, Bill thought. And he'd enjoy it, too.

Especially when it came to Mr. Lamb.

King turned back to the door, opened it, and they walked up a flight of stairs until they were in the manager's office. There was a huge desk, a refrigerator, a computer, a wall-mounted video screen. The entire south wall was a window made out of mirrored one-way glass that looked over the store below. Cool air from a hidden vent blew into the room, keeping the air temperature even more comfortable than that of the rest of the building. "Like it?" King asked.

Bill nodded.

"Excellent! Want to sit in your chair?"

Bill shook his head. He'd gone through this in the simulation, but it was different being here in real life, and he didn't yet feel comfortable. It would take him some time to get used to all of this.

"After the tour, then." King walked around the desk, pressed a key on the computer. A section of the wall opposite the window slid open, revealing an elevator. King grinned. "Pretty neat, huh?" He walked over to the elevator, got in. "Come on."

Reluctantly, Bill followed him into the small cubicle.

King pressed a button labeled NM. "The rest of you wait here," he said. "We'll be back."

The doors closed. The elevator dropped. Bill looked over at Newman King, then immediately looked away, not wanting to see that face this close. He smelled chalk, dust.

"They don't teach you this part in the training," King said. "I like to do this myself."

"What is it?"

King smiled. "You'll see."

The elevator continued descending—how far down were they going?—and the CEO stared up at the lighted numbers above the sliding doors. He was still smiling, practically bouncing on his heels with amused excitement.

The elevator stopped.

The doors opened.

They were in what looked like an enormous lunchroom, a white-walled, white-floored, white-ceilinged rectangular chamber filled with parallel rows of long white tables. At the far end was a silver counter and a darkened kitchen. There were fluorescent lights in the ceiling, but only about half of them were turned on, and the huge room was filled with a dim, diffused illumination.

Seated at the center tables, unmoving, was a group of men dressed all in black.

The Night Managers.

There were forty or fifty of them, maybe more. Cups of coffee sat on the tables before them, but the cups remained untouched, and the Night Managers sat with their hands folded, unmoving. Even in the dim light, their faces looked white, and there was no expression on them. The room was completely silent, the only sounds coming from King and himself.

Bill knew the Night Managers were his to use as he saw fit, his own private Store army, but they still scared him, and he felt a slight shiver of cold fear as he looked at them. If he had been taught about them in his training, if he had had the opportunity to work with them at the Black Tower, he might have felt differently, might have already been used to working with them, but as it was they seemed just as frightening to him now as they did before he went to Dallas.

King clapped his hands. As one, the heads of the Night Managers turned toward him. He clapped twice more, and the Night Managers' heads swiveled back to their original positions.

The CEO laughed. "Isn't that great? You try it."

Bill shook his head. "No—"

"Come on!" King clapped his hands three times and the Night Managers stood up. Four times and they sat back down again. "It's fun! Go ahead!"

Bill clapped, and the Night Managers' heads turned toward him. He clapped three times and they stood.

What were the Night Managers? he wondered. Zombies? Vampires?

No. It was nothing so simple. They weren't monsters. They weren't mythical undead creatures. They weren't corpses that had been brought back to life through magic or alchemy or science. They were men. They were . . . victims of The Store. Men that The Store had captured.

The Store had captured their souls.

I owe my soul to the company store.

Old Tennessee Ernie Ford had been more right than he'd known.

"Clap again!" King said. "Five times!"

Bill clapped five times and the Night Managers sat down in their original positions.

"Great, huh?" King clapped once, stomped his foot on the floor, and the Night Managers yelled "Yes!" in unison.

"Isn't it fun?"

It was kind of fun, Bill had to admit. And the Night Managers no longer seemed quite so frightening to him.

"So what are they supposed to do?" he asked. "Why are they here?"

"They have the run of The Store at night. And they'll audit the day's doings. And if they find something they don't like, they will tell you. Other than that, they're yours to use as you wish. Security guards, police, fill-in clerks—they can do it all. And they'll respond to voice commands, too."

King stomped his feet twice, and the Night Mangers yelled, "That's right!"

"But the clapping and stomping are more fun." He turned toward Bill. "The details are spelled out in your *Concordance*." He put a strangely formed arm around Bill's shoulder. "Come on. Let's go back to your office and finish up our business. I want to return to Dallas before nightfall."

They stepped into the elevator.

The yes-men had remained unmoving, were in exactly the same positions they'd been in when he and King had left. They came to life when the CEO entered the office, talking to each other, going over papers.

"Any questions?" King asked.

Bill shook his head.

"I guess that's it, then. The hotline number is in your *Concordance* should any problems arise." One of the yes-men placed an *Employee's Bible* and a *Manager's Concordance* on the desk. "And here's your contract." The CEO handed Bill a copy of one of the multipage documents he'd signed back in Dallas.

"Take care of my store," King said. "Don't fuck it up."

He strode out of the office, the other men following close behind, and Bill stood at the window and watched as they emerged from the door in the wall below and moved purposely down the main aisle of The Store toward the entrance.

He stayed by the window, staring, looking at all of the different people in all of the different departments of the store.

His store.

A few minutes after King and his cronies had gone, Mr. Lamb emerged from his office behind the Customer Service counter. He stared up at the window, and though Bill knew the personnel manager could not see him, could see only mirrored glass, it felt as though Lamb was looking right at him, and he had to force himself not to move aside and hide.

Mr. Lamb disappeared back into his office, and a moment later the phone on Bill's desk rang.

He walked over, answered the phone. It was Mr. Lamb. In a voice so obsequious that it had to be sarcastic, the personnel manager told Bill how excited he was to be working with him and how honored he was to have him as his manager. "I've taken the liberty of asking all of The Store's employees to gather in the assembly corridor downstairs so that you can meet with them and lay out the groundwork for your regime."

"Not downstairs," Bill said. "Tell them to line up by the front entrance. Next to the shopping carts."

"I think the assembly corridor is better—"

"Who's manager here, Mr. Lamb? You or me?" He was gratified to hear silence on the other end of the line. "I'll be down in five minutes."

A moment later, the personnel manager's voice echoed over the PA system: "All employees will gather at the front entrance of The Store immediately. This is not a drill. Repeat. All employees will gather at the front entrance of The Store immediately. This is not a drill."

Bill looked around his office one more time, then walked downstairs. On the floor, employees were already scurrying toward the front of the store. He smiled to himself. He was the manager here; he was the boss. Everyone in this building worked for him.

He liked that.

He reached the front entrance, and everyone immediately snapped to attention. His troops were before him, clad all in black, and he felt an involuntary rush of power as he scanned their faces. They were his to command in any way that he saw fit, and he could use them to make his Store run perfectly, the way he wanted. The real world was messy, chaotic, but here, in the world of The Store, that didn't have to be the case. Here in *Juniper,* that didn't have to be the case. He could remake this town in his own image, he could—

He shook his head, closed his eyes.

What was he thinking? That wasn't why he had done this. That wasn't why he was here. He did not want to remake Juniper in his own image. He wanted to return it to the town it had been before The Store's arrival. He wanted to use his new power for good.

He opened his eyes, saw the employees all staring at him, some with fear, some with hope, some with a fanatic determination that made him extremely uncomfortable.

"Get back to work," he said quietly.

Mr. Lamb stepped forward. "Mr. Davis—" he began.

"Get back to work," he ordered. "Everybody."

Once again, there was scurrying as employees returned to their departments.

The personnel manager walked up to him. "I must say, Mr. Davis, that I do not approve of this sort of micromanagement. I have always been in charge of—"

"I don't want to talk to you, Mr. Lamb."

"Mr. King himself appointed me—"

"I don't want to talk to you, Mr. Lamb."

"If it's about your daughters—"

"Of course it's about my daughters!" Bill turned on him, enraged. "What the fuck do you think it's about, you little prick?"

"Hey! Language!"

He turned to see Holly, from the old café, standing next to the shopping carts, smiling at him. She was wearing a Store uniform, but she still looked like the same Holly, unchanged, untouched, and there was a mischievous gleam in her eye. He stared at her, and it was like unexpectedly coming across a friend in a foreign land. He found himself smiling back at her. "Holly," he said. "How've you been?"

"As well as can be expected, I guess."

Customers had been let in by this time—on whose orders he did not know—and he glanced around at them. They seemed nervous, cowed, intimidated. None were walking alone; directors were leading them through The Store as though they were the docile residents of a nursing home.

I can change that, he thought. I'm the manager. I can change that policy.

He turned back toward the personnel manager. "Mr. Lamb?" he said.

"What?" the other man said belligerently.

"You're fired."

The change that came over him was immediate. A look of panic crossed his face. "Please!" he said beseechingly. "I'll do anything you say! I won't disagree with you! I won't try to tell you my opinions!"

"Mr. Walker!" Bill called out. "Mr. Keyes!"

The other two men had been standing nearby, trying to be unobtrusive, and they hurried over.

"You're fired. You're all fired."

The three stood trembling and terrified before him.

"No!" Mr. Lamb said. "Please!"

"You gentlemen no longer work for The Store."

Mr. Lamb fell first. His body stiffened and toppled forward. He made no effort to stop his fall, did not put his hands out in front of him, and his face hit the floor with a loud smack. Like dominoes, Walker and Keyes stiffened and fell as well, Walker forward, Keyes backward.

Bill didn't know what to do, didn't know how to react, didn't know what was going on. He dropped to his knees, tried to feel Lamb's wrist for a pulse, but there was none. He wanted to scream for help, wanted to order someone to call an ambulance, but he knew that all three men were dead, that nothing could save them or bring them back.

The Store had been their lives.

Bill stood, backed away. Several directors and their customers looked at the unmoving men as they passed by, but none of them stopped, and none exhibited more than a mild curiosity.

Bill turned toward Holly. She smiled at him. There

was no fear on her face, no confusion, only a look of satisfaction. "Ding dong, the witch is dead."

He nodded. He wanted to feel bad, wanted to feel remorse, wanted to feel . . . something, but he shared Holly's satisfaction, and he thought: This is for Ben.

An employee Bill didn't know came running up, looked at the men on the floor, then looked over at Bill. "I'll take care of this, sir. Don't worry about it."

He ran off the way he'd come, and a moment later his voice sounded over the loudspeaker.

"Cleanup in aisle one!"

He went home after the bodies had been taken away.

He wanted to see Ginny and Shannon.

He'd called first, from The Store, unable to wait, needing to know if everything was all right, and he practically wept when he heard his wife's voice.

How was he going to face her?

He'd been supplied with a company car, a boxy black sedan, and he took it, speeding home as quickly as he could. Ginny was waiting for him in the drive, and he threw the car into park, jumped out of the vehicle, and ran into her arms. They were both crying, hugging each other crazily, kissing.

"Where's Shannon?" he asked.

"Over at Diane's." Ginny wiped the tears from her eyes, smiled. "Mr. Lamb fired her."

"I fired Mr. Lamb."

"You're really the manager now?"

"I really am."

"Where's Sam?"

He licked his lips. "She's been transferred to Dallas."

Ginny faced him. "Do you think she'll be all right?"

"I don't know," he admitted.

He suddenly remembered when Sam had been ten years old and he'd taken her hiking and she'd twisted her little ankle and he'd given her a piggyback ride all the way home.

Ginny took a deep breath. "Will we ever see her again?"

He looked at her. "I don't know."

He saw Sam as she'd looked in June, at her graduation, smiling up at them from the field as she'd accepted her diploma.

Ginny reached out, hugged him again. He hugged her back, held her tightly, thought of what had happened last night in his suite. What had he done? Why had he been so stupid? Why couldn't he have been stronger? He blinked back the tears that were welling up in his eyes.

"I'm glad you're back," she said.

"I am, too," he said, starting to cry. "I am, too."

THIRTY-THREE

1

He found that he did not really want to change The Store.

When he was on the outside looking in, he had not realized what being manager of The Store entailed. He had not understood the rigorous demands of the job. There were sales quotas that had to be reached, a payroll that had to be met, people who had to be instructed and guided, a thousand little daily decisions that had to be made. As much as he hated to admit it, The Store was the engine that drove the town, and that meant that the entire economy of Juniper was now resting on his shoulders. He sympathized with his old concerns, but he realized now that the inconvenience of a few individuals had to be weighed against the needs of many.

Of course there was no way he could ever condone what had happened in the past: the disappearances, the fires, the systematic destruction of enemies and rivals. But, as King said, that was all over and done with. This was the beginning of a new day, and he was going to legitimize The Store in Juniper.

He reviewed some of The Store's practices, those that seemed to him somewhat suspect, but on closer examination, he saw that all of them were necessary. He had not liked the idea of having Security monitor every square inch of the floor, letting employees spy even on customers' most intimate acts, but shrinkage—theft and shoplifting—were major problems for any retailer and were a primary source of revenue loss. Besides, while people needed privacy at home, there was no reason they needed it when they were on Store property, shopping.

Directors, too, were a concept that had offended him, but he understood that despite his personal prejudice against them, they were a valid retail tool and enabled customers—elderly customers in particular—to easily find what they were looking for. The directors made shopping quicker and more efficient.

All the way down the line, the things that had seemed wrong to him proved to be not only legitimate and worthwhile but indispensable.

The Store's policies weren't as bad as he'd thought.

Ginny didn't seem thrilled. She disagreed with his decisions even after he explained them to her, and she seemed to think that he had sold out, that he had been brainwashed back in Dallas.

The best sex he'd ever had.

She still loved him, of course, and was grateful to have him back, but she was wary of him, not open and honest the way she had been, and he vowed to himself that after he got The Store shaped up, he would work on repairing their relationship.

He owed her at least that much.

At The Store, he hired new employees to replace Mr. Lamb, Mr. Walker, and Mr. Keyes. He fired some of the clerks who were not fitting in and replaced them with others who would be better able to take orders.

He had not been able to bring himself to meet with the Night Managers. He was still a little afraid of them, and though they seemed to be doing a fine job with their nighttime audits, and the reports they left each morning on his desk were both thorough and easy to follow, he could not help thinking of what he had seen in New Mexico, of the rumors Shannon had told him. He was their boss, yes, but he did not understand them and he did not know how to deal with them or what to do with them.

Still, they were part of his Store, part of his responsibility, and as King had shown him, he had absolute power over them. He should try to utilize their services and incorporate them into his management strategy.

He sat in his office for an entire morning, reading his *Manager's Concordance,* trying to learn everything he

could about the Night Managers. There was no clue as
to their origins, of course, but there were examples of
how to use them, as well as a detailed description of the
commands that would control their actions.

He'd wanted to switch the locations of two departments ever since he'd returned. Shoes and Children's
Clothing seemed to him to be in the wrong places. But
swapping them, moving all of the merchandise and fix-
tures, would take up a lot of time and require a lot of
effort. He would either have to disrupt normal operations for a day and inconvenience shoppers or pay overtime to employees who stayed after their regular shift in
order to do the job.

But he realized now that the Night Managers could
do it.

It was a legitimate solution to a legitimate problem,
and it also enabled him to ease into using the Night
Managers, feel out the situation.

He closed the *Concordance,* leaned back in his chair,
and stared up at the ceiling. Part of him wanted to bring
along someone else, a subordinate, but he realized that
he was being weak, and he knew that this was something
he had to do on his own. He took a deep breath and
forced himself to get out of the chair and pick up the
Concordance.

He took the elevator down to their room.

The air seemed colder, the lunchroom light dimmer
than before. He was not scared, exactly, but he felt uneasy, and he stood close to the open elevator door as
he stared across the long room toward the tables where
the back-clad figures sat.

As before, there were coffee cups before them, although once again the figures remained unmoving, staring straight ahead, not drinking, not even touching the
cups.

He wished Newman King was here with him.

Licking his suddenly dry lips, Bill opened the *Concordance* to the page he had marked. He cleared his throat,
yelled out, "One! Two! Three!"

The three Night Managers nearest him stood.

He walked forward slowly, stopping when he reached

the edge of the tables. He looked down at the book again, stomped his foot three times.

The closest Night Manager turned to face him.

It was Ben.

Bill sucked in his breath, a wave of nausea passing over him. He suddenly felt weak. He stared at his friend. All color had been drained from the editor's face, all emotion, all expression, all trace of humanity. There was only a blank look of dull mindlessness on the features that had once belonged to Ben and an automatonic demeanor identical to that of all the other Night Managers.

Bill peered into his friend's vacant eyes, saw nothing there. He felt hollow himself, empty, lost. A profound grief was threatening to settle over him, a bitter despair that he knew would be overwhelming, so he gave in to the other emotions within him: hatred and anger. Blind hatred and searing anger directed not only at Newman King but at himself.

What had he been doing? Who had he been kidding? Ginny was right. He had been suckered, he had been co-opted, he had been corrupted. The Store had not changed. The Store could not change. *He* had changed. He had bought into King's bullshit and had allowed himself to believe that The Store was different than he'd thought, than he'd known. He had put blinders on and had rationalized his involvement. He had been seduced by the power, by the luxury

—the best sex he'd ever had

—by the promises and assurances of Newman King, and while his initial motives had been pure, he had embraced his new job unthinkingly, without considering the moral consequences. He had even begun believing the lies that had been perpetrated in order to continue The Store's reign.

But no more.

He saw The Store now for what it was, for what it always had been, and he hated himself for swerving from the path, for going against what he knew was right. He had betrayed not only Ginny, but Ben, Street, the town.

Himself.

He wasn't going to resign, though. He wasn't going to quit. He was going back to his original plan. King had given him complete autonomy over the Juniper Store and he was going to use it to return things to the way they were. He was going to strip The Store of its power and reverse the changes it had made to the town. He was going to downsize The Store until it was what it should have been in the first place—a discount retail outlet. No more, no less.

It was Ben who had brought him to this point, who had made him realize what he was doing, and he stared at his friend, feeling again the emptiness, the sadness.

He moved forward, put a hand on Ben's shoulder, felt the cold even through the layers of black material.

"Thank you," he said softly.

The Night Manager did not respond.

He called a meeting that afternoon of every Store employee. Every department manager, director, stock boy, secretary, clerk, custodian, cook, waitress, security monitor. The first thing he told them was that there would be no more uniforms. Everyone was expected to wear nice clothes—skirts for the females, shirt and tie for the males—but uniforms were out. Instead, everyone would be issued a simple name tag.

There were murmurs and whispers, expressions of surprise and disbelief. He caught Holly's eye, saw her smile and give him a thumbs-up sign.

There would be no more directors, he told them. There were cries of protest against this, but he explained that there would be no layoffs, either. Not for those employees who wanted to work for the new Store. The directors would be reassigned to other positions. Jobs would be found for them.

The meeting lasted most of the afternoon. It was not merely a speech to the troops, but a true dialogue, and though there was some reluctance at first, he got almost all of them involved in the discussion, making them believe that he really was going to change the way The Store operated and letting them know that their input was valuable, necessary, that he did not know the details of how everything worked and would appreciate their comments, suggestions, and help in modifying the workplace.

That night, tired but happy, he returned home and told Ginny what had happened. She was horrified by the story of Ben but was thrilled that he was finally going to start loosening The Store's grip on the town and dismantling its fiefdom.

"Do you think you can do it?" she asked.

"Watch me."

It would take some time to sort through all of the tangled webs woven by The Store, discover all of the city services that it had taken over, all of the work that had been contracted out to it, all of the other businesses that were being bankrolled and overseen by the corporation, but Bill vowed to track everything down and put it right.

He closed The Store for a week while they took inventory. The employees, in teams of two, cataloged every item on every shelf, entering the data into hand-held computers, and he himself sorted the information on his own PC. He wiped whole sections off The Store map, returning items to The Store's corporate warehouse, replaced them with more appropriate stock from traditional distributors until The Store's inventory more closely approximated that of ordinary discount retailers.

"You don't think King's going to put a stop to this?" Ginny asked him one night. "You don't think he's going to find out and come after you?"

"He'll try."

She hugged him close. "You can't hope to fight someone like that. Some*thing* like that. He's way out of your league."

"Don't worry," he told her.

"I just don't want anything to happen to you." She paused. "Or to Sam."

He looked at her.

"She's working at his corporate offices. God knows what he'll do to her when he finds out."

"He told me I could do this," Bill said. "It's how he suckered me into working for him. He said the store was mine to do anything I want with."

"What if he changes his mind?"

"I'll deal with that when I come to it."

He fired twenty-six people over the next three days, fully a third of The Store's workforce. He did not trust them, did not feel they could adapt, was sure they preferred King's ways, and he did not want them working for him. That was one advantage of having absolute power over his Store. He did not have to give legitimate reasons for firing someone, did not have to have valid cause. He could simply kick someone out and banish them from the premises. He felt a small thrill of satisfaction, a return of the old sense of power, as he told some of the more belligerent employees to get out, they were through, but he refused to allow himself to enjoy it, forced himself to remain impartial and above it all, to think only about the good of the town and not his own petty emotional gratification.

Some things remained unresolved. The transients, for example. No one would tell him where the homeless people who had been rounded up by the sweeps had been taken or what had happened to them. He questioned everyone, but they all claimed ignorance.

Perhaps it was just as well.

He was not sure he wanted to know.

Then there were the Night Managers.

They were one of the big problems. He had not gone down to their lunchroom since finding Ben, had purposely stayed away, but he knew he could not avoid them forever. They continued to roam The Store at night, to audit and report on what was happening, and their reports were becoming increasingly less objective. There were no conclusions drawn, no adjectives used, only facts and figures, but the way those facts and figures were presented bespoke criticism, and he knew that he was going to have to confront the Night Managers sometime.

On Friday, he went down there again, this time with Ginny, and though she wanted to see Ben, he made her stay by the elevator door and did not tell the Night Managers to move from their stationary positions at the tables. He had read and reread *The Manager's Concordance*, but there was nothing in it about firing or getting rid of the Night Managers, and he knew that if he was going to get rid of them, he'd have to figure something out on his own.

The two of them stood next to the wall, staring across the long, dimly lit room.

Ginny shivered. "They're spookier than I thought they'd be."

He nodded.

"Are they . . . dead?"

"I don't know," he admitted. "I don't think so, but . . . I don't know what they are."

"Maybe we should try to talk to Ben, try to jog his memory or something."

"No," Bill said.

"Have you looked at all of them? Maybe some of the others are people we know . . . knew."

Now it was Bill's turn to shiver. "Let's just do this and get out of here." He cleared his throat, took a deep breath. "You're fired," he announced loudly. "All of you."

The Night Managers remained unmoving.

"You no longer work for The Store!"

No response.

"I relieve you of your duties!"

Nothing.

"Get out of here! Hit the road! Get off The Store's property! Fuck off!"

"It's not working," Ginny said.

"I know that!" he snapped at her.

She pulled away from him, and he apologized immediately. "I'm sorry. I just . . . I'm sorry."

She nodded, obviously understanding.

"You have any ideas?" he asked.

" 'Leave?' " she said.

"Leave!" he repeated loudly.

Nothing.

He continued shouting orders, screaming at them, but only succeeded in making a contingent of Night Managers in the middle of the group walk over to the steel counter next to the kitchen.

"Let's go," Ginny said. "I don't like it down here."

He nodded dejectedly, and the two of them stepped back into the elevator.

In the seconds before the elevator doors closed, he saw the contingent of Night Managers walk away from the kitchen, back to their brethren, carrying new cups of coffee.

On their own.

2

He had rescinded the curfew several days ago and people were again allowed outside at night, but the fear was still there, and he drove home on an empty road, seeing no other vehicles, even downtown.

There was supposed to be an election in a few weeks to choose a new town council, but no one had as yet indicated that they would run for any of the positions.

After what had happened to the last two councils, maybe people thought the job was cursed.

Ginny and Shannon were both home, waiting for him, and they ate together. Meat loaf and mashed potatoes. He tried to be cheerful, they all did, but as always Sam's absence seemed the most acute at mealtime, and they drifted off into silence, thinking their own thoughts as they ate.

They had not heard from her since her transfer to Dallas, and he prayed that nothing had happened to her.

School had started yesterday, and Ginny already had homework to grade and Shannon already had homework to do, so he spent the evening alone, numbing his brain with a video game on the PC. He was on the fourth level of Alienblaster when Ginny came barging into the room, shutting the door behind her. She hurried over to the window, pulled open the drapes.

"What's this?" Bill said.

"Night Managers."

He stood. "What?"

She turned toward him, her face white, blanched. "Look outside."

He did. "I don't see anything."

"Turn off the light."

He did so and again stared out the window. His eyes adjusted, and now he could see them, behind the trees, just as she'd said.

The Night Managers.

They were watching his house.

An involuntary shiver passed through him, goose bumps popping up on his arms.

Ginny pulled the drapes shut. "They're spying on us!"

Bill took a deep breath. "They're spying on me."

"Can't you call them off?"

He nodded. "I should be able to. But I didn't order them here."

"What's that mean?"

"I think it means King's coming."

"What's he going to do?"

"I don't know." Bill looked around the floor, picked up his shoes and socks. "But I'd better get down to The Store and meet him."

She grabbed his arm. "No! You can't go!"

He pulled away. "I have to."

"What if he—"

"I have to," he repeated. He quickly walked out of the room and down the hall. He stopped in the living room to put on his shoes and socks, then checked to make sure all of the doors and windows were closed and locked. "Don't open anything. Don't let anyone in." He looked around. "You still have that baseball bat somewhere?"

She nodded.

"Get it. Just in case."

Shannon had walked into the living room from her bedroom. "What is it? What's going on?"

"The Night Managers," Ginny said. "They're surrounding the house."

"Oh, God." Shannon started crying. "Oh, God. I knew it. I knew it."

"Just stay calm," Bill told them. "I'm going to The Store. Hopefully, they'll follow me. I think that's why they're here."

"What's going to happen?"

He sucked in his breath. "I think Newman King wants to meet with me."

Shannon's sobs grew stronger. She ran across the living room, threw her arms around her father. "Don't go!" she pleaded. "It's a trick. It's a trap."

"Maybe you should wait until morning," Ginny suggested.

"And maybe he'll come here."

"At least it's your home turf."

"The Store's my home turf. It's my Store. Besides, I don't want him here."

"Maybe we should come with you. There's safety in numbers. And we're female. He might not—"

"He doesn't care what you are." Bill hugged his daughter, kissed her forehead, then moved over to Ginny, pulling her close. He kissed her forehead, her cheeks, her lips. "I'll be back as soon as I can."

"What if you never come back?" Shannon sobbed.

"I'll be back."

The Store's parking lot was empty when he arrived, but the lights were on inside, and through the front doors he could see Night Managers moving through the aisles.

He felt cold, frightened, but he forced himself to get out of the car and used his key to open the doors and let himself in.

The Night Managers were walking quickly through the building, moving up and down the aisles, between the racks. They were supposed to be auditing the day's events, taking inventory and recording transactions, but they did not stop moving even for a second and did not even appear to be looking at any of the merchandise.

They just kept walking.

The Store was completely silent save for their footsteps, and the lack of Muzak, the lack of air-conditioning noise, the lack of any other sound whatsoever was extremely unnerving. Bill walked forward slowly, up the main aisle.

The lights snapped off. Behind him, he heard a metallic click. There was a sudden breeze, a rush of cold air, and he quickly turned around.

King stood in the doorway, backlit by the headlights of his limo.

"Bill," King said. "Nice to see you again."

There was no joy in his voice, no friendliness, only a hard, dangerous flatness that sounded completely inhuman. He stood just inside the building, alone, unmoving, a dark, frightening figure, little more than a silhouette. The strangeness of his body, so obvious up close, was also visible in the peculiar outline of his form, and Bill was filled with an instant, instinctive fear. But he held his ground, faced King. "Good evening," he said calmly.

The lights came back on, and the CEO strode up the aisle toward him.

Stage tricks. King was using theatrical lighting in order to draw attention to himself.

The smallness of it, the mundane practicality of the dramatic convention somehow made Bill feel less afraid.

"What do you think you're doing?" King asked.

"Standing here."

"I mean, what are you doing with The Store?"

"My job."

The two of them faced each other. Again, Bill noticed the strangeness of King's skin, the artificiality of his teeth, the ferocity in his eyes. He looked away, unable to gaze for more than a few seconds upon that unnatural visage.

"This is not the way you were trained to manage a Store."

"No, but I decided to do it this way. I thought it would be best for Juniper."

King practically shouted. "I decide what's best!"

"I don't think it can be that standardized. I think things have to be tailored to the individual communities. Things aren't the same here in Arizona as they are, say, in Ohio—"

"They're the same everywhere!" King stepped forward, and Bill quickly moved back. Wind swirled between them. "I will not have you thwarting the will of

The Store and jeopardizing its future on some personal whim!"

Bill was terrified, having a tough time maintaining his false calm front, but he forced his voice to stay level. "I'll run this Store the way I see fit."

"Then you will not run this Store at all!"

"You gave me complete autonomy," Bill said. "It's in my contract."

"You're not managing it properly. Obviously, I misjudged you. You're not Store material."

"What are you going to do? Take it away from me?" Bill paused. "Are you going back on your word? Are you going to break your contract?"

"You fucker," King said softly. "You worthless piece of shit."

Bill held his ground, said nothing.

A Night Manager passed between them, walking.

For a brief second, it looked as though King was about to attack. He glared at Bill, his muscles tensing, fists balling up. On his head, his *hair* seemed to be moving.

Then he smiled. He glanced casually around the store. "Did I tell you we're expanding? In addition to sushi and espresso bars, we're going to have brothels attached to our stores. There's a lot of money to be made in the sex trade. It's the last bastion of pure unexploited commerce in this country. It's about time someone franchised it and marketed it."

Bill had a sick, sinking feeling in the pit of his stomach. He thought he knew where this was going.

King was suddenly holding a videocassette in his hand. He tossed it to Bill. "Your last night in Dallas. It's one of our training materials." He grinned. "You might want to look at it."

Bill dropped it on the floor, crushed it beneath his boot.

King was holding another one. He laughed. "Let's look at it together, shall we?"

Next to one of the front checkout stands was a television and VCR, a display used to sell Disney videocassettes. King walk over, popped out the *Sleeping*

Beauty tape in the machine and put in his own. He turned on the television.

The room had been pitch-black, but there was none of the red-or green-tinted monochrome that characterized most film shot in the dark. Indeed, the images on the screen were dim but color-perfect, the angle straight-on. The camera had obviously been hidden behind the mirror over the dresser, and Bill watched as a nude woman entered the suite. She was looking down at the ground, hair obscuring her face, but though he could not see her features, he did see for the first time her breasts, her pubic hair, and he felt shamed and embarrassed as he thought about touching her there, as he recalled what he'd done with her.

The best sex he'd ever had.

He wanted to look away but couldn't, and he exhaled loudly as he realized that he'd been holding his breath. On the screen, the woman climbed onto the bed, straddled his chest, looked up at the camera.

It was Sam.

The revelation was so shocking, so totally unexpected, that for a full thirty seconds he had no reaction, no response at all. He simply stood there stupidly, continuing to watch the screen as his daughter began working on him.

Then he was flooded with emotion: humiliation, anguish, self-loathing, disgust. He was filled with a despair blacker than anything he had ever known, a horror so profound and all-consuming that he had not known he could experience anything like it. Beneath that, or on top of it, or mixed in with it, was an agonizing grief for Sam, a bone-deep sorrow for what she had done, what had happened to her, what he had *allowed* to happen to her.

And overriding everything was a pure, hard hatred for Newman King.

He turned toward the CEO.

"She's going to be one of our best hookers," King mused.

Bill rushed him. There was no plan, no thought behind it, only a blind desire to do damage, a need to kill. He was acting on impulse, following instinct, and his feet were pumping furiously, fists railing. He threw himself at King—

And then he was on the floor, stunned, shaking his head. A Night Manager passed in front of him, kept walking. He wasn't sure what had happened, but the television was off, he was lying on the ground, and King was standing in the open doorway, on his way out.

The CEO smiled. "I'll be sending a copy to your wife." He paused. "Unless you fall back in line."

"This is my store!" Bill said.

"No. It's *my* store. I let you play with it."

"Fuck you!" Bill yelled. He tried to get to his feet, was overtaken by dizziness, fell.

"I'll give you a day to think about it."

And then King was gone.

Bill lay on the floor, screaming with rage, sobbing, hating himself, wanting to kill King, wanting to kill himself, wanting some sort of violence. He tried to stand, was finally able to do so, and was a hairbreadth away from going over to the Sporting Goods department, grabbing a gun, and ending it all.

But something held him back.

He didn't know what it was, didn't know why, but he stood in the middle of the aisle as around him the Night Managers continued walking. He saw Ben, saw another face he thought he recognized but couldn't quite place.

There'd been something different about King this time, he realized. He'd seemed genuinely angry at one point, rattled by Bill's rebellion and initiative. He'd shown, for the first time, human emotions. And that made him seem . . .

Less in control.

Weaker.

Maybe he wasn't invincible.

Bill stared through the still-open doors, into the dark night outside. He suddenly understood what had happened here.

Nothing.

He hadn't been killed, he hadn't even been fired— although King clearly possessed the power to do both.

He'd been right. King was not able to break the contract. The contract gave him complete autonomy over this Store, and there was nothing King could do about it. The CEO could try to force him to quit, could try to blackmail him into leaving, but he could not be fired, and obviously he could not be harmed. The contract protected him.

He was in.

Bill felt an absurd sense of exhilaration. This was the first time, no doubt, that someone had stood up to King, the first time that the training had not taken, and it was clear that the CEO had not expected this, had not prepared for something of this nature. Bill was not something that King had planned for. He could not be bribed and he would not be blackmailed. He would stand tall and fight, do what he knew was right. He would come clean with Ginny, he would continue with his rehabilitation of the Juniper Store, and he would go up against Newman King.

What about the managers of the other Stores? They could do the same thing. They could stand up to King as well, run their Stores their way, do what they wanted with their towns.

King could be broken.

What would he do if all of the managers broke away? If they all defied him and started doing things the way they wanted? Would he destroy them? Or would he be so weakened by the loss of power that he would become impotent?

He would still own the corporation, of course. He would still be incredibly rich. He would still be able to hire new managers if the old ones quit or died off. But would the dissipation of his influence over day-to-day retail operations siphon off his dark power?

Bill thought of Mr. Lamb, Mr. Walker, Mr. Keyes.

Maybe he would die.

There were still tears drying on his face, still sickened horror in his heart, but there was hope there as well, an optimism that hadn't existed before.

He was still slightly woozy as he walked, but his sense of purpose overcame the lingering effects of whatever

King had hit him with, and he went through the doors, locking them behind him, and out to his car.

He drove home.

Ginny and Shannon were waiting anxiously in the living room when he arrived, and he hugged them both and told them everything was all right, and sent Shannon into her bedroom so he and Ginny could talk.

He told her what happened his last night in Dallas.

He should have come clean before, but he'd been afraid. He hadn't had the guts. He'd been a moral coward, and in that sense he had still been a part of King's team. He told her everything now, though, and she grew increasingly quiet as he described his encounter. He explained that he'd been awakened, that the woman had already been on top of him, and that he'd had no choice in the matter. He was tempted to let her think that he'd been helpless and overpowered, forced into it, but he was determined to be honest with her, and he told her that he had had an opportunity to stop it but had not. He emphasized that this was after two weeks of King's so-called training, after the deprivation and the rewards, but while he made sure she knew the context, he did not avoid his own complicity, his own responsibility for what had happened.

He did not tell her it was Sam, though. It was a lie, he knew, but it was a lie that he felt was justified. They might be able to get past an incidence of adultery, but their marriage would not survive an incidence of incest. Ginny would never be able to live with him, knowing that he had had sex with their daughter.

He would have a tough time living with that himself.

Bill was crying by the time he was finished, but Ginny was stone-faced, and he thought then that their marriage was probably over. He didn't blame her. He understood her feelings. He'd feel the same way.

Still, he was glad he'd told her. It might ruin his life, but at least it liberated him from the influence of Newman King. At least he knew now that he was free to do as he chose without having to worry about his misdeeds coming to light.

Ginny was still not speaking, still staring at him with

that hard, unreadable face, and he continued, explaining what had happened tonight in The Store, describing Newman King's anger, the CEO's inability to break the contract he had made, the possibility that he could be defeated.

Afterward, Bill collapsed on the couch, exhausted, emotionally drained.

Ginny continued to stare at him. "I understand," she said finally. "I'm not sure I can forgive and I definitely won't forget, but we'll wait until all this is through before sorting it out. Right now, our first priority is to get rid of Newman King. And to get Sam back."

Sam.

Bill swallowed, nodded.

"I think your idea's good. I don't know if it'll bring down his whole corporation, but taking the individual Stores away from him is bound to hurt him. I think you need to contact the other managers."

"I'm going to."

They stared at each other in silence. Bill wished he knew what she was thinking, but her face was unreadable to him. He took a deep breath. "Where do you want me to—" He cleared his throat. "Where should I sleep?"

She looked at him, thought for a moment. "The bed, I guess." She held up a hand. "This doesn't mean I forgive you, but I understand that these are not normal circumstances."

"I—"

"And I don't want Shannon to know. As I said, we'll sort it out afterward."

Bill nodded.

Ginny sighed, and now there was a tear in her eye. She wiped it away with one strong finger. "Come on," she said. "Let's go to bed."

3

He was in his office at The Store the next morning, paging through the rambling, incoherent notes his predecessor had left on the computer, when the phone rang. His personal line. He picked it up immediately. "Hello?"

"Bill?" It was Ginny. "I got a package from Sam. Federal Express."

His heart lurched in his chest.

"I haven't opened it yet. I thought you might want to be here."

"I'll be right over," he said.

She'd opened the package by the time he got there, but she had not watched the videotape, and she sat there, solemn and pinched, holding it in her hand.

She looked at him when he walked in, thought for a moment, then handed him the tape. "I'm not sure this is something I want to see," she said.

"It's not," Bill told her.

She nodded. "Do what you want with it."

He dropped the videocassette onto the floor and stomped on it, breaking it into pieces. He picked up the pieces, unspooled the tape, threw everything into the big garbage can in the garage.

"Have you called any managers yet?" Ginny asked.

He shook his head. "I've been trying to get up the courage. I just keep thinking, what if they're on his side? What if they don't want to do anything differently than the way he tells them? What if they decide to come after me on their own, on his behalf. The contract prohibits him from harming me. I don't think it applies to them."

"Didn't he say his worst enemies make the best managers?"

"Yes," Bill admitted.

"Then how about the other managers you met in that training course? You got along with them, right? Why don't you start there?"

He nodded. "That's a good idea." He sighed. "But King's probably blackmailing everyone. Just in case the training didn't take. He sets us up, then uses it against us."

"But if they're strong enough to stand up to him, if they're strong enough to admit their mistakes and face what they did wrong and accept the consequences . . ." She left the sentence unfinished.

"It might work," Bill said. "I'll contact them."

"But be careful."

"I know. King's probably monitoring my E-mail, bugging my phones. I need to find another way to get through to them."

"Mail," she said. "Regular mail. Or Federal Express."

"The old-fashioned way."

"It's secure."

"As long as the other managers don't have a Mr. Lamb opening their mail for them."

"It's a chance we have to take."

He was still nodding. "We might be able to pull this off."

She kissed him. For the first time since he'd told her about his betrayal. "Think positive."

"We *will* be able to pull this off."

"That's the spirit."

He'd been provided with a list of all of the other Stores in the United States, as well as a business number for each, but there were no managers' names listed, and he sure didn't want to talk to them while they were at work.

He ended up calling each Store, asking the manager's name, then dialing information for each area and obtaining the managers' home phones. Two were unlisted, and he let those slide. He called the rest individually, at night or in the early morning, and though he was awkward and hesitant at first, not sure how to bring up what he needed to say, it became easier as he went along, and he discovered that most of the managers were like him, forced into their positions, unwilling participants, and most of them secretly hated Newman King.

A few of those he dialed seemed suspicious as he felt them out over the phone, and for those he invented some business-related reason why he'd called. They might be willing to go along with the scheme, but they might also be King loyalists, and he couldn't take a chance of trusting them if he wasn't a hundred percent positive.

He was lucky that the first manager he called, Mitch

Grey, the man to whom he'd spoken most often in the training classes, seemed to hate Newman King almost as much as he himself did. Mitch was now in Ohio, and he caught on to the idea right away. He even offered to help contact other managers.

"I'm going to put together a package," Bill explained. "Send it through the mail to everyone's house. I'll describe what happened here. I'd like to have some sort of simultaneous switchover, a prearranged time when all the managers take over their Stores at once and start rolling back what King's done. I've been doing things gradually here, sequentially, but if we all did that, it might give him time to prepare, time to come up with something, a way to fight us. I'd like to catch him completely by surprise. And I think we really might be able to hurt him if we drain his power all at once."

Mitch was silent for a moment. "What do you think he is?"

"I don't know," Bill admitted.

"Why do you think he's doing this?"

"I don't know."

"You really think we can fight something like that?"

"We can try."

"But do you think we'll win?"

"Yes," Bill said. "I do."

Mass firings, he decided that night, were the best way to signal the start of the war. Get rid of all King loyalists at every Store in one fell swoop, then immediately start cutting back on The Store's power. He wrote out a tentative schedule, an outline, and saved it.

The next morning, he called more managers.

Within two weeks, it was all set.

Videotapes, ostensibly from Sam, had been arriving by Federal Express each day, but he and Ginny destroyed them all without watching them. King called his office daily, left voice mail and E-mail messages, sent unordered merchandise that had to be shipped back, contacted employees at home, ordering them to carry out his will, offering them promotions, did everything he legitimately could to destabilize Bill's power, but Bill had chosen wisely in his hirings and firings and the loyalty held fast. The Store's influence was almost completely gone outside the borders of its property, and slowly but surely Juniper was sloughing off the yoke of Store oppression.

Not all of the managers were on board, but most were. He and Mitch had together contacted over two hundred managers, and only ten had been so obviously despotic that they hadn't even been approached. Another fifteen seemed borderline, and so, just to be on the safe side, they hadn't mentioned anything to them. But the other 175 were solidly in their corner, willing to do what it took to topple King, willing to endure humiliation and embarrassment, the ravaging of their personal lives, in the service of the greater good.

Bill was proud of them all.

The plan was for the participating Store managers to call a special meeting of all their employees Sunday morning at five o'clock Pacific time, six o'clock Mountain time, seven o'clock Central time, and eight o'clock Eastern time, so that all of the meetings would correspond and occur exactly at the same moment, no matter what time zone the individual Stores were in. Sunday was chosen because it was the day that The Store opened latest.

Besides, Sunday was supposed to be the Lord's day.

And the God connection couldn't hurt.

King's people would be fired at the meetings, directors reassigned, security departments dismantled. Inventory should have been taken at each of the Stores by that time, and the managers would sign chargeback forms and order invoices in order to instantly change, at least on paper, the contents of The Stores' stock.

It was a bold plan, and even if the results didn't turn out exactly the way they intended, it was still a hell of an organizational achievement.

And it was bound to hurt King.

The only question was, how much?

Sunday morning, Bill and Ginny and Shannon awoke early. Ginny made breakfast, Shannon watched TV, Bill read the newspaper, and all three of them tried to pretend that this was an ordinary day, that nothing momentous was going on, but they were all anxious and nervous, quieter than usual, and the countdown to the hour seemed to take forever.

The time came.

Went.

In the kitchen, Ginny washed the dishes; on the television, *Heathcliff* sequed into *Bugs Bunny*. There was no big change in the fabric of existence, no earthquake or lightning, no killer wind or sonic boom. There was no way to tell if everything had occurred as planned—or if anything had happened—and Bill paced nervously around the living room, out of the house, into the garage, down the drive, back to the house, clenching and unclenching his fists, waiting a full forty-five minutes before deciding to call Mitch.

The phone rang just as he was about to pick up the receiver and dial.

He grabbed it excitedly. "Hello?" he said.

"It's done." Mitch. "Everything went according to plan here, and I called a couple other managers and they said the same."

"Everyone's supposed to check in."

"They will."

"Any difference? Any change?"

Mitch was silent for a moment. "I don't know. I didn't *feel* anything, if that's what you mean. I don't . . . I don't know."

"I guess we'll have to wait."

"You could try calling Dallas, ask to speak to Newman King."

Bill chuckled. "I think I'll wait."

"I'll call back if anything happens."

Over the next hour and a half, they all checked in. Bill didn't know what was going on in Dallas, but in small towns all over the United States, the devolution of The Store's power had begun. He was the impetus behind it, and he felt a surge of pride as the last manager, from a little town in Vermont, checked in.

"What do we do now?" Shannon asked.

"Go on with our lives. And wait."

"For what?"

"Newman King."

"What do you think he's going to do?" Ginny asked.

He shrugged. "We'll have to wait and see."

He called a meeting himself that night, closing The Store early, in order to tell his employees what had happened. He'd shared the news with a few of them throughout the day—the ones he talked to, the ones with whom he had come into contact—but he wanted to let them all know that the managers had rebelled, that Stores all over the country had seceded from the corporation. It was possible there were still some King supporters among his employees, but he had no problem with them knowing what went down. The worst they could do was inform on him, tell King. And he had the feeling King already knew everything.

Maybe King was dead, he thought.

He remembered Lamb and Walker and Keyes, falling to the floor.

No. It was too much to hope for.

The CEO would not go so easily.

If King was not dead, he was undoubtedly pissed, and Bill was not at all sure that his power came solely from the Stores he controlled. He thought of that arm with too many bones, those deep wild eyes in the white plastic face, and he shivered.

For the first time in several days, he allowed himself to think about Sam. She'd never been far from his mind, but she'd had to share space in his thoughts with other concerns, and he'd only been able to contemplate her in short spurts.

The memories of her were tainted, though, his fatherly feelings for her overlaid with a guilty shame, and he was unable to think of her without seeing that image on the video, without remembering how she'd felt in his bed. It was uncomfortable to think of her now even as a child, and he wondered what was going to happen when she returned, how they were going to act toward each other. Maybe she'd been hypnotized and would remember none of it. Maybe the two of them would just avoid the subject, never speak of it, pretend it didn't occur.

Maybe she wouldn't return at all.

Maybe King had had her "terminated."

No, he thought. Anything but that.

He tried to remember her the way she was before. Before The Store. She'd been a kind and gentle girl. Smart, pretty, thoughtful, nice. Even-tempered even as a baby. A girl with a great future ahead of her.

And King and Lamb and all of their cohorts had turned her into a conscienceless automaton, willing to do whatever they told her.

He was glad Lamb had died. And Walker. And Keyes. And if he could see Newman King die as well, he would be a happy man.

Maybe King would commit suicide, he thought hopefully. Maybe he would kill himself.

Bill stood before the assembled employees. He climbed atop one of the tables in the espresso bar and faced the men and women, boys and girls, who were packed into the junction of aisles and rows in front of him. He'd gathered them here rather than downstairs in the assembly corridor or one of the multipurpose rooms because he wanted to emphasize the difference between the old Store and the new Store, and he was gratified to see no fear or hatred on any of their faces, only expectant interest and curiosity.

The tenor of The Store really had changed.

He raised his hands for silence, announced what had happened, what the managers had done. He explained that nearly all of the stores in the chain had renounced the old ways and that from now on they would be managed and operated individually. "The corporation's power has been decentralized," he said, "and everyone is using us as an example."

A cheer went up.

"As most of you know, I have had my little disagreements with the corporate office in the past—"

Laughter.

"—and I am gratified that Newman King will no longer be able to dictate how we operate. His tyranny over Juniper is ended."

"The King is dead!" someone yelled, and everyone cheered.

"Long live the King."

The voice was like thunder, like that of a god, and it cut through the noise like a knife, instantly silencing the assembled employees. The clapping stopped, the cheering disappeared, and all heads turned toward the source of the voice.

Newman King.

He stood in the center aisle, looking toward the espresso bar.

Looking straight at Bill.

"You little shit," he said.

The lights in the building dimmed.

Bill held his ground as King strode down the aisle toward him. The Store was silent, the only sound King's boot heels clicking on the tiled floor.

The crowd parted nervously before him as he approached. The CEO drew closer, and Bill saw that his face had begun to corrode. The plastic teeth were gone, replaced by decayed stumps. The skin was now yellowish white and stretched thin in places, blackness visible beneath it.

Only the eyes remained the same, and Bill could sense the burning intensity radiating from them and he was afraid.

What was he? Bill thought.

King raised his hand, snapped his fingers, and instantly, from the opposite end of The Store, came the Night Managers. They did not spread out and begin walking past racks and displays like they usually did, but marched forward en masse.

King was at the front of the espresso bar now, but he made no effort to move any closer. He stood at its edge, looking at Bill on top of the table. "I *built* The Store," he spit out. "I made it! I invented it!"

"You ruined it!" a brave soul in the crowd called out. A kid.

King swiveled, turned, cast a withering glance at the assembled employees. "I made you!" King said. "I gave you jobs! I made you what you are today!"

He turned his attention back toward Bill, and Bill was frightened, but he heard the anger in the CEO's voice, felt the panic, the desperation. King was dying, he realized. Just like Lamb and Walker and Keyes. And he felt a small twinge of satisfaction at the thought.

King advanced slowly. "I should've killed you when I had the chance, pussy boy. But instead I took you under my wing, trained you, allowed you to be a manager."

"You shouldn't've used my daughter," Bill said, holding his ground.

"That whore!" King roared.

Hatred and anger drove away what was left of the fear. "You have no power here," Bill said coldly. "This is *my* Store. Get the fuck out."

In front of the espresso bar, the Night Managers were moving forward, passing through the rapidly dispersing crowd. Employees were slinking away, hiding behind racks of clothing, backing up the aisles. Several headed for the doors, making a run for it.

"I will not allow you to do this," King said. "I will not allow you to take The Store away from me."

"You killed my friends. You killed my town."

"It's *my* Store!"

Bill was thrown back, off the table, against the counter at the rear of the bar, and all of the breath was knocked out of him. King had not touched him, but *something* had shoved him backward, a force that had not put pressure on any one part of his body but had slammed into all of him equally, an overwhelming wall of unseen energy.

King continued to advance, his decaying face a terrifying mask of rage and hate that Bill knew was only a milder version of the real face beneath it.

Bill sucked in his breath, stood to face King. He wanted to run, but he knew he couldn't, and he—

—was thrown back again, the force this time slamming into his chest and midsection, feeling like a cannonball.

"I *am* The Store!" King cried.

Once more, Bill staggered to his feet. He stood proudly, breathing painfully. "The Store is ours," he said. "And *this* Store is *mine*!"

He was flattened against the counter this time, pinned in place by unseen energy. Through teary eyes he saw more employees fleeing, saw the Night Managers press forward.

King smiled at him, and the sight was truly terrifying to behold. "How come you didn't get rid of the Night Managers, huh? Why didn't you terminate them?" King looked at him, the smile turning into a snarl. "Because you couldn't! They're not yours, they're The Store's. They're mine."

Bill struggled, strained, broke free of the grip of whatever was holding him. King was standing directly in front of him at this point, and the CEO pushed him back, but there was no accompanying invisible force, no bolt of power. There was only the pressure of King's hands, strong and cold and unnaturally bony.

Bill grabbed one of King's arms, thrust it away.

The CEO looked at Bill, confused.

Bill shoved him.

King did not move back at all, was not thrown even the least bit off balance, and Bill felt only iron immobility against his hand muscles as he shoved, but for the first time, he saw what looked like fear on King's face. It lasted only a second, was preceded and then replaced by anger, but it had been there, however briefly, and even as King threw him to the floor, Bill smiled. "You have no power here," he said.

In a rage, King whirled around toward the Night Managers gathered behind him. He snapped his fingers, clapped his hands, pointed. "Kill him!" the CEO ordered.

The black-clad managers remained in place, unmoving.

"Kill him!" King screamed.

And the Night Managers turned on him.

Bill scrambled to his feet, backing up against the counter.

King was confused, taken completely by surprise, and he stumbled, falling. Bill was equally surprised, and he did not know what to say, did not know what to do. His eyes darted toward the converging aisles in front of the espresso bar, and he saw that most of the remaining employees were not running away, not moving forward to watch, but remained in place, waiting to see what happened next.

King was trying to get up, trying to right himself, but the Night Managers had completely surrounded him now, and they were kicking, hitting, punching.

They *were* The Store's, Bill realized.

They were his.

And they were protecting him.

One of them withdrew from his black garb a knife.

"No!" King cried.

More knives were drawn.

Bill should have been happy. He should have felt good. This was what he'd wanted. This was what he'd been hoping for. But somehow it didn't seem right. The Night Managers, who were victims of The Store, were also part of The Store. They had turned against Newman King, but they were using his tactics. They were his creations, his children.

In a sudden wave, the Night Managers moved in, dozens of knives flashing in the dim light. The knives disappeared, reappeared, and they were covered with red. There was the sickening sluicing sound of blood and rent flesh. Between the moving, shifting forms of the Night Managers, Bill saw the body of Newman King jerk once, the head rising, then collapse, unmoving.

A black inky shadow moved upward from the melee, fluttering wildly, dissipating in the air, and the Night Managers, as one, bent and stood, the contingent in the center picking up the limp dead body of Newman King. Holding it aloft, they moved out of the espresso bar and began walking silently down the center aisle of The Store toward the door that led to the basements.

Bill remained flattened against the side of the kitchen counter for several shocked seconds before finally straightening and facing the employees who were left. The looks of disgust and startled confusion that greeted him must have mirrored his own. Sucking in his breath, he strode between the overturned tables and out into the center aisle. He faced the departing Night Managers.

"Stop!" he ordered.

As one, the Night Managers halted.

He ran to catch up with them, other employees following. Near the back of the group, amidst a cadre of unrecognized faces, he saw Ben. Like his brethren, Ben's face was blank, impassive, and dotted with small splatters of blood. But the corners of his mouth appeared to be turned up a fraction, and it seemed as though he was smiling.

Bill looked up at the body of Newman King, then back at the Night Manager who had once been his friend.

"You're fired," he said softly.

Ben collapsed.

There was no transformation, no change in expression or appearance, only an immediate slumping to the floor, as though the Night Manager had been an electric toy and his power cord had just been yanked out of the socket.

Bill thought for a moment. "You're all fired!" he said loudly.

The Night Managers dropped.

He did not know if he was killing them or doing them a favor, if he was freeing trapped souls or merely pulling the plug on mindless robots, but he knew that, whatever it was, it was the right thing to do.

There was no place for Night Managers anymore.

In front of him, the aisle was now blocked by unmoving black-clad bodies that stretched half the length of The Store.

They would have to walk down another aisle just to be able to get out of the building.

He turned back toward the employees. "Come on," he said. "Let's walk around."

"I think Jim went to call the cops," someone said.

Bill nodded tiredly. "Good." He walked around a display of breadmakers, down a short row to the next aisle, and trudged toward The Store entrance. Outside, through the open doors, in the dark parking lot, he could see a crowd of people milling about, waiting. There were already the sounds of sirens in the distance.

He turned to look back at the Night Managers as he

crossed the center aisle. In the center of the blackness was a lone light figure.

"The King *is* dead," Holly said behind him.

He turned to look at her, nodded. "Yeah. He is."

*   *   *

Back at home, Ginny and Shannon were watching the news on TV, and both of them screamed and threw their arms around him the second he walked through the door.

"Thank God," Ginny cried. "Thank God."

Shannon hugged him. "We thought you were dead, Dad!"

"No, we didn't!"

"I did!"

"I'm fine," Bill said.

"You've got to see this." Ginny led him over to the television, pointing at the screen.

The Black Tower was collapsing.

He turned back toward Ginny, heart pounding. "What about—?"

"Sam?" Ginny smiled. "She called. She's fine."

"She's coming home!" Shannon said.

She's coming home.

Bill's stomach twisted. He forced himself to seem happy, excited, but it felt false, strained. He wanted her back, of course, wanted her home, but . . .

But he didn't know what he was going to say to her.

He felt Ginny's hand on his arm. "I guess it worked, huh?"

He nodded.

"Do you think Newman King—"

"He's dead."

"What happened?" Shannon asked.

Bill shook his head.

"What?"

"I'll tell you guys later." He turned his attention back to the television. CNN was cutting between the Black Tower and property on the south side of Dallas that was owned by Newman King and was supposed to be the site of the first Store in a major metropolitan area.

The Tower was collapsing into a sinkhole. Police had

blocked off a square-block area, and two cross streets were almost buried under falling debris. But it was the empty property, the vacant lot, that was the most fascinating, because dogs and cats, rats and rattlesnakes, birds and bats were all being drawn to the land and dropping dead. Police had the area cordoned off, but people were even walking onto the property and falling in their tracks. The news cameras captured several of them on tape.

"He *was* The Store," Bill said, staring at the screen.

"What?" Ginny asked him.

He turned away from the television, looked at her, smiled. "Nothing," he said.

"Is it over?" she asked.

Bill nodded, threw an arm around her, held her close, and for the first time in a long while, he felt happy. "Yes," he said. "It's over."

EPILOGUE

1

For weeks, the Internet had been buzzing with news of The Store and the bodies. Photos from all over the country of the people who had driven, walked, or crawled to the parking lots of the individual Stores had been electronically transmitted and transferred, scanned and analyzed. The conspiracy theorists and the UFO fanatics had had a field day, postulating outrageously complex scenarios that conformed to their preconceived ideas and at the same time explained the Store occurrences. Even legitimate news agencies had given the story play, although they were strangely silent on the causes, and their usual experts were not publicly offering any opinions.

In Juniper, sixteen men and women, all Store employees, had crawled to the parking lot to die.

Several dozen animals had done the same.

Street had returned. He'd seen the commotion on the news, from the trailer he'd been renting in Bishop, California, and he'd known that it was finally safe to come back. He'd driven to Juniper the next day, reopened his shop as if nothing out of the ordinary had occurred. He let Bill know he was back in town not by stopping by, not by calling, but by leaving an E-mail message: "Want to play chess tonight?"

Bill had driven to the electronics shop immediately after reading the E-mail, and Street filled him in on what had occurred the night he'd left. Bill, in turn, explained what had become of Ben.

They were silent for a moment after that, each of them thinking of their lost friend, then Street walked into the back, pulled out two beers from the fridge, and the two of them toasted their old companion.

Bill had missed his deadline on the human resources documentation, but it was no big deal. The city for which the package was intended was in no great hurry, and besides, it was the first deadline he had ever missed. His supervisors at Automated Interface assumed that it was because they had not given him enough lead time, and his deadline had since been readjusted.

He was well on the way to meeting it.

And that was that. Life was already settling back into its normal routine. A new town council had been elected last week, and though it was a tricky business and the town had had to hire an outside lawyer and accountant to sort through the red tape, the police department was once again a municipal agency, and most of the remaining Store-sponsored "reforms" were on their way to being rescinded. There'd been a town meeting in the gym the night before last, with Ted, the new mayor, presiding, and though it went against the basic instincts of most of the people present, they'd agreed unanimously to levy on themselves a temporary one-cent sales tax until Juniper was in the black again.

The Store was still open. Bill had resigned, and Russ Nolan, an employee who was somewhere in the chain of command, somewhere on the management fast track, had been appointed temporary manager. He'd no doubt been gung ho for all of the old ways, but he'd adapted, changed, and he seemed fairly levelheaded.

No one knew how long The Store would stay open, though. There were rumors that the entire chain would be bought out by Federated or Wal-Mart or Kmart. When Bill called Mitch, the manager could not substantiate any of those stories, but he did not automatically discount them.

Another rumor had Safeway or Basha's buying the old Buy-and-Save and converting it to one of their stores. While Bill had no desire to see another corporate chain open up an outlet in Juniper *ever,* Ginny seemed excited by the prospect, and he had to admit that he wasn't about to put up any real fight against it.

He didn't have much fight left in him.

He and Ginny were still healing. They'd talked through what had happened. Many, many times. On the surface, everything was fine, everything was back to normal. And neither of them had brought up Dallas in several weeks. But it was still there, between them, and Bill did not think it would ever entirely go away.

He understood that, though.

He could live with that.

It was late, after midnight, after sex. Shannon was fast asleep in her room down the hall, and the door to their own bedroom was closed and locked. They lay in bed, naked atop the covers, and Ginny traced the brand on his buttocks, her fingers lightly following the ridges. He'd been permanently marked by The Store, and while he and Ginny had talked about having the brand removed by a plastic surgeon, he had decided that he was going to keep it. It no longer hurt, and he wanted the scar.

To remind him.

So he would never forget.

"Where do you think Sam is now?" Ginny's voice was soft.

He rolled over, sat up. "I don't know."

"She said she was going to come back."

A hot flush of shame crept over Bill's face, and he looked away from her, saying nothing.

"You think she's all right?"

"I hope so."

"But do you *think* so?"

"I don't know," he admitted.

Ginny began sobbing quietly, her shoulders heaving, tears rolling down her cheeks, but only a muffled inhalation of breath escaping from her mouth. He leaned over, pulled her to him, hugged her tightly.

"We'll get through it," he said. "We'll survive."

He was crying, too, suddenly, and she pulled back, looked at him, wiped the tears from his cheeks as he wiped the tears from hers.

"Yes," she said.

And, through the tears, they smiled.

2

They'd been traveling for most of the day, hadn't seen a real town since Juneau, hadn't seen a building since an hour or so after that. Pavement had ended long ago, and though the four-wheel-drive Explorer was having no problem handling the rocks and ruts of the muddy road, Cindy Redmon didn't like being this far away from everything, this far out in the middle of nowhere. She appreciated Ray's desire for a unique honeymoon, and the idea of an idyllic week in the woods had definitely appealed to the romantic within her, but the reality of Alaska was not quite what she'd expected. It was beautiful, yes. As picturesque as the brochures and books had led them to believe. But it was cold as well. And remote. And the farther they went into the woods, the less comfortable she felt with the knowledge that the CB was their only lifeline to civilization.

What if there was an accident?

What if one of them had a heart attack or choked on a piece of salmon?

Ray, seeming to sense her mood, smiled over at her. "Don't worry, hon. Everything'll be fine."

And then they rounded a curve, and in a small clearing carved out from a stand of monstrous trees, they saw The Market.

They were silent, both of them. It wasn't a particularly impressive place. It wouldn't have stood out in a real city, in a real state, in a civilized area of the nation. But here, in the backwoods of Alaska, it seemed downright miraculous, and she stared at the small building as Ray slowed the Explorer. It was about the size of a convenience store and was built in the same style, with a flat front and an upward-sloping roof. But there were no windows, only a one-door entrance and cinder block wall. Strangest of all was the sign, a brightly lit freestanding rectangle bearing the name of the place in green-on-white letters: THE MARKET.

"The Market," Ray said. "What the hell kind of name is that?"

"Got *your* attention," she pointed out.

He laughed. "Didn't need a sign to do that. Not way out here." He pulled up in front of the building. "Feels like *Apocalypse Now* or something, doesn't it? That part where they think they're out in the middle of the jungle and come across that high-tech stage with the USO show?"

He was right. There was some of that surrealism here. But there was something else as well, something she didn't like, something that was beginning to make her feel very uncomfortable.

"Let's go," she said. "Let's get out of here. I don't like this place."

"Let's at least check it out first."

"I don't want to."

"Come on."

"What if there're crazy survivalists in there? Or some psychotic cannibal? Norman Bates or Jeffrey Dahmer could be hiding in there for all we know."

He laughed. "I'll take that chance." He opened the door, got out of the vehicle. "I'm going in, get me some bait. You want something?"

She shook her head.

"Sure you don't want to come?"

She nodded.

She watched him clomp through the partially hardened mud, open the heavy wooden door, and step inside.

She shouldn't have let him go, she thought. She should have made him keep on driving.

She held her breath and didn't realize that she was gripping the armrest until he emerged from The Market a few minutes later carrying a large grocery sack.

A large grocery sack?

He got into the Explorer and put the sack down between them, looking dazed.

"What is all this?" she asked as he started the vehicle. "What did you buy?" She dug through the sack, drew out a comic book, a box of Cream of Wheat, a pair of socks, a Tom T. Hall cassette. "I thought you were going to pick up some bait."

"Shut up," he said, and there was something in his

voice that put her on edge, that made her not want to ask any more. "Let's just get out of here."

He peeled out, bouncing through a half-frozen puddle and over a rocky bump. He kept his eyes on the road ahead, not looking around, not looking at her, not looking back, and the expression on his mouth was grim.

Before they hit the next curve, before the close-growing trees obscured the view behind them completely, she turned around in her seat and squinted through the dusty back window, her eyes focusing on a hint of movement.

The door to the building swung open.

And, in a sight she would never forget, she thought she saw the proprietor of The Market.

Born in Arizona shortly after his mother attended the world premiere of *Psycho*, **Bentley Little** is the Bram Stoker Award–winning author of several novels and *The Collection*, a book of short stories. He has worked as a technical writer, reporter/photographer, library assistant, sales clerk, phonebook deliveryman, video arcade attendant, newspaper deliveryman, furniture mover, and rodeo gatekeeper. The son of a Russian artist and an American educator, he and his Chinese wife were married by the justice of the peace in Tombstone, Arizona.